The Winter Order

Robert Seutter

I0545626

Hart & Swan Publishing
Los Angeles

Copyright

First published in the US in 2024 by Hart & Swan Publishing (Los Angeles, CA 91361)

Hart & Swan Publishing

www.hartandswan.com

First edition: November 2024

Cover photograph © 2016 Robert Seutter
Front and back cover layout: Gillian Cameron
Layout, editing, and proofreading: Cat Ellen
Editing and proofreading: RJ Ryan-Seutter

Science Fiction & Fantasy > Fantasy > Paranormal & Urban > Urban

Literature & Fiction > Genre Fiction > Holidays

Science Fiction & Fantasy > Fantasy > Dark Fantasy

Christmas fiction, Santa fantasy, Urban horror, Krampus origin, Vampire fiction, historical fiction, modern Faeries

ISBN: 978-1-965599-01-3

Table of Contents

Dedication

To RJ
My Lady Cat
and the Christmas Community

Forward

Somewhere around the fourth chapter of Robert Seutter's excellent new book, "The Winter Order," I experienced an unexpected emotion. While it was clear within the first couple chapters that Seutter was on to something completely fresh and new in the Christmas and Santa Claus genre, my emotions up until chapter four were decidedly positive. Seutter seemed to effortlessly breathe new life into the long-established Santa Claus legend. I even marveled upon discovering that Rick "The Beast" had been inspired by my career in pro-wrestling. Then, gradually, I began to feel the telltale twinges of envy, slight at first, then stronger with each passing page.

For a little context, I, like Seutter, am a Christmas performer with a dedication to my portrayal of Santa Claus. I am drawn to the storytelling aspect of the Santa portrayal and consider myself something of a Christmas historian. I've also done some writing - having authored five books that hit the New York Times bestseller list, with two of those books hitting the #1 spot. Although it's been almost twenty years since the publication of my last novel, the creation of some type of sweeping Santa Claus saga had long been a definite interest of mine. Yes, I had truly hoped that my love for Christmas, commitment to the Santa craft, vivid imagination, and penchant for storytelling would be apparent on every page.

Whether I am capable of actually doing such a thing remains to be seen. I can tell you for sure that Robert Seutter has already accomplished this lofty feat and done so in a way so decidedly different and unique that my twinges of envy have become more than matched by my deep levels of appreciation for what Seutter brings to the Christmas table. Drawing upon his deep love for Christmas lore, Seutter expertly moves his epic tale through present-day small-town North Dakota under siege, planting seeds along the way, weaving narratives together in effortless fashion, and allowing the reader to connect many of the dots throughout.

There's a saying among Christmas performers: *Create your own North Pole.* Create a magical land in your mind so real that it cannot help but feel authentic to children in that magic age. But creating one's own North Pole, no matter how magical and believable for wee lads and lasses, is usually (at least to some extent) a tinkering with the well-known tales of the season: Putting one's own twists on well-traveled Yuletide tales, deciding which Rankin/Bass classics, beloved song lyrics, and children's storybooks to cull from.

Robert Seutter brings entire new worlds to life in the pages of "The Winter Order," maintaining honor for the Santa legend and those who dedicate themselves to spreading joy through St. Nick's likeness. And in his depiction of the Krampus character, constructs an origin story for the ages – kind of an "Incredible Hulk" #181, for those who love Christmas fiction.

Yes, I felt a little envious of Robert Seutter while I was reading "The Winter Order." The vast majority of readers will feel only appreciation.

Mick Foley

August 20, 2024

1.   In the Chair

Santa Abe checked the mirror once more before adjusting his collar. Picking up a brush, he fluffed the fur on his collar, then tucked some errant hairs back into his beard. With a tilt of his hat, he gave himself a jolly wink, tossed a breath strip into his mouth, and headed to the door.

Seth, the security guard, was waiting for him with the cart.

"You ready to roll, Big C?"

"Like a rock star, Seth."

Seth smiled, putting on his security hat with the extra non-regulation elf ears pinned on either side. Turning up the Christmas music on the cart, they sped out into the mall.

They arrived promptly at "Santa's House," and Abe could see that the line was already pretty long. He smiled. Busy was always better than boring.

After an hour, they had hammered through most of the photo reservations. It was then that Abe spotted the Saldanas, a local family that Abe had come to know the past few years. They had joined the farming community in North Dakota before the oil boom and were well-known in the area. Abe grinned. They had a tradition of sharing homemade tamales during the holidays, maybe he would get lucky. His smile faltered slightly when he noticed that one of the younger boys was hanging back, something he found a bit odd. As the photo manager brought up the next family, he shifted back to his jolly persona, disengaging the beard-snagging hand of a three-month-old.

Eventually, the Saldanas came up for their photos, individual and otherwise. Abe watched the young boy, who had remained at the back of the group. It was obvious from his body language that he was still a believer. Curious.

"Ricky, don't be shy," Ricky's mother said. Ricky rolled his eyes.

"I'm not, Mom. I just want to talk to Santa alone. Okay?"

His mother cocked her head and glanced at Santa. Abe nodded with a smile. There were plenty of the required adults in the area.

"Absolutely. Come on up Rick. But let's get the photo out of the way first, okay?"

The boy dutifully clambered up onto Santa's knee and smiled wide for the photo. Mom and the rest of the kids moved to inspect the photo as it resolved on the nearby display.

"Merry Christmas, Ricky. Feliz Navidad!" said Abe.

Ricky looked both ways and leaned in, "Santa, I need your help." Abe nodded thoughtfully, giving him his complete attention.

"Of course, what I can do? Did you want something special for Christmas?"

"I need a stake and a hammer," he said quietly, his face gone deadly serious.

Abe blinked. Was this some sort of joke? It certainly didn't feel like one.

"I'm sorry, Ricky, a stake? Are you doing some woodworking? Or is this some nerf toy? Some sort of game or something?"

Ricky's shoulders slumped as he shook his head. He looked straight into Abe's eyes.

"No. A vampire is eating my sister, Monica. I need a pointy wooden stake and a hammer." He thought for a moment then continued, "Maybe I need a bunch of them. I don't know. I took some holy water from church, and I have those red beads with a cross on them. So, if you could get me some stakes real soon, that would be cool."

Abe took a moment to look at the young boy on his knee. It was obvious that Ricky's concern was genuine, but he had no idea how to address a request like this. For some reason, deep in his heart, something about the boy felt truthful, as though there was something very real about what the boy was saying.

"Well, I think it's wonderful that you want to help your sister. But as you know, fighting vampires is usually something that's done by grown-ups. Maybe this is some sort of game your sister is playing?"

Ricky shook his head no, a bit irritated.

"No one will believe me, and my sister just told me to shut up about it. It's not a game. She's at home sick, and I know he's a vampire."

"How do you know this?"

"He came in through her window, and her room is way up high. I was hiding in her closet, because I was planning on scaring her. But then he came in. His face changed, and he bit her on the neck. I was really scared." He looked at Abe intently, "I could see him, but not in the mirror. And that means he's a vampire, right? Santa, can you help me? Or my sister? Please?"

Abe took a deep breath. He tried not to talk down to children if he could avoid it. Honestly, they were often more intelligent than their parents. The mother was turning around to look at them, and almost unbidden, the words came to him.

"Okay, Ricky, Santa will see what he can do. Stay away from the bad guy for now. Until then, can you be good and have a happy Christmas? Would you like a candy cane?"

The young boy nodded happily, gave Santa a heartfelt hug, and then jumped off his lap, candy cane in hand.

For some reason, Abe felt strange, as if something in his heart had changed.

The mother leaned over, "What was that about? Did he need something special for Christmas?"

Abe checked first to see if the boy was gone.

"He's really worried about his sister. He says she's sick." Tears welled in the mother's eyes.

"That's so sweet. His sister Monica stayed home sick. She's been feeling really tired lately. We think it's mono, but we are waiting for the blood tests to come back from the doctor."

Abe nodded and patted her hand.

"I'll keep her in my prayers. Hopefully, it's nothing too serious." He handed her two candy canes. "This one's for you, and the other one is for Monica. I hope you and your family have a wonderful Christmas!"

Mrs. Saldana leaned over and gave Santa a hug.

"We brought a plate of tamales for you. We gave them to your chief elf. You do you like tamales?"

Abe gave her a big smile, "I love them. You can also put them out for Santa with the cookies on Christmas Eve. Thank you so very much."

She turned to herd her kids back into the noisy mall, stopping briefly to give her little son Ricky a big hug.

As Abe watched them go, he wondered why he didn't say more. The rest of the shift flowed past. But as it did, Ricky's words kept floating up in his brain.

"A vampire is eating my sister."

* * *

2. The Moon on the Breast of the New Fallen Snow

Parked down the street from the Saldanas' house, Abe sat parked in his car, which now smelled of the homemade tamales he had just devoured. Even cold, they had been delicious.

In his mind, any number of scenarios ran through his head, among them being the likeliness of a Sheriff asking why he was there, then arresting him as some sort of stalker. Another part of his brain felt very distant and removed as he sat in the cold, occasionally running his heater just enough to keep the window defrosted. This, he decided, was just plain nuts. He sighed.

Abe watched the big house with many cars parked in the expanded driveway, framed by several steep snowbanks. The house was decorated simply, with colorful tinsel garlands, a few strings of old lights, and a plastic poinsettia wreath on the front door. It was a tall house for rural North Dakota, and it was obvious that as the family had grown, the house had grown to accommodate them. The front porch light was golden on the packed snow and seemed warm, inviting.

Feeling the fatigue from a long shift, he checked his watch and was surprised to see it was nearly midnight. By the time he got home, washed all the makeup out of his beard and ate something, sleep was going to be in short supply. Abe sighed, but just as he leaned forward to put the car in gear, he paused. There, moving rapidly down the block, a dark figure sprinted toward the home. The night was black against black, only the dimly lit snow providing a silhouette as the stranger darted past. Suddenly all the tiredness Abe had been feeling was gone.

The figure came from the opposite side of the road, and Abe watched as it lightly skipped over one of the snowbanks then trod to the side of the multi-story house. He could make out a man of a lithe build, wearing a jacket that looked far too light for the bitter North Dakota winter. The man looked both ways, then leapt straight up, clearing three entire stories. The figure grabbed the windowsill over the top of the window, then tapped on the glass. Soon, the room lit up from within.

Abe's heart was now solidly in his throat. His eyes confirmed what his brain couldn't explain, and he watched as the window slid open and the man nimbly slipped in. The window slid closed behind him, and the room went dark.

Abe sat alone in his car. His hands were shaking, his heart pounding sorely in his chest. Time passed. After a few moments, he took several deep breaths, and after saying a small prayer to God (and whomever else might be listening), he turned the engine over and headed home.

As he drove, he shook his head, glancing at himself in the mirror.

"Are you telling me there are frickin' vampires in LaMoure, North Dakota?" he finally said out loud. Wide blue eyes looked back at him in the mirror. "Apparently so." Talking out loud seemed to help. "So, what now?"

He turned down the street towards his house and tipped the empty tamale plate into a garbage bag. He glanced back in the mirror

"Proof: One weird observation does not make it real."

NPR's *Prairie Home Companion Christmas Show* crackled faintly on the radio. The sound of a folksy, choral version of *Silver Bells* eased his heart out of racing.

Abe exited his car, plugged in the tank heater cord hanging out from his hood, and collected his gear. His first stop was the bathroom. As he set to work scrubbing his face, he had ample time to study his reflection.

Proof, he thought. He'd have to get proof. Something to indicate that he wasn't just hallucinating.

Mentally and physically exhausted, he finished his regular "de-Santa-fication" routine, then collapsed on his bed. For the first time in many years, he said his nightly prayers. They seemed clumsy in his mouth.

* * *

3.   So, What's New with You?

The next evening, following his shift, Abe was out running a few errands. With work leaving so little free time, it was easy to let the important things fall by the wayside. With both hands full of groceries, Abe struggled to open the trunk to his car. His gaze drifted across the street to his favorite burger joint and deciding that he wasn't going to make it to January on cookies alone, he decided he'd stop by for a quick bite.

The place was warm and familiar, with its cracked leather upholstery and nostalgic wallpaper. Abe had just sunk into his regular booth when his blood ran cold. There, second window from the last, sat the man who had paid a visit to the Saldanas' house the night before. Something about the way the man moved and that far-too-thin jacket had caught Abe's eye. Other people seemed to be completely ignoring the man and his two companions. One was a younger, slender woman in a fluffy faux-fur coat, the other a gruff, burly-looking biker type.

A few minutes later, the group stood to leave. Abe pretended to dig into his fries as they walked past, but as they did, he glanced into the opposing mirror. All three of them were notably absent. No one else seemed to notice.

Abe took a deep breath and turned to look over his shoulder. He could see the three of them continue to walk on, then disappear around a corner.

He turned back to check his own reflection in the mirror. It was there, looking back at him with alarm.

* * *

Abe spent another day watching and waiting. He did not spy any more reflection-less people, but he knew in his heart of hearts what he had seen. Now he had some decisions to make.

He was certain that if he told the local law enforcement about vampires running amok, he would probably lose his position at the mall very quickly, possibly even placed under surveillance in a psych ward. Being put in a mental hospital did not scare him that much, however, and while losing his Santa income would hurt, this was obviously more important.

But the idea of ending his Christmas Season, his favorite time of the year? It left his heart feeling heavy. Still, how long did Ricky Saldana's sister have?

Back at home, he did a little research online. While there seemed to be a billion hits on *vampires*, none of the results seemed relevant to the problem at hand.

Finally, not knowing what else to do, he decided to call one of his mentors, Santa Ron. He figured he was the only person who would be willing to listen to a story this crazy. Santas as a community had more than their share of zany characters, and in particular Ron had seen a lot of life, made some interesting friends along the way. Regardless, Abe *had* to tell someone. He hit speed-dial.

"Hey, Big Man!"

"Hey, Mr. Abe, how is your gig going?" asked Ron.

Abe shook his head and looked at the phone. In for a penny, as they say.

"It's been interesting. You're doing evening gigs right now, right?"

"Yup. Did you want to get together for some food?"

"Sounds great. I need to pick your brain on something. I'll discuss it when we see each other."

Ron chuckled, "Harold's, say 10:00 in the morning?"

"That'll work. See you then."

"Ho-ho-ho!"

Abe again thanked his lucky stars that he had run into Ron. The man had helped him become a Santa and had been a good friend. Abe hoped he wasn't about to lose him, either as a confidant or as a Brother in Red.

* * *

4. Lunch Date

Abe fidgeted nervously with the silverware. He had asked their usual waitress to place them in the back corner, away from foot traffic, where they would draw less attention. This close to Christmas, having two full-on Santa Claus look-alikes was bound to be confusing for the little kids. What would begin as interruptions from people who wanted "just one photo" always turned into more questions, then a quick video message, plus a Santa selfie or three. Fortunately, most folks seemed to be out shopping, giving them the run of the place.

He regarded his newly whitened beard and hair in a table knife reflection. They made him seem much older than he felt. He shook his head. What he was about to tell Ron seemed patently insane, more so in cool morning light.

Ron was what they called an "A-list" Santa. The older man had come from the west coast, as he said, "to get away from the rat race and phonies." His move to North Dakota surprised a lot of people, but even here, Santa Ron was now a "name" amongst his peers.

He had helped Abe make the jump to pro, and even got him some of the nicest gigs Abe had now. A blast of cold, dry air accompanied the looming form of Ron as he lumbered through the doorway. Santa Ron was six-foot-five, and he made everyone feel like a kid next to him.

"A-yup, that's a storm coming in for sure. We'll have six inches by tomorrow. Sure, the kids will love it," Ron said, as he peeled off his long green parka.

"I got us a pot of coffee, and Tina said she will come back for your order in a bit," responded Abe.

Ron sat down, unwound a bright red scarf, and untucked a beard that was the envy of many of his peers. His craggy face held two sharp blue eyes. Ron had always been very direct, and today was no different.

"You look like you've hit a bump in the road. Something wrong with your mall shifts?"

Abe sighed and took a sip of coffee. Ron raised a shaggy white eyebrow.

"You didn't mess with that cute little elf with the black hair, did you? I told you when I saw her that she was trouble in a basket."

"No, in fact the mall gig is going great," Abe answered and shook his head. "Even though I'm a newer Santa on the block, everyone is really treating me well, and people seem happy. Thanks again for that. And no, I've made it clear to Miss

Perky that I'm not going for the bait, even though she's still flirting with me like crazy."

"The suit is like catnip for some women," Ron laughed.

"Yeah, well, you and I both know that outside of the suit, we just look like chubby old white guys."

"So why the long face?" Ron smirked blithely.

Abe took another sip, grimaced, and put the cup down.

"I value our friendship, Ron, and I really want you to take what I am about to say with a pound of salt. This is complete crazy talk, and I can't believe I am saying this."

"Ho-kay." Ron's eyebrows shot up, and he smiled at his junior. "I've seen a lot of stuff in my day. I lived in California. Go ahead, lay it out."

Abe opened both of his hands and stared down into the coffee cup.

"About a week ago, the third day into the gig. We were just starting to get lines, and it was coming on five or six when I saw a big family I recognized join the queue. We do most of the family poses, and then I go back to ask the kids what they wanted for Christmas individually."

Ron nodded, "Did you know this family?"

Abe lifted his eyes from the coffee cup, blurting it all out.

"Yup. I know them, sorta. I don't live too far away from them. When I moved here from Fargo, I saw them around, at the store, that sort of thing. Talked to their Dad once or twice, mostly good folks, big extended family, and about ten cars on their property. Anyway, one of their little boys, Ricky, clearly a believer, climbs up on my knee. He looks around to see that no one else is looking, and then whispers into my ear. And he says, 'Santa, I need your help. Can I have a wooden stake and a mallet for Christmas?'" Abe looked at Ron pointedly as he recounted the remainder of his story.

"I hear in Santa School, they cover some of the awkward questions, like 'Are you the real Santa?' and 'Can you bring my family back together?' or 'Can you bring back my dead dog Rover?' But I'm pretty sure they didn't cover vampires. Did I miss something?"

Ron's gaze stayed steady, and he didn't laugh it off. Instead, he was quiet for a moment.

"What did you say?"

"What could I do? You know that we don't have long with the kids. I mean, it wasn't that busy, but his mom was heading out."

"And? What did you say?"

"I handed him a candy cane and said, 'Santa will see what he can do.'"

Ron nodded, adding more cream and sugar to his coffee, stirring quietly.

Abe waited but Ron said nothing, his face stoic.

"Ron, I know that if we suspect abuse, we tell them to go to a mandated reporter—a teacher, a doctor, a cop, or a fireman. It's not our place as Santa to deal with this. But something about this kid, it just stuck with me. He was being too intense for that age. I could feel it in my gut. Something was wrong."

Ron carefully brushed his mustache aside and sipped his coffee.

"So, you decided to do something?"

Abe sighed, "Yeah. I mean, I knew where they lived, so I figured it wouldn't be too big of a deal if I just parked nearby and, ya know, looked around a bit. I mean, I didn't know what else to do."

"And?"

"And, yeah, well, I was watching the house. Just before I was ready to give up and go home, I see this young guy zip across their lawn. He looked kinda buff, and he's wearing a thin leather jacket. Then he jumps straight up to the third floor. He hangs off the eaves, the window opens, and he's in, no time flat. Then the lights go out." Abe shook his head. "I've been trying to make sense of it all, and I can't." He put his hands flat on the table.

"So, I start checking out the neighborhood, and the next night, I happen to see the same young guy who did the jump, and he's with a couple other people who do not look like locals. I don't know why. I am sitting there, eating a burger, I look at them walk by, then I look for them in the mirror across the aisle. Except I can't see 'em. They are not there. In the mirror! But then I shoot a glance over my shoulder, and sure enough, they're there.

"I know, I know. This sounds like a bad movie. But I kid you not. I think that kid is right. I think there are vampires here, right here in LaMoure, North Dakota."

Abe jumped and spilled a bit of coffee as Tina the waitress suddenly bustled in.

"How are my favorite Santas?" She swapped out the coffee decanter for another one without asking and whipped out her pad. "Big Ron, you want the same? Chicken fried steak?"

Ron smiled, "Yup. Extra gravy. Thank you, Tina."

She turned to Abe, "You're looking pretty skinny for your line of work. What can I get you?"

"I'm not that hungry. Can I get some strawberry rhubarb pie, if you still have any?"

Tina smiled, "Been saving that last bit just for you."

As she started to head off, Ron shot a glance at Abe and asked the waitress in a jocular voice, "Hey Tina, a quick question. Do you think there are vampires in LaMoure?"

Tina turned and smiled and adjusted one of the many pins on her apron.

"Vampires?" She paused and considered the question with a smile, "Well, since the big oil boom, we've got about three to four times the number of people in town. A lot of people coming and going. So, vampires? Sure, why not?" She tilted her head at the other full rooms in the diner.

"We got boomers, rig rats, pimps, hookers, hustlers of all sorts nowadays. It's kinda hard for all of us old townies to deal with." She raised an eyebrow, "Besides, I'm looking at two Santas here. I believe in you, so why not a couple fang-boys?" She mock hissed, smiled, and went off to fill their orders.

Abe gaped at Ron, "Really? I'm scared out of my gourd, and you openly asked our waitress?"

"Sure. Besides, if you really want to know what's going on in a town, ask a group of kids, a hairstylist, or a bartender," Ron beamed.

Abe nodded. Ron did always seem to know what was going on.

Their food appeared in front of them with a wink from Tina, and Ron waited until they were alone again.

"And yeah, Abe, honestly, I'm not completely surprised, although this took a lot less time than I expected."

"What? That kids ask Santa for weapons to deal with real monsters?" Abe leaned back.

"Sort of. The simple truth is, once we put on the Red Suit and we make Santa come to life for folks, it's kinda like ringing a bell. One that you really can't un-ring. Being a true-hearted Santa is sort of like making a magical contract with the universe. Belief is a powerful force."

Ron paused to look Abe steadily in the eye, not laughing.

"And don't take this wrong, but I knew from the minute I met you that you were meant to wear the Red Suit. After a while, you just know. You can sense it. Guys that decide to do it for real, the ones who really invest in the role, they're *different*. People tend to treat us *differently* as well. Then you start to see things a bit *differently*, especially after people start sharing tiny bits of their lives with you. All those kids giving you their trust and hugs. Old folks sharing their memories. All kinds of people with their troubles, prayers. It's a powerful force, my friend. There's power in the old traditions and stories, and..." Ron stopped.

Abe's eyes narrowed, "And?"

Ron leaned back, rolled his shoulders, and sighed.

"And I was hoping I would never have to have this conversation with you. At least, not until you were a few years down the road. But since we're going there, I'll trade you weirdness for weirdness. As you know, there's all sorts of Santas: Black, white, brown, gay, male, female, straight, LGBT, all sorts of Santa type characters of every ethnic variety, culture, you name it."

Ron tilted his head and studied Abe.

"But YOU, Abe Wykowski, need to know that Santa really exists. Although, probably not quite in the way you might think."

Abe said nothing. This was not the conversation he had imagined having this morning. Tina popped over with more food, then disappeared just as quickly. Ron picked up where he left off.

"Here's the deal: Magic exists. Most people subconsciously train themselves all their lives not to see it. But you've had one of the older people with Down's Syndrome come visit you, right?" When Abe nodded, Ron continued, "Their belief, it hits you like a hammer, doesn't it? You would rather crawl across a mile of broken glass than to shatter that belief."

"True. It's intense."

Ron waved to the Christmas scene painted on the diner window.

"Belief is a big part of that magic. All those weird little coincidences that happen during the Christmas season? There are little bits of magic involved. And yeah, there really are vampires and werewolves and things that go bump in the night. And ghosts, Christmas is big on ghosts. Since you have some of that belief wrapped around you, you're starting to notice things."

Abe had been picking at his pie, but he put his fork down. His eyes were incredulous.

"Really, Ron? Really? Somehow, I expected the, 'It's not your job to be a social worker, Santa,' and 'Maybe it's time you go and see a head doctor' speech. Instead, you tell me straight up to my face that magic and vampires and all that crap exists? That there really is a Santa? So, which one? Saint Nicholas in his tomb? The jolly Coca-Cola trademark Santa? Or maybe the guy who shows up with Krampus, the demon who drags kids to hell? How are Rudolph and the gang doing these days?"

Abe shook his head and started to get up. Ron put a hand the size of a baseball glove on Abe's shoulder and pulled him back down.

"You're not far off there, Abe, and you were right to talk to me. If you want to save that boy's sister and their family, if you want to figure out whatever else is going on, you're gonna need to sit and listen. I'm serious."

Ron's face had taken on an intensity that Abe had never seen before. It reminded him that Ron had once been an Army combat vet and, after that, a cop for twenty years. The big man leaned closer and spoke lower.

"Yes, magic and all of that exists. Believe me, I've seen some very weird stuff. Most of the professional Santas know about it, but we don't talk about it, at least not openly. Anybody who deals with belief on a regular basis experiences this. Priests, healers, so on and so forth. It's mostly weird synchronicities, the little flashes of insight. For most folks, it's really intangible. Not that many of us in day-to-day life, on this side, deal with the stuff on the other side of the veil."

"The veil?"

"It's hard to describe. For most people, it's kind of like being colorblind to a particular color, or not being able to hear a particular pitch. As kids get older, most of them learn to tune the magic out. Our world does touch on other, um... places."

Ron paused and looked around to see if anybody was paying attention to them. *White Christmas* started to play in the background.

"Santa does exist. But he's more of a guiding spirit. When someone is really channeling the Spirit of Christmas, doing something important, that touches on one of the Big Man's aspects. And then powerful stuff can happen."

Abe put his face in his hands and rubbed his eyes. Ron waited. Abe lifted his face slowly to look at him.

"So how does that figure here?"

"As you know, there are a bunch of Santa organizations. The Brotherhood of the Red Suit goes back quite a ways, but what you may not know is that some of them go *waaay* back. Some long before what we call Santa Claus was running around in a red suit, being pulled by the reindeer. For most of the Santas, it's just about the social and business side of the Santa organizations. It's still important, all the good pro-bono work we do, like the Santa's Heart charity. We all go to the dinners so we can grump, keep tabs on one another, help each other out, try to keep standards up, gossip, bitch, all that." Ron paused and rubbed his palm absent-mindedly.

"But when one of us occasionally runs into something that smacks of something truly weird, of a magical nature, if it looks like something that the local authorities can't or won't believe you, help you–well for that, there is a secret organization." The big guy paused to sip some coffee.

"It's called The Winter Order or the Order for short, and I'm a member."

"The Order?" Abe looked at Ron with a deadpan expression.

Ron nodded, "The Winter Order. Okay, technically *Ordo Hiemalis Sancti Nicolai Thaumaturgi*. That translates to the 'Winter Order of Saint Nikolas, the Wonder Worker.'"

"And they can help us?" Abe asked, somewhat surprised at Ron's Latin.

"Maybe," Ron leaned back and opened his hands uncertainly. "There are some serious catches to this. The Order was created a long time ago, hundreds of years ago, and some of the rules they operate under are strange. When you haven't dealt with things like they've had to, the rules can seem very bizarre to us in the modern world. And you need to know, they have very limited resources."

"How old?" Abe ate another bite of pie and held up his fork.

Ron tilted his head, "I'm not certain, but as you know, St. Nicholas dates back to around the third century, and there is a lot of that tradition involved in all this. The Order isn't completely Christian. Which helps, considering they have a track record of working with, how do I say this? Other beings."

"So, how do we get them on the Bat-Phone? Is it the Reindeer-Phone in this case?" Abe raised his eyebrows.

Ron held up his hand and started counting off fingers.

"First, we need to give them proof that we actually have a problem. That can be trickier than it sounds. And rough. A member (me) needs to present you and your proof to the council." Ron ticked the second finger, "Secondly, anybody who invokes the aid of the Order has to be willing to become a member. If you ask for help, you must be willing to give it; and, once in, you're in for life, or until you retire."

Abe leaned back and started to say something. Ron made a calming gesture as he cut off Abe's questions.

"There are active and reserve roles; but it also means that your name goes into a pool of names. You will probably have to get some training, and someday you will be tasked to do something to help some other member. That means going on missions to help others, usually."

"Third, the Order will only come to your aid if you vow to see the problem to its end. That means you have to be willing to fight. To prove your courage, to be in the thick of it. You can't bail when things go horribly wrong, and believe me, they can."

Abe studied Ron's face carefully.

"You seem to know a lot about this. So, you're an active member?"

Ron rubbed a scar on his hand and nodded slowly.

"Yup. We had a problem down in Long Beach a while back, and I needed their help. I've helped in a few places since then."

Abe looked out the window and said nothing, watching the people go by, huddling up as they were whipped by the wind and snow.

"So, what happens if someone needs help, the Order reaches out, and someone turns out to be lame? 'Not Order Material.' Someone like me, who might or might not be a wuss."

The big man chuckled but nodded his head gravely.

"I mentioned that the Order is old, right? A long time ago, there were things like trial by ordeal or trial by combat. Those sorts of things may not make a lot of sense to you and me these days, but to the people of the time and the beings they were dealing with, they had to agree on some common ideology. Imagine if today, before you joined the military and went through boot camp, you had to face some sort of lethal challenge before they even agreed to train you.

"Centuries ago, the Order was part of a magical agreement, with other magical beings and groups in the world. That agreement is called the Compact, with various sides agreeing to certain rules. When that Compact was made, there was a group of Fay who ended up owing us some favors, and that's where the Elves came in. Anyway, that's why the Yule season is safer for most of us, because it was part of that Compact. At least, in some countries, anyway. People subconsciously know or feel this, even if they don't know why." Ron leaned back, closed his eyes, and recited.

> *"Some say that ever, 'gainst that season comes*
> *Wherein our Saviour's birth is celebrated,*
> *The bird of dawning singeth all night long:*
> *And then, they say, no spirit dares stir abroad;*
> *The nights are wholesome; then no planets strike,*
> *No fairy takes, nor witch hath power to charm,*
> *So hallow'd and so gracious is the time."*

"Shakespeare, Hamlet, I think, Scene 1 Act 1," Ron added. Abe gave him a small round of applause.

"Nice. Very theatrical, sir."

Ron gave him a sheepish smile, continuing.

"Even Shakespeare knew that, but what folks don't know is that this peace is partially due to the work of the members of the Order, over many centuries."

"Because of the Compact?"

"Right, the Compact. Magical rules." Ron pointed at Abe.

"One is that the person who first gets asked for help has a much greater chance of invoking supernatural help. It's a magic thing. That boy asked you. You said yes, and that could make a big difference. History has shown time and time again that if the person who got asked is willing to step up, there is a much better chance of success."

Abe wiped up some pie with his finger.

"Sort of like a wish or something?"

"More like the rules in a fairy tale. The handsome prince is not allowed to sub-contract." Ron sipped his drink.

"And you need to know that the Order has had its jolly ass handed to it many times. Thousands of folks have died, spread out over the centuries. Sometimes the Bad Guys or the monsters win."

He gave Abe a raised eyebrow and slight grin.

"That said, most of the things that go bump in the night think twice about bumping us. Why? Because. We. Bump. *Back*."

"So, what if the person who was asked for help can't or won't step up?"

A look of sadness flashed across Ron's face.

"It happens. A lot of the time the Order must pick and choose which Christmas folk to help. If someone else who is not a Santa is the champion, or the Santa or helper is not willing to fight, then the Order must make a judgment call. A lot of times, it means the non-Christmas champion is on their own. The Order will try to help in a limited way, but...." Ron opened his palms in an ambiguous gesture.

Abe shivered as he felt another cold blast of air accompanying another customer.

"Okay. First, why Santa or Christmas performers? Why not just anybody who signs up?" he asked.

"It doesn't always have to be Santas. Back in the old days, it could be any warrior and pledge who had sworn to the Order. They had plenty of knights, clerics, scholars, and wise women, but as the centuries passed, the Order has diminished in size. Ironically, in the last two hundred years, belief in Santa has only grown with the population. We have more belief in Santa than ever, if not for Christmas altogether. Belief translates to power. Anybody who has helped keep the magic of Christmas alive stands a better chance of using that magic. You've felt it."

Abe nodded. He had, even if couldn't put a name to it before.

"A 'true Christmas performer,' in both heart and mind, tends to be most powerful. That energy can gather around them. Anyway, long story." Ron didn't volunteer anything more.

"Let's say that I believe that vampires are real, and that there is a group of bad-ass Kringles out there who might help us with this. How do I get them involved?"

Ron ate a big bite of chicken fried steak and hooked a thumb to the wind and cold outside.

"Well first, we need some physical proof. We need some actual fangs or maybe claws from a creature, that would do in a pinch. But here's a big newsflash: Vampires are as tough and as mean as it gets, and there are different kinds. They have different flavors, abilities, and honestly? If we run into an older one, we don't stand much of a chance. If we're lucky, we are dealing with a newer one that's not all that clever. Most times, it's hard to tell by looking at them."

Abe stopped poking at his pie crust and looked over at Ron.

"Wait, you said 'we?'"

Ron looked at him with a wry half smile.

"What kind of Santa would I be if I knew there were vampires eating kids in my town? *Ho-ho-ho, the fang-boy has got to go.*"

5. How to Catch a Vampire

Abe looked around the cab of Ron's massive truck. It could've well had its own zip code, and the white vehicle moved with a grace that belied its immense size. He peeked behind Ron, at the bags of items strewn over the rear seat and peered into the darkness of the covered truck bed.

"Okay, I gotta know. What's in the bags?"

"We need to catch one of them, and there are some things you should know. Not all vamps are the same, and there's a whole host of different vampiric creatures. Yours sounds like a typical traveler type, probably from House of the Wheel. Let's hope it is. I'm not prepared to deal with a Russian Dhampir, not by a long shot."

Abe slowly turned to look at Ron.

"Wait, catch? Ron, kidnapping is illegal the last time I checked. And what happens if we are wrong, and he's not a vampire?"

"We won't be kidnapping anyone." The big man shrugged, "You need to take him out, as in kill him. Back in the ancient days, this process was sort of like an *einvigi* or trial by ordeal."

Abe stared at Ron blankly.

"For lack of a better word, it's a duel. If you win, you'll stand a much better chance of the Order backing you. Plus, you'll find out if he's a vamp pretty quickly. Trust me."

Ron kept glancing in his mirrors and looking about, a bit more than Abe felt comfortable with.

"If we're lucky, he's a young vampire. The older they are, the more powerful vampires become. After a lifetime or two, they can get annoyingly fast, tough, and strong. That, and they have abilities. The adolescent ones are about twice as capable as a normal human. Most of them are able to grow claws and fangs, but not all. Bullets and other projectiles will do some decent damage, and silver burns the shit out of them. They all hate holy water, the real sanctified stuff. When it comes to religion, authenticity matters a lot. Brandishing a cross might drive back a young one, but if you're not a true, wholehearted believer, an elder vampire will just slap it out of your hand and go to town on your ass. So being steadfast in your faith is a really good thing."

The big truck powered down the road, leaving a cloud of snow behind. It was already getting dark when Ron turned into Fat Eddy's burger joint and parked at the far end of the lot. He reached to snag a bag off the back seat and started fishing out a few select items.

"Baby vamps have little control over their bloodlust and need to feed a lot, especially if they aren't killing their victims. Yours seems to be fond of his young lady. Seems he's got enough control that he hasn't killed her thus far, which means he's older, too. From what you told me, I'm guessing this place is along his route. Regular feedings mean she's *maybe* only got a few days left to live. If the parents are smart, they'll get her to a hospital, but once a vamp puts the bite on someone, they're capable of tracking them."

"What makes you think he isn't, you know," Abe mimed a pair of fangs hitting his palm.

"Turning her? Vampires rarely make new vampires. It really pisses off the older ones if one is made without permission."

Abe was visibly uncertain, leading Ron to gesture to the town around them.

"Don't forget your vamp is probably feeding on others, too." Ron unwrapped some items and handed them to Abe. "So, if you want to save the girl and the town, you can start putting this gear on."

Abe looked down at the heavy weight vest in his hands.

"Uh, why am I weighing myself down?"

"Put it on," Ron continued pulling out gear.

Abe did as he was asked and was happy that the truck was big enough to accommodate his shuffling. As he put it on, he noticed that the weight vest had many odd seams and ridges.

Ron reached over and connected some cables to an anchoring point, then started fastening something around Abe's neck. Abe shrugged back on his coat, along with some hefty new gloves and other accessories. Ron pulled Abe's hands to him.

"These are reinforced gloves. If you notice, there are metal circles on the knuckles and fingers. Those cables connect to the vest, which is loaded with hi-capacity iridium/lithium batteries all throughout. You throw the switch on the back of your wrist, and you'll be ready to rock and roll. There's enough juice in it to kill a person several times over. Needless to say, don't touch any of your exposed skin, and avoid rolling in any puddles if you can help it.

"I also just put a silver-plated, high-gauge steel gorget on your neck, and those glasses are specially made. Don't take 'em off. If a vamp is trying to put the stare on you, you can actually see their eyes shimmer."

Ron reached over and stuffed some things into Abe's pockets.

"In your left pocket is a 45-caliber semi-auto pistol. It's got frangible silver rounds in it, and that can hurt it big time. Though, honestly, if it spots you first, you might not even have time to get it out. A vamp's senses are twice as sensitive as ours, and they can smell fear and blood from a distance. Hence, in the other pocket, a big can of bear spray. The good stuff."

Abe pulled out the pistol and the bear spray. All of this seemed very surreal. He snapped back only when Ron continued, stuffing both back into their pockets.

"Also, in the pocket are some carbon fiber zip ties, plus a silvered and blessed knife. Oh, and some stakes. Remember, don't hesitate."

Abe's eyes were getting wider and wider.

"Ron, I really don't know if I'm up for this."

"Abe, don't you have multiple belts in martial arts? I mean, we did meet at Master Kim's in Fargo. You teach Aikido to the kids now in the off-season for chrissake."

"Yeah, I was a Seabee and a combat engineer too, but I've been in only a few real fights as an adult. In the Seabees, we built stuff and blew it up. This, this is a whole new level of crazy! I am not a Jarhead-Seal-Special Ops kinda guy."

Ron took a deep breath and looked out at the dark. He spoke matter-of-factly.

"Do you want to save that boy? Cuz after that girl gets sucked dry, there's a good chance the vamp will come back with its friends for the rest of that family. It's been invited across the threshold, which means it can invite in its buddies now." Ron took Abe by the shoulder.

"Abe, here's the deal. You already accepted the Contract. That kid asked for your help, and for better or worse, you said yes. To invoke the Order, the Santa who got the plea for aid must prove that the problem exists. We could wait and see if we could find some of their other victims, but this is North Dakota in winter. These creeps are probably just taking the bodies and shoving them in snowbanks or under the lake ice. Come spring, those vamps will be long gone, and so might the bodies of their victims. We need evidence? We find it ourselves, before it's too late."

Ron turned suddenly and looked out the window to his left.

"There's your boy." Ron handed Abe a mirror. "Don't look out my window, look at him in the mirror with the glasses on."

Abe spotted his Casanova, tawny Latino and well-built, walking down the road with purpose. There was still enough light to make him out under the streetlamps, and looking closely at the mirror through the glasses, the smooth face now appeared wrinkly as moldered leather, pulled thin against the skull as if in rictus, eyes dark, feral, and sunken.

Abe's hands trembled as he handed the mirror back to Ron.

"Holy crap."

"Yup."

"These glasses, they're like that movie...."

"*They Live* with Roddy Piper, a classic. The glasses allow you to see their images in reflection. Just don't wear them too often, they will give you a splitting migraine."

Ron backed up the truck, which had been idling its diesel engine like a giant purring cat, and wheeled out of the parking lot back towards the Saldanas' house.

"Let's break it down. Your vamp has got a mile of semi-dark road to walk, but keep in mind, cold don't bother a vamp much. You're going to just happen to be walking the other way, and with any luck, he'll go for you because, 'Hey, middle of the night, rural road. Why not?' When he does, he might try a couple different tactics. He might try the eyes or he could try talking to you, ask you to help him with something, then jump you. Young vamps ain't subtle, so expect it to try and sucker punch you, cut you with its claws, what have you. When it cold cocks you, it'll throw you into the shadows and feed. When it does, you have to juice up, slap your gloves on him, and hold on tight. Just like a dead frog, its muscles are going to kick fierce. With any luck, you won't make any skin-to-skin contact while you're zapping him. Once you get him down, you stay on him until I get there. Do what you need to do, stake it, stab it, anything. Whatever you do, *DON'T LET UP*. I'll get to you as soon as I can."

Abe felt his insides go liquid as Ron's big truck rolled past the dark figure walking down the road and Ron drove him to where he was going to ambush him. No, *It*. A part of his brain yammered that what was happening at that moment was completely crazy and that he would be going to jail for a long, long time. On the other hand, if the man really was a vampire, there was a very good chance it would snap him up like a wolf with a rabbit and make a snack out of him. The truck pulled over by a shabby looking stand of jack pines.

"Here's your stop." Ron looked at him intently, "Abe, we wouldn't be here now if I didn't think you could do this. You can." Ron dimmed the interior lights and pointed.

"God be with you. Oh, and say a prayer. Never hurts to be on the up and up."

"Ron, how are you sure he's going to go after me? I'm not a small guy."

"He will." Ron gave a short low chuckle, "You'll stink of fear, adrenaline, and blood, and that's sweet nectar to a hungry bloodsucker."

"Wait, what?"

That's when the much bigger man slapped him. Hard.

Abe's head rang and his face stung. He looked at Ron angrily, momentarily considering turning on the shock gloves.

"What the ACTUAL FUCK, Ron?"

Ron just turned the rearview mirror so Abe could see it. Abe's face was red, and there was a thin cut on his cheek. He was bleeding.

"Head in the Game, Abe. Get out. Stay safe, my friend."

Before the slap could really register, Abe was outside in the darkness, the chill of a North Dakotan winter rushing to greet him. The truck rumbled off as he stepped over the mounds of snow on the stretch of icy sidewalk. A scant few mercury lights offered meager pools of yellow light along his path. Somewhere off in the distance, Abe could hear a dog barking. In the distance, a dark figure was walking his way.

Abe took a second to internalize the fact that Ron was good to his word. Sure, he was scared out of his mind, standing there, shivering, stinking of fresh blood. He could feel the cut on his face stinging in the cold, and instinctively pulled the scarf up to hide it, along with his beard. As he did, he noticed the metal contact points on his glove. He swallowed hard and fumbled for the rubberized switch on his wrist. There was a click, and he was suddenly very conscious of what to do with his hands, trying hard to focus his remaining mental energy on walking normally.

The wind came up and blew curls of old crystalized snow across the icy sidewalk. After what felt like an agonizingly long time, then quick as a flash, he was walking past his target. Abe tried to be casual and focused on ignoring the blood drying on his sleeve and face. As they walked past each other, Abe muttered a hopefully casual greeting.

"Evening."

The man just nodded and walked past him. Abe kept walking, the hair on his neck standing straight up, his heart pounding. His mind raced with options of what to do now.

"Excuse me?"

Abe heard a lightly accented voice ask behind him. He stopped and turned. The man held up a cigarette.

"Do you have a light?"

Abe tried to spot the man's eyes, which seemed dark and hidden.

"Uh, yeah, I think so. Hang on."

Abe looked down and started to pat his pockets, and at that moment the monster struck. It was a blur. A sudden blow connected with his chest, so strong and fast, it drove the wind out of him. Abe felt like a volleyball that had been expertly spiked. The heavy batteries in the vest absorbed a great deal of the force, but Abe felt himself fly through the air backwards and the horizon spun madly.

When his eyes refocused and he dragged in a breath, he realized that in almost no time he had been dragged a hundred yards across a field and into a copse of trees. The vampire kept the momentum going until Abe felt himself lifted and slammed against a tree. It had been a mere handful of seconds. Now he could see the vampire's eyes.

With the glasses Ron had given him, he saw two images superimposed, fading back and forth between the square and open features of a young man and a drawn, corpse-like face, lips pulled back to show a set of sharp incisors set amongst jagged teeth. The creature's eyes were completely black, glinting and piercing, hard as obsidian. Almost absentmindedly, the creature lifted him off his feet, and he felt his neck being pinned by a powerful hand.

"*Esté quietos, y voy a ser rápido,*" the guttural voice croaked.

Something deep and primal screamed inside him as the creature's jaw unhinged and it went to tear his throat out.

If not for the vest and the metal gorget covering his throat, Abe would have already taken too much damage to remain conscious. Already dizzy from lack of air, his fear and adrenaline forced him to start kicking and swinging without even thinking. The vampire looked at him quizzically, surprised that Abe could move. Its surprise grew measurably as Abe's hand slapped down on the clawed appendage cruelly seizing his throat.

There was a smell of ozone and a strange hissing scream as the vampire buckled and lurched backwards, letting go. Unfortunately, the vampire had damaged the insulating layer on Abe's collar, and Abe managed to catch some of the electrical shock to himself. The two of them flew apart, leaving Abe to gasp for breath. The vampire toppled to the ground, looking dazed.

Abe coughed, throat still spasming from the shock. Knowing he had only a fraction of a second to act, he threw himself forward in a sloppy tackle. The vampire was startled as Abe grappled the creature's head, hands pressed to its forehead. When he connected this time, there was a crackling sound. The vampire convulsed wildly, back arching, flipping Abe backwards and breaking contact again. When it could move, the creature hobbled towards the trees.

Abe was thrown rolling and was slowed by surrounding brush. He twisted the switch on his glove off and grabbed frantically for his pockets. The thick gloves and parka did not help as, flailing, he searched for a weapon and finally withdrew the can of bear mace. Scrambling to keep up with his attacker, Abe pulled the pin, and a 20-foot line of brightly fluorescent spray flew from the can as he pulled the trigger. Unfortunately for the vampire, it had just chosen that moment to turn and look for Abe, and it caught a face full of burning capsicum-powered hell. It shrieked and started clawing at its face, swearing colorfully in Spanish.

However, his victory was short lived when he moved to reposition. Abe's foot caught tree root and with a *thud*, he went down. Even with its face dripping with caustic fluid, the vampire's head whipped around at the sound and it snarled. It was crystal clear at that moment that he had merely sent the creature into a frenzy. It was on him in an instant, biting and clawing at him, striking him like a cat batted a mouse on the ground. Abe did his best to roll with the blows and prayed for a moment to do anything.

Suddenly there was a loud *boom* followed by another as the vampire spun away. The noise was deafening. Abe looked down at the gun in his free hand. Without even thinking, he had pulled the pistol and shot. Abe rolled over on his shoulder, saw the vampire starting to get up, and emptied the rest of the clip.

Boom, boom, boom, boom!

The crisp air made the pistol sound like a cannon going off. Abe got to his feet. The vampire, despite being shot repeatedly, was still crawling, the bullet holes in its torso smoking. It cried out to him, in an all too human voice.

"¡No más! ¡No más! ¡Por favor!"

Abe hesitated. That was a mistake.

In a moment frozen in time, Abe saw pine needles, dirt, and snow fly as the creature launched towards him. The two of them whirled back through the pine branches, and the gun was swatted out of Abe's hands. As the vampire threw a flurry of clawing attacks, Abe brought his arms up to protect his face. The vampire wrenched his hand out the way, and Abe vaguely heard a small *click* as the glove circuit snapped.

For a second the vampire's face was only a few inches away, and Abe smelled death and rot and he saw angry obsidian eyes and a twisted, cavernous mouth full of fangs. Abe brought up his hands to strike both temples, and the electricity from the glove arced as his hands met skin. Again, the vampire spasmed and it was thrown backwards. There was a popping, snapping sound and then silence.

Abe's head roared and he spun as he tried to get up, lungs struggling to fill themselves. First one moment and then another passed. Abe staggered, not certain what was happening. His breath was a white cloud in the moonlight that was just now filtering through the trees. The pine trees were silhouetted, cold and brittle in the sub-zero temps. There was something in the tree across from Abe. He pulled the silvered knife and moved carefully forward.

In a very surreal scene, the vampire's back-arching convulsion had thrown it backwards, managing to impale itself on a thick branch. The corpse was hanging about a foot above the ground with no purchase, with about a foot or so of broken jack pine protruding from its chest. It hung there and twitched, its half-shut eyes opalescent and reflective in the milky light, like ghost moons.

Cautiously, Abe crept closer, bent down and, snaking an arm over, clamped a hand over its leg with the glove still activated. The creature gurgled and twitched, jerking listlessly. Abe held on until it stopped moving altogether. He smelled something horrible burning, and a tiny fading whine came from the vest as the batteries gave up their last.

Moving quickly, Abe pulled out the carbon fiber zip ties and trussed the creature up. When he finished, he staggered backwards to lean against a tree, trying hard not to pass out. He gave in to gravity and slumped to the ground.

Soon a deep quiet voice came over the sound of wind and distant highway noises.

"Abe, you okay?"

Abe looked up blearily at Ron.

"Yeah?"

In answer, Abe saw the big man move along the tree line towards him. Abe noted that Ron also added some gear to his wardrobe, including the large rifle in his hands. Ron approached slowly, surveying the area, and then finally stopped at Abe. Even in crunchy snow, Ron moved without making much noise.

"Abe, did you get bit? Can you function?"

Abe pulled himself off the ground with great effort.

"Yeah, I mean, no, I didn't get bitten. I can function, I think, although not for the lack of that son-a-bitch trying, though. Ya know, in the movies, they make this shit look a lot easier."

"Yeah. And for the record, you ain't finished," Ron chuckled lowly.

Abe's eyes widened. He looked over at the vampire who was attached to the tree like some grotesque Christmas ornament.

"Say what?"

Ron nodded at the tree and handed Abe a stake and a hatchet.

"You managed to pin it all right, but the stake has to go through the heart. You are about an inch or two off. Even if we buried it right now, it would come back in a few days, meaner and hungrier than ever. You need to stake it and really hammer that bad boy in. I'll do the rest."

Abe took the proffered stake and made his way over to the creature. It remained motionless, and yet, somehow, he could feel it waiting. He placed the stake over where he thought the heart was, and the opalescent eyes of the creature flew open as it began to writhe and struggle in place. Abe's heart raced and he hit the stake with the reversed side of the hatchet, hammering repeatedly. The creature's head rocked back and hissed, as the stake went through with a visceral crunch. It slumped when the stake hit the tree behind it, like a puppet with its strings cut. Abe jumped back.

Ron gently took the hatchet from Abe's hands and traded him the rifle. Ron stepped up and deftly pulled several items from his jacket. Abe watched as Ron scrawled a symbol the vampire's forehead. Then lifting its head, he pried the mouth open and stuffed something inside.

"Abe, come stand by this thing."

Numb, Abe did as was asked. Ron pulled out an old-fashioned camera, readied a flash that seemed to take forever to charge, then snapped several photos of Abe and the staked vampire.

"The lens on this camera is specially made by a monastic order in Italy. Special filter on this camera allows it to capture things that normal film cameras can't. We take these pictures and we send them to the Order. They'll probably commit to sending us a team."

After Ron stowed the camera, he motioned Abe to step back. With a couple of solid chops, Ron took the creature's head off. It tumbled into the snow, leaving an anemic trail of black goo behind. Ron kicked it into a bag and turned to Abe.

"Watch."

The rest of the vampire's body started to writhe and boil into tiny droplets, then fall apart, leaving its clothes in a heap on the ground. Ron pulled out a flask of holy water and sprinkled it over the pile, saying something that sounded like Latin. The rest of the creature disappeared in a foul-smelling cloud.

"Abe, very carefully check the pockets, full search. Take any ID and whatever else you find."

Abe found a wallet, some keys, and a stack of plastic money cards. As he rummaged, Ron cracked a tube and shook the contents around the area, then picked up the dark bag.

"Let's vamoose. And we need to be careful, heading out to the street."

"Why? Do you think the Sheriff has been called?"

"Nope. But Fish and Game might be about," Ron chuckled. "They get testy if they think you have been bagging white tail out of season. And I really don't want to explain a vampire head inna bag."

A short slog later, they made it back to the giant truck.

"Ron, why did it melt? And why did you save the head? As a trophy? And isn't that going to melt, too?"

Ron pulled the rumbling truck into a U-turn.

"Ah, magic. It's tricky to sustain, and the curse is like a binding. Once severed, the energy dissipates quick. As far as the head, well, vampires are all attached through their bloodlines. It's a big thing to them. Depending on who the Order sends to help us, we can maybe use this head to tell us which Vampire House we're dealing with. We have a few mages among the ranks, and there are some outside contractors who we can talk to. Glad I had the asphodel, too. It's an herb with special properties, and a mouthful prevents the head from going overripe."

Abe leaned against his door and sagged, exhausted. He checked his ribs. He checked his ribs and confirmed he was cooking up tomorrow's bruises. In fact, every part of him felt battered. He slipped the gorget off from around his neck and looked at where the claws had bent the metal, before dropping it on the seat in the back.

"This keeps getting weirder and weirder. I have to ask, Ron, how many Santas have you known that managed to take on a monster by themselves?"

Ron's face looked like it was carved from stone, in the light of the oncoming traffic.

"Three, including myself. Some get killed."

Abe felt a ball of anger build up in his chest.

"Then what the hell use is this process? It's stupid!"

Ron showed little or no emotion, replying as he drove.

"If it makes you feel better, I've never seen a new person take out a vampire single handedly before."

"You were watching all that!?"

"Yup. And I was ready to step in if you needed it. I almost did. You are one tough and lucky son of a bitch."

Abe pressed his aching head against the frosty cold glass of the window.

"I don't think I'm the only son of a bitch in this truck, Ron." Abe turned to watch the streetlamps blur by. He had no idea what else to say.

Ron remained silent for the rest of the drive back to Abe's car. In what seemed like no time at all, Ron was shaking him awake.

"Here's your ride. Go get some sleep. Don't invite ANYBODY into your house."

Abe groggily poured himself out of Ron's truck. He looked back at Ron.

"When will we know?"

"I should hear something back tomorrow. And Abe?"

"Yeah?"

"I pretty much felt the same way you did when I stepped up. It sucks. The Order is an ancient organization and has rules it needs to play by. Not a lot of resources. Sometimes the higher powers play their games, and we puny mortals do what we can to jump through the hoops, hanging on for dear life." Ron came around to help Abe into his car.

"If you prayed before that fight, I'd make a habit of it. You killed an actual vampire, you know that? That was real. Which means there's a battle coming and you are now in it. That anger you feel, that frustration? Hang on to it. Cuz it can help you." Ron's dark eyes looked even more tired as he patted Abe on the shoulder, "Safe home and blessings. Call you tomorrow. Drive safe." Ron closed the door of Abe's car.

With that, the big man lumbered back to his truck, looking more like a tired prophet from some forgotten age in the orange-tinted light of the parking lot. The huge truck rumbled quietly away.

Abe waited the full minute it took to defrost his windshield, feeling very exposed in a nearly empty parking lot. As he drove home, he could feel every bruise and scrape. He felt like someone had worked him over with a baseball bat. Twice. As he drove, he looked up for a moment and prayed.

"Lord, please don't let there be an article in the paper where some poor innocent guy got killed by me. Please."

When he got home, Abe said extra prayers. Then he dug out a crucifix he had inherited from his uncle, arranging it on his nightstand. By the time he pulled the covers up, he was asleep.

* * *

6. The Balloon Goes Up

When Ron got home, he methodically backed the truck into the heated garage. With a sigh, the door closed behind him. He had a lot of cleaning to do, including fixing and recharging the equipment he had lent Abe. Of course, there was also the matter of sealing a head in the tank of a magically secured, rusted water heater tank. After several hours of tidying and a change into his Frosty the Snowman pajamas, he entered the study, tapped his computer awake, and picked up a fiber-optic Christmas tree decoration.

Plugging it into his computer, he waited until the tree cycled through various colors, before settling on a soft green, his cue to pull the film roll from the camera and insert it into the photo processor. While he waited, he wrote up an account of what had happened, and once the negatives had dried, he fed them into a slot at the base of the tree. After a while, it flickered again. He began the process of logging into the Jingle Net chat room, starting with the initial password, then the hidden link, and then a secondary code. A few seconds later, the cute dancing reindeer ceased his prancing and a video call opened. Ron gave the all-clear sign to his camera, and a young woman with brightly colored hair came into frame and gave him the counter-sign in response.

"Hey, Ron."

"Hey, Freckles. Is your Dad still out?"

"Yeah, he'll be at a Tree Lighting ceremony until fairly late. They always do the photos afterwards and that takes forever. Those poor kids must be getting home exhausted."

Freckles was usually out elfing with her Dad, as her clown and princess gigs tended to dry up during the holidays. The fact that she was on the Order's encrypted site meant that her father, Santa Kyle, had her standing by just in case. Curious.

"Freckles, I Santa Ron Verletz, sworn member of the Winter Order, on behalf of Abraham Wykowski, a Santa in LaMoure, North Dakota, USA, invoke the aid of the Winter Order. In accordance with the rite, he himself was asked by a child for aid, invoking us in our Season. He provides the following as proof of his challenge."

Ron clicked the mouse and sent the files.

Freckles' smile gave way to a stern, analytical look. The file popped up on her end in short order, and her eyes told him she was looking at the photos and his account.

She answered, still pouring over them.

"Santa Ron, I have received your proofs and your request for aid. I will tender them to the Council. May the Spirit of the Season guide us."

"Thanks, Freckles."

Freckles looked at the picture and shook her head.

"Wow, it looks like this one went down hard!"

"It did. Abe and it went twenty rounds. I think Abe had more than just a little divine luck."

Freckles raised an eyebrow at Ron.

"You put Abe through the whole tradition? No help other than gear? You must think highly of him. I'm guessing there's more to this? Do you think that you just have a rando pack of vamps moving through, or some loner twos and fews, or what?"

Ron ran his fingers through his beard.

"Honestly Freckles, I'm thinking this is why I am here. Something big is happening here. I can feel it in my gut."

There was a sound off-screen and Freckles disabled the video. Ron looked at the fiber-optic Christmas tree, which was now golden, signaling a holding state.

A few minutes had passed when the screen lit up and another window popped up beside Freckles'. It was Kyle, his white hair still matted from hours of wearing a warm Santa hat for hours.

"Hey Ron," said Kyle.

"I briefed my Dad and swore him in, Ron," added Freckles.

Santa Kyle was a much shorter and rounder Santa than either Ron or Abe, but his permanent smile belied his sharp blue eyes.

"Ron, I'm happy you were able to get proof of this as soon as you did. We have had several of our scrying people ringing the bells, telling us something big is moving. One of our Volva, the Norse witches, swears that some of her rune stones stood on end tonight. So, I'm guessing that our Council is going to respond with a great big, '*Yah, sure, you betcha.*'"

"Well, I hope so. Do you know who is on deck, who can get here quick?" Ron took a deep breath.

Santa Kyle rubbed his face, thinking through the current situation.

"Probably Pastor Carl, out of Bemidji. He's old, but he's one of the old school White Light team. I worked with him back in the day. Good man. Then there is Santa Jon, out of Minneapolis. He's a Pagan, and a certified nutter and badass. He's hell on wheels with the sharp and pointies and has some mojo of his own."

Freckles, who had been quiet so far, jumped in.

"What about Skyia?"

Kyle shot a look off-screen, then turned back to his camera.

"If she'll do it? Maybe. No doubt she's the best hunter out there, but I don't know if the Council will bond her. There might be a question as to whether the Caestus binding will work properly, if the members aren't male or human," he shrugged as if to absolve himself of answering.

"I don't think the higher powers particularly care whose asses we hang on a line, Dad," Freckles rolled her eyes and turned away from the camera.

"Sorry, squirt. Truth is, much of the old magic was created by old men, and if Skyia is part Fay, that'll be even more complicated. Just sayin. If it says, 'use a blue kangaroo,' that's what you do, right?" Kyle shook his head.

Ron jumped in before Freckles started to make it more of an issue.

"Anybody else?"

"Ron, LaMoure is at the ass-end of nowhere. Hell, Fargo maybe has what? Seven semi-pro Santas and a bunch of volunteers? Last I recall, there was scary Lithuanian or Russian Santa, Morry something, out that way but nobody's seen him for years. I think he ended up clashing with the feds for some reason, and now he does acts by night, leaving stuff at the doors of the needy, fixing things anonymously, but doesn't do anything public anymore."

There was a chortle and an *Ah-Ha!* as Freckles popped back up on screen, waving a paper triumphantly. She held a bleary photo up to her camera.

"The Beast! The Beast may actually be in South Dakota."

"Come again?" Ron raised his eyebrows.

"The Beast. He's a really well-known pro-wrestler. *Aaaaand*," said Freckles with a grin, "He's a huge Santa fan. Wears the suit for charity events, keeps a room in his house with Christmas going all year round." She reached out of camera view to hand the paper to her dad, who took it reluctantly.

"Muscles do not a monster hunter make," Ron cautioned. "But if he's actually a member of the Order and he's nearby, then yay?" His face betrayed his lack of enthusiasm.

"Whatever happens Ron, you know we'll do our best," Kyle advised. "Something else you should know: They've predicted a massive snowstorm coming through the region these next few days. Kinda came out of nowhere. That could make travel to your area a real problem. If need be, could you rely on any local talent?"

Ron ran calloused fingers through his beard.

"Not really, no. We have some people here who slap on a beard during the season, and one other pro Santa who was flown in for a nearby mall. He's a good-looking, real-bearded Santa, rocks the Coca-Cola suit hard. Out from the west coast I think, Steve somebody. He's not a member of any of the Santa groups that I know of. That reminds me; if this all goes ugly, I better let him know to keep his head down and be wary."

"Yeah, that should be a fun conversation," said Freckles. *"Hi, welcome to our fair city, and oh, by the way, a bunch of guys in white beards are going to get into a turf war with a bunch of vampires. Mind your ass."*

Kyle sighed, "You are not helping, Ann," addressing Freckles pointedly.

Freckles looked seriously into the camera on her end.

"Ron, we are on the clock. Go get some sleep and Blessings."

Kyle echoed, "She's right, get some rest and God Bless. May the Spirit keep you. I've got a lot of work to do. Lord knows you've got a lot of work to do. Find yourself a team. Then, have fun finding some replacements for their gigs, at the last moment, in season."

Ron winced. Anybody who could play a convincing Santa had long since been booked up.

"Good luck, Kyle, we're going to need it."

"You bet, Ron."

Ron waved goodbye to the camera, shut down the computer, and carefully tucked the fiber optic tree away, hiding its internal encryption port. With the negatives collected and placed in his safe, he set about lighting several candles, checking his magical wards, and finished with a round of prayers.

Ron knew sleep would find him tonight. Unfortunately, so would his dreams.

* * *

7. Origins

717 CE, near what is now Hungary

Father Nicholas cast his gaze over the smoldering remains of the village, fists clenched with frustration. Tears streamed down his marred, sooty face. He had arrived too late to warn his neighbors, and now, the smell of smoke and death lingered thick in the air. The carnage had been so complete that, between the fire and the raiding, he could barely make out the identities of the corpses littering the streets. This had been a new posting, and he had barely gotten a chance to know them, let alone learn to speak their language fluently. He bowed his head and prayed, even though the rage squeezing his chest made it difficult to muster the words. Humidity caused the sticky beads of perspiration to run down his face. The songs of crows and flies were his only answer.

A moment of wandering produced an adze and a shovel. For several hours, he alternated between digging and wheeling cartloads of bodies to the selected plot, and in time, had buried all the dead he could find. The raiders had spared no one. As he worked, however, he noticed there were no bodies of young women, nor of children.

The adjacent ruin had been newly consecrated for the Saint of his own namesake, in honor of St. Nicholas of Myra. Using the burning shell of what was intended to be his new church, he created a burial mound and covered it with crackling timbers he had dragged over. The wild animals would not be digging up this grave.

As he went to pull over one last beam, he heard a cough. He whirled, startled. Picking up his shovel, he sought its source. Another cough. The smoke from his pyre was floating past the crumbled well. After searching, he found woven mats under the dirt and weeds that were hiding a small storage pit. Shovel tight in hand, he flipped the mats over, revealing the faces of several small children. They were terrified, yet one young boy peered back fiercely, a small knife outstretched. Father Nicholas fell to his knees and said a small prayer of thanks.

Following his recitation, he stepped back and called to them, but all refused to follow. Scratching his head, he decided to fetch them water, given their exhausted and sallow appearance. When he pulled up the bucket of water, he saw his reflection and realized that the mud and grime on his face made him almost unrecognizable to even himself. For the sake of recognition, he cleaned his face, then brought fresh water back to them. At that point, the children clambered out and ran to him. First one, then another, and another, and another. To his surprise, he now had ten children between three- and seven-years old clinging to him, even a little white-haired girl named Alena, who was one of the few children he had had a chance to baptize. All the children started talking, crying out for their families all at once. Father Nicholas, who had spent most of his life in study, turned his eyes up to the heavens and silently questioned God's choice of him as an erstwhile guardian.

Father Nicholas caught the flash of silver on the horizon. Horsemen, far across the fields, were closing the distance. More raiders. Nicholas quickly considered his options. There was almost no chance he could get the children to the river, and if he did, the raiders likely had boats as well. He could send them down into the hole again, but now that he had built the pyre over the grave, the raiders would know someone had returned to the area. This time, the children were sure to be found, to be killed or sold as slaves.

Spinning frantically, Nicholas saw the thunder of an oncoming summer storm brewing in the distance, with threatening clouds hanging over the nearby forest. While the raiders would not respect his church, his faith, he knew there was one place in the forest they would avoid. Raiders had no fear of his "slain God," but they stayed away from the sites of the older gods. This was a site sacred to the Old Ones. Father Nicholas had visited a while ago and, while it had been unnerving, there had been a small cave amongst the craggy hills in the woods. A hoary-haired man had been maintaining the grounds and accepting offerings.

Father Nicholas uttered a small prayer of forgiveness to the Creator for even contemplating what he was about to do. With many gestures, he scooped and loaded several of the smallest of children on the hand cart, to which he tied the two nanny goats that had approached to be milked. The older children spotted the riders on the horizon, helping to organize the youngest among them. Father Nicholas waved, and the whole group quickly trotted towards the forest. The breeze gathered as the first droplets fell from above. As they fled, he hoped that real rain would get to the village before the raiders did, fearing that their tracks would be obvious and easy to follow.

* * *

God answered his call for rain in spades. Four cold, rain-soaked hours later, Father Nicholas was pulling the rickety cart along a trail that had begun to flood. In the darkness, it was almost impossible to see where he was going. He had stacked most of the children in the cart and covered them with his cloak. Now only the brutal effort of pulling against the mud kept his teeth from chattering. Sadly, the two goats had wrestled free earlier.

The oldest boy seemed to understand where they were going, his expression halfway between discomfort and embarrassment. He quietly led Father Nicholas through a cluster of boulders and toward the side of a cliff. There, in the dusky evening light, Father Nicholas could make out carvings in the stone, the forms of old gods draped with moss, and near them, a yard of half-buried wooden statues.

Turning around, he realized that he had been pulling his wagon past a clearing of bulging trees, all wrapped with faded garlands, where the villagers had only recently stopped entombing their dead in the living wood. His stomach sank, but the boy ran forward and rattled a hanging wooden noise maker. A short time later, a dark figure stepped out of the gloom. Who or what it was exactly, Father Nicholas could not tell, except that the outer irises of the person's eyes shone a vibrant green. Muted scuffling accompanied the figure as it shambled around them, sniffing the cart. The boy bowed deeply and indicated to Father Nicholas that he should do the same. He did so. The person or creature stopped in front of him, waving a long-nailed finger, motioning to the children.

"Sssacrificessss?" it asked in a high-pitched voice.

"Uh, no. NO! Please. We are here asking for refuge," Father Nicholas was startled. He pointed to the children, "I ask on their behalf. We mean no harm. Once the raiders in the town are gone, we will be on our way. Please, these children are wet and cold, and they have been through much."

The figure stared up at the gray clouds overhead, and then looked back down at him. It reached out and tapped the wooden cross on his chest with a long black nail.

"Your white god. You love it, yesss?"

Father Nicholas shivered and took a deep breath, "Yes."

The figure waved a bony hand around at the forest surrounding them.

"The people come here no more. They come to you. Your god does not protect them. Now you come to us?" The figure pointed to Nicholas, "We name your followers Forest Killers. Iron Bringers."

Turning to face the cart, Father Nicholas could hear the rain picking up again. The temperature was dropping steeply. There was no way he would be able to stop at least a few of the children from getting very ill, possibly fatally if they did not find shelter soon. He bowed his head.

"It is true. People who follow my God do not honor your ways. But we do believe in charity, mercy, generosity. Please."

There was a snort from the dark figure.

Rain hammered down on the gathering, and the figure in the darkness swayed for a bit, as if listening. Finally, it spoke.

"Yes. Refuge we give, for as long as needed. It has been a long time since we have heard the laughter of children, and sweet is the sound to us. But there is a price. Two children we will choose to stay, to be trained in our ways. One will be sacrificed, and it will be their choice." Before Father Nicholas could say anything, one of the older boys spoke up.

"My name is Andrei. My heart is big. I will be the sacrifice."

Father Nicholas stepped between the figure and the boy.

"No."

He looked over his shoulder at the sodden boy, standing defiant.

"No, Andrei. You haven't even been baptized yet. Thank you, but no."

Andrei started to say something, but Father Nicholas stepped forward and looked into the strange eyes of the figure. Desperately, madly, he rifled through what he remembered of these people, and a story about challenges of long odds popped into his head. His thoughts turned quickly to the marauding bands outside of these woods. He had little left in the way of options.

"Rather than a sacrifice, how about a challenge? I will challenge whomever you like and offer my life as wages, be it slavery or death. Let me challenge your people, I offer my life for those I would protect. Would it not be better to see a priest of the White God dead? Or working your fields?"

The figure stepped back, a bit startled, and swayed for another long moment. The wind whistled and the rain thundered as it hit the ground.

"Agreed. A challenge. In the morning. Your life for one of theirs. Come."

Following the figure through eddies and crevasses, and slowly gaining altitude, they soon found themselves inside a long, angular cave. A false floor of timbers and mats had been installed, and it occurred to Father Nicholas, as the figure struck up a fire, that he was in a place that had probably once held hundreds of worshippers. Echoes were swallowed up by its sheer size. Outside the rain drummed.

A fire sprang up, glorious and golden red. Two more figures came out of the darkness with rough woolen blankets and bowls of hot broth. They moved the children to encircle the fire. Of the three followers of the old gods, one was a man, the other a woman, both of whom looked bird-like and ancient. A tall figure entered, bringing with it a heavy cauldron and several loads of firewood. With deft hands, the elderly pair levered up the floors and erected walls to trap heat in the big cavern. Being as close as they were to the wall of the cave, the stone itself began to heat up, blackened with the silt of hundreds of fires before. As Father Nicholas took a cup of broth, he looked up and saw that the walls were painted with hundreds and hundreds of drawings. Most of them seemed to be about the hunt, scenes consisting of strange symbols and effigies. The children, now sufficiently revived, examined the tableau in wonder, only to then collapse in a pile, falling into an exhausted sleep.

The strange eyed man hunkered down near the fire, slowly drawing lines in the ashes, while humming and speaking odd phrases. Try as he might, Father Nicholas fought to keep his eyes open. He failed.

* * *

8. The Challenge

The next morning, the children were already up and excitedly exploring. The rain had stopped, replaced by a cool mist that hung over the forest. Father Nicholas walked to the edge of the cave and the view was beautiful. The entrance itself provided a lofty vantage, hidden in the cleft in some massive rock formations, which themselves marched into a host of mountains. Spotting one of the locals, possibly the old woman from the night before, he waved to them. Where he navigated his way down, she stood, pointing to a fire and making motions for him to eat. He did so hesitantly, even though he was roaring hungry. Relenting, he scooped up a bowl of some thick, hot gruel, and said his prayers quietly.

The fire was not far from a stream, so after he finished two bowls of chewy but delicious wild grains, he washed himself and the bowl. When he returned, he could see the children were having a good time climbing the scaffolding that ran along the inside of the cave. He felt a presence behind him.

Turning, he saw several of the forest dwellers — one oddly shaped giant of a man and a tall, dark-haired woman dressed in hunting gear, a bow and quiver slung at her side. She examined him with a cold, measuring look.

Each walked up and inspected him in turn, his hands and clothes alike. At this, the children in the cave stopped laughing and turned to watch. The woman archer was last. Her nose wrinkled, and with a step back, she spat on the ground. An incredibly old woman tottered up to the group, so thickly covered in fetishes and strung adornments that it was hard to see where her skin stopped and the ornaments began. She handed him a gourd and motioned for him to drink its contents.

Father Nicholas looked back at the children.

"Andrei, whatever happens, see if you can get them back to their relatives if you can."

Andrei nodded affirmatively, if somberly.

Father Nicholas lifted the gourd and drank. It was by far the foulest, most horrible concoction he had ever tasted. Only the years of poorly made monastic food gave him the willpower to gag it all down and not vomit. Trinket woman nodded a slight *well done* to him and offered him a leaf, which he took and chewed. It was a blessing, slightly sweet, muting the flavors and numbing his taste buds. Off in the distance, he could see others drinking out of similar gourds.

The elder woman took the vessel from his hand and tugged at his shirt sleeve, motioning for him to undress. Cold and embarrassed, Father Nicholas did so, revealing a body that was pasty white and, while not scrawny, it was obvious he had little flesh to spare. He kept his cross and rosaries, despite continued prodding. As his head started to swim, a tall woman came back to look at him, while another carrying a bow regarded him with disdain. Nicholas attempted to focus his eyes on the tall woman, who was now blurry and oddly colorful. A rolling gurgle let him know his stomach was not happy.

She spoke in what he estimated to be perfect Latin, *"Mox fereris ad locum certaminis. Eligendus tibist ad quem vis pugnare. Ex arena non egredi potes et nemo te adiuvabit. Intelligisne?"*

However, his mind heard, "In a moment, they will bring you to the place of the battle. You must choose whom you will fight. You cannot leave the sand and you shall receive no aid. Do you understand?"

Father Nicholas nodded, feeling rather helpless and slightly irritated. Not only was he going to spend his moments fighting clumsily, but they had drugged him before he had had a chance to fight. It seemed terribly unsporting, really. As he walked, he quietly prayed to St. Nicholas of Myra, his namesake. The original St. Nicholas had been renowned for being resilient, a bit of a scrapper. And if ever Father Nicholas needed some of that fighting spirit, it was now. He took several deep breaths. For a moment, his stomach seemed to calm down.

They brought him to what looked like a natural arena and amphitheater where they pushed him into the center, a sandy mound mixed with mud from the recent rains. Surrounding it were hundreds upon hundreds of effigies and carved stones. As he examined them, the symbols and all the odd faces and figures seemed to be moving and changing, even peering back at him. Turning his gaze past them, he saw that the locals now looked different, ambiguous and strange. Some were misshapen and only barely humanoid, and others were quite subtle and beautiful. Even the trees and landscape seemed alive. His head swam as several warriors, some human, some not, walked into the circle and surrounded him.

The whole affair, his addled state, everything seemed strangely surreal and humorous. He staggered past one of the men, laughing, and patted one of the wooden statues. It was so old, he could barely make out the carvings on it. He noted that the statue had rusty red chains and manacles on it. Nicholas stumbled over to them, yanking on them to keep himself upright. Unfortunately, the stakes that were secured in the wood jerked free. He rocked and stepped away, chains still in hand, before running back onto the dirt. Overcompensating, he wobbled over to the mound and tottered past the figures' ranks until he was beside the wall. The beings around him made small noises but did not move to interfere.

Nicholas hefted the chain and drunkenly whirled it around. It felt rusty and solid. He felt many eyes upon him.

"Fine. I'm, fine. *urp* Fine. No, I'm fine. Dear Lord, *whoa*. The children. I must fight."

Having decided that he would practice trying to hit one of the carved figurines, he swung at the one closest in the group, swirling and snarling around him. It was the biggest, moldered and crumbling, and he hit it hard. The chains spun. Wooden and metallic crashing thundered as the manacle slammed into the wood.

Father Nicholas staggered to his knees. Angry voices crowded round his head.

"He can't do that. It is not allowed."

"He is in the spirit circle. It is not for us to choose."

Behind him there was a roaring, hissing sound. The ground shook as something massive hit the ground.

Father Nicholas pushed himself up. His head was clearing but his senses were still frayed. His eyes seemed to see with a dreadful translucent quality. He watched as the creatures around the arena recoiled, their eyes wide. Nicholas turned slowly, not wanting to see.

There, in the center of the arena, loomed a huge, cloven-hoofed shaggy creature, reminiscent of a man. It had a pair of dark, infernal horns, glowing eyes, a long snapping tail, and imposing genitalia. It lolled its head back and forth, a long, snaky tongue tasted the air, culminating in the creature beating its hairy chest with huge, clawed fists. It pointed directly at him, and Father Nicholas heard it with explicit clarity.

"Challenge accepted!"

* * *

Father Nicholas stepped towards the mound, his heart pumping madly, his senses still reeling. Halfway between laughing maniacally and crying miserably, he realized there was no chance that he could beat a creature this powerful in a physical challenge.

Instead, Nicholas decided that if he was going to die, he was going to give them all a show. If they had been angry about him defacing things, this next bit was really going to annoy them. He hoisted up the chains and flung them around his head, flogging any statue or icon within reach, chanting his morning prayers as loudly as he could. As he flailed away, he saw flashes of exotic colors, his world growing ever blurrier. He heard hisses, moans, and inhuman screams coming from all around him, some coming from the idols, others from the watchers around the circle. Out of the corner of his eye, he saw the giant shaggy creature leap his way. The very next second, he found himself batted across the ring, peppered with a torrent of welts and gashes, and flipped and tossed through the air like prey. He barely had a chance to register where the creature had sunk its claws before it had tossed him through the air and over its back, as if inconsequential.

With a bone jarring, meaty thud, he slammed against yet another column, feeling all the air leaving his body. Nicholas connected so hard that the massive stone figure was tilted back. For a hazy moment, he saw the beast turn and lower its head. Ragged gasps wracked him leaving him sucking for air, struggling to pull himself up to a kneeling position. As the creature sprinted at him, a humongous ram, Nicholas realized that one end of the iron chain was draped over the wooden arm of the neighboring totem. With blind impulse, he attempted to pull himself up and over the attack, and in that second, the creature made a serious mistake. The rain, mud, and sand had made the ground soft and treacherous. It tried to stop or turn, but it was too late, carrying its momentum into the unyielding stone idol, crashing hard enough to stun itself. There was a second loud crack and a grinding sound. Shaking its head in a daze, the creature failed to step away fast enough and the larger part of the heavy stone figure came crashing down with a heavy *whud*, pinning the creature from the waist down.

There was a chorus of distraught cries from the onlookers. Father Nicholas had only narrowly avoided being flattened by the idol himself as it fell. Feeling incredibly faint, he lowered himself back down to the dirt, leaving a bloody trail of footprints behind him. Panting, he shot a glance at the tribe and creatures playing witness to the debacle. The potion he had drunk had surely addled his brains, along with the deadly flurry of blows. It became even more obvious that many watching were not human, nor even particularly material in nature. Moreover, the collective onlookers were united in vocal, frothing anger. The thin, birdlike woman now had black feathers instead of hair, her eyes gleaming now gone black with no sclera. She pointed at him with a talon-finger and screeched in a rending voice.

"You must not stop! It is kill or be killed!"

Father Nicholas backed away from his fell-horned foe. Though it was in obvious pain, it was doing a credible job of pulling itself out from under the stone, despite being partially crushed. He scanned the arena, finding chunks of stone from their battle, but nothing of real weight. Saying a hushed prayer, he jumped onto the stone that entombed the creature. Its mouth gaped, emitting a horrible, braying scream. He scrambled off the stone and onto his captive's back before it could shift to face him, hooking the chain's end under its chin and began to twist the chain around its neck. Tears ran down Nicholas's face. He had never been a warrior, knowing only the life of a healer, a teacher. He looked up, white-knuckled hands cinching the chains even tighter, and saw the woman with the bow studying the scene intently. Her dark eyes were locked on the creature beneath him. Ever so slightly, infinitesimally, she looked up at him, and her eyes spoke the word "please." Something inside of Nicholas felt her pain.

Nicholas prayed to God for inspiration. For one amazing moment, he felt a piercing sense of clarity, as if a note in the universe was being sung and the note was himself. Everything froze. In this sweet, timeless moment, he felt peace. The images came to him then, as time resumed. Where they came from, he was not certain: It was a memory, something he remembered from his youth, a game he had played with one of his foreign brothers in his childhood monastery.

Aware of the company judging him, he turned his attention back to the strangling. The metal was burning the skin of its neck. He felt a pang of shame.

"I did not pin you, this statue did. If you promise to stop attacking me, I will help free you. I will take these chains off you, and because we are both wounded, we can have a battle of the mind."

The creature looked up at him defiantly and snarled. However, an ear cocked and it studied Nicholas. The rage in its eyes cooled, and it soon nodded its head.

Father Nicholas slipped the chain off the throat of the creature, drawing a chorus of incredulous calls from the beings surrounding the ring. Nicholas hobbled to the base of one of the broken stands. With a stray beam, he slowly levered the hefty stone idol off of his opponent. There was a *whump*, and carefully the creature pulled itself away, trying to stand. Unable to manage the feat, it slumped to one side.

Wasting no time, Nicholas took a piece of wood and scratched a circle in the sand surrounding them.

"I've been told that demons and spirits like riddles and such. You and I will play a game. If I win, you will be beaten and your life is mine. If you win, do what you will. Fair?"

The creature answered in a surprisingly deep and rich voice.

"Yes, provided I understand the game."

"Agreed."

Surrounding them, the beings outside the ring started to chant, but a wave of a feathered and clawed hand from the dark-feathered bird woman silenced them abruptly.

Father Nicholas ignored them and gathered a group of rocks together. He took a shard of bloody wood and drew a star around the two of them, and all of it within the circle.

"Here is your riddle. It's called the Pentalpha. I have nine stones that have to go to the ten intersections." He held up the first stone.

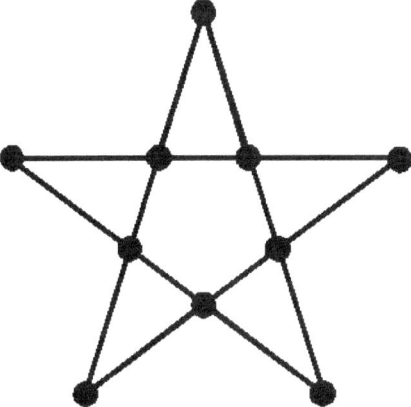

"This stone must go to two other points, before it stops. The three points must be next to each other. The points have to be in a straight line."

The creature furrowed its brow as it looked around.

"It cannot be done," it growled suspiciously, showing serious fangs.

Nicholas skipped back a bit holding up his hands.

"But it can. Ah, yes, last and final rule. The first and third point are not allowed to be occupied, but the second point is!" he added hurriedly.

A cracking voice from the Bird Woman broke the moment.

"You may issue this challenge, son of Adam. But know this, whatever happens between you two, by nightfall, there will be a final ruling."

Father Nicholas saw the Bird Woman was now perching on a higher stone, and other creatures were studying the problem with interest. Father Nicholas bowed to her. He shrugged and pointed to his own bloody legs.

"We are both seriously wounded. I don't know if we would live much longer regardless."

The Archer woman looked up to the Bird Woman.

"I will give you fresh game for three moons, if I may offer them help to them both equally. I want to see how this puzzle ends."

The Bird Woman shook her head irritated and waved a claw-like hand.

"Fine."

The herculean Goat-man propped itself up and placed the first stone. Father Nicholas picked up another and waited. The creature pointed to another juncture. Obediently, he walked over and checked with the beast to make certain he had the right point. He started placing the stones for the creature that had, only a short time ago, almost succeeded in providing him with external organs. Time stretched out. An hour passed. While most humans would have departed, the coterie of paranormal creatures stayed, watching with singular interest. A bundle was tossed in between Nicholas and the creature. While it considered its next move, Father Nicholas opened the bundle and found poultices, bandages, a skin of water, and a loaf of hard bread.

He applied some of the poultices and bandaged himself as best he could. With some effort, he tore the bread in half and partook in some water, never leaving the circle. Gingerly, he offered the rest of the items to the creature.

"My name is Nicholas."

The big creature snatched the rest of the items from him with the snarl of a big cat.

"It is bad manners to offer a name when it is not asked."

The creature followed suit, bandaging itself as best it could; however, the leg and hip would need much more than a bandage or poultice. It finished off the bread and water with a satisfied gulp.

The afternoon wore on, and Father Nicholas noted a few new observers had left, including the children who evidently had free run of the area. The creature tried over and over, but the sequence defied it.

Flies gathered and hummed in the hot sun. The holy man shook the water skin again. There was maybe a swallow left. He decided to save it.

Dusk began to fall, and the creature was becoming more and more agitated. Ominously, a large group of creatures with spears and swords gathered near the opening.

"What do you think will happen if you don't solve it by nightfall?" Father Nicholas asked the creature quietly.

It glanced up at him briefly.

"Then they will kill me."

Father Nicholas looked up at the bird woman who was transforming into more and more a black silhouette against the lavender sky.

"And if I give you the answer?"

The creature gave him a tired, toothy grin.

"Then I am likely to kill you."

* * *

Nicholas stepped back. Torches were being lit. The wind picked up, and a burning twig from one of them landed within the circle. Seizing the opportunity, he plucked it from the ground and cradled it, then used it to light a piece of wood. He held the wood aloft to help the creature see well.

There was the sound of a gong and the Bird Woman cried out.

"Enough! Black Goat, can you solve the puzzle?"

The creature dipped its head for a second.

"No."

"Mortal, do you have the answer?"

Father Nicholas bowed and picked up the rusty chain.

"I do."

He walked over, put a thick piece of wood into the manacle and then offered it to the creature.

"What is this?" it asked darkly.

Father Nicholas wrapped his hands around the chain.

"I'm helping you up. I'm assuming you would rather be standing when you meet your end? Besides, I need you to move."

The creature took the chain and, with Father Nicholas's help, managed to get to a standing position. Father Nicholas took the last blood-stained rock. He put it at the point where the creature had been lying. Taking the stick, he called out the points out working his way back to the starting point, tracing as he did. He held onto the chain as he did, keeping the creature steady.

"Theta, Eta, Zeta, Digamma, Epsilon, Delta, Gamma, Beta, and Alpha."

There was a groan and some laughter from the surrounding circle. Father Nicholas dropped the stick and nodded.

"I know. It irritated the hell out of me, when I realized that the point I was standing on was the point you had to move to."

There was a grumble of something unintelligible from the creature that Nicholas overheard being called the Black Goat. The Bird Woman stepped out of the shadows and motioned to warriors that were standing nearby.

"He must die, then the mortal can go."

Father Nicholas looked over at the Black Goat and did not drop the chain. Instead, he moved to block them.

The warriors started towards the circle drawn on the ground and the moment one of their spear points crossed the line, the circle burst into flames.

As one group, they all stepped back while flaming spear bits fell to the ground. A pulse of fire raced around the circle, and the star drawn on the ground was illuminated into flaming lines. The ground itself glowed, as did the splashes of blood and the drawings on the rock.

A high, clear voice came from a hooded figure, who approached the outermost ring to stand beside the Archer.

"Can you not see?" said the Tall Woman.

The Archer looked up at Bird Woman.

"For the record, this is not my doing."

The Tall Woman moved her hands in an intricate way and then pointed to the two in the circle. The Bird Woman hissed in response.

"What do you want?"

"It's obvious. By the rules of sacrifice and binding, by circle and star, they are bound. By fire, bound. By stone, bound. By water, bound. By the covenant of bread, bound. They have a life debt between them."

Tall Woman pulled her hood back to reveal ash colored hair and clear gray eyes. She pointed to the iron chains.

"By iron and blood, bound. And by the chains of the Binder itself, no less."

Bird Woman looked down at the Archer woman and then Tall Woman.

"You wanted to see how it ended, hrrrm?"

Archer woman gave her a wry look, a bit chagrined.

"Okay, the bread and water might have been my idea, but I did not *know* that he would share it evenly."

"Gaaah!" screeched the Bird Woman.

The clawed woman pointed to her peers. Nicholas thought he definitely saw some family resemblance.

"Why would the two of you want to help this *Nicholas*, name-saked for the defiler who broke your temples, who helped destroy the old ways? A minion of a selfish desert god? When has the desert ever loved the forest?"

Tall Woman, with her sleet gray eyes, looked calmly out at the two beings in the circle, both of whom looked tired and confused.

"I understand your anger. Heed my council: Let the two of them be healed. And just as you would have trained the children in your ways, train them for seven years as weal or way, as chance to be. Work them, teach them, then send them on their way. Keep as many of the children as you wish but keep them alive. The mortal did fight for that, did he not?"

Bird Woman cocked her head, and something unsaid flew between the two of them. Both had the look of someone facing an adversary who they would rather not fight. The feathered matriarch sniffed and spat at the ground, nodding curtly. Tall Woman spat at the same spot, causing it to hiss. The Archer stepped up to the circle and scanned it curiously.

"I see others have meddled as well."

She pointed to the massive statue that had partially pinned the Black Goat creature.

"You cannot hide from me."

She looked carefully at where the battle had happened, her eyes missing nothing.

"Winter, show yourself."

A faint ghostly form appeared and the temperature dropped. A voice like ice crystals whispering against a frozen snowbank whistled.

"They did insult my sssssstatue."

"Not with intent."

"Not sssso," said the Winter Wind. "Look at them. A bringer of ssspring and a lighter of firessss."

"For dropping the stone on them and interfering with the duel, you should give them the boon of winter," said the Archer.

The heat and swelter of this evening were obviously taking a toll on the cold weather spirit. There was a *KRaACK!* like the sound of a splintering ice sheet.

"Ssssaid and done. Sssssaid and done." With that, it faded from view, leaving the ground around the area covered in frost.

The black feathered Bird Woman hopped down from the high stone. With a swipe of her clawed hand, she walked through the fire and up to the two figures.

"Well fought and well played, although I think you two were ignorant of the forces around you. Still..." She looked at Father Nicholas.

"For seven years, you will serve us and you will learn as the children do. You will refrain from teaching your god in symbol or speech for seven years, while you dwell here."

She turned to the visibly angry Goat-man and prodded him with an angular black nail.

"You. You will heal and help us keep our lands, as well as take classes," she added offhandedly as she walked away. "Remember, both of you are now bound. If one of you dies, the other will, too. Either by the magic of your bonds, by our hands, or by falling off a rock. It makes no difference to us." She hobbled into the darkness.

The Archer walked over to the two of them.

"Take care of each other and get some rest. They will try to break you. It will be a long seven years. Heal fast and learn well. Your lives depend on it."

Then she leaned in and reached up, touching the face of the Goat-man tenderly.

"Be well, old friend. I'll see you soon." The Archer took two steps into the forest and was gone.

Standing in the dark, Father Nicholas waited for a few moments and coughed.

"Can I help you get to someplace to heal?"

In answer, the creature pulled on the iron chains and glowered down at him. It growled.

"Must you be so nice? Back there, during the duel, you could have killed me. Why did you stay your hand?"

"Sorry, it is a thing with my beliefs," Father Nicholas bowed his head. "Killing you felt wrong. That's why I played for time."

The creature stared at him and started to say something, then stopped. It growled and winced as it hopped from out the circle. Nicholas offered his shoulder and cringed as the big creature leaned on him. Together, they hopped and staggered towards a fire near the caves.

As they walked, the creature hissed and growled in pain. Nicholas paused and helped it lean against a tree. In the darkness, with smoldering eyes, the Black Goat looked down at the priest.

"My name is Krampus. I am He who dances in the woods. *Once we are no longer bound, know that I will kill you."*

Nicholas looked up at the deadly creature and sighed.

"Well then. That would mean I might have no reason to struggle to survive what happens next. You might as well kill me now. Although as I understand it, that will kill you, too." Nicholas gave the creature a rueful smile, "I don't know what happens to you, Krampus, when you die, but there's a chance that I might go to my heavenly reward, hopefully."

Nicholas looked around himself, surrounded by old gods and arcane magic, and realized that there was a chance that his God might not be that happy with him either. There came a nickering laugh from the darkness. A rich voice oozed from the Goat man.

"I will give you this, little son of Adam, you don't scare easily. Let us both survive and then see what becomes of it. Perhaps I will give YOU a challenge to solve. Those of your creed know little of magic. These are the old magicks. These are those most primal arts that can bind body AND spirit. You assume you will go to your other place. My folk live a very long time. Perhaps your shade will not be going anywhere. Think on that."

Nicholas said nothing but reaching out, offered Krampus a thick branch to help it start hobbling again.

"Why do you still keep those heavy chains and manacles? Their weight has to be hurting you."

There was no immediate answer. Finally, Krampus spoke in a low voice.

"These have your blood and my blood on them. They are things of power, made by the being called Binder. I would not have them fall into the wrong hands."

"Ah."

When they reached the fires of the followers of the older gods, they were shown piles of sweet-smelling branches and rushes to sleep on. The two of them wordlessly parted ways and found rest, but not alone. Never alone again.

* * *

9. A Matter of Time

790 CE, at a small and obscure monastery near the Danube

Abbot Nicholas lay on his deathbed, and in a thready, humorous voice, he was imparting what was left of his memories. At this point, most of what came to mind were his mistakes. Beside him sat several of the people he had met, befriended, or even saved throughout the years. Not surprisingly, most of them were now feeling their age. Andrei, tall and burly in his cloak, stood in the corner watching the flames. He was now a successful merchant, having cut one of his trips short and taken the long journey to the Abbot's remote, and hidden Third Monastery. Unfortunately, its two predecessors had been put to the torch over the past few decades. Andrei smiled to himself as notes were dutifully taken by the scribe, who was attentively listening to what Nicholas was relating. Finally, two of the healing attendants shooed the congregation out to allow the old man some rest. The group left, and Andrei along with them, but not before stopping to pat Nicholas's hand. He was already asleep.

Andrei fell in step with Sister Alena, another of the original group of children who had been saved by Nicholas those many years ago.

"He looks so frail," he said.

She nodded, "He is. He's been so strong for so long. It's hard to see him like this."

Andrei looked at the monastery being built around them. It was rumored that this location was near a magical crossroads, and odd happenings had taken place within its borders. He looked back at her.

"Third time's the charm, eh? I believe we were right to leave those other assignments. No one will find you here... If that is what you wish."

She walked over to the newly built well and drew up a bucket of fresh water. She pulled two cups from the eaves and patted the stone beside her. After filling both cups in turn, she handed him one.

"It is. It has been a long journey. After Father Nicholas was granted his freedom from the Aka, we tried to go back to the way things were. But, after all those years with the followers of the old ways, we simply could not fit in. Most of the land he had been given was already taken by someone else." She produced some dates from a bag and offered him some.

"At our second monastery, we were called to task by envoys of the various churches—the Roman faction, the Eastern factions, and so on. Their 'representatives' infiltrated and spied on us. They were aghast when they found that we were letting both males and females lead prayer, sometimes communally. We welcomed odd people and some of the wildling creatures that meant us no harm. Father Nicholas's faith had changed after his time with the green folk. It wasn't uncommon for those who were magical or blessed, cursed by being different, to make their way to him. And of course, being our Nicholas, he was always generous to a fault, and that got him in trouble."

She patted Andrei on the knee, "Most of this happened while you were out during your campaigns abroad." She reached up to touch a scar on his face. "Whoever did the healing of your face saved your eye, brother." She said it with a knowing look. Andre took her hand and held it gently.

"A witch named Csenge. Very skilled with a needle and a good storyteller, too." Andrei smiled down at Alena. Alena nodded and continued.

"For a while, Father Nicholas tried to keep the lands of the old ones and those who lived on those lands and the forests of the Black Goat safe. Some of the locals from the plains coveted it and made trouble, calling him a heretic. We barely got away before they burned down that monastery as well."

"That's irony. Saving Christians, only to then have his church burned down by 'Christians.'" Andrei spat out a date seed.

He took the measure of Alena, now a calm, slender, older woman, very different from the wild little girl he had grown up with. She nodded sadly.

"The church and the people of that town said you all burned," said Andrei, still holding her hand.

Sister Alena smiled.

"It helps to have those you call friends who understand the ways of glamour. In fact, as soon as the tower behind us gets finished, we are going to have a glamour covering the whole area. That should make it very hard for people to find us or remember us without knowing the right charm, and..."

Andrei raised an eyebrow, "And?"

"Some people have taken to calling him Nicholas Thaumaturgus, Nicholas the Wonder Worker." She cocked her head and laughed.

"Mind you, they also referred to Nicholas of Myra as such. And that other Nikolai, Sion something, down on the Black Sea." She handed him another date. "The inhabitants here call him 'the Hidden Nicholas,' but never in his presence." Alena smiled up at Andrei.

"Our people, the people of the different path, believe so much in his generosity, in his accepting and gentle heart, and in his willingness to sacrifice himself, that even some of them have even considered accepting Vows."

Andrei looked around at the monastery being erected around him. He had noticed it when he had first arrived. There was purpose here, almost like the humming of bees filling the air. Lepers, the misshapen, the broken and odd, even some folks with strange eyes, feet, or fur on their faces, they all moved about freely here.

"Vows? Interesting. So, this will be an Order that will continue beyond our Nicholas, inspired by the legends of the original."

Alena held up her hand.

"Anonymity is our way now. We have learned our lessons. One of the fundamental teachings espoused by Nicholas of Myra was anonymous giving, as with the gold for the daughters. Thus, one of the vows of our new order may be that we remain anonymous. We will give without giving notice of ourselves and help by providing a better example without seeking acclaim, and so on."

Andrei sipped the water, which was ice cold and sweet. Looking at the cup, he noted its odd shape, as well as the band of leaves imprinted around its rim and the quality of its make. The merchant in him wondered how many he could get.

"I have a feeling you are about to ask me for something."

Alena nodded.

"First, you need to know it means so much to him that you are here. To me. Your contributions, your retelling of all the confusing stories during your travels... They have been a boon to our cause." She leaned on his arm and stretched her legs.

"Our order will need agents in the world of men, people we can depend on and can point us to those in need. An emissary to those who are different and, if necessary, those who we may need to defend; in particular, children."

Andrei chuckled as he answered, "of course."

"Isn't it ironic that our Nicholas never thought he was particularly good with children, yet has such great love for them?" Alena snickered.

"He was a good father to us, albeit a bit distracted."

"We were not easy children to deal with." Alena made a face.

"True."

Both smiled quietly, remembering misadventures from long ago.

"Even now, we are establishing other Churches of St. Nicholas of Myra, as part of the mundane world and the existing churches." Alena looked intently at Andre. "You know they are going to split, don't you?"

"Yes, as if the Children of the Slain God needed more problems." Andre cracked his neck.

"The Greeks are tired of Rome. Those special children who decide they want to leave us and be part of the mortal world, they will only remember our little monastery dimly, once they leave us." Alena sighed.

Andrei rolled his shoulders and squeezed the knots of travel from his back.

"Mm. Well, I do foresee one issue. You know I am a worshipper of the old ways. What happens to the people who need to be pointed this way if they are Mohammedan, Northmen, or possessed with spirits, what have you?"

Alena's expression grew pensive, casting a glance back towards the rooms where Father Nicholas lay sleeping. A moment later, she turned back to address Andrei.

"We've come to an arrangement, I think. If they intend no harm, they can have places of prayer outside the monastery, but they cannot recruit. Neither can we, except by example. As for the spirits, it depends on whether they are spirits of the mind, or spirits of another sort. We can and will cast them out if the host is being harmed."

There was a clatter and a startled yelp as something big leapt down from the nearby wall. A towering figure slunk out from the shadows.

Andrei moved for his sword, but Alena gently stayed his hand. The monolith stepped into the light of the torches, and instantly both recognized the beast, despite the distance of many, many years. Krampus scanned the empty area, spotted them, and gave them a slight nod before heading towards the monastery.

At the sight of the woolly giant, many of the others in the clearing scattered. Undaunted, Andrei and Alena stood and followed it into the room. The two healers were busy inside, the senior most of the two brothers just finished performing the last rites.

Krampus moved into the room gracefully for someone of his size. Tasting the air, he bent down and allowed his agile tongue to briefly touch the old man's forehead. He snorted, shaking his horned head.

"It won't be long."

As others left to prepare for the rituals of passing, two more figures stood outside the room, clinging to the shadows. They peered from beside the newly completed tower, dark against the darkness. There was a fluttering gust of wind, accompanied by the smell of dew-speckled flowers in the morning. Something else landed outside the door, ever so softly, limned all about with light. It looked around at the other guests then entered the room.

Alena felt as if all the weight of the world lifted from her shoulders as the presence walked by.

"Now is the time," said the lucent figure, its voice inscrutable, exquisite.

Krampus turned to face the new attendee.

"Now I am to be Free," he said, growling.

The luminous smiled, sat down on the bed, and gently caressed Father Nicholas's face. In response, a ghostly image of Father Nicholas sat up, stretched, and looked around as if waking from a refreshing nap, looking a touch surprised and a great deal younger.

Father Nicholas looked up at Krampus.

"Krampus, old goat. It's been ages. Good to see you."

Nicolas turned to look at the person who was perched on the bed and try as he might, he could not discern the age of the individual, nor its gender, only that it seemed to shimmer as it sat.

"Oh. OH."

The Angel smiled.

"Nicholas, you have given everything our Lord could ask of you and more. You have earned your heavenly reward. However... we have a slight complication."

Everyone else in the room seemed puzzled by the statement. Krampus shook his head, and accidentally knocked some plaster down with his horns.

"Complications?" he growled.

"Indeed."

The glowing messenger reached over the bed and plucked a long box that was on the shelf, opening it.

"You recognize these, of course?"

Krampus leaned over and saw the rusty chains and manacles, the sight of which made him snarl and recoil. He did not like where this was headed.

"*Yes.*"

"Well, that is part of the problem. The two of you are very thoroughly bound together: Magically *and* spiritually."

The Angel pointed to the ghostly form of Nicholas.

"He has the right to go to his reward, but I do not think you wish to join him on his ascent, do you?"

"*Gah! No!*" Krampus visibly shuddered and knocked down more plaster.

The spirit of Nicholas made calming motions with his hands.

"Easy my friend. I have it on good authority, it is a genuinely nice place!" he said with a gentle smile.

Krampus stepped back, which was hard in the humble space of the room.

"*I have no desire to spend an eternity dwelling among your kind, stranded in your realm of purity. Meaning no offense, I would die of boredom.*"

The Angel started to say something, but Krampus cut it off.

"*You know what I mean.*"

"And that leads us to another problem," said the glowing emissary. "Belief. Belief is a powerful thing."

It kept speaking as it picked up a cloth and carefully wiped the chains, as well as other talismans in the box. It delicately removed a bell and rolled it in its palm. The trinket rang softly, at which The Angel smiled, before returning it to its resting place.

"Krampus, your domain is suffering. Ever so slowly, the beings in your domain will diminish alongside your belief, down to the last tree and forgotten sacred stone. This may take an exceptionally long time, but I do not believe it will be pleasant." It shrugged its heavenly shoulders. "At the least, you would have Nicholas in this form to keep you company, but..."

"*But?*" asked an increasingly vexed looking Krampus.

"As you know, Nicholas has done what he can to help those of the forest, the wyrd, the people and beings that are unwelcome in much of this new world. He can still do more. He has cast a pebble in a curious pond, and his belief has taken equally strange turns along the way."

At that, the Angel looked at Nicholas with a raised eyebrow, and Nicholas gave it a slightly embarrassed look.

"To sum up, there is a surprising amount of belief in you, Nicholas, hailing from a wide variety of beings." The Angel set down the box and rested his hands on the items.

"If you, Nicholas, are a Saint, and I do say 'if,' there is a very good chance that our Creator may have other plans for you."

Nicholas raised a ghostly hand, "I am glad to be of service!"

"*What a surprise,*" and Krampus rolled his bright green eyes, grumbling.

"Thank you, Nicholas." The Angel smiled. It turned to Krampus.

"If you agree to help him, I possess sight enough to tell you that Nicholas will not only help the people of your lands, but that belief in you will remain for centuries to come. Much longer, in fact, than if you are by yourself, I believe."

Krampus sucked in a deep breath, then growled lowly as distant thunder.

"We have several lives between us, and I am still in his debt. Fine. It seems I cannot be rid of you, after all, O' Son of Adam." It kicked the flagstone beneath it with a powerful hoof, and it promptly cracked in half. *"Call, Nicholas, and I will come."*

With that, the creature named Krampus stomped out of the room into the inky black night.

The Angel turned to look at Andrei and Alena. Its gaze made them feel weak and open.

"The road for your Order will be long and hard, and possibly quite bizarre. Yours is the way of the open heart, the open mind, and the open hands." It lifted a finger and the two of them drooped into a deep sleep. The Angel turned back to Nicholas.

"I can take you to your reward for a time, but I am afraid you still have more lives to touch."

Nicholas nodded, "Thank you. Uh... Forgive me, I don't think we've met. How would like to be addressed?"

The Angel smiled and helped the spirit of Nicholas to his feet.

"You can address me as Azrael. You have met a few other angels along your journey, even if you were not then aware. When His will is in harmony with the world, we do what you do. We do our best to remain unseen, as pleases the Creator."

"Azrael, as in the Angel of Death?" said Nicholas with eyes wide.

"Well, yes. I am, but there are others." The Angel looked around the room and gently straightened the body on the bed. "This was a nice change of pace for me."

Nicholas looked at himself on the bed, and then at the Angel.

Azrael sighed, "Retrieving the spirits of the dead can be somber work."

"Ah." Nicholas looked down at his ethereal form. "So, I will be helping as... a ghost?"

Azrael led him outside and nodded to the two figures standing near the tower. Nicholas noticed them and offered a friendly wave but could not make out who they were.

"Not quite," Azrael responded.

"As a Saint, you may appear as a vision, answer a select few prayers, offer counsel, and perform the occasional miracle. That would be standard. From what I've heard, you can expect to be *very* popular. I have been informed from on high that you can expect to do some work guiding spirits. That is rare. Very Old Testament, that."

Nicholas had not noticed that the two of them had walked off the mountain and were heading upward, giving him a shock when he looked down. To his astonishment, he found he was unafraid.

Nicholas turned back towards the Angel, who was beginning to transform in appearance, seeming ever more complex and powerful.

"Wait. If I am to work anonymously and my followers are working to be anonymous, how will that all work?"

"Well, we can assume that all you Nicholases are working together." Azrael shrugged, wings bobbing into sight behind him.

"Oh. I hope they don't mind."

The Angel smiled, "I believe it will be their honor." Nicholas returned the warm expression.

"Thank you. It all just sort of happened. I really don't know how."

Azrael chuckled, "You know, I asked that question to God myself. The Creator said, and I quote, 'You know, belief is a powerful thing!'"

As the two continued on their journey, behind them, bronze and silver bells rang out, lowly and slowly from the monastery. The chimes flowed down the mountains and valleys, reaching the ears of far-off neighbors, who heard them and wondered at their sweetness of tone, as well as from whence they came.

The two dark figures took their leave of the monastery tower and departed down a scraggy, long-forgotten path. Bird Woman looked over at the Tall Woman.

"Feh. Did you know this was going to happen? That your sister's friend would be kept alive, being bound to a Christian Saint?"

The Tall Woman looked at her with intense gray eyes, the color of the sea during a maelstrom.

"Not specifically. But you can't win if you don't play the game."

The Bird Woman shapeshifted into a raven and flew up to an old pine tree.

"For such long odds, you play them well," croaked the Raven.

"Always," said the stormy-eyed woman, just as she stepped into the woods. Then, she was gone.

* * *

10. Chains of a Different Sort

Modern Day, the Yule Season, LaMoure North Dakota

Cosimo Florentine, also known as "His Grace, his Excellency, or Mr. Florentine," poured the hot water over his tea with excruciating precision. The five people in the room knew that to disturb him in this ritual was to court his ire, a state of aggravation which was known to be unlimited and very, very exacting. The ticking of the grandfather clock punctuated each moment of silence. When the older gentleman finished, he brought the porcelain cup to his nose, then looked up.

"Charles, you were saying?"

Charles DuPree, head of the LaMoure Police department was sweating, this despite having been in the cold for some time and having taken off his officer's parka.

"Mr. Florentine, I have guys searching around the town, but we haven't seen anything obvious. I mean, yes, we did find a spot, and it looks like something went down there, but there was something chemical all over the incident area that burned everything up. I don't think it was your typical accelerant."

Mr. Florentine raised a patrician eyebrow, glancing at both his consigliere and the hooded attendant quietly tracing lines across a stale old book.

"Henry, Avice, what say you?"

Henry stroked his mutton chop sideburns, then motioned, drawing two more people into the room: a young man clad in a leather coat, with patterns cut into his skull-close shaved hair, and an older heavy-set woman in a rather gaudy pantsuit.

"Fredericka, if you would?" Henry asked.

The woman nodded, withdrawing a piece of pine tree bark as she bowed to Florentine, introducing the vampire in the leather coat.

"This is Vuk, on loan to us from Dmitri's house. He's a Serb, and his English isn't all that good, but he found this. He tells me that it has two scents on it: one is kindred, and he is fairly certain that the blood scent belongs to one of the kindred called Hermano. The other is human, although it smells oddly foul."

"Da, odd," the thin ferret-faced man nodded in agreement.

Henry paced across the floor and then addressed the police chief.

"Charles, as a mortal, I expect you wouldn't know this, but it takes a great deal of work to kill one of us, even a younger one. Yet, from everything you've described here, one of ours has gone missing and that is extremely troubling. We have a great investment in this town, and I cannot stress the importance that things go very smoothly over the next few days."

At that moment, the hooded figure that had been reading in the corner held out long yellow-nailed hand and beckoned for the piece of wood. Fredericka looked surprised. Henry plucked it from her hand and handed it over.

The wood disappeared under the cloak, accompanied by the mumbling of discordant vowels. A few moments later, the figure called Avice spoke in archaically accented English. Its voice sounded dry and rough from disuse.

"The one called Hermano is no more. The blood of the mortal, the magic bond is still good, but I would not count on that staying so."

"Why?" asked Henry. "Is there something magical happening in this town we did not foresee?"

In answer, the figure returned the woodchip, hands disappearing under its robe.

"Of course. We are about to do something powerful, in an age of gnats."

Avice waved a gaunt hand over its shoulder in irritation and went back to reading its book. Henry addressed Florentine.

"Your Grace, I recommend we ask each of the gathered houses to lend us some effective but subtle people to track this human down."

From another part of the room, the giant haphazardly taking apart a remote control with a knife spoke out. His sleepy demeanor and bulky physique did not hide the menace in his half-lidded eyes.

"Cosimo—I mean, Mr. Florentine—just let me take just a few of the human children. I can have some answers for you very quickly."

A snort of disgust came from under Avice's hood. Fredericka quirked an eyebrow at the massive brute, turning to face Mr. Florentine.

"Your Grace. It has taken me a long time to set up everything at the children's home. I really don't recommend anything that could potentially disturb the children or our timetable. No offense to Baron de Rais."

Baron de Rais sighed and used the sharp knife to shave the buttons off the remote, looking infinitely bored.

"Oh, my precious lamb Fredericka. If only you could offend me. I am truly hoping that someone might," he said, eyes drifting toward Avice.

"I won't take any of your precious little ones. Unless of course, his Grace wills it." He continued.

Mr. Florentine held up a hand.

"No, Rais. That won't be needed at this time." He pointed to Vuk. "Find me the person attached to the blood on that bark. Do not rest until you do." Turning to Henry, he asked, "I would assume that the one called Hermano has a sponsor here?"

"Yes, a woman named Daniela, she's out on Autry Way."

Henry consulted a small book from his pocket.

"She would be with the House of Hearts. Her sire is Master Drummer."

Florentine nodded and wrote something on a piece of paper. He then carefully stamped it and handed it to the police chief.

"That is her address, including the room number. Take some of our ghoulified officers. Wait until midday, stake her, and take her out somewhere bright, away from humans. Destroy every last speck of her. Take any remains and throw them in running water. If anybody gives you trouble, show them this note. Do you understand?"

"Yessir," the Chief of Police replied, beating a hasty retreat.

"This event has been hundreds of years in the making," Mr. Florentine addressed the rest of the room. "For all our sakes, and the sake of the effort we've put into this, I expect you all to be as thorough and as careful as possible. Understood?" Everyone nodded affirmatively.

As Vuk, Charles, and Fredericka were leaving, one of the hotel staff knocked politely on the door. A woman wheeled in a weathered trunk, and as soon as it entered the room, Avice hissed softly and shunned it. Henry thanked her and gave her a big tip, which she accepted gratefully and left quickly.

"Oh relax, even a meager practitioner like myself can handle this," Baron de Rais said as he waved his hand at Avice.

The Baron took the case from Henry and set it in a corner on a luggage stand. He pulled out a stick of some unknown material and drew some symbols and a circle surrounding it. Avice watched from the corner but said nothing. Baron de Rais opened the box. Inside was a tarnished and rather musty, worn-looking Santa suit.

Baron de Rais sharply pulled his hand back from the open trunk in the circle, as it had begun to smoke. A bitter snarl rumbled in his throat as he examined the singed flesh.

"No doubt about it: Holy relic."

"Well done, Henry," Cosimo Florentine said with a slight smile to Henry Raymond. His consiglieri bowed slightly. The Baron de Rais gave Henry a baleful eye.

Avice glided over to inspect the contents from outside the circle's barrier.

"That is the Santa suit of Father Joe, of Father Joe's Orphanages," explained Henry. "Joe was originally a fairly wealthy car dealer, becoming a believer late in life. Eventually, he sold everything to build a series of children's homes, and every year they received a visit from him in order to hand out presents to the children personally, even after spending all year collecting money to help the orphanages stay solvent. That meant thousands of good works over the years. Of course, he died almost penniless on his way to one of his homes, his station wagon full of gifts."

"Well?" Henry looked at Avice.

"Provided everything else goes as planned, these clothes will be sufficient to the task. I think we should be particularly careful with the binding chants."

The three other vampires in the room looked at each other, then back at the clothes in the trunk as the room filled with the scent of peppermint and mothballs. All nodded, their grins shining savage and empty.

* * *

11. Donuts and Coffee

Abe walked down the corridor, slogging through his second day as Santa following the fight, still aching and sorely hobbled. The incident had only happened on Sunday night, when the Christmas House had locked up early. Even though the battle with the vampire had been three days ago, it had taken a while for his body to realize just how poorly it had been treated. By the time he got to his break room, he was ready to collapse, and as he blissfully sank into the couch, he pulled his phone off its charger. There were three texts from Ron.

> *Park at Fat Eddies after your shift*
> *dress in civvies*
> *warm*

Abe went through the remainder of his shift, steadily getting more nervous. All the waiting was making him paranoid. Maybe selfishly, he had been hoping that he would not be needed for anything else, but a feeling in his gut had him feel fairly sure that was not going to be the case. As he left the set, he gave a high five to the photo manager, who in turn gave him a thumbs up and advised him to hit the chicken soup, as she had already collided with the kid-crud wall. A short time later, he sat in the dark parking lot of the restaurant, watching even more snow fall in contrast to the black of an icy North Dakota evening.

Ron's truck was announced by a low rumble before he spotted it. As it trundled around the corner, the headlights of the car sat so high that they shone directly into his window. Abe hopped into Ron's truck and, in no time at all, they were trekking down a dirt and gravel road near the outskirts of the city. Abe saw what looked like a feedlot–a sprawling warehouse with a small office visible inside. There was a sign half buried in a snowdrift that read, "...*groCo Cattle Auctions*." One of the sturdier doors of the warehouse sat wide open. Ron drove straight in.

Ron spent several moments of quiet observation before finally nodding curtly and exiting the cab. Both men swung down from the truck, strolled past the rows of bleachers stored in the massive warehouse, and ended up at a pen lit with a few floodlights. Several other vehicles were parked nearby, including a large RV and an enclosed trailer. Sharp clanking of metal informed Abe the large warehouse doors behind them had ground to a close. Outside, the winter wind buffeted the corrugated walls of the warehouse. Ron looked at Abe, shrugged, and then led them through an interior door to the small office built inside of the warehouse.

Abe's first view of the office was obstructed by piles of coats on desks. Beyond this were a few whiteboards, a small altar in the corner, and candles aglow. There was the scent of church incense, and neat little bundles of herbs and parchment hung over the doors and windows. At the farthest end of the room stood a modestly sized artificial Christmas tree, dressed scantily with worn decorations.

The men in the room turned to look at them as they entered. They stood at a table, surrounding two thoroughly plundered boxes of donuts and an industrial coffee urn that, from the smell of it, the contents had long since burnt. The biggest of them could have been a gladiator, and Abe could swear his face seemed vaguely familiar. Ron bestowed hugs on each of them in turn, all greeting him with the same good cheer, except one. Ron turned and with a wave, introduced Abe.

"Gentlemen of the Order, I would like you to meet your requestor, Abe Wykowski. This is his second year as a pro. Abe, let me introduce your Caestus crew." Ron gestured to a kindly looking elderly man with a well-coiffed beard, who appeared rather tired. "This is Pastor Carl Dengerud. He's been on several missions for the Order, and he's going to be our priest and thaumaturge."

"Greetings, Abe." Pastor Carl shook Abe's hand warmly. "I would say, 'don't mind the snow on the roof,' but since we are all Santas, looking old is the one part of the biz that I now have nailed." Carl chuckled and motioned to a table with various oils and implements on it, including a small mirror.

"I'm a thaumaturge. Roughly, it means Magical Sage in the tradition of St. Nicholas, or Nikolai Thaumaturgus, St. Nicholas the Wonder Worker. I'll be asking the help of the mighty and kindly spirits in this battle. You and I will have a chat later."

"This is Eric or just Top, known as Top Hat the Magician," Ron introduced a younger man that lacked a beard entirely, sporting short black hair. "He's what you'd call a Clark Kent, since he's a designer beard. He's also known as Santa Magic."

"Nice to see someone who isn't a complete geezer! Heya, Abe." Top spun in his chair and smiled up at Abe. "I'm the tech guy. Real magic is Carl's department, my specialty is illusion and special effects." He pointed to the trunks of gear and some computers set up on racks. "And communications. And a tiny bit of smuggling. And a little bit of pyro."

He waved his hand and a small flame appeared out of nowhere, flared, and went out.

Abe laughed, "Nice."

The goliath with the smell of alcohol on his breath walked over and hugged Abe briskly.

"I'm Jon. I'm part of the brute squad, and it'll be my job to get you trained up as best we can. For now, I'll be in charge. Carl there? He's my second in command." He turned and flipped open a case, peered back at Abe with a measuring eye, and he began digging.

"I'm the guy who gets up close and personal with the weensy beasties. Also, and you should know this: I have no problem with the White God but just to get this out in the open, I am a Norse pagan and a big fan of Tyr and Thor. My version of the 'holy father' might include an eyepatch. That said, I love mistletoe and holly just as much as the next Santa." He laughed as he flicked the charms around his neck, which included a Thor's hammer, a sword, and a cross.

Abe shot a look at Ron, who laughed as well.

"Yeah, Abe, just like with our black, gay, or Jewish Santas, the Order is what you might call... *Unitarian* in its outlook. We managed to stay pretty open minded in many respects, before it was cool."

"True," responded a heavily accented voice originating from a lean and shaggy looking man who was rapidly devouring a plate of donuts in rapid succession. His long beard and hair were tangles of gray and silver, and he was dressed as an odd mixture of deer hunter, infantryman, and Kris Kringle.

Ron reached over and picked up a cup of coffee and a donut with sprinkles, the last of its comrades, and handed them to Abe.

"Abe, this is Morozko. He's sort of a local, although I've only seen him around here a few times."

Morozko juggled his donuts and coffee to pat Abe awkwardly on the shoulder, leaving a handprint of powdered sugar residue.

"I live not too far away. I apologize for my English." He devoured a fritter in two bites. "I know that this place be trouble for long time. I have come on quest for God. I am a good tracker. You will probably die, so you should do confession every day, okay? Also, I have two doggies, Purga and V'yuga. You meet them later, they are best dogs in the world. Very smart."

Morozko looked more like a homeless person wearing a grungy Santa's cap, a stark contrast to the strutting peacock Santas Abe was used to seeing. Morozko pointed at the other Santas with a grimy finger in the midst of chewing.

"Sure, I am telling Santas here that we have big problem here, but no one listens to me." He shot Abe a helping of side-eye, and Abe felt a bit indignant for what seemed like unjustified anger. Jon cut in, his annoyance towards Morozko barely veiled.

"Right, sorry about that, Morozko. But here we are now!" Jon nudged Abe, "Abe, have you met the fifth member of the Caestus?"

Everyone's attention was pulled toward a man backing into the office. He spun his large frame around, his arms laden with two oversized boxes with fresh crullers to replace the now empty boxes on the table.

Abe thought he looked somewhat familiar, bigger than Ron and a neck thicker than Abe's leg. Hulking mass and smorgasbord of scars, thick dark beard, and shaggy hair—it all finally clicked into place for Abe.

"You're... that wrestler, mixed martial arts guy? The, uh... The Beast?"

"The one and only," he said with a nod and a small bow. "Although technically? I don't wrestle anymore. I do a lot of PR, stand up, management, and that sort of stuff these days. My name is Rick. It's a pleasure to meet you. Great job taking out a vamp on your first try, by the way."

At that there was a chorus agreement from the whole room, even a grunt from Morozko.

"By the way, I'm a newbie. This is only my third mission," Rick said to Abe with a wink.

"Hey, I'm technically not a part of your Caestus," Ron remarked as he grabbed a cup of coffee for himself. "But I think the rules will allow me to man the radio and do support, right?"

Pastor Carl looked up from the equipment he was unpacking.

"Technically, since I am a minister and can consecrate this place, we can call this our redoubt. As such, I can make you one of the attendants."

"Stupid question?" Abe interjected with a raised hand. "What is this, um...?"

"There's no stupid questions," Jon quickly answered. "This *'kai-stus,'*" he exaggerated the pronunciation, "means to strike and it comes from the Greek fighting tradition. Think of a battle glove, sometimes boasting spikes, knuckles, or blades? They would wrap them around the boxer's hands. For us, Caestus means a group of five in a magically bound fighting team." He held up his hand, slowly closed it into a firm fist, and smacked it into his palm.

"I can't imagine what the contenders back then looked like," Top said with a visible shudder. He turned to look at Rick "The Beast," who was missing a lump of his ear and several teeth. "Sound like your kind of gig?"

"Not me," Rick said with a shake of his head. "I want to keep my good looks. Besides, most of my beauty marks came from accidents in the ring, not much on purpose."

Abe looked at Jon's fist and then the rest of the men.

"Consider me educated."

"Good job finding us this place, Mr. Ron." Top surveyed their gathering. "Not a lot of people are going to be making their way out here. We get to park our vehicles inside, which is a big advantage, and that gets us out of that slushy wonderland outside. We'll need to run some power cords out for the block heaters on our vehicles, though. It ain't that warm out there in the barn."

"Plenty of power and water hook ups out there," Rick laughed. "I think they do rodeos and auctions here. I've already got a 220-line going over to my RV as we speak. I'm gonna sleep well." Top did not return the laugh.

"Yeah, good for you. But here's something weird I ran into. This is an oil boom town. Everybody and their brother is bailing out of this frozen place and heading home for the holidays. But for some reason, every one of the hotels is packed for some sort of training convention."

"That's kinda weird," Ron replied as his eyebrows shot up. "Last year, the hotels here were mostly a ghost town during the holidays. LaMoure is a newer town, so we don't see mixed generations living here. This close to the big day? All those folks that stuck around will be making a mad dash to Fargo or Minot to hop on a plane just before Christmas Eve, that or Minneapolis. A convention, this time of year? Here? That's crazy."

Morozko had the aroma of someone who spent a lot of time by a wood stove, rather than a shower. He finished devouring his last donut and brushed the crumbs out of his beard.

"I will make us some tea. Some of you are staying at hotel?" Top, Carl, and Jon raised their hands. "Da. You need to be careful. Some of peoples at hotel is *nezhit* ...undead. Mebbe vampyr. Some are ghouls, too. Or servants to them."

Simultaneously, all three of the men looked at the Russian with concern. Morozko waved his hands.

"Is not so bad. Most people there are what, food? Cattle. What is called mortals or kine. Undead bring own human servants. I been watching for a long time. I dig through dumpsters, find some nice things, too. They are not caring over much."

"Uh, gents?" Topper addressed Ron and Abe with a look of concern on his face. "I'm thinking maybe we want to just visit the rooms at our hotel, if you catch my meaning. But if we actually want to sleep, we might want to do that elsewhere?"

Abe and Ron nodded briskly.

"Yeah, not a problem. I have a couch." Abe gave Topper a weak smile.

With that chestnut of information, all the men pulled chairs out and got to work.

* * *

12. Sales Promotion

At the West Gardens Grand Ballroom, the sales training had hit fever pitch. Every one of the teams from around the country was running exhausted. The presentations arranged for the management team had been viewed by everyone, met with running cheers. Some very nice prizes, such as foreign vacations, even keys to new cars, had been doled out with great pageantry and enthusiasm. Cindi Becker had not come all the way from Tallahassee to lose.

Cindi shot a stern look at Tom, the weak link in Team Ocelot. His typos in his section of the PowerPoint had cost them points for presentation. Cindi was slightly smaller than him, a stature offset by unflinching focus and keen wit. Determination and stamina had flung them ahead, and she knew it was due to her faith in the Lord. Prudently, she decided to soften her expression and gave him a smile, which he returned wearily. A chime was rung, and the hotel staff opened the beige double doors. In the hallway outside, another perfectly serviceable buffet had been prepared. Two hundred people reached for their electronic devices in tandem, standing and shambling for the doors and their meals.

During one of her periodic glances away from her social media, she noticed one of the upper echelon types was beckoning to her. Cindi easily picked him out as he wove gracefully through the crowd, trimly clad in a perfect bespoke suit.

"Ms. Becker?"

"Yes! And you are?"

The man in the flawless outfit swept down ever so slightly.

"Michael Stevens. Ms. Becker, we've been watching your performance with your team. I have good news and bad news. Could you retrieve your jacket and other belongings from the ballroom?"

Cindi's face immediately blanched, and she turned stiff with embarrassment, to do as requested. As she walked hurriedly back, her words flooded out in a hasty explanation.

"I am *so* sorry about those typos, and I'm sure that we could tweak everything to your needs and resubmit..."

The man cut her off, waving her protestations aside.

"No, no, no Ms. Becker. Your team was chosen for you, correct? We have been watching. Simply put, some people are more inquisitive, more aggressive, singular. That would be you. Your team, Ms. Becker, is holding you back." He gently took her by the arm and led her away from the crowds scurrying for tables and wall sockets.

"Cindi, if I may use your given name? I said, 'good news and bad news.' The bad news is that your team will have to find a new leader." The courtly man paused for effect, and she could feel her eyes growing round.

"We think you are Ultra material. Yes, Ultra is real and yes, you would start out with a salary roughly three times what you were promised."

"I... I knew that certain folks were heading off for other teams, and that we wouldn't be seeing them again." Cindi started to weave a bit and felt more than a little flush.

"Indeed. The technology we are putting to use in Ultra can only be sold by an *elite* sales force. The tech market being what it is, if you accept, we have you sign some very comprehensive NDAs. That would mean saying goodbye to folks back home for a while on any electronics or social media. If all goes well, we would have you heading out of here on Christmas Day, first class, of course. You won't be seeing any of the other teams until after the holidays." He gave her a knowing smile.

"May I assume you accept?"

With a trill laugh bordering on hysteria, she nodded quickly. She had had her doubts, driving her team into the wee hours of the night, "accidentally" jamming the printer for the other teams. Sure, she might have been a tad too sharp or pointed when she had belittled the underlings on Team Ocelot, but all that was behind her now. She was going to be in the ranks of the elite, the Ultra sales force. God had once again chosen her to be rewarded. Cindi Becker adjusted her jacket and smiled.

"Michael, I hope you know that you're making the right decision in picking me."

"Of course," Michael nodded.

They came around a corner, and there were six other people she recognized from the training. They all had similar "I've just been secretly told I've won the lottery" smiles.

Michael steered them all towards a handsome small woman wearing a pinstriped suit and prim corseted vest, who bowed slightly.

"Ladies and gentlemen, this is one of our VPs, Ms. Angela. She'll be accompanying you to our private corporate lodgings. You'll be back in a few hours, after the briefing. If you would, take a moment to send out a few emails letting people know you will be away from electronics for a short while. Please avoid anything too specific," he said with a cheeky smile. "You could say that the upcoming storm is causing problems."

Everyone nodded and whipped out their smartphones. All obeyed cheerfully, including Cindi. Michael congratulated everyone again, then departed.

Angela smiled at the smug group and pointed to Cindi.

"Ms. Becker let's start with you. Let's get you signed up and seated. Come this way."

Giddily, Cindi joined Angela and stepped out the large utility doors of the hotel, out onto one of the massive utilitarian loading docks. The wind was bitter cold. Cindi smiled excitedly, but then frowned as she noticed she could not see a van or limo, instead only a pair of dumpsters and a blocky in-town delivery truck.

She finally noticed the four other people standing on the loading dock, awaiting their arrival. None matched the stately dress of the delegates from Ultra, and each had eerily iridescent eyes. Angela removed her glasses and looked up at Cindi, taking her plump hand gently in hers. She bent down and kissed the back of it, before giving it a reassuring pat. The kiss on Cindi's hand felt like cool fire, and although it startled her, Angela simply smiled as if everything was completely normal.

"Cindi don't worry. You're Ultra now! Everything is going to be just fine."

The words seemed distant, Cindi's head spinning, a numbness spreading up her arm. Angela's voice became so relaxing, she could barely focus her eyes. The small woman led her by the hand, guiding her toward the truck, still offering pleasantries.

Yet something, somewhere in the back of Cindi's mind felt that primordial thrum of anxiety, crying that something was dreadfully wrong. Still, she could not concentrate, her brain feeling as though it were stuffed with cotton.

Angela nodded to the group of four on the dock, who easily lifted Cindi into the darkness of the back of the truck, and then shackled her to the ceiling. Frigid cold cut deep in the shadowy recesses where they hung her. Cindi wanted to scream, but she could barely move. Weakly, she looked up at the two pinprick wounds on her hand and watched her blood creep down her arm from where Angela had inflicted them. For some reason, this seemed important, but she was hard-pressed to remember why.

Another person was brought in and shackled next to her, then another.

Cindi vaguely registered the irregular clunking of the rolling steel door before it slammed down and locked. The truck lurched away, battering her with the bodies of other helpless passengers.

On the dock, Angela turned to the other ghouls and vampires and gave them a shark-like grin. Having repeated the process so many times, she withdrew a napkin from her breast pocket and dabbed at the blood on her lips.

"This is why I adore the Midwest. Where else can you find Ultra-grade in this economy?"

One of the ghouls grinned and lit up a cigarette, handing it to her.

"You had to put the bite on that big one?"

"Yeah. Miss Corn-Fed Pink Pantsuit was a bit too ornery, and it's better not to take chances. Most of the others, I could just use the eyes on."

A fellow vampire came up and bummed a cigarette as well.

"So, that makes, what? About 40 head a day? Are we going to have enough kine to last the length of this whole deal?"

Angela shrugged.

"I'd guess so. His Excellency doesn't tolerate loose ends. If he says the math works out, then it does. If we need to, we can always hit the mall. This time of year, the Mall is always packed."

* * *

13. Where Three Roads Meet

1239 AD, somewhere north and east of Bratislava, Holy Roman Empire

Brother Bernard and Sister Aleta watched the Abbot with concerned eyes. He had packed the holy relics into his saddlebags himself and spoken little during the journey. The old man seemed lost in prayer and his eyes had a driven aspect to them, when they were open.

Riding ahead of them were the many warriors who had traveled from various countries around the world to find peace at their monastery. It was obvious that Commander Magnus was not permitting rest among the militias and fighting brethren of St. Nicholas. Sister Aleta heard horses behind them speed up, trotting faster to keep pace. A couple of small wagons pulled their encampment's kit, led by non-militant members of the order. Some of those who had only joined the order a short while ago finally made it to the front.

Padraig, a young man of only twelve winters, rode up alongside them on his mule, his cloak drawn tight over his shoulders.

"Do ye not feel it?"

Bernard looked over at Aleta and gave her a small, wry smile.

"And what would that be, oh Mendicant Padraig?"

"I ken that we are being watched. That... spirits are keep apace wi' us."

Sister Aleta wagged a finger at him.

"While that is true, some of those spirits take umbrage at being noticed. So, we shall not discuss this loudly nor will we endeavor to spot them."

"Yes ma'am," Padraig croaked and blushed. The boy had originally come from Hibernia, followed by Britain, an environment where female clergy rarely spoke in front of their male counterparts.

Brother Bernard leaned back to check on the rest of their baggage train, taking the chance to use his second sight and scan the area. The young lad was right. An uncommon amount of fay activity swirled around the caravan. After he took a moment to observe them, he caught a glimpse of what seemed to be another band of figures leading their own group of horses. Bernard noted that the others were working hard to stay in the shadows.

As he straightened up, he turned to Sister Aleta. Having known her all his life, he could read that she sensed them too.

"What does your ever-sensitive nose tell you, Sister Aleta?"

She raised an eyebrow and shot a look at the young companion.

"That someone very nearby needs to take advantage of the lavender soap in his saddle bag at the next river."

Padraig's eyes were like saucers.

"Coo! You can smell the soap in me bags from that far? That's a miracle!"

"Or perhaps she knows that Brother Bertram would not have let you go with us without the tools to make certain we are clean?" Bernard laughed. "Or that we just had Mother Embry deliver some lovely lavender soap not long ago?"

Aleta shook her head with a small amount of exasperation.

"Padraig, we shan't be stopping at the next fording long enough for you to bathe, but you really do need to. Tell the others we will be coming to a river soon, and to prepare for it," said Bernard.

Padraig nodded, wheeled his pony, and trotted away.

Bernard watched him go with a blithe expression. The Hibernian youth obviously thought this was all a grand adventure. However, the purpose of this journey was gravely serious and equally dangerous.

"My brother," Aleta said with a small cough. "Must you always explain everything as some stale fact?"

"No, Aleta, my sister dear," Bernard answered with a shrug. "I could have told him that you have a shaggier, less amicable side. That, since puberty, you can smell everything. That would rather drain the mystery of the thing, don't you think?" he finished with a sprightly look. "Now that you mentioned it, what *is* your nose telling you?"

Aleta inclined her head towards the other mysterious travelers.

"The wind has been switching back and forth, but... Blood-drinkers. Un-life. Maybe a witch and some Unseelie."

"Oh, ahem. Perhaps I should tell the Abbot?" Bernard asked quietly. Aleta nodded at him.

Both trotted up to the Abbot, who was walking slowly behind the warriors who were all leading their horses in kind. His eyes seemed distant. Aleta waited a moment then coughed softly.

"Father, a moment of your time?"

It took a few moments for him to react. When he did, he looked quite startled, as if he had been innumerable leagues away in a world of thought, but quickly settled into a genuine smile.

"It's nice to see the two of you doing something together. Our Sister Aleta is always away and you, Bernard, are always up in that tower."

Bernard and Aleta both regarded him warmly, as the man had been like a parent to the both of them. The elderly man was exhausted and it showed. They waited until there was some distance between them and the nearby troops before reporting their observations.

"Ah, yes. That would be Duke Cosimo and his coterie. You are right. They are creatures of the dark, *neamh-mairbh* or *murfeo* as Padraig would call them. They are also coming to be signatories to this agreement. I have no desire to be anywhere near them but fortunately, or unfortunately, we are currently under truce."

Aleta scrutinized him, attempting to keep the skepticism from showing on her face.

"Is this not the group we were sending all those letters to? In Venice? I ran my paws bloody delivering all those missives."

Father Abbot smiled.

"Yes," the Abbot replied with a smile. "That Cosimo fellow is a great proponent of flowery letters, ornate vellum, and fancy seals. Thank you, oh swift runner." He reached up and patted Aleta's hand affectionately.

"If it is of any consequence to you, I've had all those letters soaked and scraped, and I am having a palimpsest handbook made for you out of the collection. I'll give it to you after we get back."

Aleta clapped her hands and gave him a delighted gasp.

Both men knew how much she loved a chance to practice her own scribal arts. High quality vellum was hard to come by, even if it was second hand.

"We will leave them behind a bit when we pass the ford," the Abbot continued to Bernard. "As magical creatures, possibly spirits of a pestilent nature, crossing a water boundary is probably going to be a bit problematic for them."

The Abbot climbed back up onto his horse.

"We should take good advantage of that time, get to the place where we want to make camp as soon as we can, get our wards up, and particularly our blessing, aye? I want to make certain we all pray together at Vespers and at Compline. That means everybody, I mean *everybody*. Tell Commander Magnus that I want *all* in our company to participate in our worship. We cannot afford otherwise."

"Yes, Father Abbot."

With that, the elder reentered the caravan. Bernard pivoted his horse toward Aleta.

"Perhaps there is time for a stroll in the woods?"

"A good idea, Brother-Brother," Aleta replied with a warm smile. "I will see you at camp. Come collect my horse in a bit, could you?"

Bernard slipped her a smirk. It was indeed like old times for the two of them.

* * *

14. Harmless Woodland Creatures

Aleta tied the reins to her horse's saddle and bid it to stay quiet for a moment. The world rose to meet her open senses. After a lengthy pause, she was fairly certain that this area was abuzz with activity, both mortal and arcane. As far as she could tell, she was currently alone. She promptly stripped and stowed her things, then pulled one of her spare bundles out of her pack and buried it in the leaves. Her backup contained a tunic, trews, crucifix, a blessed silver knife with accompanying soapstone, and coins in a waxed pouch. Several more prepared bundles sat in her saddle. It was part and parcel of being a skin changer.

"A naked person generally has very little authority in polite society."

She was sure a famous man had once said that, though she could never place the quote. She took her horse and spoke to it quietly.

"Frik, after I leave, I need you to go find the rest of our horses and wait for Bernard. Do you understand?"

The older horse tossed its head and pawed the ground. She gave it a tight hug, then an apple for good measure.

Looking around carefully once more, she said a small prayer and pulled open the tiny bag around her neck with reverence, being certain not to let any direct sunlight in. A second later, her eyes having adjusted, she could see the reflection of the tiny moon mirror stored inside the bag next to some small charms. When she was greeted with that familiar twinge, she carefully sealed it back up and allowed the change to seize her eye, slither down her spine, and begin to sew its transformative mana into the sinews of her body.

A few minutes later, a brawny, mottled wolf ran up and sniffed the muzzle of Frik the horse, giving a wag of its tail. In answer, the horse tilted its head in recognition, before turning to trot towards the traveling denizens of the abbey.

The wolven Aleta turned and sprinted in the direction of the dark caravan. Even if she were seen, no one would notice the small bag buried in the thick fur surrounding her collar, she hoped. A short time later, she had located the other party. Just as the Abbot had predicted, they were having problems crossing the magical boundary of the river. In this case, their solution was creative and unique.

Aleta saw many dozens of small figures, rushing up and down the riverbed, grabbing stones, sometimes thrice their size, building a rudimentary dam. All of them moved with unnatural speed. She found the nearest patch of brush, crept in, and smelled—watching and listening. As the creatures moved, they failed to notice the wolf eyeing them from the shrubbery, or at least, it failed to concern them.

Aleta the Wolf, however, possessed eyes that were exceedingly observant. She made a mental inventory of the creatures helping to build the dam. A good majority consisted of the dark tomtin, along with a smattering of redcaps, goblins, and other fairies she did not recognize. On the close side of the riverbank stood an uncanny antlered creature observing, if not supervising, the operation. As she studied it, she mused that it could perhaps be some sort of magical construct. It had an odd look about it, even for something of Fay origin. Her lupine form was not so adept at color distinction, but it was far better suited at seeing in the darkness than her human half. In order to see the creatures at all, she relied on the pressed four-leaf clover, water-bored stone, and cold-iron cross resting in her charm bag. She doubted any human watching what transpired would have seen much, save for the stones tumbling and a great rushing wind.

In a fairly short time, the dam was complete, and a human minion darted across the new road that had been formed.

Aleta watched as the minion shook something out of an earthenware jug that smelled of distant roads and long-crystallized resins. Once it had dusted a path across the stones, the dark caravan gingerly made its way across. One of the riders peeled away as it reached the other side, headed toward the pronged form in the shadows. She followed quietly, sharply aware that the woods were chock full of dark Fay of every shape and size.

After a careful approach from downwind, she was close enough to hear that the rider was speaking with the strange creature. From this angle, she recognized the mounted figure as one of the assistants to the chief vampire. Petru ...something. She had first seen him while delivering messages to their estate in Florence. Now he was dressed in the latest fashions of the regions, a state hardly practical while on the march. Like most vampires, he valued style over substance. And of course, dark hooded robes. Miserable weather would hold little in the way of practical repercussions.

Aleta tried to remember what House this vampire hailed from, what his abilities could be; unfortunately, nothing sprang to mind. The antlered creature was surrounded by smaller Fay, many of whom bore clubs, flails, and whips. Many erratically sniffed and twitched, squinting around the tree line furtively. Their master looked like an effigy of a man cast of straw, clay, and meat, with four hooved legs and antlers sprouted from a head caught between the skull of a horse and a human. As the creature turned to look around, Aleta saw smoldering red dots where the eyes were meant to be, its massive torso and arms bulging as it distorted. It held a massive flail in one of its topmost limbs, as easily as a child holds a toy rattle. The tiny fairies wrattled and birred, so much twitching amongst the leaves about them. She felt a chill claw up her spine and crouched lower.

Petru seemed unconcerned about the small Fay encircling their meeting and spoke to the construct as if he did this sort of thing all the time.

"....and the preparations for the offerings. You will use the contents in this bag, please." Petru handed the bag down to one of the redcaps near his horse, his steed rocking back in terror.

The voice of wind and sorrow answered him.

"It will be done."

"Done... done... done," the Fay in the area echoed back in response.

It was overpowering in its eeriness, and Aleta had to stop herself from letting her hackles rise. Even Petru seemed a little nervous at the sound but continued.

"Lord Ruprecht, I cannot stress this enough. My master is NOT to be hurt, nor are any of those in my caravan. When I signal, your forces and mine will destroy all of the humans. The spoils recovered are yours by right, with the exception of the items belonging to the Abbot. Again, we must not settle for anything short of complete annihilation, understand?"

The lilting voice spoke again.

"And your master will give the signal?"

Petru looked around at the unblinking eyes of the Fay in the woods and noted how hard and flinty they were, how dreadfully hungry the unseelie faces looked.

"Uhm, no. That task will fall to me. When this handkerchief is dropped to the ground, that will be the time. Remember, this must be done before the break of day. The forces of the Order will be no easy meat."

"Meat... meat... meat..." the Fay around them repeated until the sound was swallowed up by the canopy of the forest.

Petru nodded his head to them with a thin smile.

"Yes. Meat. And bright, red human blood and cries of terror most sweet."

At this, their number started to hop about and brandish their weapons.

"Sweet... sweet... sweet...."

The massive creature bowed its antlered head slightly and turned to leave. The mass of little creatures followed it back into the forest, scuttling and blurring.

Petru sat on his horse and allowed himself a shiver. Making for the road, he soon fell in with the chief vampire, who was riding in a covered litter carried by servitors.

Aleta padded alongside them, ghosting her way through the brush. With her keen ears, she listened as Petru pulled up to the litter and addressed the regent inside.

"Master, I have paid the dark Fay for their help with the dam. It has already been reopened, and they will help us rebuild it when we leave."

A dry, urbane voice emanated from within the canvas.

"Well done, Petru. I must say, the initiative you have shown working with the Others has proven to be quite a boon for us. Congratulations."

Petru's face lit up.

"Thank you, Master. It is my hope that someday soon, you will reconsider my petition to form a new House, which will include those of the Unseelie line. Among those of us who would join it, we have favored the name 'the House of Dark Winds'. I hope that soon we can show our worth to you and the other houses"

"Very descriptive, Petru," hummed the Lord from his concealment. "However, as I have said before, much has conspired to take place at once, and these things do take time. Did your 'friends' still desire to have one of theirs join me at the stone tonight?"

Petru looked away, smiling ever so slightly to himself, and Aleta saw it.

"Most assuredly, Master."

"Very well, then."

With that, Petru rode ahead. The noise and dust kicked up by the dark caravan managed to distract Aleta, so that she did not notice what was behind her until it was too late. One moment she was slowly slinking from bush to bush, only to find herself next being bludgeoned across the torso, throwing her off her feet.

When she spun around, she saw a humongous black wolf staring at her, with several more hovering behind. Their foul scent told her that these were either skin-changers like herself, possibly vampires belonging to the House of the Wheel, or a pack of wolves that had been ghoulified and blood-bonded. Briefly, Aleta attempted to appear as an ordinary wolf, a low-ranking omega. This pack's answer was to move closer, fangs exposed. Aleta waited for a fraction of a second, then did something no ordinary wolf would do. With a sharp pirouette, she kicked a paw full of mud into the alpha's face, then bolted away, knowing she was no longer running just for her life but also for those of her family.

* * *

15. At the Crossroads

It was close to midnight when the large group of warriors, priests, and members of the Order of St. Nikolai Thaumaturgus arrived at the crossroads. The smell of petrichor on loam permeated the woods dense with overgrowth, scenting the air. This location had been used for centuries as a meeting place for trade and parley. It was also bordered by an ancient standing ring and a wide forest, as well as a nearby river. Three roads met, marked by boulders near the towering oak, ash, and linden trees. From the oak hung several bleached skeletons, signs of warning dangling around their necks. The members of the Order spotted them in the light of their torches and lanterns, crossing themselves instinctively as they passed by. All of them had been blessed and prepared themselves as best they were able before arriving, but as far as they were concerned, an extra token of piety never hurt. In the center of the road rested a large, flat stone, roughly thirty hands across, and the lip resting at waist height. On its face sat a cloth atop which sat a bell.

Brother Bernard advanced with care, offering a slight bow. Producing a plate from the bag at his side, he carefully arranged some bread, salt, and a cup of burgundy wine. Satisfied, he leaned over and lifted the bell, giving it one small, decisive strike. The tone of it was high, sweet and pure, and it echoed over the road, soundwaves quavering in the damp, cool night air.

He returned to his group and waited, though not for long. From the road to their left, two figures approached, laying objects on the stone, including a candlelit lantern. Bernard watched their movements closely, and while he was merely human, he had spent many years at the top of his tower watching the stars, resulting in plentiful headaches by day but superb vision at night. The group on the left belonged to that dark caravan which had been tailing them. Few were discernible as guards outright, but there seemed to be a great many forms hanging back, beyond the range of the light.

Bernard closed his eyes then reopened them, studying the silhouettes against the ivory starlight, and could now see the black procession had grown much larger in number, and a vast number were not all shaped like men. It occurred to him that the lantern was a gesture of courtesy to the humans, as the vampires and others in the shadows had little need of it.

The most slender of two visitors stood perfectly still and straight, as the second, stouter figure ran forward to complete the first part of the offering. After checking for a nod from its placid companion, it too rang the bell. This time as the bell sang out, it seemed as though vibrations echoed as shards, bouncing off the stones in the area like shrapnel. The two figures slipped back into their group as well, as if part of a court procession.

There was a murmur from the assembled warriors in the Order, as it seemed that hundreds of fleeting shapes and some truly massive ones ignored the road entirely. The hoard blurred—a whirling, roaring stygian river that swirled around them then the stone beside them—before retreating back to the forest to disappear into silence. Even then, among the trees nearest the Order, glimpses could be seen in foxfire glimmer. The Fay of the Seelie Court had made their entrance.

New faces, those of creatures only mentioned in children's tales or perhaps glimpsed ambiguously while walking alone, revealed themselves by the light of the lantern. A soft, teal luminescence streamed from the forest, and a contingent of the Fay nobility paraded forth, their path lit by wisps of faerie lights. A dour creature approached the table, its appearance half manlike, half that of a wild boar, and laid a large leaf piled high with an assortment of nuts and fruit on its face. It looked back at the two most regal of the creatures, who nodded. The creature rang the bell.

This time, the ringing swelled and ebbed, slowly lowering in tone. The atmosphere had been dead calm until that moment, as a violent wind suddenly sprang up around the congregation. It was as if hundreds of unseen wings were fluttering, and a dark and inscrutable form emerged from the center of the slab. Off in the distance, things howled and bayed in the night.

It was possibly an old woman dressed in a hooded mantle, but it was hard to tell. One certainty was the gleam of the sable eyes peering back at them from the darkness of the hood. A voice croaked from everywhere and nowhere. It might have been from the figure on the rock.

"It Begins."

Another displaced voice called out.

"Have the offerings been made upon the Oath stone?"

Yet another responded, as if from someplace deep and far away.

"They have."

"Good," said a voice like rasping steel. "Now."

> *"At the crossroads, rituals crafted*
> *At the crossroads, words convened*
> *At the crossroads, pacts contracted*
> *At the crossroads, my rule shall be."*

The three skeletons hanging from the tree chimed in with giggling, leathery voices.

> *"An' so it is said!"*
> *"And zo it will be!"*
> *"An' so it's doon!"*

The figure on the rock pointed a staff at the skeletons and said, "Hush, you."

The entity rapped on the stone three times.

"This be my road, my place, my peace, my power. You have invoked the old ways, made your offerings, and thus are bound by them. Any who breaks my peace will be my meat. Until the bell is rung, you shall... talk."

This concluded with the figure stepping back and disappearing into the shadows. Yet somehow, Bernard knew she was still very much present. He was also nearly certain who had been invoked, including her name. Hecate was a renowned goddess of ancient magic, and while not as powerful as she once was, crossroads were still her dominion. The power thrummed in the road beneath their feet, leaving him disinclined to challenge it.

The Abbot approached the stone, and as he did, he bowed.

"My name is Klaas, and I will speak as the head of the Order of Nikolai Thaumaturgus, of the Christian God, as a man of God, and as a son of Adam. The beliefs and spirit of my order travel with me. Who will speak with me?"

Another shadow parted with the dark, and it revealed itself to be a man of average height, with thin, hawkish features. His manner of dress was subtle, understatedly lavish in that way indicative of true wealth. His eyes did not reflect light like a human's, instead having an opal-shine like a nocturnal predator. The figure stepped carefully forward.

"This damn mud is ruining my shoes," said the person dryly. "Ahem. I am Duke Cosimo Florentine of the House of Measures, of the beings of shadow. I once was a son of Adam but am no longer. I will speak for those who ally themselves with me now or those who kneel before my power. Who else will speak with us?"

A petite individual stepped out of the woods, and although it looked like a beautiful young lady from the waist up, the entirety of its lower extremities were replete with smooth, polished scales which shone iridescent in the torchlight.

"I am Melusine, as some have come to know me. I shall speak for the children of the five elements and for the nobles of the Fay realms, as much as any do."

The Abbot nodded to both the figures and leaned against the rock.

"We are this evening to address one issue: The hunting of humans. Know that the people of my Order have promised that no harm shall come to those who would do no injury to us."

"It is true," Duke Cosimo admitted. "Your Order has even gone so far as to offer some protection for those others of your species would consider abominations. Also truth, the natural order of things is that the strong prey on the weak. My ilk must feed on humans every now and then. That is our nature, just as you feed on beasts of the forest or cull your livestock."

Melusine looked at both of them and spoke with a voice both beautiful and alien.

"Once, the children of ages were everywhere. In time, the sons and daughters of Adam and their human gods, both old and new, have driven us further and further from our lands. We were killed by flame and iron, they destroyed root and thorn, and now they foul and desecrate our homes. The song of your bells hurts our ears."

"You and yours," she said pointing to Duke Cosimo, "hunt the humans then bring their wrath down upon us! Forests burn, ancient sites upturned, because of you and yours."

Melusine rounded on the Abbot.

"While your order may have some respect for the old ways, they help those who only know the way of the Desert God, the White God of flame and iron. Those of mixed blood, those who follow the wyrding way, are killed and tortured." As she spoke, Melusine grew larger, and larger.

Abbot Klaas held up his hands and made calming gestures.

"The truth, as always, is a matter of perception. I have no desire to see humans killed by anyone, including other humans. Some grievances are beyond the purview of what we are here to discuss." He paused and took a deep breath.

"I do not speak for the human kings, nor the Holy Roman Church. I acknowledge that both of those powers would either control you or, failing that, destroy you. They may well attempt to do so. All my Order and followers can do is provide what quiet works and diplomacy we can, to try and tip the scales towards peace and cooperation between us. Even, perhaps, offer haven. But because some forces in this world will not honor any boundaries, including ours, we will use our swords and prayers to defend and protect ourselves when needed."

He pointed a hand back at his followers.

"My brethren and I ask you, what would you have of us that we may share honest peace?"

The Vampire Duke Cosimo answered first. His voice was cultured and fluid.

"Our two sides are much alike Abbot Klaas. We both play at being hidden yet partake of the outside world. While you may not like our methods, the results of our efforts have borne fruit. Are not the roads safer? Is not commerce flowing, artists patronized, and yes, even the Church growing ever wealthier? I would ask the following: Allow me to install one of mine within your monastery. Then, turn a blind eye when the occasional small harvest comes to pass. When someone who is not a signatory to this agreement comes to harm you and yours, we will aid you, help you deal with them."

Melusine studied the Abbot but said nothing.

Abbot Klaas turned to look back at his group. He could see the outline of his forces' commander listening, and he could sense, if not see, that the man's jaw muscles were clenched. Klaas knew full well that Magnus had lost two children to vampires only a few years ago. The Abbot turned back to look at Duke Cosimo.

"This I cannot do. To make such a deal with you would be to play God, as to who lived, how many, and why. Regarding taking someone who has been touched by the dark into our church, well, that has proven problematic but generally people come to us when they have lost all hope. Should someone of your... community wish our help? They are welcome, provided they mean no harm. And no harm would naturally also mean no spying."

Klaas turned to face Melusine and was about to say something when something low and fast came barreling down the third road, pursued very closely by a pack of black shadows. Melusine waved a hand as the figure shot towards the Abbot, causing the wolf to stumble and slide, rolling to a stop at the man's feet.

The black wolves charged forward, none seeming to care about the meeting they were interrupting, intent on killing the wolf that was Aleta.

Brother Bernard spotted the wolf now gasping the Abbot's feet. He quickly grabbed an older man named Cormac, one of the Knights of Saint Nikolai.

"We must defend the Abbot and the gray wolf!"

Sir Cormac heaved the great sword off his back and headed towards the Abbot, moving fast for a man his size. Duke Cosimo backed up a few paces as did Melusine. Klaas pulled up his crucifix and, stepping over the wolf, brought it up before the onslaught.

"This being claims my protection and, by the Grace of God, she shall have it." With that, a soft white light began to emanate from him. The pack of black wolves slowed down. A few seconds later, the knight was now standing resolute beside the Abbot, his great sword at the ready. At the sight of the white light, the Fay in the forest keened, and the dark contingent hissed.

"Something about this is very odd, be ready," whispered Brother Bernard to Magnus, who was next to him and back in battle formation. Magnus replied with a nod. Around them, the warriors of St. Nikolai quietly prepared for battle.

"Pardon me for just a moment," Abbot Klaas said politely, looking briefly at the ambassadors of the Dark and the Fay.

The Abbot swept his cloak from off his shoulders and laid it across the panting wolf, then whispered to it. A few seconds later, a disheveled woman stood up, wrapped in the cloak. A murmur went through the ranks, as well as the surrounding creatures. The black wolves growled and started to inch closer.

Sister Aleta pulled the cloak about her, exhausted, and whispered to the Abbot.

"Among the black caravan, there are ones who have broken the rules of the Oath rock. They do not wish any agreement made. They did something to the offering." With that, she sagged against the holy man, barely conscious.

Duke Cosimo and Melusine both boasted keen hearing and had started to move. Melusine retreated back to the forest, while Duke Cosimo stepped forward, leaning in and carefully poking the bread that was part of the dark contingent's offering. At his touch, the bread lost its shape and glamour, dissolving into sand.

The High Lord of the Vampires snarled and whirled.

"How Dare You!"

This he said not to the Abbot but his own accompaniment and to a particular vampire named Petru.

Petru said nothing but allowed a handkerchief to slip from between his fingers.

Casting his gaze down at the ground, the visage that rose to meet the irate Duke was changed, now that of a monster in full, gnashing frenzy. Petru, thirty other vampires, and hundreds of screaming, hissing dark fairies flew towards the Order.

Duke Cosimo turned to look at the Abbot and Melusine. He bowed.

"My apologies," he said and then vanished.

The Abbot, despite his age, quickly scooped up Aleta, placed her on the sacred stone, and began to pray. Cormac spun and put himself in front of the holy man, just as the pack of wolves leapt to attack them.

The night filled with cries of battle and screams of pain and fury. The dark Fay were deadly accurate with their whizzing, deadly elf shot, using razor sharp bronze or eldritch blades to dismantle larger foes with inhuman strength and swiftness. To their dismay, the human infantry were soon made brutally aware of the gaps in their leg armor. Various vampires of several houses ripped into the ranks, snatching them bodily and tossing them away as the human warriors tried to keep their battle formation square. In the blackness, men screamed for aid.

Commander Magnus pulled something from a leather case and rang it.

The old clerical bell had a very different tone from the previous one, a note that sounded defiant and resounding. It rang out and filled the air with a searing radiance. Immediately, the dark Fay and vampires retreated backwards outside its range, barely a stone's throw away, screaming and snarling at the humans. Their eyes were screwed shut, skin smoking. Orders among files flew, the knights and warriors of St. Nicholas moving to fill the gaps in the line. But in the rush of the first wave, the creatures of the dark had cut the Order's ranks almost in half, and in the interior of the square, there were many wounded. Out in the darkness, the human warriors could hear the screams of the ones who had been dragged further into the night, fated to be tortured and devoured.

Standing just outside of the glow, the creatures who had met the blades of the humans found that the human weapons and shields they carried were edged with cold iron or silver and had been blessed to boot. The cursed undead licked their wounds to staunch the smoking and burning.

Magnus turned to his lieutenants.

"Torches up. Second file, I want a poll axe or glaive every third man." He handed the bell to one of the brothers who acted as a healer for his troops.

"Brother Colum, I want you to pray, and ring that bell every minute or so."

The brother took the bell and moved to the center of the group.

Just out of the light of the torches, the vampire Petru turned and looked at the boiling mass of unseelie creatures and various vampires in full hunting mode. He called to them in a thick, sing-songy voice.

"Tonight, we fight for our existence. We have always ruled the night, and it is time these cattle learned to fear us again. Let the bell ring till our ears bleed, let their swords burn like flaming brands, they have already lost half of their number, and it is many hours till dawn. Our victory is assured. We will drink their blood and dance in their entrails tonight! Can you not smell their fear? Can you not taste their desperation on the wind?"

Petru turned to a glowering red cap next to him.

"We shall be clever, my friends. A short distance back, there were many stones the size of human heads back by the path. Bring them here now, as many as you can find."

The red cap zipped away, followed by others. To the larger vampiric creatures, Petru pointed towards the center of the square.

"In the center is their bellringer. I will give an untouched, matched set of young redheaded Scottish girls to the creature who takes him out with a stone. I will give you even more if you crush that bell." Snarls of hunger and laughter answered him in assent.

Back at the Oath stone, Aleta was too exhausted to do anything except shiver, collapsed upon the biting cold of the rock's surface. The pack of ghoulish wolves had been chasing her most of the day, never tiring, never giving up. Fast and relentless, but not terribly bright. The Abbot continued praying with great strength, his voice rich and powerful, and the air around him seeming to ripple. The Knight Cormac had already killed two of the black wolves, but not without getting bitten repeatedly himself, and the wolves had set about weaving back and forth, waiting for an opening. Aleta looked over and saw the Vampire Lord watching quietly, as were the Fay in the woods.

She knew that the Lord, should he enter the fray, would probably kill them all in short order, but had yet to do so. They had met before, and he had always spoken to her civilly, if aloofly.

"Duke Cosimo, your people broke the truce. Why do you not stop them?"

"I don't control these Unseelie. Right now, the kindred that attack the holy warriors are dying as well. I shall wait until this resolves itself and deal with the survivors."

Aleta felt tears of frustration course down her cheeks, and she caught a glimpse of something shining on the big rock next to her. She leaned over and there, lying next to the other offerings, was a knife wrought in black obsidian, wrapped in leather with a bone handle. Weak as she was, she wanted a weapon. She reached over to pick it up, and a large, feminine hand, scarified in arcane symbols, extended out of the darkness, batting her hand away. Aleta looked up and saw the shape of the black crone looming over her. A hoarse voice whispered in her ear.

"Touch it again and die, skin changer. That offering was done in good faith and is therefore mine."

Aleta felt fear such as she had never felt before. Cold sweat broke out all over her body, and she scrambled back.

"My apologies, great one. Why do you not punish the ones who have transgressed against you?" she asked in a trembling voice. A voice both ancient and frightful answered her.

"Think that I, who suckled at the teat of magic itself, am to be fooled by a glamour, no matter how carefully wrought? Blood is being shed, something I have missed, and hungry grass shall drink its fill. This I like at my crossroads. The humans are being tested. The fiends in the dark, who stand by and watch, are too being weighed and measured. Stay on this rock and watch, little one."

Aleta curled herself into a ball, and resolved to defend the back of the Abbot, who was chanting with quiet conviction.

Not far away, the forces had rallied for a second round of battle. Magnus saw the forces draw close again and then heard small whistling sounds.

"Shields! Center ranks, turtle!" he cried out.

Out of the night sky dropped hefty stones the size of melons, and more warriors went down with crushed shoulders and smashed helms. The big kite shields the warriors had not been built to bear the brunt of such heavy attacks, and the shields themselves cracked and gave way, as did many of the arms behind them.

Petru smiled and waved at the vampires. Some of the largest night creatures lumbered up to join his ranks.

"That's the way! Keep throwing!" he laughed.

They answered with grunts and growls, as they heaved the stones aloft. The Knight commander knew that his battle formation was crumbling.

"Dress lines and ready to attack! To the right flank, March! *Feuer und tod!*" he called out.

From inside the battle formation, three objects were hurled in the direction of the aggressors. Each connected with the crowd in turn, bathing them in blossoming fire. The flame sprung up amidst the creatures and was rapidly spreading as shrieking Fay and vampires fought madly to get away from it, only spreading it even faster. Brother Bernard watched in mute horror, for the flasks had been created by him, and he had wondered at the claims of the old Arabic instructions. The Greek translations penned by mad old Khālid ibn Yazīd were indeed as accurate as they were potent. Unfortunately, Brother Bernard now had no other flasks, nor any other tricks up his sleeve.

The vampire Petru nearly bolted himself, cursing himself for that deep and instinctual fear of fire inherent to his species, something few vampires ever overcame. Instead, he gathered his colleagues, stepped behind their lines, and slew those at sword length who were running madly on fire. Fangs bared, he snapped to face those who were thinking of leaving the field. Petru reached down and grabbed some of the distraught small folk.

"Ah, my friends, thank you for volunteering. Ready your knife."

Using his vampiric strength, Petru pitched them screaming into the center of the human's battle formation. More chaos ensued.

Anarchy and fire were spreading through the night, and the human lines were holding fast, despite the magical creatures' strength in numbers. Sadly, one of many heavy stones had finally sailed to meet its mark, colliding with Brother Colum, who had been praying and ringing the accursed bell relentlessly like a machine. Petru grinned, delivering a triumphant shout that echoed among his remaining colleagues. The fairies and vampires skirted the burning earth and gathered to finish them off.

From out of the darkness behind the human forces came the strange figure with deadly stag horns and a massive flail. Despite their efforts, the corner of the Order's battle square soon crumpled. Aleta saw the creature first and prepared to jump off the stone, to run to her brother's aid.

The Knight Cormac had forced the wolves away at great cost, and the Abbot was starting to bend at the knees. He staggered and Aleta heard him faintly say, "...and your will be done. Amen."

The Abbot finished his prayer, now almost completely exhausted. In his mind, he softly cried out. *Lord, help us.* To his surprise, a quiet voice responded in his mind with dry humor.

"Well, I am not the almighty, but He has asked if I might lend you some help."

"Who?" the Abbot answered in confusion, feeling even weaker.

"I am Nicholas, the founder of our order. The Almighty has given me permission to look in on things once in a while and help if I can."

"Nicholas, take this body, help us in our hour of need," the Abbot said.

The voice of Nicholas responded quietly.

"Possession is a demonic thing. Saints and angels, we don't take bodies. However, if you like, we can guide you and provide you with aid. The decision will always fall to you. Would you like some help?"

"Yes, in the name of the Almighty, yes," the Abbot responded fervently with a nod.

The voice of Nicholas responded by chanting an ancient prayer, and the Abbot felt energy well up within him, like a vast ocean tide filling a bay.

Aleta was just bending down to pick up the exhausted Abbot, when suddenly he stood back up under his own power. As she helped him stand, she marveled as a golden light surrounded and infused the priest. He patted her hand confidently, and she felt instantly calm. It was the Abbot she knew but, somehow, more.

Abbot Klaas looked sad but calm and he reached into a small pouch. He pulled out a set of rusty manacles on thick, heavy rusty chains and he called out loudly.

"Krampus, dancer in the woods, we have need of you. Honor our agreement and help us!" A dust storm of wind and leaves swirled up to surround the stone.

Suddenly, a booming roar tore across the battlefield, deep and primal and, for a moment, everyone stopped to look. Charging out onto the flame-lit battlefield, the creature known as Krampus fully revealed itself. It was twice the size it had been when Aleta had seen it as a small child, and it was moving with incredible speed. Krampus tackled the horned stag creature, and the ground shook when the two beings met. With a spin, Krampus grabbed the wicked horns and wrenched the creature into the dirt, snapping its neck.

Aleta watched as the Abbot, who seemed empowered and bright, impossibly withdrew a full-sized crozier from the same bag that had held the heavy chains and stepped calmly towards the ranks of the vampires and dark Fay. A voice clear and powerful poured forth the flowing words.

"Ágios o Theós, Ágios ischyrós, Ágios athánatos, eléison imás."

Undeterred by screeching of the night creatures, the Abbot steadily advanced, a bright glowing crozier in one hand, chains held tightly in the other. As he walked, he touched one fallen warrior then another, each opening their eyes, bewildered, rising in his wake. No stone or bolt came close to him, and with a cry, the warriors of the Order of St. Nicholas rallied.

The holy man turned and touched the crozier to the sword of Cormac, walking behind him.

"Vade et esto lux in mundo," which Aleta heard as, "Go and be a light in this world."

The knight bowed humbly, then turned and started towards the ranks of the undead at a run. As the first vampires turned to fight him, they slowed as they approached. Their eyes grew wide, as if unable to stop whatever was hindering them. With a practiced turn of his wrists, the mighty swordsman pivoted his hips under the great sword, bringing the blade down his side, and then swiveling across the other shoulder. The two vampires he caught with the sword instantly crumbled in a cloud of dust. Several of the vampires on the field who saw this immediately turned and fled into the night.

Across the battleground, the being known as Krampus was enjoying itself immensely as it tore into the meatiest of the Fay creatures. The horned creature reeled back and bellowed in a wordless cry that all wildest creatures know.

"CHALLENGE ME!"

Aleta looked over her shoulders and saw a collection of the brighter Fay leaving the forest, moving to intercept the dark ones. As swift as they had been to attack, the dark creatures were now fleeing in droves.

Soon the battle was over, and the Abbot drifted about, gently touching wounded warriors. As he did, elf-shot was expelled from their bodies and the magical injuries reverted to normal ones. The Abbot turned to the Knight Commander of St. Nikolai and bowed.

"Commander Magnus. It is not within our power to fully restore those who have fallen in this battle. They are returned to you until dawn. Use them to protect you and yours until then. Blessings and thanks to you. I'm afraid I am going to be very weak in a moment. Good luck."

In his mind, the Abbot heard the voice of Nicholas.

"Brother, I must be going. Thank you and good luck."

"Thank you," Klaas responded as he felt his vitality fade and looked for a place to sit down.

Moment after moment passed. The newly restored warriors were strangely quiet as they helped the remaining troops and members of their caravan reform.

Across the field, the vampire Petru had headed into the green. As he scrambled towards the darkness of the forest, a slim figure stepped out to meet him.

"Duke Cosimo!"

"Petru."

The younger vampire was afraid, but still slightly defiant.

"I do not regret attempting what I did. I only regret failing. We could have made the civilized world ours!"

"I don't think you thought this out," the Duke replied. "Had it occurred to you that their priest could tap into all that belief? That font of energy fed by the prayers of the countless little old women praying away over this Earth? No? Of course not." The arch-vampire moved to walk alongside Petru.

"As you know, I have my spies and my mages. That loathsome bell the humans used; it has a very unique property. Should it touch any other bell, the other will ring no matter how far away, when the master bell is struck. The human commander, Magnus I believe, had made certain that I knew of this. He, of course, had plans of his own devising."

"I don't understand," Petru admitted as he shook his head slowly.

Duke Cosimo abruptly spun face to face with Petru.

"No, you don't! Magnus told me that he had bells linked and agents placed all over the Empires, people who would until daybreak then seek out and destroy all our kindred and their hidden holdings should those bells ring. Now, because of you, they have been! Ring, ring, ring! Idiot." He turned and started walking again.

The ancient vampire gestured to the ranks of human warriors gathered, a spot of light in the darkness.

"Did you really think that such a large congregation of humans would agree to meet a host of vampires in a field in the middle of nowhere without a plan? You've made one of the classic blunders, the classic error of assuming that good people cannot also be clever. There is a reason why monsters fear the mob. The cost of this will be very dear, dear indeed!"

"My apologies, my master." The courtier Petru's face turned even whiter.

Duke Cosimo's eyes narrowed down to golden pinpricks, and he nodded gracefully. For Petru, what followed was a burst of blinding pain and a loss of consciousness.

When Petru slowly came to, he was unable to move or speak. Waves of pain told him that his body was shattered, having been stuffed tightly into the trunk of a large tree. Stakes of living wood had been very carefully plunged through his mangled body, pinning him. Duke Cosimo stood, waiting for Petru's eyes to focus.

"Apology accepted."

Cosimo looked up at the branches of the tree, then back at the hapless vampire, who was unable to do or say anything, apart from moving his eyes.

"It was the tradition long ago, for humans to entomb their dead in the hearts of the trees of this area. The trees here grow quickly, sealing the open spaces inside them. They fill with a sap that cures into a hard resin after many centuries. Decades, perhaps centuries from now, I shall come back and find you encased in amber. You will still be here, aware, in agony as the tree crushes you, and as the sun tortures you daily and, of course, you will be mad with hunger. When the ages have visited their torment upon you, I might, in fact, allow you to serve me again. As a paperweight."

And with that, Duke Cosimo, Arch Vampire of the House of Measures, faded into the shadows. Petru could only scream soundlessly, and scream and scream.

* * *

Stars wheeled overhead.

At the Oath stone, the three sides reconvened. This time, Duke Cosimo brought a plate himself and set it down. The crone figure stepped out of the darkness and peered at them all.

"Duke Cosimo, you have been let down by your associates. They have not won the day."

"My apologies to all here. This battle was not my intention."

The crone chuckled, a sound like shaken gravel.

"Intention or no, you have broken my rules and, for that, there will be penalties."

Cosimo started to object but thought better of it.

"Understood."

The crone turned towards Abbot Klaas. He was now fully himself again, barely able to stand as a result.

"What would you claim as your vengeance rights?"

The Abbot shook his head wearily.

"Vengeance is the Lord's province, not mine. But I would say this. For every person of my group who was struck down, every life lost, let the agreement here last a hundred years."

Duke Cosimo looked like someone who had something very delicate and personal caught in a sausage grinder and had just felt the handle begin to turn. The Abbot smiled slightly.

"For not stopping this battle, let it be said that any of the Vampiric Houses and their allies can no longer hunt or interfere with those of the Order of St. Nikolai. That our order, during a season at our mutual discretion and when petitioned by an innocent, may do what is necessary to protect and defend those who share in our principles. Furthermore..."

This went on for some time. Aleta saw a book being passed to Brother Colum, who came forward to scribe, despite being sorely battered. The Knight Cormac stood guard with his newly blessed sword and watched as the man pulled out a very handsome leather-covered box, then set about writing swiftly and discreetly. Time passed. Soon the blanket of the evening sky slipped to reveal the indigo of encroaching sunrise, still the negotiations persisted.

The Crone motioned to the Fay in the woods and Melusine, their spokesperson, came forward.

"What penalty will the dark Fay who deconsecrated my fields and grounds pay, those who would break the rules of my roads?"

"Their lives are forfeit," Melusine replied as she bowed, "to be done with as the human wishes."

The Abbot was looking more and more weary, and the powerful presence that had been within him was slowly diminishing, like a candle fading. Brother Bernard stepped forward.

"Allow me, Abbot?" The old man nodded.

"We have no desire to destroy them, yet they have slain many of ours. As recompense, they may serve us, to do good deeds and works as we see fit, a hundred years for each one of our fallen. To honor our intent and not twist our words, to work without recompense or entrapment, and to honor the generosity of our Order for not destroying them. Let the sound of bells fill them with happiness, and may both the Unseelie and Seelie be bound by the same rules as the Vampire Houses."

"Not bad!" the Abbot said with a chuckle and an approving grin.

"I'm not certain," Melusine answered with a frown.

The Crone could be seen more clearly as the light began to fill the sky overhead. Voice stern, she pointed a long, tattooed finger at the Fay being.

"Allow me to give you certainty then. For allowing the glamour to be used at my Oath stone and not stopping the battle, I fine you the penalty of twice the punishment. May an equal share of Fay creatures from the Seelie side now serve this Order as well."

Melusine let out a cry and in the woods behind her, much howling and wailing could be heard.

The Crone stabbed a finger down at the parchment.

"The Dawn comes," she intoned with a voice like iron. "Let the three sides sign this compact and let this be done. I grow weary of you all."

The three sides did as they were told, their contract magically sealed and consecrated. The forces of the dark contingent, as well as that of the Fay, moved into the thick forest following the lingering shadows, taking their wounded and dead with them. Krampus approached the Abbot and the two spoke together briefly. Then, claiming the abominable skull with its rack of sharp antlers as a souvenir, Krampus headed off into the woods, chuckling to itself.

As the sun rose, the air brimming with the ballads of morning birds, the Abbot led everyone in their Morning Prayer. When the light of dawn kissed the faces of those who had been temporarily restored, they crumpled and fell where they had been kneeling in prayer, looks of peace on their faces, to move no longer.

Aleta watched as Brother Colum finished dusting the ink on the page.

"I am very fond of the scribal arts. I could not help but notice how fast and sure your words were, and your attention to detail. What is your name?"

He bowed, and carefully stowed the new document in a sturdy sleeve.

"They call me Brother Colum. You can thank the brothers of St. Columbanus for my hand. I was once of the green isles, land of great scribes."

Aleta bowed to him. She turned to address the big knight who had defended them. "And you? What is your name?"

"Cormac. Sir Cormac to some."

Aleta gave him a big smile.

"Aleta. I am skin-changer and a Sister of the Order. Why is there doubt about being a knight? "

"As a young man, I was abducted and learned new ways on the merchant routes. I finally made my way home and was knighted. Unfortunately, the local church found out that my mother was Jewish, and that led to some complications." The two of them left Brother Colum, stepping away in deep conversation.

Brother Colum finished his task and handed the case to the Abbot.

"Father Abbot, may I ask an odd question?"

The Abbot inspected the document and case mindfully, nodding in satisfaction.

"Of course, Brother. You have a good memory and a fast and fair hand."

"Thank you, Abbot. What will the Order of the 'Hidden Nicholas' do with the help of all those elves and whatnot?"

The Abbot shrugged as he pressed his signet ring into the soft wax, placing a warding rune on the case.

"Who knows? They are beings of amazing abilities, and our Lord does work in mysterious ways."

He handed the case back and sat down, his face gray, utterly exhausted. His head sagged to his chest, and his eyes closed. Brother Colum waved to the others, who came over and lifted him gently, even reverently.

On the long journey back, the Abbot Klaas quietly passed away, to the sadness of all who had been present. Shortly thereafter, Brother Bernard the Scholar was made the Abbot of the Hidden St. Nicholas, now called St. Nicholas the Wonderworker.

* * *

16. Intermezzo

Years and then decades and finally centuries slipped by, all while slowly the strength of the military hand of the Order diminished. The Order itself became a secret, a canon of stories that passed into legend. Occasionally, those oddest, most magical of folks who believed in the ideas of Nicholas the Wonderworker found their way to those quiet, shrouded places. Through the years, the stories of the Order and the monastery of the Hidden St. Nicholas were forgotten more and more as a certain jolly old elf took the stage.

* * *

17. Mall Time

Modern Day Yule Season, LaMoure, North Dakota

The Avalon Mall in LaMoure was so new that there were places where the paint was still drying, and even a few of the shops had not yet been filled with tenants. The color scheme was chrome and white, with all the balconies and crossways filled with silver, red, and green decorations. There were thousands of people inside, trapped in the bustle, away from their homes for last-minute shopping missions. Despite the sentimental music resonating in every storefront, the people inside looked more determined than cheerful. Bing and Bowie sang "Little Drummer Boy" and the tune bounced around the high arches.

Abe adjusted the scarf around his face to better hide his beard and followed Ron, who cut through the crowd like a snowplow. Ron had a scarf hiding his distinctive facial hair as well. Both were wearing non-holiday colors and ball caps.

In the world of Christmas performers, Abe knew it was considered very bad manners to look like Santa in a mall that had someone else working that gig. The taboo was so strongly observed during the season, one rarely risked venturing somewhere there might possibly be another Santa. It was part of the code to never confuse the kids if one could avoid it. For Abe, he felt like he was secretly playing hookie. It was one of the weirdest things about being a Santa. Being one himself, he rarely got a chance to see other Clauses working with an audience in real life. With so much riding on finding work this time of year, a real bearded Santa could hardly spare the time.

Ron stopped for a second, the tide of people swirling past them. He pointed towards a utility hallway, and they swam their way over. Standing at the front was a bored looking security guard, relaxing in a cart, texting. He looked up, raised an eyebrow, and smiled. He nodded, being in on the joke.

"Santa."

"Santa."

"Go on in, Santa is expecting you," he chuckled and went back to his phone.

Abe and Ron walked down the hallway, and the din and the Christmas music decreased significantly. They found the door Ron was looking for, on which he tapped out the rhythm to "Jingle Bells." The door popped open.

Another Santa looked out at them and gave them a huge grin. The man was older than Abe, more rotund, but much friendlier looking than Ron and he had a magnificent beard. It was obvious he was still in Santa mode, despite being out of his jacket and wearing a sweat-stained T-shirt. His face was still made up, a healthy dusting of glitter twinkling in his beard.

"Hang on, hang on, gents. Be right with you. Grab a chair or a couch. There're beverages in the fridge and a ton of snacks on the table."

The older Santa pulled the cold packs from his ice vest and stuffed them into the freezer in the minifridge, then disappeared into the bathroom. Abe looked around. The room was, for all intents and purposes, indiscernible from a studio apartment except for the obvious department store ceiling. It was a pretty sweet arrangement. He had seen and heard of a lot worse.

Their host came back looking fresher in a clean T-shirt, speaking quickly while prepping a meal in the microwave.

"Ron, I was hoping you would come by. You know I don't get a chance to get out much with the schedule they have me on. It's crazy, I don't get many visitors that I don't have to 'Ho-Ho' at, besides the security folks, the cleaning crews, and photo crew. I hope you don't mind if I eat while I chat, because I'm on 'til ten, if you can believe it. This break is only fifteen minutes, sad to say."

"Eat, Steve. We totally understand." Ron gave Steve a quick hug then gestured to Abe, who was already seated.

"Santa Steve, meet your competition over at the Fairfield Mall. This is Santa Abe Wykowski, who filled in for Len, who might've had a stroke, we think. Abe and occasionally Santa Mitch are hot seating it over there."

Santa Steve extended a hearty handshake to Abe and offered him a brownie, which Abe took.

"Nice to meetcha, Abe. Nice looking 34th street beard you've got there. I hear this is your first year doing the malls. How's it going?"

Abe laughed and looked around at the spiffy apartment Steve had settled into.

"They have us downstairs in an old security office. Bleak and cold, full of cleaning supplies and Easter decorations. This is pretty swank."

Steve nodded as he fished his microwave dinner out, devouring it before it could cool.

"Yeah, this is about the nicest I've had in a location. The truth is I'm the only Santa, and I'm doing ten- to twelve-hour days. Sometimes longer. It's dark and cold out there in the real world, and not much to see right now, from what I hear tell. They flew me in and, not too long from now, they fly me back out. Believe you me, I will sleep the whole way home."

Ron snagged a beer out of the fridge, saw the wistful eye on Steve, and swapped it for a diet ginger ale. Abe nodded in agreement. They both knew that "beer-breath Santa" was a no-no.

"Abe, Steve here is out of the Los Angeles area. They saw his photos and the management team paid top dollar to have him turn down his gig in California and come up here."

"Ron, didn't they know you were up here?" Steve said, eyeing Ron. "I cannot believe they didn't offer you this gig first, cuz if they low-balled you by bringing me in...." He trailed off, shaking his head and looking concerned.

"Nope, no worries there, Steve," Ron said with a wave of his hands. "My mall days are mostly behind me. I'm just doing photo work and home visits these days, maybe the occasional corporate and charity event."

"Must be nice," Steve said with a laugh. "I admit, I really needed the money so that's why I am here, doing the grind. Thank God I've not hit the snot-wall yet."

At that, all three of the Santas in the room knocked on wood. It wasn't a question of *if* they would get sick during the season, it was a question of when and how hard.

Ron got a serious look on his face, leaned forward, and revealed the ring he was wearing to Steve.

Steve looked at it and wiped his face, being careful to get everything out of his mustache and not smear his make-up.

"Holy cow, Ron. Is this official Order business?" Steve whistled low.

"Steve, I know you haven't had much to do with the Santa organizations since the Santa wars..." Ron started when Steve cut him off.

"Damn straight. I don't have a lot of time for all that political drama-llama stuff. They can take all that bunkum and shove it where the sleigh don't fly."

"So, Steve. You know how once you've worn the suit for a while, you start to notice things?"

Steve lost his cheerful demeanor, and just looked very, very, tired.

"Yeah, I know. Like that thing with you and Skip." Steve lost his cheerful demeanor and just looked very tired.

"Abe, I'll have to tell you later," Ron said with a wince.

Steve looked at the ring and then up at the clock. His demeanor was all business.

"Talk quick, Ron."

"There is something big going down in town, and we're not sure what. Abe here spotted at least three vampires, and we have at least one confirmed."

"No shit?" Steve's eyes widened and he looked at Abe.

"No shit," Abe answered with a nod.

Steve closed his eyes in thought.

"Come to think of it, I may have caught some glimpses of some stuff. More than a couple people here with odd eyes. A few folks that the light hit the wrong way as they walked by. Oh, and a big, tall elf lady. Maybe a little Spanish fairy lady with wings. Her boyfriend looked a bit um, wolfy, now that I think about it."

Steve tossed his empty dinner tray, wiped the table down, and started preparing himself for his last session for the night.

"I hope you don't mind talking to me while I prep." Steve started brushing the fur on his jacket, making everything North Pole spiffy again.

"The thing is, there's a fair number of Native Americans up this way that I don't know anything about. So, I ain't going to throw any stones. If it don't mess with my mall or my customers, I ain't messing back." Steve stepped into the bathroom, leaving the door open for the conversation.

Abe looked unhappy, but Ron just walked over to the bathroom door frame and spoke over the sound of running water.

"Steve, we want you to pull out after tonight's shift. The Order has a small contingency fund. We can't fully repay you for breaking this contract, but we can give you a stipend and a flight out of here tonight. We can fake a medical emergency, and I have a driver who's ready to get you on a plane home."

Steve came out of the bathroom drying his hands, his face was clearly paler.

"What the hell, Ron? If I break this contract, I doubt any of the photo companies will pick me up again next year. Besides that, I have a special gig happening the night after Christmas day. They're paying me five grand to show up at a special Christmas for an orphanage. I saw two vans full of toys. The kids aren't getting their Christmas presents until the second day after Christmas. It's going to be a huge deal, press, media, everything."

"Steve, that's kind of weird, don't you think? Making all those kids wait like that?" Abe shook his head.

"Yeah, I brought that up to them. They said they tried to get everything together before Christmas and just could not do it. But the corporation is giving a ton of money to the charity that runs the orphanage, and they want the kids to feel like Santa is doing something special, just for them."

Steve sat down at his makeup mirror and applied a few touches here and there, sprucing up his hair, reddening his cheeks.

Ron walked over behind him and looked at Steve in the mirror.

"Veritas, truth, Steve. I'm being deadly serious." Ron spun Steve's chair around, eyes attentive and hard.

"If you stay, you may die. There are bad hombres in town, and we already know something is up. We'll stick around until after you get off shift. Abe can pack you up in the meantime. If you come with us, we'll get you out of this town. The gears are turning on something really sinister, and the Order is trying to protect you and all those people who might want to come see you. You need to listen to me."

The older Santa said nothing as he put fresh cold packs in his cool vest and put it on. Abe and Ron watched as the Santa coat and belt went on. Steve looked in the full-length mirror at the door, adjusted his suit, popped a breath strip into his mouth, and then put his Santa cap and gloves on. Abe and Ron knew the ritual well. Santa Steve turned and faced the two men.

"Gents, you go ahead and make yourself at home here, and stay as long as you like. My North Pole is your North Pole." He gave them a small smile. "Here's the thing. The rumor mill says that the Order has done some good things, and occasionally has done some messed up things. I've heard some pretty crazy stuff."

Steve shot one last glance at the clock and looked at Ron with a raised eyebrow, who gave him a shrug in return.

"You know that I don't belong to any of the fraternal organizations for a reason. I'm not a joiner, never have been. And I'm too old to change my ways. I appreciate you two coming here, I really do.

"But there's a lot of people out there that want to see Santa," Steve commented with a thumb hooked over his shoulder. "An orphanage full of kids that I'm going to deliver presents to. I really need the money, I won't lie, but that's not why I wear the suit. I suspect that's not why you wear the suit, either. You are my brothers in red, I can tell, but I'm going to put my faith in the big man upstairs for now. I'm here for the season."

Santa Steve shook hands with them, kissed the first two fingers of his gloved right hand, touched them on the crucifix plaque by the door, bowed quickly, and then headed out, giving the bells hanging on his belt a good ringing. He called out loudly as he walked toward the noise and lights of the mall. Abe and Ron followed out into the utility hallway to watch him go.

"Jeremy, start the cart and let 'em know Reindeer One is on the roll. Maybe we can swing by the food vendors, and I can snag you and the crew some cinnamon pretzels."

"Yessir, Mr. C!" the voice down the hallway cheerfully replied.

Santa Steve turned back to give Ron and Abe a perfect holly-jolly smile, a finger salute, and then he disappeared around the corner.

"Ho-Ho-Ho, and awaaaay we go!"

Ron grabbed his scarf then pulled the door closed behind them as they left, checking to make certain it was locked. Abe bundled up as they exited.

"Well, that went as well as expected," said Ron as they headed into the throngs of shoppers. Abe shuffled quickly to stay in Ron's wake.

"You expected this?"

"Yup. As Santas, these old guys, they get grumpier, more curmudgeonly, and not afraid of much of anything except looking bad or disappointing kids. It's odd, the big hearts paired with the stubbornness."

"That might explain all the bickering on social media," said Abe.

"Ayup."

The automatic doors of the mall slid open, and the frigid wind hit like a frozen hammer. The scarves were no longer just disguises.

"I'm gonna drop you off at base camp and swing back in case he changes his mind," Ron called out over the wind. "You tell them what you heard here. I'll probably see you tomorrow morning."

In no time at all, the massive truck was flying along the salted highway leading to their headquarters. Abe broke the silence, as per usual.

"Ron, is it just me or is there something weird about this? Why fly Steve all the way from California? Why make those kids wait two days?"

Ron cracked his neck and drove steadily. The windshield wipers beat a steady tempo against the snow and slush.

"Well, there's no accounting for an agency's tastes, but I've seen them pay top dollar for specific Santas before, so that's not as weird as you might think. Steve is a veteran Santa, but I know some of the ones that they passed over who are just as pretty, closer, and that they could've gotten for way less money than they're paying for Stevey-boy. As to the kids? Yeah, there's something kinda weird about that."

Thirty minutes later, Abe was sitting down in front of three of the Caestus members–Jon, Carl and Top–at their new center of operations. Top was typing rapidly, and Jon and Carl each had looks of consternation, attentively listening to what Abe had to say.

"Damn," said Jon.

"I don't know Steve very well, but yeah, from what I know, he ain't going to budge. Which means we have at least one non-Order Santa on the playing field, which can complicate things. Well, besides Ron, of course."

"I agree, the thing with the kids sounds darn fishy," Pastor Carl replies, nodding slowly. He closed his eyes for a moment, concentrating. He stroked his beard contemplatively before opening his eyes again.

"I can tell you one thing: Belief is a powerful force. The days leading up to Christmas, Santa Claus grows in spiritual power. The day or so after Christmas—for most westerners that is—Santa would be at his lowest ebb, at least here in the US. Not because people aren't thinking about him, but because everyone believes he oughta be exhausted after his evening of gift-giving. So, if 250 million people think you would be tired, I suspect that belief would make it so."

There was a high sound warbling outside and Jon stood up, peering outside.

"That was fast: Compass Rose is back. Fellas, secure your papers, and Pastor, mind your flames if you would."

Top scurried over to secure things, grinning broadly.

"Abe, this next part is going to seem pretty cool to the newly initiated," Jon said quickly, "but for right now, say nothing. No matter what you see, say and do nothing. Just watch."

Jon opened up a window and a blast of cold air shot in along with nothing more than a blur.

Seconds later, standing on the table was a miniature person with wings, dressed in a tiny vintage aviator's cap, complete with goggles. From head to toe, it stood roughly about four inches high. The figure blurred back and forth. Abe's eyes struggled to focus on it.

Jon set down an enormous plate of junk food, a pile of Twinkies, Ho-Hos, and other treats.

The warrior Santa, the little fairy talking in a language full of round, swooping vowels that Abe assumed was either Gaelic or Norwegian, but he could not quite say—all this pressed deep on Abe's heart, where a small part of him was doing cartwheels and yelling, "I do believe, I do believe!" Outwardly, he tried not to move or barely even breathe.

After a few snatches of conversation, Jon set a wide piece of paper on the desk and snapped a pencil at the tip before placing it on the paper. Abe tried to follow as the small figure darted about on the paper, covering it with tiny squiggles and dots.

When it finished, it looked up at Jon then over at Abe. It was finally standing perfectly still, and Abe could now see very clearly. Abe was surprised to feel the hairs on the back of his neck stand up. Consciously, he knew the perfect geometric shapes comprising its face should have added to something resembling a human. The taut, angular features, the completely black eyes without any hint of white, and an expression that never resembled anything described as friendly—one could almost be forgiven for seeing a predator staring back.

Jon immediately started unwrapping the food to distract it, and the creature devoured each morsel as soon as it cleared the plastic. Abe shivered again.

Jon rolled up the drawing to secure it, said something in the strange language, and walked over to open the window again. The fairy blurred like a comet, whizzing out the window before it was barely opened.

"Bet that blew your frikken mind," Top remarked to Abe.

Abe made no attempt to hide his awestruck expression.

"Yeah, that little guy was... was intense."

"Little lady, Abe," said Jon. "Compass Rose is a lady, but gender is kind of beside the point when you're dealing with the Fay. Compass Rose is one of the more powerful of the Seelie Fay, and I have a deal going with her." Jon finished latching the window tight.

"With the Fay, don't let their size confuse you. Kinda like spiders or frogs, they can be small, but still very powerful. Also, when she's around, you say nothing to her, take nothing from her, and give nothing to her unless I clear it first, got it?"

"You got it," Abe agreed. He thought back on how fast the mountain of food that had disappeared, as if it was dissolving in a high speed timelapse, and shuddered.

Jon rolled the paper back out again, pinning the corners with office supplies. All over the paper were fine drawings, hundreds of dots and swirls and lines. All the men leaned over to inspect it. Jon scratched his head.

"That was the first time Compass Rose has ever offered to draw something for me. I'll be danged if I understand what this all means."

Top took out his tablet and snapped a few pictures of the drawings. Carl found a ruler and started methodically cataloging all the different shapes.

"This could take a while, Abe," Jon explained. "Morozko and Rick are out running a little recon. I could use you on watch tonight, if that's okay with you. So go get a few hours sleep if you can. There's a cot set up in the other room. Oh, and Abe?"

"Yeah?"

"Prayers, whatever hoodoo that you do do? Do it. Before you go to sleep and when you wake up. Got it?"

"Got it."

Abe found the cot, then contemplated getting down on his knees like he did when he was a child. The memory of the look the fairy gave him made his hair stand on end, and he decided that a little bit of extra humility might not be a bad idea.

* * *

18. Vewwy-Vewwy Quiet

It had taken Rick "The Beast" some time to get to the coordinates. Per his usual luck, he was wading through deep snow, on his way to meet with the Mad Russian. After slogging through the dark copse of trees and snow drifts, Morozko suddenly appeared in front of him as if by magic, his two dogs now at Rick's back, studying him intently. Rick started to say something, but the long-bearded man held up a finger to quiet him.

Morozko gestured and his two dogs, V'yuga and Purga, immediately stopped investigating Rick and silently came to his side. With a couple of soft clicks, Morozko dispatched the pair ahead of the men and motioned for Rick to follow.

The two Santas made their way into the darkness. As they moved, Rick saw Morozko slow, then pulled the camo bow limb covers off of the recurve-limb crossbow. With a few experienced gestures, he cleared the flight groove, cocked the bow, and loaded a bolt into it. Rick decided he was going to give the man some room, waiting patiently at a distance. Morozko moved forward.

A few minutes later, one of the dogs came trotting back. It had found something. Morozko started to follow it, motioning for Rick to stay put as he did so. Rick waited. Snow started to collect on his shoulders, and somehow Rick did not feel it was at all "Christmas-y." The whole area had a feeling of something darker and more primal.

Finally the other dog came back to Rick, looking up at him as if to say, "Well, are you coming?" Rick nodded and followed, his big boots crunching through the snow, nowhere as quiet as the Russian's.

As they rounded the bend, the dog's ears cocked back, and it suddenly lunged into the darkness. Rick had no idea what was going on, but he certainly was not going to be left behind. He did his best to sprint after the dog.

Once around the corner, he beheld an interesting sight. The Russian was kneeling, in the process of cutting the head off of someone on the ground with a long, curved blade. The torso had a crossbow quarrel through its heart, and the two dogs were nearby, tense and entirely focused on a dark mass just a stone's throw away. In the darkness, it looked like some things were bent over a body, and guttural, chewing noises could be heard, the sound dampened by the fresh fallen powder.

Morozko, still staying down, turned and quickly made gestures for *blade work* and *monster*, pointing at the scene. Rick slung his shotgun and shrugged the big Dane axe off his back, quickly flipped the leather cover off, and started trotting. Morozko melted into the brush to his left.

The two ghouls that were feasting on the body had only just registered the two dogs, when the colossal frame of the professional fighter loomed out of the darkness.

The dogs ran to pin the ghouls, taking them in the legs. Rick brought the axe around in a wide serpentine arc, and the first ghoul's head went flying off with alacrity and a look of surprise. The second ghoul started to yell something and went for a gun, but as the axe sailed to the conclusion of its arc, it plowed through its collarbone and embedded itself in the ghoul's torso. Rick put a size 16 boot on the ghoul's chest and yanked the axe free. Despite being nearly bifurcated, the creature clawed at Rick's leg, digging pointed fingertips into him with amazing strength. The axe swung down to cleave the thrall's neck, and Rick realized with consternation that he had embedded the axe, yet again. He swore under his breath.

With the slam of a car door and a flash of light, a car that had been parked on the road roared to life. As the headlights flicked on, the car sent piercing white beams flooding into the night. There was a curse behind Rick of something in Russian, and despite getting a brief moment to turn his face, Rick was blinded.

Rick could hear the car flying towards him and, in an act of desperation, he lifted the axe, ghoul and all, throwing himself backwards. There was a *Ba-BUMP-Bam* as the car hit the ghoul and clipped Rick's hip, throwing him further back away from the road. Rick found himself night-blind, spinning, and then dangling over and sliding into a gravel-filled snowbank.

Rick heard a whistle and a chorus of mad barking. He struggled upright and, sure enough, his left leg was definitely torqued. To the ghoul's credit, part of its arm and hand were still attached to his leg. Annoyed, he peeled the gore off and went to look for his axe, which had hurtled into the snowbank with him. As he hobbled, he heard a *tonk* as his boot hit wood and metal, and he immediately bent down to uncover it.

A few seconds later, Rick stood upright again, his big hand closed on the metal studded shaft of the old axe. For a second, he looked upwards and thanked the Almighty for his luck. Using the axe as a walking stick, he lurched back towards the scene and waited for his eyes to clear. The car continued barreling down the road, its taillights vanishing in the distance.

"Zko?" Rick called out quietly.

"Stay where you are," Morozko's voice answered back in a whisper.

As his eyes readjusted to the darkness, he heard some short staccato barks, followed by another muffled *thunk*.

"Nice work, Mr. Beast," Morozko complimented Rick when he arrived a few minutes later.

Rick looked around and noted the bodies near him. Some of them looked inexplicably different.

"Ghouls, and... what or who were these?"

"Chop heads first," Morozko said as he made a chopping motion with his hand, "and I explain."

Rick painfully limped from body to body, making certain the heads had been completely severed from their respective hosts. Morozko picked one from somebody who looked the most important, plied it with herbs, and stuffed it into a plastic bag.

Their first tasks completed, Morozko set about laboriously hauling all the remains up and over an embankment, to the top of the hill.

Rick could hear splashing which was odd, considering everything in North Dakota had long since frozen over by this time. With the assistance of his blood-spattered crutch, he got halfway up the hill and could finally see what was going on. This was no common hill; it was part of a retaining wall for a slurry pool full of foul-smelling mining wastes below. The water and mud from fracking were so densely polluted, nothing in this square of black oiliness was capable of freezing. As his night vision returned, Rick realized that the expanse of the pit contained dozens upon dozens of mostly submerged bodies, frozen in various states of decay. It was the stuff of nightmares.

Rick immediately started hobbling his way back down. Morozko caught up with him and tapped him on his shoulder.

"No, Mr. Beast. This way."

"Wait, what? And please, call me Rick. What just happened?"

Morozko led him back up the road to a wide chain link fence covered with "No Trespassing" signs. The hefty gate sat ajar, and an industrial work truck was parked there with its doors wide open. There were several squat buildings that had steam pouring up from their chimneys, and a network of massive pipes weaving between the structures.

"When I am scouting for Jon, I see the vampir and ghouls. They find boy and girl who are kissing, and they decide to have snack. I call you. I am too late, cannot save them, but I shoot the vampir first. You killed two dead men, but that third son of whore ghoul, that one just went away, away in car of boy and girl," said Morozko as he put the crossbow away.

At the mention of the car, Rick's hip started to throb with serious intensity.

"Oh! Oh, damn. Maybe we should have just snuck away?"

"Da, maybe," Morozko said with a shrug, looking sad and exhausted. "But I know this girl. That is why I call you for backup. She's very nice to me, works in bakery, gives me old bread for nothing. I cannot let them turn her, and ghouls are not clean killers. Bad way to die. I am very sorry, Rick." The old man reached down to pet his dogs, both of whom looked at him with concern.

"I am old and soft Grandfather Winter now. She remind me of my *snegurochka*, my winter-granddaughter, and so I must stop this. But I... I am too late."

Rick now officially felt horrible. The man had been trying to save his friend.

The wrestler bent down to scrub his hands cleaner in the snow. Once he'd sufficiently scrubbed off the stinking ghoul blood, he patted the Russian on the shoulder awkwardly.

"Right. What now?"

In answer, Morozko gave a piercing whistle, and his two dogs barked in response.

"Now we go and go quick. You are hurt. We are done with 'snoop-ink and poop-ink.' That son of a syphilitic sailor, it run back to ghoul nest. The vampirs send peoples to investigate. You go take truck, I will clean area and close gate, yes?" Rick grimly nodded at Morozko.

Walking around on slippery ground with a bad hip was something he would rather have left to the younger members, a sentiment that grew each time he slipped and fell to his knees, the scars that littered his body aching sharply each time he collided with the ground. Finally, he lurched over to the truck, and sure enough, the doors were still open, the keys dangling in the ignition. Rick stopped for a moment and flipped open the latch on the upper part of the enclosed truck bed. The grooved floor had blood on it, but even more worrying were two reels of brightly colored det cord, empty boxes of industrial plastic explosives, and sealed tubs packed full of blasting caps. He bungeed the whole mess over to the wall of the truck and carefully shut the truck's gate.

There was a crunch in the gravel, and Rick turned to see Morozko looking even more bedraggled. The two dogs jumped into the back of the cab, looking very pleased with themselves. Morozko tilted his head and laughed.

"You sit, I drive. I live here, I know where to go."

Rick did as the man said. As they were leaving, they stopped to secure the gates behind them.

Morozko drove carefully, leaving Rick free to turn the heater on. As they approached the highway, he noticed a ring of keys now lying between them.

"So, the vampires had keys to that site? They've been using this site to dispose of bodies for a while now?"

"Da."

It grew quiet in the cab again. Morozko reached back and petted his dogs, who stuck their heads over the seats seeking more attention.

"They are 'Best Dogs in World,'" said Morozko.

"I am inclined to agree," Rick chuckled.

"No, seriously. 'Best Dogs in World.'"

Apparently, petting and driving was something that the Russian was used to. He rubbed the muzzle of one and then the other.

"This one is named Purga and this one is named V'yuga. Their names are meaning Blizzard and Snowstorm. They love the weather, even with the grandmother being jackal. They think they are back home at work."

"A jackal?" asked Rick.

"Da, special Russian dogs. Very few in world. They are called Sulimov dogs. Bred with jackal. Best noses in world. They are trained to find explosives. I help train some, and these two, I train to find vampir back home. They tell me there is many bombs, many bad things here."

Rick slowly turned from the dogs to look at the Russian. The man flashed him a wolfish grin.

"Wait, what? How long ago?"

"Some time ago. What? I tell people, but they no come."

"What about the police? FBI?"

Morozko looked at him pitiably, as if explaining the world to a child.

"Da, Mr. Beast? You think you can take all the people back there in black pond, make them disappear, and no one does nothing? In my country, people disappear all of the time. Everyone corrupt. You go to police, maybe you disappear. Here is no different. Police here work for vampirs. Me, I am just crazy Russian Santa who live out in woods. They send people to come find me, but they never do. I am here. You are here. Best dogs are here. Now, we find out maybe what is really going on, have some real fun, *da? Pravo mal'chiki?*"

Rick had no idea what Morozko had just said, but the dogs barked and wagged their tails excitedly. Rick simply nodded, then started digging through the truck's glove compartment, hoping for some ibuprofen, anything that would help with the throbbing in his hip or his head.

* * *

19. On Prairie Rose Lane

Halford looked at Bill the Ghoul with a frustrated expression and flagging control, intermittently glancing at the vampire who was Bill's master. Travis was of the House of Swords, and while vampires of his bloodline could make ghouls easily, the "gift" did not bequeath them any extra brains.

"Mr. Travis, could I get a little help here? Before I pass this information on, we need to be very certain about the facts of what we're going to share."

Travis walked over, grabbed Bill by the chin, and stared into his eyes.

"REMEMBER."

Bill dutifully recited, word for word, his description of what had happened to him last.

Halford interrupted his recounting.

"Bill, are you certain they both had beards? White beards?"

"Yes. One was all grey and super duper long, like that one dude… Gandalf! And the other big guy, I only saw him for a sec, but he looked familiar. He had a beard down to about here," he said, indicating a beard about four to five inches long. "You know, kinda a Santa beard."

Halford turned to Travis, his face grim. "I don't think your assistant will be coming back, nor will the men that accompanied him."

Travis snarled. Bill, trying to appease his master, remembered one other fact.

"Oh, and the tall guy? The one with the axe. I swear he looked just like this one guy from WMA."

Travis's head snapped to attention, and he hurriedly dug his smartphone out of his pocket. A very short time later, he showed a picture to Bill the Ghoul, who nodded with a childlike grin.

"Hey! How cool is that! The Beast makes a good-looking Santa!"

Travis shook his head and growled, responding with low clipped words.

"Not. Cool. You moron. You stupid *fucking meat-sack*. That Santa just iced two of our people, and one of them was your friend. Go get the rest of the squad, tell them to arm up, then meet us outside. Move!"

Bill, having been rooted to the spot during the scolding, now scrambled to do master's bidding. After his hasty exit, Travis turned his attention back to Halford. Travis was uncertain where he stood in the pecking order when compared to Halford, who was a moderately powerful vampire from the House of Words.

"Sorry about that," said Travis. He rubbed his eyes as though his palm to stave away the impending migraine.

"He's not my ghoul. One of mine would have come back with the heads of whoever attacked them. But at least this moron survived long enough to report back here. Whoever they ran into, they knew what they were dealing with."

Halford picked up his phone and got ready to make a call.

"Yeah, that amount of preparation is why I have a bad feeling about this. Go find the slayers and bring back the heads those beards were attached too. I am calling Mr. Raymond."

* * *

In the warm amber light of the LorenCo Executive suites, Henry Raymond stood by a lavish fireplace, jotting down notes, listening on a phone.

"Thank you, Mr. Halford. I will call you back shortly. Please remain available."

Henry took the phone off speaker, hung up, and slipped the device into his pocket. With a heavy sigh, he turned and looked at some of the other leaders of the vampire community in the room. Two more had just arrived. Henry nodded to Drummer from the House of Hearts and Dmitri from the House of the Wheel.

"You all heard that, correct?" The assembled vampires nodded.

"Is Avice available?" asked Dmitri. "Perhaps his spells could help us find them fairly quickly, if he was inclined to help?"

Henry shook his head.

"No. Avice, as always, works for himself. Even then, he needs to concentrate on getting the ritual ready. From what I understand, it's fairly involved, and there are bindings and such that need to be absolutely perfect."

Baron de Rais stood up and stretched. He gave them all a sardonic, indolent look.

"Well, then. I think we know what this means."

"The Order?" Drummer suggested.

"The Order. Although to be honest with you, I'm surprised that there are any of them left," the Baron chuckled. "Everyone knows that vampires and Santa Claus are only real in the movies."

Henry stopped pacing as the door opened and Duke Cosimo Florentine swept into the room.

The whipcord-thin nobleman raised an eyebrow as he surveyed the gathering. Hands clasped behind his back, he padded over the fireplace and stood there a moment without speaking. A lengthy pause ensued, the enigmatic Duke gazing at the log below, crackling and popping at his feet. Most of the other vampires stood well away from it. The Arch Vampire spoke in a matter-of-fact tone.

"I heard. We have been found out, my friends, although to what extent remains to be seen. Due to the nature of our current undertaking, it's hardly surprising that powers on high are moving a few of their own. Henry, find them, or find one of them and make them talk. Avoid killing them if you can. Let's get this resolved before it can evolve into something even more problematic. As of this moment, we are all on the clock. Tomorrow is Christmas Eve, and then we have forty-eight hours before the ritual can be completed." Duke Florentine turned to Baron de Rais.

"Baron, you have an absolute talent for creating chaos and destruction. That is why I'm telling you in no uncertain terms: I want you to reign it in. Take anybody who is not essential to maintaining our schedule, anyone you need from the various houses. Find them."

Duke Cosimo pointed straight at Baron de Rais, who loomed more like a grizzly bear than a subordinate.

"Do NOT make waves. Get Marcus to have his security force scouring the area but emphasize the need to keep this local. We can't have word getting around that people are hunting Santas. Am I clearly understood?"

"Understood, Your Grace," Baron de Rais affirmed, smiling coolly and completing a stately bow.

Duke Florentine turned to Henry.

"Put our sacrifice under double guard. The minute he finishes in the market, I want him sedated and brought here, and put under constant surveillance. He is not to be hurt or despoiled in any way. Likewise, that actor we hired to play the role of our shaggy friend. I want him watched and under protection as well. Have him brought here when you collect our Santa."

Duke Florentine stopped for a second, acknowledging the newly arrived heads of Houses.

"Master Drummer, do you know of Daniela? I believe she is one of your kith."

"Yes. A brilliant dancer," Drummer responded warily.

"No longer. I believe one of her fledglings was hunting without permission, an act which likely exposed our presence. As she failed to control him, despite my direct orders, she is no longer. This was my decision."

Drummer flinched and his face grew hard, but he said nothing, bowing instead. Despite the warmth of the fireplace, the room had gotten decidedly chillier.

Duke Florentine caught the eyes of all the people in the room. His gaze shifted to the small Christmas tree decorating a table at the center of the room.

"Most of you know this: I was there when the Compact of the Powers was signed. Back in those days, it's true, we walked more openly. There were no radios, no telephones, no cameras. Guns hadn't even left Cathay yet. Back then, people did not mock 'kindly old men with white beards.'

"Those men who still clung to life after the decades of plague, of famine, mindless brutality, they were filled with cunning, ever watchful. Some of them even had powers of their own. It was the proposition of those men not to hunt monsters outside of the Yule season. In exchange, we agreed not to hunt them without justifiable cause. We signed a magical compact, a treaty if you will.

"Many hundreds of years have passed, few humans still truly believe in magic, and while that is fortunate for us, there are more people believing in Santa Claus than ever."

The Duke bent down to carefully rearrange a small ornament on the tree. Straightening himself, he looked at the others.

"Whole industries now exist to propagate this belief, this Yule season. While commercialism has changed the face of this holiday, it's no excuse to take this lightly. Wherever it originates, belief means power." His brow furrowed slightly.

"If we are lucky, we are only dealing with a Caestus, a group of five from the Order, and they have no idea what is really going on here. Hopefully, we haven't attracted the attention of any of the high rollers." He glanced upward.

"The aim is to do what needs to be done before they can comprehend the true scope of our plan."

He made eye contact with each of the Heads of the Vampiric Houses in turn.

"We must do this swiftly, subtly. If we can, we shall claim a reward many of us have longed for over many centuries. With that in mind, know that I will. *Not*. Tolerate failure. Understood?"

All the people in the room bowed to the ancient vampire, once the de facto ruler of Europe at large.

Duke Cosimo Florentine stalked from the room.

Henry turned to the rest of them.

"Alright, Rais, I will coordinate your resources. The game is afoot. Let's see if we can find them before they can find us."

Sir Gilles de Montmorency-Laval, the Baron de Rais, a Knight and one of the most horrifically deviant serial killers of children in the 14th century, nodded politely, but his eyes were alight with sharp intent. The smile on his face was small and capricious.

"Henry, you know as well as I, the reason Cosimo keeps me around is sometimes you need a reason people don't go into the woods. It's a purpose I'm happy to serve. These are our woods. I will find them, have no fear."

Henry's face said little, but his eyes spoke volumes. He nodded to the Baron.

"Remember what our Master said. Swift and subtle. *Subtilis. Sotil. Subtle.*"

In answer, the Baron looked at the other vampires in the room, and said to some of them, "You. You, and you, with me." The vampires he picked nodded in the affirmative, but all seemed thoroughly repulsed when his back was turned.

* * *

Back at the base of operations in the warehouse, the Caestus had pulled together and the information from Rick and Morozko had been delivered. Everyone stood around the big table with grim faces as the reality of their situation sank in. Carl tended to Rick's injuries as they spoke.

Jon snapped on some heavy-duty purple gloves. Shaking a bag out onto the table, the newly acquired vampire head rolled out. He inspected their trophy delicately. Lifting a blue lip with the tip of a broken pencil, even rows of jagged teeth shown beneath discolored gums. After a moment, he turned around and shook his head.

"Top, check out the bicuspids on this one."

Top leaned around his computer monitor and snapped a picture with his phone.

"Jon, that's a classic sharkface if ever I saw one."

"Sharkface?" Abe asked.

"Remember the vamp you fought had kind of a pronounced muzzle look on him when he vamped out?" Jon answered. "There are a bunch of vampire clans, or houses as they call them. When they vamp out, they all look different. Their bloodlines all track back to their first generation, and each bloodline of vampires has different abilities."

Abe looked at the multiple sharp teeth in the mouth of the head in front of him.

"So, *is* there a House Sharkface?"

Top laughed.

"No, they call themselves the House of Measures. Big into quiet money, bankers, control freaks of the highest order. Most of them have eidetic memories. This one looks fairly young." Top paused to look at Abe seriously.

"Hey, I don't want to scare you too much, but this will all be in your training, provided you find a chance to get it. In the meantime, try to remember the following." Top ticked off each one on his fingers as he went.

"There are seven main houses that we know of. I just mentioned that the ones with faces like sharks, that's House of Measures. If the vamp has teenie fangs, claws, and looks mostly human, then it's probably House of Dance. If they have really big eyes, look all washed out and gray, that's House of the Scholars. If they act and look bug-nuts crazy, kinda twitchy and twisted up, that's House of Mirrors. House of Swords usually emulates some kind of predator, but they can't go full animal form. If they look like TV announcers, all glamtastic and innocuous looking, but grow claws like needles, that's House of Words. Finally, if they look rough with long claws and a muzzle with some nasty fangs, vis-à-vis your first blood, then that's the House of the Wheel." Top looked around, "Did I forget any?"

"Believe it or not, I think it's important to note that there *are* some vampires we'd classify as good people," Carl mentioned. "Given that the Vampiric Houses and the humans both want them dead, though, you rarely see them come out of hiding."

Carl continued tending to Rick and added, "But, yeah, those houses are the main types. Old world European, broadly speaking, but we do have to deal with something outside those castes every now and again. Sometimes, it can get a little gray."

"So, why are the different types of vampire significant?" Abe asked as he gingerly stepped away from the severed head.

Pastor Carl stood up and tossed some wet wipes to Rick.

"Two reasons. Different types of vamps have different powers. Practically speaking, that makes taking out a mixed group more difficult. Also, vampires usually don't like any other clans in their territory, except for the House of the Wheel, who seem to be allowed everywhere. Now we know there are at least two different kinds here, along with a handful of ghouls, which means..."

Top picked up the line from Carl.

"Which means that, according to the Compact, we are officially allowed to ask for even more help. Possibly a whole Caestus or more."

"That's good, right?" Abe smiled.

Jon finished stacking gear and walked over to Abe, patting him on the shoulder.

"Technically, yes. Keep in mind, this city is pretty damn remote. Whatever help we are going to get, it had better be close by. Speaking of which, call our friend Ron, ask him to come back to the shop."

Abe picked up his cell and passed the message on via text.

Rick stood up gingerly, wincing as he buckled his pants. One leg of the pants was missing entirely from the knee down, revealing fresh white bandages.

"Much better, Pastor. Thank you!" He turned to look at the others.

"Guys, from the number of victims we saw, we know we're dealing with something out of the ordinary. They had a LorenCo company truck, explosives, and the keys to that toxic waste dump turned boneyard, fer Chrissake. As I understand it, LorenCo helped build this town, which means there's a good chance that that company is infiltrated."

A tray was carried in from the other room, several tiny cups of black coffee resting on it. Morozko gave them all a knowing look.

"This is coffee the way we drink it at home. Is very strong. You will need it."

He set the tray down and lifted one of the cups to his lips delicately. He blew on it, and a rich aroma perfumed the air.

"I told them at Order home office. I said to them, 'this town is full of vampires, some bad shit will happen here.'" He shrugged and drank more of his coffee.

"I think we are all going to die, but we should make monsters remember us forever. We are the Order. Order of Nikolas Thaumaturgus. We will show them what it is like to fuck with Father Christmas."

Pastor Carl came over to join them and took one of the tiny cups. "Merry Christmas!"

All the others picked one up and joined him in the toast.

Jon's nose wrinkled as he put his empty cup back down, "Yow."

"Pastor, now is the time, I think."

Carl stepped out and came back a minute later clad in a robe, a silk stole around his neck, beautifully embroidered in the olden way, and carrying a small box. Out of the box came a bell, as well as a small round disk with an odd looking cross on it, and faded letters that looked like Greek. He addressed Jon.

"First, I think we need to swear Abe into the Order."

In answer, Jon fetched a bearded axe, with its ornate wire wrapped haft, inlaid runes, and rows of neat metal studs.

"Normally we do this over a sword, but right now, my axe is the prettiest weapon in the room, I think. Do you mind swearing over her?"

"Nope," Abe answered with a smile. "I've already taken the Santa Claus Oath, by the way."

"Good man, I knew I liked you. It's very similar. Repeat after me: I swear myself to the Hidden Order of St. Nicholas, inspired by the gift giver of Myra, in the tradition of the wonder worker of Aka..."

A few minutes later, every silverback in the room was thumping Abe on the back and giving him hugs, each of them saying, "Welcome, Brother."

Pastor Carl raised his hands to get everyone's attention again.

"Gentlemen, I hate to rush this but the clock is ticking. We five together, here in a circle."

Pastor Carl instructed everyone to reach in and touch the bell. Jon picked up the medallion and had it passed around three times. As they did, each of them was sworn to the service of the Caestus, to answer the call of the innocent, and the oath of St. Nicholas Thaumaturges. Abe handed him the medallion last, and the pastor reached down, picked up the bell, and while chanting, rang it three times. The sound of it was pure and sweet, seeming to go on forever.

"Abraham, with the blessings of the Highest and the love of St. Nicholas the Wonder Worker, we are pledged to help you with your cause. May this circle not be broken. May this Caestus of Jon, Carl, Rick, Morozko, and Top help those who called up on us. May God bless and protect us all."

The lights in the room seemed to get brighter. Abe felt something warm and hopeful rush through him, and his hand seemed to tingle. For a moment, there was... peace.

Outside, the dogs could be heard singing out in harmony, and for a moment, the room was filled with the sound of winter breeze and the hiss of a space heater. Off in the night, ever so faintly, the sound of Christmas music echoed from somewhere unseen, fading slowly. Abe felt a burning sensation on his right hand. The design of the medallion was now branded on his hand with faint red lines.

Pastor Carl blessed him and patted his hand.

"Don't worry. Only people who are meant to see it can. It'll go away after the mission is completed. It means you are an official member of this Caestus, Abe. Your Caestus. It's like being deputized. You have the ability to ask things, and people will often recognize it as an act of good, although they may not know why. Think of it as a badge or an ID. You are going to feel really weird for the next few days. I've done a few of these, and each one is different, but this convocation? Very powerful, I think. Go, have a cookie and drink something."

Pastor Carl sagged and wobbled over to a nearby stool.

Abe did feel different, as if something had been set in motion in his chest, something that felt ultimately vindicating. The feeling resonated within him like a low E on a bass guitar. He was in search of a cookie when Top took him by the sleeve and pulled him outside into the warehouse.

"Notice anything?"

Abe looked around before guessing, "That I forgot my hot cocoa?"

Top trotted over to the door, packed some loose powder into his palm, and returned, handing the snowball to Abe.

"Now?"

Abe examined the snowball, but it took a second for him to realize.

"It feels cool, but not freezing?"

"Yup!" Top grinned as he replied. "One of the perks of rolling with a Caestus of St. Nicholas. Cold doesn't bother us, or at least not as much. We can help others out as well. It's that whole *'heat was in the very sod which the Saint has printed'* thing. The blessing of the Caestus gives us certain abilities. You won't slip on ice or fall off of a roof, despite what happens in the movies. It gives you extra stamina, agility, and strength when you need it. It also gives you a basic version of second sight, so the magical stuff is less likely to blindside you. Whatever you do, don't take it for granted or misuse it." He looked past Abe's shoulder.

"Whup. Time to suit up. One more thing. You never know how your ability might manifest, so that's a nice little surprise waiting for you."

"You mean like superpowers?" Abe tried waving his hands, but nothing seemed to happen. "Nope."

"Check this out."

Top removed the hat he was wearing and passed it over his face. When he brought it back up, he now had a perfect "Miracle of 34th Street" Santa beard and mustache, complete with snowy eyebrows. Even his eye color had changed. Top dropped the hat over his face, lifted it back, and the Santa beard and mustache had vanished.

"Okay, that was amazing!" Abe declared.

"I was hoping that would work," Tom said with a giant grin. "You never know. Let's head back in."

Abe chuckled to himself as they walked through the door.

"What?" Top quirked an eyebrow.

"Now I can use a line from one of my favorite movies. *'We're on a mission from God!'*"

"Then I get to say one, too," replied Top. "'The one thing about living in Santa Carla, I never could never stomach... all the damn vampires!'"

"Lost Boys, nice. Hey, at least Jake and Elwood live and save the orphanage."

"True. They do end up in prison."

"Ooh. Good point."

As they came back in, Jon called them over.

"Gentlemen, I think we've figured out what Compass Rose was trying to tell us, in a weird, topographical way."

Everyone gathered around the table.

"What ho, Supreme Claus-mander?" asked Top.

Jon rolled his eyes.

"These seem to be channels of magic... ley lines, dragon lines, lines of power, if you will."

He then laid a sheet of plastic over the map, and more lines appeared. It was not immediately obvious, but Abe traced things with his finger.

"Wait. There are some similarities between some of the ley lines and a lot of these tunnels and power lines, right? I see a lot of geometric shapes here."

"I hope this is just a coincidence," Pastor Carl commented, "but it was a tradition with the free-masons and other secret societies, to design cities with arcane patterns. In fact, Washington DC has some of that going on."

"Coincidence, surely," said as Rick leaned over and smiled a gap-toothed grin. Ever the progressive, Abe thought.

Top pointed to bunches of dots congregated near the city center, and in a second, more affluent area.

"And what are all these markers?"

Jon said what all the Santas in the room had feared he would.

"Bad guys. I think. Maybe. Vamps."

"Crap. Somebody canceled Christmas," said Top.

Abe looked at the dots. There were a lot of them.

"Why are there that many vampires in LaMoure, North Dakota?"

Jon reached down and smoothed out the map.

"That's the question, isn't it? This entire county has been invaded, and we have no clue as to why."

* * *

20. Out of the Pan

The lines at the S-Mart were finally thinning down to a manageable level. Ron had fueled up his monster of a truck and had packed many useful goodies in it. He was now picking up the last of the provisions, some tanks of propane for his camp heater, and some more ammo, of course. The clerk who was waiting on him looked exhausted.

"You going hunting?"

"Yup, leaving right after Christmas, I think. Maybe get some winter pheasant up at game ranch. The double aught and slugs are going into retirement, sadly. Bit worried that regulations may change next year. Better safe than sorry."

"Good idea. Got a lot of folks stocking up. Me, I was just worried that maybe you were going to 'down-source' some reindeer."

Ron gave the clerk a Santa-worthy smile.

"Nope. Everything is fine on that end. You have yourself a Merry Christmas."

With that, he took the heavily laden grocery cart and started wheeling it out. As he rolled by an aisle, he saw a younger man who appeared lost, clutching a satchel in both hands. The man spotted Ron and his thick white beard (even though it had been stuffed down into his coat) and with a smile, the man approached Ron.

"Excuse me, sir? Pardon my asking, but do you know where the small button batteries are, you know, the ones that are about the size of dime? Like watch batteries."

Ron pointed to a sign hanging three aisles over.

"Check in the old folks' section, down by the walking sticks and such. I think they sell most of those for hearing aids and so on."

"Thanks," the young man answered, nodding thankfully. "I flew all the way in from Los Angeles and forgot to bring some spares for my mask."

"Mask?"

"Oh yeah. I think you might know who this is, in fact."

He opened the padded bag he was carrying and revealed to Ron a fur-covered visage, complete with horns and fangs. Ron leaned back, eyes wide.

"Wow, that's a nice one! You came all the way to LaMoure in winter to play Krampus? That's brave. Why do you need batteries?"

The young man smiled at meeting a kindred spirit.

"See, I knew you were a Santa. Heh heh. I'm doing like, a corporate party, and the eyes in the mask actually glow, but something happened and the batteries

I had are dead as hell. So, I asked the event coordinator and her driver if we could run out from the hotel and grab some fresh ones." He gestured to the two people waiting near the front of the store.

Ron followed the young man's gesture and made eye contact with the two figures. Ron's stomach did a flip flop. Some instinct told Ron he was in great danger. The cold feeling in his gut burbled the word "vampires" repeatedly. Continuing as nonchalantly as he could, he leaned over and patted the young man on the shoulder.

"Good luck on your gig. I hope they put some pictures in the paper, although I doubt many people in this town even know what a Krampus is. Folks around here are pretty conservative. Out of the suit, I would recommend you openly wear a crucifix, even if it's just to make the locals feel more at ease." Ron started to push his cart back towards the exit and turned back one more time.

"Oh, and there's a storm brewing. When a big storm comes in around here, power often goes out, making ATMs and card readers useless. So if I were you, I would stock up on a lot of goodies and keep some cash on hand, just in case."

"Good idea! Thanks a lot, and Merry Christmas, Santa."

Ron gave him a big smile but internally, he winced. At the word "Santa," he looked back at the front of the store. He could no longer spot the female partner that had been by the front door. Ron said a small prayer and asked for some extra help from St. Nicholas. His cart trundled out the door and into the icy cold. He looked around and, seeing nothing unusual, he decided to head for his truck. A few hurried moments later, the basket sat empty, the bags were tossed in, and Ron was climbing up into his large truck.

As he reached to slam the door shut, a set of finely manicured nails swooped in to arrest its momentum, a petite woman holding it open easily.

"Hey, Santa. Big truck you got here. Compensating for something?"

"Ho ho! Nope, Santa is a big man and so he needs a big truck." Ron leaned over to pat her hand.

His hand came down atop hers and the silver rosary beads he had palmed burned her hand immediately, the sizzle audible from where he was sitting. She immediately hissed and jumped back lithely, clutching her hand.

"*Hkkkkkk.* Bad move, old man. That hurt."

"My sincerest apologies!"

Ron took the fraction of a second he had bought with rosary to fire through his coat. The booms reverberated through the truck and parking lot twice, a .500 Smith & Wesson snub nose revolver cracking off point blank into the woman's meager frame. In any other person's hand, their wrist would likely have broken, but the gun was almost to scale in the hands of its wielder who was six foot, five inches tall. The two fragmenting rounds of blessed silver ammunition impacted the bloodsucker with enough force to knock her ten feet backwards, shredding her chest and collarbone.

Ron slammed the truck out of neutral and stomped hard on the gas pedal. The mighty steed bellowed and as he flew across the parking lot, he saw the vampire stop rolling, obviously trying to get up. Ron flew into the oncoming traffic, narrowly missing several small economy cars, before his heart climbed back down out of his mouth. The ringing in his ears paired exquisitely with the smell of cordite and melted plastic that pervaded the inside of the cab. Peering down at the pocket of the parka he had shot through, he almost laughed when he noticed it was smoldering. Calmly, he patted out the burning embers.

Just then, a text came in from Abe. He glanced at it.

Watch out. More than one kind of baddie in town. Possibly lots of bad guys. Caestus says that something big is going down, to come back to shop ASAP. Danger Will Robinson. Danger.

"No shit," Ron said to no one in particular.

Having got away from the traffic, he had started back towards the auction house when he noticed that he was being followed by a large, dark gray security truck with LorenCo markings. Ron sighed deeply and changed directions, doing his best to think fast and run through his options.

One, he could run for it. The tanks on his truck were completely full, plus he could plow through ditches and snow where most other vehicles could not. It might help that there was a storm on the horizon. Two, he could lead them back to the shop, and the Caestus could offer the vampires a warm reception. Unfortunately, that would give up the Order's location. Three, he could run for holy ground then try to hold them off. Ron was about to call the Order when he noticed the LaMoure police cars falling in behind him. There were no lights flashing, and another LorenCo security SUV had joined the party. The fact that five vehicles were now following him made his next thought even more chilling.

If the vampires had the police in their pocket, there was a pretty good chance his phone was compromised by now. He had about twenty minutes before he was going to be beyond the city limits, out onto the bleak night of the cold high plains.

He called Abe, who responded promptly.

"Ron, did you get my text?"

"Yup. You might want to put me on speaker, cuz your phone is crap."

Back in the warehouse, Abe's eyebrows shot up. Ron had never mentioned his phone being bad before. He thumbed it to speakerphone, walked to the conference table, and waved everyone to silence.

"Yeah, I got it. Can you hear me?" Top, Carl, and Jon all leaned in close as well, staying silent.

"Yup. Abe, I have to leave for a bit. Maybe go find a place to do a little praying, tune up my Christmas Spirit. Ya know? Funny thing. I was at the S-Mart, and I ran into a professional Krampus reenactor. How cool is that?"

"Very cool!" said Abe.

Abe looked at the other men who cocked their heads and looked at each other. Top looked at the phone in Abe's hand and ran for his computers. They all could hear Ron doing something while the truck rumbled through the winter streets. Ron continued.

"Well, Herr Krampus says he's here for a corporate gig, shopping with two folks, and one of the people showing him around stopped by my truck just to say 'Hi!' to Santa. Nice lady, great smile, real graceful. I gave her a couple of my Santa souvenirs. Guess I still have the looks! But meeting her made me think for a bit, which got me feeling down, and so I'm deciding to head out of town. I'm tired of all the traffic tickets, cop cars, company cars, all that.

"I think it's time for me to go someplace quiet, pray a bit, and get into the Christmas Spirit. After season, maybe go catch some fish."

In the operation center, the men at the table were busy taking notes and looking at the city map. Abe said a small prayer for his friend. Pastor Carl held up a hastily drawn note.

Vamps probably listening. Say goodbye.

"Okay Ron, are you sure you don't want some company?" said Abe.

"Nope, you have a lot of things to attend to, and there's a lot going on in LaMoure this year. You be your Santa best, believe in the power of the suit! Tell all the folks to keep me in their prayers and have a great Christmas! Do yourself a favor, toss the electronics, and get some quality time in. Be good, do good, Abe," said Ron in a deep, jolly voice.

"You got it, Ron. Drive safe. Merry Christmas, amigo!" said Abe. He turned his head so that the others could not see his eyes tearing up. Abe had a sinking feeling in his stomach. After a moment's hesitation, he flicked the phone off.

Top gently leaned over and snagged the phone, expertly rooted the battery out and placed it into an uncommonly thick bag.

The Caestus leader, Jon, looked around the room.

"Okay, it's obvious he's being chased. What did you all catch?"

"Well, the part with the Krampus is really odd," Pastor Carl answered. "That makes me think something magic is happening. Maybe a ritual or something?"

"Sounds like he's going to run for holy ground," Top suggested. "Depending on how close they are, it could be his only hope. That part about making friends, avoiding tickets. I'm guessing vamps and cops. They might've even turned some officers. He wanted Abe to toss his phone, so that makes me think that they may be intercepting phone calls. Bastards. I hope Ron's 'souvenirs' made a lasting impression."

"Yes?" Jon nodded to Morozko who was holding up a hand.

"He said nice smile. Very graceful. Woman from House of Dance? I think he tells us he was being followed, five cars or five peoples." Morozko drew a shape in the air. "Fish? There is no place to ice fish around here, not for dozens of kilometers."

"Sorry, I don't follow?" Jon cocked his head.

"Da, fish. Iota, Chi, Theta, Epsilon, Sigma—in Greek, they are ichthys but means fish. Fish is secret symbol of Christians in ancient times. Five letters, five cars, maybe five vampires?"

"*Suuuurrre?*" Jon tentatively agreed. He looked at Abe. Abe nodded.

"Yeah, that actually sounds like Ron. He was really up on that stuff. Are we going to go help him or what?"

"Abe, I hate to say this, but if he's saying what I think he's saying, the cops are in the vamps' pockets." Jon reached down and finished arming himself. "He'll have a roadblock waiting for him, if we show up looking like Santas, they're going to take us out, too. The last thing I want on the news is footage of an armed gang of Santas shooting cops. By the time we catch up with him, I don't know if there'll be anything we can do. If the vamps really were listening to our calls, then that message probably just got them a step closer to finding this place. So, I think we're going to have to grab our gear and move this whole operation into Rick's RV."

Abe shook his head and his eyes got hard. The whole group could see the defiance in his face.

"No, dammit, is that how the good guys do things? Up and leaving one of their own swinging in the wind?"

Jon stopped what he was doing long enough to look back at Abe with a mixture of sternness and understanding.

"I didn't say we weren't going to help, but right now, our options are limited. If the vamps have the phone network and the cops, that changes things a lot."

"By 'a lot,' he means 'completely screwed,'" Top added.

"Not helping." Jon glared at Top.

At that, Jon pulled down a wooden box, sticky with peeling shellac, and set it at the center of the table. Taking a deep breath, he withdrew what looked like two intricately carved wooden bracelets.

"Rick, do you have any food in your RV—rice or oatmeal in particular?"

"Hello, Santa?" Rick patted his belly in answer. "I have the good stuff!"

"Excellent," Jon responded and gave him a small grim smile. "I need you to make two big bowls as fast as you can. Extra sugar and cream, berries if you got them. And Rick, this is important: There MUST be a big pat of butter on the top of each of them. Right now. We need this yesterday."

Well practiced in the art of shrugging off injuries, the bandaged fighter chuckled and ran.

"Got it!"

"Really?" Abe interrupted. "Now is the time for oatmeal?"

Jon gave Abe an annoyed look.

"My powers in a Caestus are runes and summoning," Jon explained and gave Abe an annoyed look. "In this case, I am summoning some Fay. And believe me when I say, asking the Fay to help in a crisis? It's just as likely to blow up in your face as pulling the pin in Mr. Hand Grenade and not tossing him. The Fay are all about the rules and traditions. Mess it up, and you're in trouble."

Jon turned to Carl and Top.

"Top, see if you can sync with Ron's phone and get us a GPS location ASAP. Carl, let's get packed up and ready to move. This place is spent. Then, if you would, see if you can put a prayer of protection on Ron."

The Pastor grunted his assent. Top took the bagged phone and some electronic devices of dubious legality and made his way outside. The old Pastor clasped Abe's shoulder.

"I have an old prayer that one of my Catholic brethren gave me a while ago. It might do just the trick. Let's start packing everything back up again—we're going mobile."

Morozko and his dogs kept watch outside and in a surprisingly short amount of time, the command area for the Caestus was transferred to the inside of the RV. Things were cramped, sure, but it was a top-end RV, and the interior was like being in a nice, if rather linear, walnut-paneled, leather-seated apartment. As the team got ready to pull out of the warehouse, Jon beckoned Abe over.

"The place is empty again, but we still have something to do, quickly. Abe, I want you to watch something. Same as before, you say and do nothing. Period. Got me? Please, go stand in the corner and watch the table."

Their resident Norse warrior pulled a cell phone out and fiddled with it for a second, then put the two bowls of steaming hot porridge on a low table, along with a small bag and the two carved bracelets. He put his hand on top of the bracelets, a faint glow building beneath his palm.

"Jeg innkalle Nisse til meg. Hedre dine løfter om gammel. Jeg spør i gamle måter for din hjelp!"

Jon swayed slightly yet managed to keep his hands in place. Abe almost jumped out of his skin as the locked door suddenly opened, a gust of cold wind heralding the arrival of two small men, each about three feet tall swept into the room. Both had gray cloaks covering sky blue coats, and tall, elongated red knit hats. Their eyes were dark and shimmering, their beards lengthy and full.

Jon bowed to them and conversed in yet another language Abe did not understand. The exchange must have gone well, though, as the little men bowed and proceeded to wolf down the bowls of porridge with slender, ornate spoons. After they finished, the two of them looked at each other, then bowed again to Jon.

Jon showed them a picture of Ron and his truck on his cellphone, which fascinated them. Back and forth they went, until Jon bowed to them one last time, offering them the two bracelets. This seemed to delight them. The two small creatures had turned and started to leave, when one of them stopped in front of Abe. The little man cocked his head and smiled.

"Det er på tide du kom tilbake!" It gave him a wink, and the two little men were gone.

Jon waited for a moment and whispered what must have been a blessing. After he was finished, he addressed Abe.

"Those are Nisse. Don't let their small size fool you, they're very powerful. We were lucky, in that there's a fair number of Norwegian settlers in the upper Midwest. Hurray for Norwegian bachelor farmers. They didn't have a problem getting here."

After snagging the bowls and doing a quick inspection of the site, Jon made for the door.

"Get the lights."

A definitive clunk sounded out and the warehouse plunged into darkness. Abe felt a touch of fear in his heart. Abe wanted nothing more than for his friend to be okay.

Abe jogged over to Jon's SUV.

"What did that little guy say to me?"

"It was a bit odd, really." Jon shot him a look as the two of them buckled in. "Then again, the Fay are always a strange lot."

"Oh?"

Jon revved the motor and started cranking the wheel to the left.

"He said, 'It's about time you got back!' or something like that."

"And that means?"

"No idea."

The auction office and warehouse now sat dark, looking much colder and desolate as the small convoy of vehicles pulled out. The base grew smaller and smaller in the rear-view mirror of the RV, until it was nothing more than a memory.

* * *

21. Into the Fire

Out on Hwy-2, the four police officers looked at each other nervously. Stopping a felon out on a North Dakota road was not par for the course, but not entirely unusual either. The North Dakota highway patrol was stretched pretty thin, as were any nearby Reservation police, who probably would not have been inclined to join them in this venture.

What unnerved the police officers were the four strangers–three men and one woman dressed in military style black and gray tactical gear, LorenCo patches emblazoned on their chests. They had pulled their SUVs up to support the police cruisers and were now arranging themselves in firing positions. The highway was unusually wide for this part of North Dakota, two lanes traveling in both directions with a deep ditch between them. Sgt. Burke headed over to the LorenCo man who seemed to be in charge.

"We appreciate you coming out to back us up. I'm Sgt. Burke, LaMoure PD."

"Not a problem. I'm Captain Lambert, LorenCo Security International. According to the reports, the suspect shot one of our employees, and the city charter allows us to assist you wherever possible."

Burke looked over at the LorenCo people, who seemed unphased by the knife-sharp icy wind.

"I understand, but I just need to point this out: This is a law enforcement matter. If we can catch him, lock him up, that's exactly what we are going to do. Your folks, I'm sure they're well trained, but they are not authorized law enforcement officers for this area, and we want to arrest this person legitimately," he said, eyeing the captain of the detail. He continued.

"We need to make sure nothing happens that the DA can take advantage of later. With any luck, our spike strip takes out his tires, he goes into the ditch, airbags go off–Boom, we got him. Cool? "

"Got it," Captain Lambert said non-committedly.

Sgt. Burke walked back to his truck but could not help noticing that all the LorenCo people were carrying the latest model XM7 assault weapons, which were supposed to only be for military use. He kept just a basic bolt action 30.06 hunting rifle in his trunk, and his men were outfitted with shotguns and pistols. The LorenCo people had always made him very uneasy. A small army of security folks always seemed like overkill for a city in North Dakota, "Homeland Security" or no. Sgt. Burke got back into his vehicle and cranked up the heater. A few seconds later, he straightened himself and called his other police officers over, lowering the window.

"Each of us will spend 10 minutes in a car warming up, while the other three are outside." He jerked a thumb at the private security folks. "As for the Dirty-Water folks over there, they aren't in a playful mood. Keep an eye on them, and don't let them push you around."

The other policemen nodded and got back to their positions. It was not long until, off in the distance, they saw the lights of a civilian truck hurtling down the asphalt.

Burke jumped out of his police SUV.

"Show time! Let's get ready, and keep our guns holstered for now."

Out of the corner of his eyes, he saw the security captain throw some call signs, and the other team took rifle positions. Sgt. Burke growled in annoyance, knowing this had every chance of going sideways.

* * *

22. In the Giant Truck

Santa Ron reached down and made certain that everything stowed inside the cab had been tied down, at least, as best as he could manage one-handed. Behind him, he saw the police cars and security vehicles slowly backing down. He slowed as well as he got closer to the roadblock. The vehicles obstructing the path ahead suddenly bloomed with blinding lights and a loud voice crackled over a loudspeaker.

"STOP YOUR VEHICLE NOW. PARK AND TURN OFF YOUR VEHICLE AND KEEP YOUR HANDS ON THE WHEEL. YOU ARE UNDER ARREST."

Ron slowed the truck to a crawl and said a small prayer, peering through his windshield. Not far past the roadblock, somewhere close by was the Holy Trinity Church—a tiny, dilapidated chapel made of fieldstones, built by early prairie pioneers. It was a small, often forgotten place on the long roads leading out of LaMoure county. Ron reached over and put on his Santa hat with a look of stony determination, then concealed it with the hood of his parka.

Ron gave himself a devil-may-care grin in his rearview mirror and launched into song, projecting the first line in a growling, sonorous baritone.

"Oh, the weather outside is frightful...!"

He threw the truck into low gear and shifted it into all terrain mode. Ron floored it, the lyrics of the second line resounding throughout the cab.

"But the fire is sooo delightful...."

Up until then, Sgt. Burke had been watching the truck decelerate beside his own V6. Good, he thought. It seemed to be complying with his orders. What a shock it was, then, when the behemoth roared and drove straight down into the median between the roads with jets of snow flying in every direction.

"Sonofabitch!" Sgt. Burke keyed his radio. "He's running. Hold your fire unless he attempts to ram!"

Behind him, the security forces opened with their assault rifles. *TAKTAKAKTAKA!!*

Caught in the moment, the other police officers drew their weapons and opened fire as well, a barrage of high velocity rounds shredding the truck.

Sgt. Burke screamed at his men over the PA.

"Stop firing! No one told you to fire!" but no one was listening.

In the truck, Ron ducked down, a veritable smorgasbord of bullets and pellet shot punching through his windshields on the front and doors of his truck. Glass rained down on his head, and while he struggled to stay as low as he could, he was forced to pop up occasionally in order to aim for the opposing two lanes.

The truck hit the frozen snow drifts and launched itself over the side, careening wildly. For a second, it lost traction and started to spin out, but swiftly caught its footing again, sending chunks of dirty slush and gravel pouring on his assailants. Ron did his best to stay behind his dashboard as it disintegrated around him. The massive truck neatly clipped the corner of one of the security vehicles, sending it careening away, then zoomed past the roadblock, leaving a cloud of steam behind. Ron continued to sing, a bit off key.

> *"And since we've no place to goooo, let it snow, (crack! spang!) let it snow, let it snow..."*

The hull of the truck rang continuously with each consecutive volley, his onboard dash alarms making a variety of unhappy chirps and beeps. A ricochet managed to rebound across Ron's back shoulder, bringing with it a burning line of pain. Undeterred, he kept the pedal pressed flat to the floor.

Ron chanced a glance out the windshield, now little more than a patchwork of spider web cracks. Off in the distance, he thought he could make out the outline of the church. Somehow, the truck seemed to have found the farmers' frontage road underneath the snow, and the massive diesel engine churned through the snowdrifts. The sound of gunfire faded behind him.

Back at the roadblock, the LorenCo Captain Lambert snarled at his subordinates.

"I pay you assholes too much. Get the trucks turned. Stay on the highway, and don't try to off-road it. Once you get down there, follow on foot, but DO NOT go near the church."

His face was starting to take on a pronounced predatory shape. The vampire hooked a thumb at the police officers.

"Get these fucking yokels down there as well. Let them take the lead for now. Turnbull, you take my ride."

As the security forces ran to do his bidding, Captain Lambert, a vampire with the House of Swords, strapped down his weapons and blurred away from the vehicle. As it ran, the shadowy figure started to transform once shaded from the glare of the lights, hands and arms extending, legs stretching into wicked curves. The creature ignored the roads and instead, easily loped across the dark snowy fields towards the church, fast as night and twice as deadly.

* * *

23. Little Church on the Prairie

Ron stuffed a t-shirt inside his parka in an attempt to staunch the blood running down his back. With a short jab, he knocked the remaining glass out of his side window. To his surprise, he had almost arrived at the church.

With his headlights shot out and his front window now a jigsaw puzzle, it was becoming difficult to navigate. Ron saw some irregular bumps in the snow whiz by, only realizing at the last minute that the church overlooked a graveyard, and he was seeing snow-covered tombstones. He spun the wheel of the truck to avoid hitting them and pulled further onto the sparsely plowed road. Now on his final approach, faintly twinkling Christmas lights wrapped around the historic building sign guided him into the small parking lot. The chain surrounding the gate was a mere suggestion, the truck sailing through it like a piece of string. Ron drove the truck as close as he could to the church, finally lurching to a stop next to an old metal horse post. Grabbing the bags out of the back seat, he fell out of his truck, scrambled to his feet, and ran for the church. Out of the corner of his eye, he saw something dark moving across the field, barreling towards him. Holding onto the bag's strap, he fired with his off hand.

"Lord, guide my hand!"

There was a *BOOM!* and a foot of flame erupted from the .500 pistol. He kept running, though near blind, having ruined his night vision. Ron lurched over the new state-mandated wheelchair ramp and kept going.

As his eyes readjusted, he looked over to spot that the misshapen creature was still pursuing him out of darkness, only now it was compensating for a noticeable limp.

"Tag, fang-boy," Ron muttered with a small smile.

Ron spun past around the great big church bell mounted in a display on the grounds and did not even bother trying for the church doors. With a heave, he tore the security bars off the window, and he threw himself bodily at the stained-glass behind it. Unfortunately, the glass buckled and broke, but did not give way. The church had been built for North Dakota weather, and the even windows were heavily reinforced. Ron bounced backwards and landed on his ass.

"Oh, fer cryin out loud!"

In the distance, he could see a myriad of flashing lights getting closer, and around the corner, something that looked vaguely like an over-extended hyena came towards him, its two eyes glowing like harvest moons. Ron noticed that its limp was already almost gone. Ron struggled to his feet as the creature closed the distance quickly.

An inhuman voice gurgled from the creature.

"Not having a good day, Santa? Why don't you cram your fat ass through the chimney?"

Ron smiled darkly, cocking the pistol he had just recovered from the snow.

"Rude."

The pistol thundered again. The vampire had anticipated the shot, however, and the bullet missed it narrowly as it lunged sideways. Ron felt a rushing wind as a muzzle full of razor-sharp teeth snapped shut less than an inch from his throat.

Suddenly, there was a whistling *CRACK!* as two pounds of slate fieldstone hit the creature in the head with crippling force, spinning it away.

"Kjør NÅ!" Ron heard from somewhere out in the darkness.

Ron did not speak Norwegian, but he had a pretty good idea of what it might mean. He ran.

The haggard Santa sped past the vampire as it was trying to reshape its head, and this time he ran to the back of the church. Ron blew the lock apart with the pistol and yanked open the door. As he launched himself through the doorframe, behind him a long, clawed arm lashed out to ensnare him. As it reached, it crossed the threshold of the church and the whole limb burst into flames.

The creature howled in pain, bellowing in frothing rage.

"Mother *fuckerrrr! Aurruaghhkhk!*"

Ron slammed the door shut, then proceeded to jam a handy snow shovel into the latch to keep it from opening.

"Now, now, language! We don't want to be on Santa's naughty list, do we?"

In answer, there was a hard *CLICK*.

BRRRRRT!

Ron dove into the small coat room as the back door was perforated with automatic weapons fire behind him. The rounds ricocheted around the inside of the small stone church.

A voice answered, now a bit more human.

"Your choice, Santa. This is a pretty old church. It'd be a shame to burn it down around your ears. The police will be here soon, and they'll want to talk you out. You and I both know that's not going to happen. Even if you do make it till morning, once you hit jail, you're done."

Ron started to flip pews and tables down to make himself shields from any more ricochets. He called out, responding to the voice outside.

"Sounds like you have all the answers, friend. Why don't we wait 'til sunrise, discuss this over breakfast, eh?"

BRA-TATATAT!

Another burst of machine gunfire caved in another window, shards of colored glass flying everywhere. The heavy oak pews he had set up thudded and splintered around him.

* * *

24. Waiting Game

Ron quickly took inventory. He had some ammunition, but most of the rounds were for the rifle back in the truck. With two speed loads left, aside from the two still chambered in the pistol, all he had was the blessed knife in his boot; very little when compared to an army of vampires, ghouls, and cops.

Silently, he watched as the lights of the police vehicles flashed brighter and brighter, shining disconcertingly through the tattered stained glass of the church windows. He had no idea who had thrown the stone outside, but he suspected someone had lent him magical assistance. Pressing his wounded back to the wood with a weighty creak, he sent up a small prayer of thanks to whomever helped him.

Outside, the distant crackle of police radios, chatter, and sounds of shuffling feet all became clearer. He took a moment to get up and check the other rooms of the church—there was not much to search. Apparently, the early pioneers were extremely efficient—show up, pray, and leave. As a result, the trappings of the church were fairly basic. Ron found a basin full of holy water and few other items of interest, so proceeded to get busy. The work kept him from thinking about the pain in his shoulders and the blood running down his back and arm. As he worked, he started singing again, quietly to himself.

"You better not shout, you better not cry...."

* * *

25. Visions of Sugarplums

After being invited in by the staff, Mr. Florentine walked quietly into the big house. It was brightly painted and spacious, every inch of the expansive foyer actively studied by two bodyguards flanking him efficiently. Standing in the largest room was an enormous Christmas tree, decorated with hundreds of ornaments, a majority of them hand-made by children.

Fredericka was now wearing a nicely tailored fur coat, matching hat, and earrings that looked like little poinsettias. Beside her were two of the staff for Open Arms Home, a slender young woman with long chestnut hair and a heavyset older woman who looked very put upon. Fredericka curtsied, stepped forward, and cheerily introduced them.

"Mr. Florentine, I am so happy you could stop by, especially as busy as you are. May I introduce the head counselor, Mrs. Schmidt," she said, pointing to the older woman, "and the president of the nonprofit, Ms. Berold."

Mr. Florentine inclined his head graciously at both women.

"I am so honored to be here, and I have heard so much about all your good works. Thank you all for staying so late."

The two women smiled, and Ms. Berold stepped forward.

"Mr. Florentine, I am speaking truthfully when I say that the contributions you have made, they've made a huge difference in the lives of these children, and I daresay, the whole state."

Mr. Florentine took her hand briefly.

"I could do no less." He turned to the older woman. "Mrs. Schmidt, I was wondering if I could see them."

"Well, I suppose. You need to know, they were all out late and are exhausted. I'm certain they are very much asleep."

"I understand. However, I won't be able to see them tomorrow, I am afraid."

"It's no problem. Please, this way."

A short time later, the guests were shown from room to room, checking in on dozens of sleeping children along the way. Ms. Berold excitedly noted that each room had an animal theme. As they were finishing, Mr. Florentine stopped to carefully tuck a young boy's arm back onto his bed. All the women beamed at him.

"Do you have children of your own?" asked Mrs. Schmidt.

"Ah, you're a flatterer. I am older than I look. But yes, I have children, grandchildren, and adopted children who are near and dear to my heart."

"But none so young as these, Mr. Florentine?" Fredericka gently closed the door behind them.

"True," the dapper older man sighed. "That is why it is so important that these young ones get an extra special Christmas. It's a part of parenthood I miss dearly."

Mrs. Schmidt stopped for a moment to look at their kindly old benefactor.

"That actually has been somewhat of a problem. It's been hard to convince them that Santa won't be coming for them on Christmas Eve. We limit their TV, but they do seem to get the message regardless."

Ms. Berold shot the older woman a warning look. Mrs. Schmidt continued hastily.

"But we do understand you have something special planned for the children!"

For a second, there was a flicker of irritation on Mr. Florentine's face, but it was gone in a flash.

"Mrs. Schmidt. I am so sorry, and I know this must be trying. But understand that I am from Italy, and in Italy, the children get their presents on Epiphany, which is January sixth. So, I understand what it is to wait. These children, they only have to wait an extra day. I can guarantee it will be worth the delay. Look at it this way: Back home, our presents are delivered by La Befana, a kind but ugly old witch." He laughed, finishing his thought with a mirthful wiggle of the eyebrows. "I believe they would be very confused by that!"

"But we will have Santa Claus at the event?" Mrs. Schmidt asked as she smiled uncertainly.

"Indeed. In fact, I want them to get no presents whatsoever until the night of Christmas Day. We have arranged to have the most amazing, most real Santa Claus come for them.

"Ladies, it means a great deal to me that they believe, that they are excited to see Santa Claus when he arrives. I promise you, there will be presents for them, and for you and your staff... *sarà meraviglioso!*"

"Trust me," Fredericka added emphatically, "I've seen what is being planned. We will send some shuttle buses to collect you and bring you to the LorenCo Center, and they have a room that is being set up for you. The buses are being decorated, and we have some of our employees so excited, they have even begun wearing their elf costumes at work."

"Don't worry, we can do this," Ms. Berold reassured Mrs. Schmidt with a pat on the shoulder. "It will be their most magical Christmas ever! And who deserves it more than they do?"

"I guess," the older woman said in resignation.

Mr. Florentine made a motion with his hand, and a sheaf of envelopes was handed to Mrs. Schmidt.

"These are for you, the other counselors, and your staff. You truly deserve them. We could have waited, but I thought maybe you might want this for extra Christmas cheer, *si*?"

Mrs. Schmidt blushed and went to hug him, but the bodyguard stepped forward ever so politely.

"My apologies," said Mr. Florentine with a chuckle. "Ms. Berold, will you walk me to the car?"

"Of course."

Outside, in the darkness, Florentine's demeanor changed. Gone was the charming old man, replaced by the spider who made puppets of popes and kings. He turned to Ms. Berold.

"Elaysa, I trust you have this handled? I need true believers, churning out hope just as strongly as their little hearts can bear. Mrs. Schmidt looks exactly like the type of woman who would allow just a small Christmas present in. That absolutely cannot happen."

Elaysa gently touched his arm with a reassuring smile on her face.

"I understand, Grandfather. If she causes me any problems, I have two more Kindred with me who can either give her the eyes or even a bite of control, if need be."

"Hmph." Duke Florentine frowned slightly. "To be truthful, we want the children to be as far away from any other forms of magic up to the last. Avoid it if you can."

"Of course, your Excellency," she said with a glimmer of mischievousness. He reached out and took her hand, squeezing it as he had in her childhood.

"With any luck, we will be out of this god-forsaken, frozen hellhole soon enough. Next, it will be back to Milan. Who knows? I might even be able to enjoy a walk with you on a sunny day on the beach once we reach the Riviera."

"That would be wonderful!"

Duke Florentine held her hand a moment longer.

"I know that this assignment has been a long one, and I truly appreciate your hard work. I hope none of the Kindred has given you any problems or questioned your authority. You are my family and of my line, and if they challenge you, they will also contend with me." He shook his head. "It's rather amazing, so many of them enjoying immortality, still choosing idiocy."

"The curse of success, I think. No, Grandfather. I still get the occasional sideways look, but your reputation and my training have helped me maintain the needed order among our agents. All the kith and kindred know who I am." She gave him a smirk.

"You should get into the limo. It's cold here, and it can be rough for someone your age."

He returned her smile for a fraction of a second.

"Ah, yes. Fragile as an old paper kite, I am."

"Ciao." She pulled him down by the arm, planting a kiss on his cheek with a familiarity few had ever known. Indeed, as one of the last of his direct descendants, she knew she was precious to him.

"Ciao!" He bowed to her and slipped into the idling car.

Once inside the armored luxury vehicle, Duke Florentine looked at his assistant. "Take me to the site. I want to see how Avice is doing with the ritual. At once!"

26. Hunting

Baron de Rais watched as the neighborhood slowly rolled by. The developments were so new, there were whole streets of partially constructed buildings. He turned again to the vampire of the House of the Wheel, who was helping coordinate the search.

"Marcos, you've told me six times now, nothing has been spotted. Surely a group of fat, senile, bearded men can't be that stealthy."

Marcos twitched ever so slightly and coughed to cover the tremor in his voice. The Baron had been known to kill his underlings once in a great while. There were even rumors he had eaten them.

"No, your Excellency. We have tried putting drones up, but they are freezing up, and we have a cyber team watching every camera in the city. The AI surveillance software will flag them if they are near a camera long enough. But it is brutal winter weather, and it's normal right now for faces to be covered and bodies all bundled up. They are probably huddled up somewhere well-fortified, waiting for daybreak. We have a team trying to extract one of them from a church at the outskirts of the town. He made it to holy ground, so we have some members of the local law enforcement working to remove him. Since they are local and have families, that could be problematic, seeing as they aren't on our payroll. I've been assured the situation will be resolved soon."

The Baron took one of his daggerlike claws and etched a filthy word into the glass.

"I tire of this, Marcos. Stop the car and fetch me the black bag in the trunk. Avice is not the only sorcerer in our ranks, and I doubt one little scrying spell will cause too much trouble. Have three of our kind keep watch—you are with me. Oh, and hand me those maps."

Once pulled over, the Baron stepped out of the limousine-style SUV. He started to walk down the street, casting this way and that, until a smile of satisfaction crept onto his chapped lips. He motioned to Marcos.

"Follow but stay hidden in the shadows. Have the vehicles pulled around the block, this will take some time. And increase that to four of our kind keeping watch, one on every corner."

Marcos issued the commands, and a few minutes later, the two vampires were making their way towards a new ranch house. Effortlessly, they leapt over the tall fence, landing in the frost blanketed backyard. Almost as soon as they were over the wall, a pet door that led into the garage swung open, and a large black labrador charged out, snarling and barking loudly. A second later, Marcos stuffed the former pet's dead body under the snow-covered picnic table. Other dogs in the neighborhood started barking as well, but they all blended in with the sounds of the distant highway.

Marcos hung back by the swing set, watching the Baron. Baron de Rais was carefully sniffing at each window, finally choosing one. After having donned a Santa hat and a set of false whiskers pulled out of the bag, he quietly tapped at the window. A few moments later, a tousled haired girl with beautiful dark eyes peeked out of the curtain. The Baron smiled and pointed towards the back door, and held up a finger to his mouth with a smile. The girl's eyes widened, and she gave him a delighted grin. The curtain dropped and a minute later, the back door opened. She looked up at the Baron.

"Santa! Where is your red suit?"

In a voice rich and sweet, the Baron nodded and bent down to her level.

"That's a very good question. Christmas is coming soon and I am having it cleaned, right here in this town. I heard there was a special present you wanted, and I thought I would drop some of the very best ones off while I was nearby. May I come in?"

The girl gave him a delighted smile, reached out, and took his hand.

"Come in, Santa!"

Baron shot Marcos a predatory grin. As he stepped across the threshold, the Baron whispered under his breath, "Marcos, you and all our colleagues are welcome within, too."

Baron Gilles de Rais accompanied the young lady into the kitchen.

"You are so nice. I have some special presents for you all, and you are going to be so helpful."

A short while later, Marcos stepped out of the master bedroom, adjusting his jacket. He made his way to the living room, where the Baron was practicing his dark arts.

Baron de Rais finished the last part of his incantation.

"....*et in vos hoc nomen.*"

The lights in the room dimmed and dark energy flickered in the air itself. Baron de Rais pushed one of the bodies out the way, which fell on the floor with a *fwump*. With arcane gestures, he sprinkled blood on the maps lying scattered around the dining room table, watching carefully to see the directions the spatters were taking.

"You may speak," the Baron said to Marcos, "now that we are focused. Blood of a virgin always works best for these sorts of things. Screw those idiotic pendulums." With that, he did some hand motions again, and flicked more blood from his fingertips.

Marcos bent over and studied the maps. There were four concentrations of bright red droplets. One was by the old church outside of town, two were in the city proper, one sat squarely at the mall, and another was in a housing area. The fourth, however, looked to be comprised of two lines. As he watched, the blood crawled across the surface of the plasticized map.

"Your Excellency, this one here. It seems a bit strange. That one is moving?"

Baron de Rais pulled up a stool and bent over to study it.

"*Incroyable.*"

He looked up at Marcos with a mildly impressed look, absentmindedly licking the blood off his fingers.

"The last time I used this spell, we were still using horses and buggies. Whomever that is, they are moving fast enough that the spell caught the motion."

The Baron tilted his head and studied the geography.

"What does this symbol mean?"

"A large truck stop, Lord Baron."

"That makes sense. Earlier, you mentioned the phones we were tracking went dead. Now, we see the followers of the Fat Man moving in the darkest night. I suspect that at least one of them has been flushed, risking it at this hour. Let us see if we can't catch a few juicy little fishies. Oh, and investigate these others, besides the one in the mall. That one is ours."

"As you wish. What about the remaining family members?"

"Thrall the woman, feed the man and the old woman to our people, and save the remaining two children for me. But keep them here. Tidy this all up. I greatly dislike being told to clean up after myself. Have one of ours stay to mind the lot of them, until the absolute last minute. If necessary, of course, kill them, and put them under the covers of that trailer out back. In this cold, they should keep until spring."

Marcos nodded and did as he was instructed. As he gave orders, he watched as the Baron tiptoed daintily over bodies and away from the diabolist symbols painted in blood on the table. The Baron snagged a bottle of wine, popped it, and mixed it with the blood from his chalice. He sniffed the slurry appreciatively. Draining it, he turned back to Marcos.

"Lively now, Marcos. I want to catch the mobile one as soon as possible. The hunt calls."

When they got to the waiting car, Marcos looked over his shoulder.

"Lord Baron, I was wondering why you put the Santa guise on to gain us entry, rather than use your gaze to compel her will."

"Well observed. Drive." As the luxury SUV headed down the road, the Baron answered him.

"Several reasons. One, the powers I invoked hate the Order even more than we do. It takes a great deal of energy to cast during this season. They appreciate the joke. Secondly, she was a true believer, and that helps with the magical law of attraction. I wanted thoughts concerning Christmas to cross her mind last, to help me locate any Santas. And third, I had just always wanted to do that, and I am a darkly humorous individual. It will make for a great conversation starter at parties."

"Ah."

As the car accelerated through the night, Baron de Rais leaned back, looking very pleased with himself. The night was looking up.

* * *

27. In the Wind

Across the town, two different camps became gradually aware of dark magicks being carried on the winter night winds. The spindly figure of Avice had been examining the room where the event would take place, when the rather skeletal looking vampire stood straighter, and turning his head slowly with a slight hiss. Avice stared at the vampire lord in the doorway.

His Excellency, Vampire Archduke Cosimo Florentine looked downright silly with fluffy sterile protection bags on his feet. He was inspecting the ludicrously expensive and delicate laser etched designs engraved on the floor.

"Amazing. In the old days, it would have taken years for them to do something this beautiful, this sophisticated... and you say this was done in a day?" He looked up, "Avice? Is there a problem?"

Avice looked completely spent from his work, dressed in a threadbare robe and smelled of candle soot, dust, and old books.

"YES! Your great lumbering village idiot, buffoon, jackanape, that whore's son, obscene, grease-swollen, oath-breaking..."

Duke Cosimo put his hand in his face and rubbed his eyes tiredly.

"Yes, yes, Baron de Rais. What is the problem?"

With a long arm, Avice waved in a general direction.

"Any magically aware creature within a thousand miles just heard the noise he created with his blundering diabolist magicks."

"Are you sure it was him?" inquired the Duke.

There came a sniff from within the hood of the figure.

"I would know that discordancy anywhere. If I had not already taken precautions, he could have endangered this whole ritual. As it is, he just created a great deal of magical noise that the higher powers will be taking notice of."

There was a low, feral growl from Duke Cosimo. His finely manicured fingernails dug deep grooves into the bridge of his nose. After a moment, he was his gracious self again.

"You are ever wise and learned, Avice. Thank you for taking precautions, magister. While he may be a hammer where a scalpel is needed, perhaps he has found the location of that Caestus for us?"

Avice swayed a bit and looked as if he was listening to something else, saying nothing. The Duke waited only a moment and then continued.

"In any case..." Duke Cosimo said, pausing to look at his watch.

"It is now officially the day before Christmas, and in a very short time, all the ingredients for your great work will arrive. I will attend to Baron de Rais. Please, let my assistants know if you need anything"

Avice nodded, turning his sights on the restraining posts that were being brought into the room.

Duke Cosimo stepped back out into the hall of the LorenCo Stadium center and glared at his staff. "Bring me to Rais, now!"

* * *

28. Rolling Thunder

The Caestus team picked out a place to spend the night once they had stopped rolling. Rick brought down the interior lights so it was harder to see inside. Morozko sat in the passenger chair, quietly praying to himself in Russian, while his dogs were happily running around inside the plush RV. Pastor Carl was securing the space by strategically placing candles around the room, and had already blessed and marked all the windows and doors. Behind the RV, Top followed at a distance with his trailer and Jon with his bulky Jeep. The plan was to head to one of the overflow parking lots behind the three big box-marts. The stores had brought in extra staff for the holidays, so few extra RVs and trailers likely would not be noticed in the chaos.

However to get there, most of the vehicles need fuel, and so they stopped at the newly renovated Truck Rite next to the highway. It was big, it had its own market, showers, several restaurants, and plenty of choices for fuel. It also had the advantage of a "civilian" section for those who were not professional truck drivers, which diversified what supplies they might replenish there. A glowing oasis in the night, the team eagerly pulled into the lot, greeted by the familiar crackle of overplayed holiday music.

Rick pulled up to a pump, and wearing his scarf and hat, he got the diesel pump working in short order. He climbed back inside out of the cold.

"It takes a lot to fill this behemoth, and that pump is running pretty slow."

A nondescript man in a Florida Marlin's cap tapped on his door. Rick started to reach for his gun, but stopped as the man pressed his hand against the glass, where the Caestus sigil shone on his palm. Rick opened up the door and the man hopped in, and as he took off his cap, he turned back into Top. Abe and Jon piled in a minute later. It was obvious Abe was still tense.

"Still thinking about Ron, right?" Jon asked.

"Hell yes, we need to do something."

"Abe, we are. I know my friends are out there lending him a hand, and Pastor Carl is cooking up something as well. The longer Ron keeps their attention out there, the less they can focus on us here."

"Hey guys, since we have a moment," Jon interrupted and started emptying a bag, "I dragged out some of my special headsets for us. With these, our line of sight can extend about a block or so, provided nothing gets in the way. If something does, we're looking at maybe a hundred feet."

Once everyone was comfortable with how to use them, Top addressed Rick.

"Big Man, are you our designated Coca-Cola Santa?"

"I guess so? Want me to break out my bag?"

"Yes, please."

Rick stepped back to the RV bedroom and came out with his Santa hat, jacket, and bag and set the gear down beside them on the couch. Despite not being in full Santa garb, the air about him had changed. With a demeanor of sureness and warmth, he was now one of the Santas, complete with beautiful flowing beard and twinkling eyes.

"Ho-ho-ho! What would you like for Christmas, young sir?"

Top grinned and held out a piece of paper.

"Why Santa, I've brought you a list! Could I have twelve of these phones, with chargers and earbuds, active on a GSM network?"

Santa Rick returned the smile, eyebrow raised.

"Have you been good this year?"

"Well, I am trying to do better."

"Good enough," Santa replied with a confident smile.

Santa Rick reached into the large bag and began to pull out one wrapped present after another. Soon, the couch was covered in a heap of wrapped boxes and envelopes.

"May I ask?" Morozko watched with great fascination.

"Yes, go ahead, but only for what we need for this mission. Oh, and it has to be something that someone has actually given as a present on Christmas. Also, you need to be truly thankful."

"Da," Morozko said and cleared his throat.

"Father Christmas, may I have some of the nice booties for my doggies, the ones with rough pads on them for traction? Also, do you have the good 7N14 151 grain ammunitions? With nice blessed silver tips? That would be most lovely." The old Russian man stepped back and sat down, looking uncertain for the first time. He then added, "Oh, and some good tea. Dilmah, Ceylon tea, if it is not asking too much. *Spasibo*!"

Surprising most of them, Santa Rick looked dejected.

"What's wrong?" Abe asked as he leaned in.

"I know what my role is here for the Caestus, what my ability means. But this... while I know that it's necessary, it always hurts. Every time I pull a weapon or ammo out of the bag, it makes me really uncomfortable. Christmas is not about violence."

Abe nodded, "Got it."

"Well, we've got a job to do," Rick concluded and squared his shoulders. "Let's see what the elves came up with." After rummaging through the bag, out came two nice insulated dog jackets and booties to match, followed by a pair of rawhide chew toys with bright red ribbons. Two heavy boxes were next, Rick handing them to Morozko with a smile.

"Well, you gotta thank the kind Appalachians and the gun aficionados out there. Ammo for Christmas, Morozko. *Aaand*, your tea!" Rick handed the last box over with a flourish.

"*Spasibo!*" Morozko exclaimed as he collected his treasures and left the queue.

Jon nudged Abe.

"Abe, I noticed you have a .45, but that's about it. Maybe you want to ask Santa Rick for a hand-to-hand weapon?"

Abe looked around sheepishly.

"Sure? So Santa, I'm going to be fighting some bad guys, I think. Any chance you've got something in that bag that will help me protect myself?"

Santa Rick stroked his beard and smiled.

"I'm certain we can find something, here we go."

Rick reached into the bag and pulled out an old-fashioned Christmas stocking, complete with a candy cane poking out the top.

"Thank you, Santa," replied Abe. Making a point not to spill its contents, Abe carefully took the stocking. He looked surprised and tiny bit underwhelmed.

Abe set the stocking down beside him, and then as an afterthought, reached down to tug on the candy cane. As he did so, something shiny caught his eye, and the more he pulled, the heavier it felt in his hand. All the men stood back, and Abe was forced to stand as he finished unsheathing a great sword. Pastor Carl was beside himself laughing, and Jon and Top looked at each other stupefied.

"Looks like you have one heck of a candy cane there, Abe," Jon sputtered.

"I think that might be a choking hazard!" Top said with a laugh.

Jon stepped past the tip of the sword, closely examining the crossbar-hilt. Pastor Carl leaned over to study it as well.

"God be praised, Abe! This is a famous sword belonging to one of the original Knight Commanders. It has a long and illustrious lineage, and it normally hangs in the hall back in our primary monastery. It's called *Illuminator*, or the Sword of Light, and it is a powerful magical armament."

Abe staggered slightly as he found the proper balance of the weapon, his shocked expression remaining even as he tipped the sword back into the stocking. With a gentle push, the blade slid smoothly out of view, and when he lifted his hand away, there was the candy cane again.

Pastor Carl said a blessing under his breath.

"Abe, you should know that this sword would not have been presented to you without a reason."

Jon reached down and picked up the sheath, which hung from a loop on the top cuff just like any half-filled stocking.

"Huh, that's a slick trick!" Jon looked over at the other men with a new grave expression on his face.

"It isn't enough to be a badass, no offense to Abe here. This sword showing up means we are about to be in some very deep kimchi." Abe was still staring at the stocking in disbelief. Jon asked, "Abe, do you have any training with a sword? A European great sword?"

"Maybe? I practiced all sorts of sword katas, but we were doing mainly Chinese swords when I was getting my martial art degrees. I did some live-action roleplaying and reenactment back in the day, but those guys played a bit rough for my taste. Honestly, I've not done a lot with anything this size, but I did do some spear training."

The warrior patted him on the shoulder.

"We won't have time to train you properly right now, but just make certain you have room to swing it before you draw it."

"Like they said in the Banderas version of that Zorro movie, 'The pointy end goes into the other guy!'" Top added, while busily ripping open blister packs.

Abe gave him a sardonic look as he picked up the stocking with a couple of fingers.

"As always, Top, your insights astound."

"It could be worse. Remember in Star Wars, old Ben Kenobi gave Luke a lightsaber, and Luke immediately pointed it at his face. At least with that, you won't risk impromptu laser eye surgery."

"Thanks."

"Don't mention it!" said Top cheerily. "I always knew Santa Claus would be Gryffyndor!"

Pastor Carl gave him a giddy smile.

"So, either you get to fight Moldy-Wart or you chop the head off of a giant snake." Both Abe and Top turned to look at the aging Lutheran minister enthusiastically.

"Did he just make a geek reference?"

"He did!"

"What? I'm a fan of the Lovecraft works," Pastor Carl responded defensively. "I love to read. Besides, I live in Minnesota." He hooked a thumb towards the window. "When this is what you deal with six months out of the year, you learn to read or ice-fish. Or both, you betcha."

Santa Rick pulled out another box.

"Ho ho! Abe, I think these are yours as well."

Abe turned his attention from the stocking and opened the new box. Inside were a set of articulated finger gauntlets, old and battered, mended with silver rivets and very fine chainmail. After some small adjustments, Abe found they fit him surprisingly well. Jon pointed to the mesh in the palm.

"This makes sense. It'll allow you half-hand with that sword. Two-handers were more of a Renaissance weapon, and the Illuminator pre-dates those by about three or four hundred years. The cruciform hilt on the sword is fairly small, and it doesn't have the flukes to protect your hands either."

Jon turned over Abe's hands to examine the gauntlets further.

"Huh. Check out the etchings on the back. Bears. These must have been a pair of the original Commander Cormac's. Interesting. Stories abound with conflicting information. Some say he was buried with full honors, in his armor and with a ceremonial sword. Others say that, in the end, he turned into a bear and ran into the woods."

Abe practiced flexing in them. For a man of his size, it was rare to find something that fit so well.

"Well, I don't know much about fighting with this stuff, but I'm happy to have these." He patted Santa Rick on the knee. "Thank you so much, Santa. I will do my best to honor these gifts."

Santa Rick smiled broadly. A timer went off and everybody jumped.

"I have to go finish at the pump," Rick explained, who seemed to be his usual self, headed towards the door. Top jumped up.

"Rick!"

"What?" Rick asked as he turned around, one hand on the RV door.

"Your Santa suit?" Top pointed to his hat and coat. "We don't want to tip our hand, right?"

The older Santas in the RV all blinked in unison. Years of Santa meetings had made them somewhat oblivious to the garb while in season.

"Oh, crud. Right. That would have been really dumb."

With the exception of Abe, the other members of the Caestus seemed nonplussed. Top just smiled.

"Man, you real beards really are used to the 24/7 thing, ain'tcha?" He held out his hand to Rick. "Here, I'll take care of the pump and you go put your gear away. Keep that bag handy."

"Can you get us some snacks, too?" Rick added, as he passed him his credit card. "Protein. Eggnog, if they have it. Go nuts but make it quick."

"Roger that," Top said and smiled as he climbed out of the RV to disconnect the diesel pump and head into the store.

A few minutes later, Top watched from the store as the big RV pulled away from the pump. His hands were full with two baskets stuffed with a few hard-boiled eggs, a quart of eggnog, a few sports drinks, and several bags of junk food. A crackle from a police radio made him look over his shoulder, where he spotted two cops, along with two others who wore dark civilian clothes and stern, cadaverous expressions. Top went back to paying the clerk, frequently glancing up at the anti-shoplifting mirror. As to be expected, the gruesome twosome had no reflections. A chill ran down his spine. Top thanked the clerk and started to head outside, when he saw there was a sizable security force across the lot conducting inspections vehicle by vehicle.

He turned and went back to the counter, setting down the bags.

"Can I leave these here while I hit the bathroom?"

"Sure," the clerk agreed.

Top turned and jogged for the restroom, tapping the mic on his headset.

"Guys, look outside. The place is crawling with vamps and cops, and they're searching door to door." Glancing out the windows both ways, he saw the hired security forming blockades in each direction.

Top pretended to look casually at a phone card dispenser by the window.

"They're setting up roadblocks. Southeast corner of the road south is still open, but you have to go *now*," he whispered.

Jon's voice in his ear spoke solemnly.

"Top, can you make it back?"

"I don't think so. I'm gonna make for my truck, meet up with you guys later. Seriously, you have to leave."

Inside the RV, Jon and the others confirmed Top's observations. Rick was the first to act, hopping into the driver's seat and preparing himself.

"Guys, are we doing this? Do we stay or do we go?" he called back.

Abe had watched as Jon's expression hardened in that short time. Having pulled his hat over his face, he was already stepping out into the chill.

"Go. I'll find you."

Morozko hastily pulled some things from the satchel he was carrying, while Pastor Carl started praying. The old Russian set a very businesslike silver-headed mace on the counter. The two dogs were now very alert and standing next to him, waiting.

Inside, Top dove into the bathroom, did a quick check, and then flipped his hat, altering his appearance. He now looked like a middle-aged Latino truck driver, tired and exhausted. As he exited the store and made a beeline towards his own truck, he saw the big RV slowly roll out of the parking lot.

Some of the police started towards their squad car, looking like they were going to go after the RV. Top said a small prayer under his breath, then saw two of the dark-clothed civilians start to move with purpose as well.

"Damn. Double damn," quietly hissed Top.

They had spotted Jon walking towards the truck. One of them walked past him, the other giving a short, sharp whistle to the cops.

"God this is fucking stupid," Top said to no one in particular. He reached into his jacket and flipped a small tube towards the vampires. With a resounding flash of actinic light, there was a *ka-KRACK!* as the flashbang went off.

Top yelled, "Ninja-Out!" as a huge cloud of smoke rolled forth, and all hell broke loose.

The two vampires were momentarily stunned, and all the security forces and cops pulled their guns, charging into Top's surrounding area. Out by the pumps, Jon saw the flash and started walking very briskly to his truck.

Top barely made it back into the store and dove behind a rack of pastries. The two vampires followed him into the building in a blur. There was a gust of wind, the ringing of the bell, but when Top looked up at the anti-theft mirror, they did not show.

Top rolled over and pulled his hat over his face again, shifting back into his previous guise, popping up just as one of the vampires grabbed him. The other vampire shook his head.

"No, shorter. Mexican guy."

The vampire let him go, and the two of them darted down the hall.

Top went back to the counter and grabbed his groceries.

"What the hell is going on?" he said to the clerk.

"Some asshole tossing fireworks. Really? In a gas station? Place is crawling with cops. Bad move for him, I hope they find his ass."

"Crazy. Merry Christmas."

"You, too." The clerk waved goodbye.

At this point, various truckers and some of the people who had been sleeping in their cars started to move about. The area began to fill with police, LorenCo security, and people who were poorly disguised "undercover security."

About twenty truckers were being corralled towards the side of the diner, two of the Latino truckers being interrogated in particular by the cops. Top skirted the around pumps and snuck right past them all, headed towards his truck. Seconds after escaping the small fueling island, however, three shadows materialized out of the darkness. All were outfitted in tidy LorenCo Security suits.

"Good evening," rumbled the largest.

Top nodded and started to sidestep them.

"Evening," he replied.

In his mind, Top started to consider options, but none seemed very promising. One of the shadows slid to block his way.

"Excuse me. We are looking for someone, or some people who look like Santa. They might have been around here recently." said suit two.

Top readjusted the bags in his hands, and smiled, getting into character as a crochety old man.

"What, like uh, like a Santa? No, no, not around here. Although, if you wait until tonight, you may get lucky! Are you police?"

The biggest of the shadows stepped forward, its eyes glowing opalescent.

"We are the authorities here. What an interesting cologne you are wearing, sir," said the figure. As he stepped into the light, he revealed the fleshy face of Baron de Rais.

Top dropped his bags, staggering back.

Baron de Rais smiled and tapped his nose, now advancing.

"It is a peculiar blend, eh? I detect notes of peppermint, church incense, and... do I detect the slightest hint of spirit gum? Ah, and fear? Yes. Fear. How lovely."

Top lifted his arms, rotated his hands, and suddenly a stream of white doves flew from his sleeves, fluttering wildly. Being true predators, the vampires were stunned for a fraction of a second, as they tracked them. When they looked back, there were two bags of groceries on the ground, but there was no Top.

The doves flitted into the night. The vampires started to move, but Baron de Rais held up a pudgy hand, one eyebrow raised.

"Wait."

Head cocked, what followed was a tiny splash, then a dizzying blur. Baron de Rais was suddenly next to the fuel island, Top dangling in his left hand.

"Not bad, illusionist, but I've seen better. Too bad about the snow and puddles. I know, I know, you were in a hurry."

Top hung like a kitten grabbed by the neck. He smiled roguishly.

"Everyone's a critic these days. Hey, Tons o' Fun, what's that on your face?"

Baron de Rais looked at him questioningly.

"Probably bloo...."

At that moment, Top tapped the edge of his hat and a shower of holy water sprayed from it, pouring across Baron de Rais's face.

As it smoked and bubbled, Top struggled to escape, but the Baron had the good sense to slam him against a pump, brutally. The big vampire seethed in anger.

"*Merde*! You!" he said to one of the other vampires. "Come take this idiot out of my hand. Keep him alive!"

The two other vampires rushed to do as they were bid, oblivious as Jon's Jeep came hurtling past the pump, hitting them squarely, refusing to slow down. One vampire flattened against the wall, the other knocked wide, skipping across the asphalt like a marble.

Top took that second to reach into his jacket, but Baron de Rais reacted much faster, slapping him sharply. Top dangled loosely in the Baron's grip, a puppet whose strings had suddenly been cut.

Jon swore mightily as he saw Top go limp in his rearview mirror. He knew he could spin around and try to rescue Top, but only if he could rely on Top's help. The other vampires would recover too quickly. Instead, Jon cornered dangerously, sling-shotting through the entrance into the truck stop, going the wrong way on purpose and scaring the hell out of an oncoming Swift truck driver. Once back on the highway, he slowed down to perform a bootlegger's reverse, and then headed down the road, speeding up to a hundred miles an hour.

While the police scrambled to catch the rogue driver, Baron de Rais waited until several more of the vampire security team arrived. Marcus pulled around in the limo, and de Rais casually tossed the unconscious body of Top inside.

"Strip him, search him. I want two guards watching him at all times. Give him any medical attention he needs and make certain he is bound and gagged. I will be along shortly to interrogate him."

Marcus motioned to one of the security people who pulled out handcuffs and climbed in back as well.

"Yes, Lord Baron."

Baron de Rais twitched as Marcus's cell phone began to ring. Marcus answered, listening to it briefly.

"Baron, Duke Cosimo. He sounds annoyed."

Baron de Rais took the phone awkwardly, always having disliked this new technology.

"Yes?"

The voice of the archduke was monotone as ever, paper dry.

"Does the concept of subtlety confuse you, Gilles?"

Baron de Rais quietly snarled, motioning everyone else to their tasks.

"My apologies, however, you wanted results, and I got them. In fact, I am sending one of the Order to you—an unbearded one, strange as that seems. Another magic wielder. In any event, it is obvious that they have one of their teams in the area now. The first is still pinned down in the church, and another is fleeing in a truck, with the gendarmes in hot pursuit."

There was a slight pause before the Duke responded.

"Good, but their teams are usually drawn in groups of five. You are possibly three short, assuming that the one driving away belongs to them. Any one of those left free could cause an unacceptable delay. The ritual will commence at midnight, and it continues until culmination the following midnight, Christmas Day. It. Cannot. Be. Interrupted. Need I remind you that you will not have much in the way of Kindred resources come daybreak?"

"No," grumbled Baron de Rais.

"I don't care which one you break, but I want those Santas found and dealt with."

"Of course," said the Baron, fingering the burns the holy water left behind.

Click.

Baron de Rais handed the phone back to Marcus, as one would a dead rat.

"A slight change of plans. We need the one we just captured conscious as soon as possible. I don't care what it takes."

"I will take him to our resort, let the doctors earn their keep." Marcos glanced up at the brightening sky. "And I will find one of our best officers to take over for us."

"I shall join you shortly," Baron de Rais responded. "I spotted some kine sleeping in that vehicle over there, and suddenly find myself tremendously hungry. I don't know what it is about this time of year, but I can never stay on my diet."

Marcus gave him a thin smile, motioned, and the black vehicle sped away.

The Baron strolled over to a family van parked between two big rigs, stuffed with people swaddled against pillows. He casually broke the glass on one of the doors, and then oozed inside to feed. The screams that ensued were buried under the sound of dozens of huge diesel truck engines idling. Any police or security forces that did hear them offered nothing but silence.

* * *

29. The Lorica

At the Holy Trinity Church out on the plains, the sky was starting to tinge gray, and Captain Lambert had shifted back to human form. The man inside the church had turned out to be remarkably resourceful. Lambert witnessed everyone who had approached the church pelted by large stones, all flung with brutal force. Curiously, they could not tell where the stones were coming from.

Sgt. Burke jogged over to the security team leader, as it was obvious that Lambert's team was gearing up for a full-on tactical assault.

"Captain, can I ask what you and your folks are doing?"

"It should be fairly obvious, Sergeant. You have a killer in there, we're putting an end to this."

"Uh-huh. And if I call my commanding officer, he's going to tell me to let you do this?"

"You're sharp, Sgt. Burke."

Sgt. Burke looked at his officers and then at the LorenCo militia. The security team was much better equipped, and most of them looked like juiced mercenaries spoiling for a fight.

Sgt. Burke stepped closer to the security team commander.

"I ain't too sure what's going on here, but I suspect you, personally, are not going to be going into that church."

Captain Lambert turned to stare at Sgt. Burke with eyes alert and inhuman, with all the softness of volcanic obsidian. When he spoke, he made no effort to hide his elongated teeth.

"Sergeant, I like you. You're a cut above the other nimrods you have in your force who are, for the most part, thick as bricks. But even a brick has its uses and a lot of them work for me. So, the best thing you can do right now is get into your truck and drive away.

"Or barring that, help us get the suspect out and turn him over to us. I'll see to it that when promotion time comes around, you get one. Maybe you join our team and make about five times what you make now."

Burke's face blanched when he saw the Captain's true nature, but he did not step back. He glanced back at the various cops and security personnel, who were all waiting expectantly.

"Rather than have your folks blow the hell out of a historic landmark church, let me see what I can do. Give me ten minutes."

Captain Lambert turned his gaze up to the sky.

"Ten minutes. After that, the Church is going to need some major renovations."

Sgt. Burke handed his duty pistol to one of his officers, waved a stained white handkerchief over his head, and started walking towards the church. There was a *wa-tack!* as a rock the size of baseball smashed to bits at his feet the second he got within shouting range of the church. He jumped back with a yelp.

"Whoa! Yeah, yeah, truce! I just want to talk! I am unarmed!"

There was a rustle then a tired, deep voice answered from the church.

"What do you want?"

"You need to come out. In a few minutes, they're going to blow this place apart, and you're either going to either die in a hail of gunfire or get roasted to death when their grenades 'accidentally' lights the place on fire."

"You know what they are, right?" the deep voice said with a dry chuckle.

"I have no clue, honestly; but they don't seem inclined to wait you out, fella. If you surrender yourself to me, I will do my best to keep you alive, and that way we don't risk losing another state landmark."

"Yeah, sorry about the church. Holy ground is about the only thing that will keep 'em at bay right now," said Ron as he carefully took a piece of glass to see if he could spot the person speaking.

"Right, listen, you need to do what I say," Sgt. Burke continued. "I have five more minutes to get you out, and then these folks are going to bring their full weight to bear. I would say this is your best chance."

There was the sound of shuffling from within the Church, and the deep voice called back to him.

"Yeah, honestly, that's not going to happen. They would take me away from you as soon as I came out. I'm tossing you a note."

An object was gently rolled across the frozen grass, landing near Sgt. Burke's feet. It was a water bottle with a note taped around it. Trepidatiously, the sergeant crouched and gave it a look.

> *They are vampires and their minions*
> *The town is full of them right now and not certain why*
> *You need to go home get your family and get out of town*
> *I am going to try to keep them here until daybreak*
> *Thanks for trying*
> *God bless.*

Sgt. Burke reread the note then stuffed it into his jacket. For a brief instant, the police officer and the old man caught a glimpse of each other. Burke nodded once. Ron nodded as well, disappearing back behind the craggy stone wall.

For the audience behind him, Burke spoke loudly.

"Yeah, sorry, you get no helicopter, no money, and I'm fairly certain this is not going to go well for you. Please come out! Last chance! Please!"

"Time's up, sergeant," Captain Lambert called out from behind Sgt. Burke.

Sgt. Burke shook his head, and in front of himself where it could not readily be seen, he gave the church a thumbs up.

With that, he turned and walked back. When he arrived at the vehicles, Sgt. Burked noticed that two of his officers had decided to "assist" the LorenCo forces. He addressed his remaining two officers.

"Holly, Martin. This is no longer our operation. Grab your gear, your cars, and let's head back to the shop." The two police traded confused and angry looks, but a few minutes later, Burke and his officers were shrinking in the distance.

Ron watched them disappear from the window of the church.

"Looks like it's just us, now!" he shouted.

"Looks like!" said Lambert, now showing a lot of fang.

Captain Lambert gave the church a malicious grin, as he pumped a CN tear gas grenade–a type notorious for starting fires–into the building.

Shhhakooompf. POOF! Shhhhhhh.

At that point, the security force surrounded the building and poured a torrent of rounds into the shattered windows, filling the church with bullets, tear gas, flash bangs, and smoke grenades, a Vietnam battle in a box. Parts of the building were already starting to ignite, and the rounds bounced off the field stones inside like maddened hornets.

Ron scurried up to the roof where a small wooden alcove awaited him and positioned himself down by a small vent. In his mind, he prayed for dawn to come, but smoke had already begun to spill around him, building firelight faintly dancing among the surrounding trees. The roof was a bad place to be, but the pinball machine of bullets bouncing below was worse. Through the vent, he spotted something behind the security force.

Near one of the vehicles, he saw a tiny man with a red hat making motions with his hands, possibly imitating a moose or a reindeer. Ron shook his head. The gas was making him hallucinate. He looked again, and still the little man went through the same gestures, pointing to the left side of the church.

Ron looked behind him to see the roof sag where the beams below weakened, the building now fully engulfed. If he was going to move, this would be his final chance. With a steadying breath, he took a running leap, and landed in an area that was still untouched. Picking up a burning chair, he threw it out one of the side windows, and due to the barrage gun fire earlier, the chair sailed through with little effort. Ron clenched his fists and followed it.

He landed outside on the snowy field, and two of the security team immediately spotted him.

Just as they swung their rifles to target him across the fields, there came an immense herd of deer. As they bounced and rolled toward the mass of cars, the bucks with heftiest antlers wasted no time attacking the humans with guns. The herd flew by, and having jumped to his feet, Ron sprinted alongside them.

Captain Lambert heard the crash of the chair going through the window. Furious, he rounded the corner and saw the fast-moving herd of deer streaming by. He knew that his target was amongst them but was unable to spot him in the fray. With a cry, he ran forward, his assault rifle blazing.

Ron was almost off the church property, running toward the rising sun, when two of the deer around him went down kicking and screaming. Two more high velocity bullets tore through him next, prompting Ron to spin, and empty his revolver at Captain Lambert. The creature gave an unholy shriek when the blessed, silver frangible rounds hit him. However, the frenzied vampire ignored the burning holes in his thigh and arm as he ran towards the Santa. Ron lurched and toppled behind one of the snow-capped gravestones.

Lambert limped laboriously as he came around to rip the throat out of the man. A steadying hand placed on the nearby stone, he picked Ron up. As the vampire did so, he started to smoke.

Ron chuckled in gasping pain.

"Hey, dummy. Graveyards are consecrated ground, too."

The hyena-like vampire moved forward and stuck a clawed hand deep under the big man's rib cage, lifting him up off his feet. But as his head lolled back, the captive produced something small and round that glinted softly in the light of the burning church. It was a light bulb filled with holy water. Ron slammed it home, catching him full in the face. The vampire Lambert went to his knees, clawing at his face, screaming.

"Merry Christmas!" gasped the bearded man. "Sorry I didn't have time to wrap it." Slumped against a gravestone, he spat, "Good luck finding your way home, blind, as the sun rises." The big man laughed, coughed, and crumpled.

The vampire struggled to its feet, smoking, and stumbled out of the tiny graveyard. As it did, it heard screaming behind him, both human and otherwise.

Something incredibly strong snatched the vampire by the ankle, and a few seconds later, Lambert was lying on the ground, staked, a shard of deer antler through his chest. Captain Lambert was paralyzed and unable to move, as were several of his men.

As the sun started to rise, though paralyzed, Lambert could see two small creatures, with the appearance of little men in red caps, sadly trying to help the wounded deer rise and leave.

One of them walked over to watch as Lambert's body disintegrated in the morning sun, watching the process dispassionately. The Nisse may not have cared about the church all that much, nor the mortal they had been summoned to help, but the deer were children of the woods. And about them, the Nisse cared very much indeed.

* * *

30. Rough Morning

Without knowing why, Abe knew Ron was dead. The sun was up, and Jon had just joined them. The four men all looked exhausted.

Rick handed him a cup of coffee and a piece of toast. Abe took the drink but set the toast down. No, Abe did not feel much like eating.

"They caught Top. So, anything he had on him, like our radios? They're compromised. I don't know if he's still alive, but there was a gigantic son-of-bitch, who I swear I've seen before someplace," said Jon.

"Damn. I think I handed Top one of my company cards," Rick said and winced.

"Yeah, you did," said Abe.

Pastor Carl looked old and fragile. He started a small prayer, and the four remaining men bowed their heads for a moment, praying together in the early morning light. The day before Christmas had begun, and the sound of a waking city rose in the background. After he finished, the pastor poured some coffee for himself.

"I had to sleep for a few hours. I kind of wish I hadn't. I had some dreams, visions almost. There was some wretched creature doing horrible things to a family. Some sort of dark ritual. And I caught a glimpse of a herd of deer, and Ron was with them, which was part of my protection prayer for him. I am hoping he got out of that situation."

"I'm sorry, Pastor. I think I felt him... pass on," Abe said with a crack in his voice.

All the men looked at Abe, started to form their questions, and each decided against it.

"Well, part of our special gear is back there, at that truck stop," Jon sighed. "I don't have the keys to Top's trailer or truck anyway. Let's hope it'll be okay. Aside from the fact that we need to find Top and get him back as quickly as possible, he was our tech guru. He's also the only one of us that doesn't look like Santa right now."

Rick surveyed his desk in the RV.

"I have my computer and a dedicated and encrypted satellite phone. I can get us online with HQ. Since it's a sat phone, I don't think anyone'll be able to trace it very easily."

"Okay, that's good news," Jon said and gave him a weary smile. "A lucky break for us. Let's get them on the horn and see if we can get some help out here. Give them a report on what's going on."

Morozko stood up and stretched. He walked to the front of the RV and said something in Russian to his dogs. Once he had let them outside, he left the door slightly ajar. The air whistled in, crisp and cold, and it smelled like the fresh cut pine trees in the tented Christmas lot nearby.

"I am going to go outside, maybe talk to a friend or two. I will be back in one hour or so. Is okay?"

Jon nodded, handing Morozko one of the burner phones Top had been setting up, and wrote down some numbers on a card.

"Call if you have problems, then ditch the phone."

Morozko took it, offered Jon a pat on the shoulder, and headed out toward the shopping center.

A rhythmic beeping caught Rick's attention. He sat down at his desk, flipped open his laptop, and yanked the head off a Santa and Rudolph statue, plugging it into the computer.

A few minutes and several encrypted websites later, Rudolph's nose glowed green, and a video call popped on screen. It was Santa Kyle.

"Greetings, gentlemen. I'm kinda surprised to be hearing from you."

Rick got out of the chair, giving it over to Jon.

"How so?"

"Word was that an ice storm came through your way, took out most of the phones and such."

"Nope. The weather has been a bit rough, but no ice storms. There's a big one on the way, though."

"Then I guess somebody has been knocking out communications around LaMoure. Bring me up to date."

As Jon recounted the evening and their best guess at everyone's status, Kyle took notes and asked a few clarifying questions.

"Well, there's no doubt that we'll be pulling out the stops to get you guys some help up there. If we have one member down, one captured, and the town is full of vampires, then we need to act fast. But then again you are out in the middle of nowhere, and it's the day before Christmas...." Kyle opened his hands in a gesture of "what now?"

Jon started to say something, but Kyle cut him off.

"I'm not saying I don't have members who would leave their Santa chairs to help you, far from it. If Ron is down and Top is in the hands of the enemy, you couldn't stop them from heading your way. I honestly don't know what other resources the Order can send your way."

Kyle looked away from the video camera, examining another monitor. He called out over his shoulder, to another room out of view.

"Sweetie, can you help me here?"

Freckles came into view, drying her bright red hair. She waved at the camera briefly.

"Hey guys!" Freckles leaned over at the second monitor off to the side. "Dad, that means you have someone who wants to join your conversation. It's the Knight Commander."

"Well, heck yeah, bring her in! Some help?"

Freckles took the back of her Dad's chair and bodily pushed him out the way, then leaned over and started typing quickly, which was a sight that did improve the morale of the team a bit. She stood up and nudged her dad's chair to wheel back into place.

"Here you go, tap that. Just so you know, two of these connections are being bounced off satellite, so you could lose them at any moment."

Another screen opened up on the laptop in the RV, showing an intense looking woman with graying auburn hair and sharp blue-green eyes. Her face had a deep tan and the squint of someone who spent a lot of time outdoors.

"Honori gloriaeque Nominis."

"Et mei et ordinis nostri," Jon responded back. "Good to see you, Commander Lira." The commander nodded at the video camera.

"Kyle, go ahead and just read out that report you were going to send me, then send it anyway. Jon, take notes if you would, see if there's anything important you want to add."

Kyle read back the report and Jon chimed in with some small additions. When they were done, the Commander cocked her head and looked at the camera curiously.

"Pastor Carl, deer? That was your invocation?"

Pastor Carl leaned into view of the camera with a pleased look.

"One of our Catholic brethren recommended the *Fáed Fíada*, also known as the Breast Plate or Lorica of St. Patrick. It was also called 'The Deer's Cry.' Legend has it that Patrick used it to disguise himself and his followers as deer to get him out of enemy territory. I figured it was worth a shot, but I had no idea it would summon deer. I thought it might just protect him, making him look like one and offering him a little protection. My Latin isn't as good as it could be. My sincere apologies."

"I don't think my little friends, the Nisse, are going to be very happy with what happened to the deer," Jon said to Carl. "I think we will need to make some amends on this one."

"If we get through this," Pastor Carl replied, "I will happily pay for a few truckloads of hay and feed and some salt licks, delivered to wherever they want. We could even plant some apple trees for them."

Lira, Knight Commander of the Winter Order, checked her notes and addressed the video conference again.

"Pastor Carl, Top was sworn to the Caestus. You should be able to track him through your bond. No luck?"

"I tried. I started the minute I heard he was taken. I was scrying, but I could only sense him for about ten minutes and then he was gone. By that, I mean something blocked my connection. To sever a connection that strong, I'm assuming it was magic with intention."

She made a note, and then looked back up at the camera.

"Abe, could you lean into the camera view, please?"

Lira's tiny image on the screen smiled somberly as Abe squeezed in near the laptop.

"Abraham, I wanted to welcome you to the Order of Nikolai Thaumaturgus, also known as the Winter Order, and tell you that we are glad to have you. But I have to admit that while most missions are rough, but you have certainly found us a doozy."

"My biggest thanks, Ma'am. To everyone else, too."

"The fact that the sword Illuminator has come to you is indicative of the strength of your belief. It's a great honor to carry it, so do try to conduct yourself in a worthy manner."

"I'll do my best."

The woman turned to check something off screen, and then faced her camera again.

"Caestus, hang on a minute while Kyle and I speak with a few others. Keep the line open."

Abe stood up again to look at the others.

"The Commander of the Order is a woman? She looks like she would be a tough Mrs. Claus. I'm guessing she's a career military type?"

"Oh yeah," Jon laughed. "A while ago, there was a big problem in Belgium, and she was one of the U.S. officers attached to a NATO mission. It turned out to be a lot more outlandish than any of the mundanes ever wanted to deal with, so the Order helped them out.

"She heard the call kind of like you did, Abe. Now, she's in charge of our strategic operations. The Abbot is our spiritual head, but we've had a few Abbesses over the centuries as well. The fact that she's involved means we have their full attention, I think."

There was a tap at the door followed by Morozko climbing back inside, along with two damp but very happy dogs. He gave an awkward hug to Abe.

"Your friend, Ron, is no more. I am sorry. I have friend of a friend who says he gave them hell out at the old church. Maybe four vampires, many ghouls, and two bad police dead, maybe more.

"Police have picture of your truck, Jon. Good thing is out here, your truck model is very popular. Bad news, your front grill is bent and town is not so big. Also, funny thing: all LorenCo trucks, cars, all driving around town conducting business. Something big, no one is quite certain what is happening, not sure where."

The computer connection chimed and the picture reappeared. Kyle and the Knight Commander looked out. Her eyebrows shot up as she spotted Morozko.

"*Privetstviye, kapitan. Kto zakazal sumasshedshego Deda Moroza?*" she said, laughing.

"Crazy Father Christmas, am I, hmm? What can I say, I knew I was going somewhere, I was only hoping for someplace a little nicer. Nice to see you too, Commander." He gave her the same summary he just gave the men.

"Damn," she said. "I was hoping I could bind a second Caestus around Brother Ron. He was one of our best, and we will be praying for him tonight." She switched to screensharing, and several photos came up on Rick's laptop.

"Do any of you recognize any of these?"

The men leaned over to scrutinize the photos, despite their poor quality.

Jon pointed to several.

"I saw the one in the top right in a car, and that bigger guy with the long hair, upper left? That's the one that grabbed Top."

Abe and Rick both recognized one, and Morozko pointed out three more.

The Commander sighed and rubbed her face.

"I'll send dossiers to you for review. You didn't pick out Duke Cosimo Florentine, Lord of all the Vampiric Houses, but you have recognized enough to prove we have at least five houses involved there. If that is the case, it's all but assured he's there as well. What's worse is that the crusty brute is Gilles de Montmorency-Laval, Baron de Rais. A truly twisted, evil knight, pedophile, devil-worshiper, and sorcerer, we're fairly certain he hails from around the 14th century. He is Cosimo's pet monster, and one of the scariest creatures we've ever encountered. When vampires step out of line, this is the bogeyman that Florentine sends to deal with them. It's no wonder Top had problems with him.

"As you probably already figured out, something truly momentous is going down in your neck of the woods, and your team is going to have to find out what that is and stick a wrench in it.

"I will have our magisters here start working on divinations and prayers of protection for your team. I can put word out to get whomever we can headed in your direction, but I don't really see any point in sending in non-Order assets at this time, as it sounds like they own the local law enforcement.

"That said, I do know of an ally or two who might be able to help. Possibly... hmm, maybe one civilian could be of use to you, but we don't need to mention the words vampire or magic to him."

"Any idea of what the Vampiric Houses might be up to?" Jon queried.

"My money is on a big magical ritual of some sort. Why else be out in North Dakota on Christmas Eve? It's not like the House of Measures is lacking in money, or the House of Wheels are lacking in places to hunt."

"Our Caestus will do what we can to mess with their plans," Jon said with a thumbs up at the camera. "I'm going to have my team sleep for a few hours while we have some sun, then we can find out what they've got cooking. For now, let's assume that this computer we're on isn't compromised. I'll have Abe give Freckles all the numbers for the phones, so we can communicate out in the field on a limited basis."

"I'll see if I can get the Santas at the malls in your town to get the hell out of dodge," Kyle volunteered. "Right now, I'm going to figure out how to pull together another Caestus, somehow, some way."

"Jon, do you have any more Fay friends you can ask favors from?" the Commander asked.

"No. Wait, well... none that I think would be able to get here in time. I do have a small flying fairie who is helpful, but she's a bit scary. Why?"

"Well, if she can open a Way, you could probably get Ilbereth there for a moment or two on Christmas Eve, if we can make a case for you. Get some sleep and promise what you have to. Ilbereth isn't a combat specialist, but he's well versed in some useful skills. Good luck, and may God and St. Nicholas protect you."

"Likewise, Commander. Abe, can you read these phone numbers off to Freckles?" Jon relinquished the desk to Abe and slouched into the RV couch.

Abe wrapped up the details for Freckles and turned around when the video screen closed out.

"Who's Ilbereth?" Abe asked Jon.

"You like *Lord of the Rings*?" Jon chuckled.

"Sure."

"Lord Tolkien was a bit of a savant. He wrote about the North Pole and Father Christmas in letters to his kids. In the letters, he mentions an elf who helps Santa named Ilbereth, who was one of the Elves who is known to us in the Order, as coincidence would have it. Maybe J.R.R. had some connections."

"Oh. Is Ilbereth a bad ass like Legolas?"

"I have no idea, but I'd take a willing Fay's help anytime I can get it. Because of the compact, we can ask for their help with relative safety.

"Now you crash for ninety minutes, Abe. We need to go find the bad guys and rescue Top, if we're able. A little sleep is better than no sleep at all."

"Yessir."

* * *

The city of LaMoure, North Dakota bustled with a vengeance. People fled the town hoping to make it out of the city and to destinations further on, such as Billings or Bismarck, before the expected storm came in and blocked the roads for days to come.

Many of the newer residents wore looks of fear and concern, having heard that winter storms in North Dakota were serious business. Shopping carts were packed full of extra supplies, alongside hasty last-minute Christmas presents. Lines were abysmally long. There was sparse news about the drunk man who fought with the police on the edge of the town. An observant few noticed more jets flying in with passing interest. LaMoure had recently acquired both a renovated airport for the commercial flights and new private runways, much larger than those belonging to other cities of equitable size. People watched the increased air traffic and smiled. LaMoure was an unexpected happening boom town.

Abe was dreaming fitfully, a towel draped over his face.

He found himself in oppressive darkness. It was cold and damp, and it looked like it had been devoid of life for a very long time. Abe spotted a glimmer of light far in the recesses of the void. The cold chilled him like nothing he had felt before. The luster drew him closer and closer and there, within a faint circle of light, curled up in the darkness, he found a young girl. The light was coming from a bundle of reeds held by an older indigenous woman, all wrapped in a buffalo robe. The elder looked up at him as he came forward and stopped him by holding up a finger.

"This little one is quite lost. She has been badly used by those who the sky will not accept. She thinks it was your doing, feels very pained that she was tricked, that her family was hurt because of it. She is a daughter of my many daughters, and so she found her way here."

Abe bowed his head, not knowing what else to do.

"What do you want me to do?" Abe answered with his head bowed.

The old woman adjusted her robe and blew on the bundle.

"Ask her."

Abe got down on one knee, just within the light.

"Hey, there."

The girl looked over her knee, then cringed. Something in the way she recoiled made part of Abe's soul twist. He had forgotten that he looked like Santa.

"Hi. You look very sad. What can I do to help you?"

In answer, the little girl hesitantly held out a hand, still refusing to look at him. Abe gently reached out to touch it. As he did, a wave of raw fear, incomprehensible horror, and violent pain swept over him, as what the Baron had done to her and her family flowed into him. Abe sank to the floor, crossed his legs, but did not let go of her hand. Eventually the images stopped, but every word, every emotion, every image, everything was engraved in his memory. Tears burned down his face. Abe took a deep breath and gently let go of her hand to stand up.

He turned to the old woman, barely able to meet her eyes for more than a moment.

"Can you help me find her house?"

The old woman looked down at the little girl.

"She can. If she gets lost, look to the birds."

Abe bent down again and spoke to the little girl.

"What should I call you?"

"Trish."

"Trish, if I can get us back to the town, can you show me where your family lives?"

She stood up and wiped her face.

"Yes."

The old woman bent down and tied something around Trish's neck.

"Little one. You were brave to have come all this way. You must be brave a little while longer. Know that you are always welcome here."

The little girl gave the old woman a hug, and for the briefest of moments, the darkness receded.

"You're the good one, right?" Trish asked Abe.

Abe held out his hand.

"Trish, I don't think your friend would let me come anywhere near you if I wasn't."

The old woman gave him a raised eyebrow but said nothing. Soon, the little girl had Abe by the hand, and he felt the two of them rushing back towards the world.

Abe abruptly sat up in the RV, his face bathed in sweat and tears.

He looked around the RV. Rick, Jon, and Pastor Carl were all still fast asleep. Quietly, he grabbed his jacket and his new Christmas stocking. He jotted a message on a sticky note and attached it to the door. Letting himself out quickly, he squinted in the gray-white sun. Sitting in a lawn chair was the Russian, beard hidden under a scarf. Morozko's dogs were watching Abe intently. Morozko lifted up the brim of his hat to also study Abe.

"You need to do something."

"Right away."

The older man reached into his coat pocket and tossed Abe some keys.

"Down at end of lot is plumbing truck, it says 'Ryan Plumbing.' If you are lucky, it will start. Come back soon, we will leave in afternoon."

Abe ran down the parking lot.

* * *

31. Long Night, Longer Day

Abe was not familiar with these housing tracks.

"Slow down, you're going too fast," said the young girl's voice in his ear.

Abe slowed, and after many turns and accidental circles, he heard the voice of Trish again.

"That's Maggie's, I got to go on an overnight at her house. Go up there and go... left." Abe almost zoomed past the turn, forcing him to crank the wheel sideways. He was halfway down the street, when suddenly he saw police lights in his rearview mirror.

Abe's heart sank. He had been caught in a truck that did not belong to him, and in a town where the cops were owned by vampires. Fumbling in his coat pocket, he withdrew the .45 caliber pistol, then proceeded to stuff it under a blanket of food wrappers on the truck's ratty bench seat. Once he had eased to a stop on the shoulder, he rolled down the window and waited for the police officer to walk up.

The officer had one hand casually on his hip as he craned down to take inventory of the driver and the inside of the truck.

"Afternoon, Santa. Took that turn a bit harder than you intended, I think. Have we been hitting the eggnog a little hard today? You have a busy night ahead, y'know."

"I do indeed have a busy night tonight," Abe replied and gave him a jovial smile.

The officer got a bit closer and looked around the inside of the cab.

"Santa, I've seen you at the other mall, haven't I? Not the big one, the Fairfield, I think."

"You'd be correct. Did you bring your kids there? If so, I hope the photos came out okay."

The officer stepped forward to look at something out of Abe's view, then stepped back again.

"My sister's kids, actually. They loved you. They think you're the real deal."

"Thanks."

The officer looked around to see if there was anybody paying close attention. Suddenly, there was a gun in his hand.

"Santa, you want to tell me why you're driving Pat Ryan's truck? And why I can see the empty holster in your jacket?"

The officer had done a good job of distracting Abe while he had armed himself, now having him dead to rights.

Abe's smile became very forced.

"If I tell you, you are not going to believe me."

"Go on." The officer never wavered.

"A little girl's family has been attacked by vampires. Some of them are still alive, I think. The vampires have already done some heinous stuff, I've been told, and I only have a very short time to rescue them, if I can." Abe took a deep breath and opened his hands, keeping them flushed with the steering wheel. As he rotated his hand, the Caestus symbol became visible.

Ever so slowly, the officer took his own pistol and put it back into his holster.

"My name is Sgt. Burke. Believe me, if this had happened a few days ago, this all woulda gone down a whole lot different. But, recently, I seen some things that I can't explain for the life of me. If it's okay with you, I think I should go with you. I've never been as unsure of what to do as I am right now, but I know evil when I see it. If those sons-a-bitches take over this town, as a lawman, that'll be on my head. Monsters, no monsters, I'm not just going to let Santa go fight some vampires without backup, not if I can help it."

"You believe me?" Abe's eyes were wide with disbelief.

Sgt. Burke nodded sadly.

"Yup. Sorry to say, I don't think I can get on the horn to ask for any backup, if you know what I mean."

Abe gave him a relieved smile.

"Yeah. Here's the thing, I have about thirty minutes to deal with this and then I have to go."

The sergeant phoned in something about going on break over his radio.

"Why, you have some official Santa business you have to attend to?"

"You could say that."

"I'll follow you, then."

And with that, the two of them drove a few more blocks, and then he heard Trish.

"That's my house. They have all the curtains closed."

Abe parked up the street a bit. As he sat and looked at what should have been a cozy, nondescript suburban home, he swallowed hard, reliving the memories he had inherited from Trish. He had a general idea of the layout of the house, but not where everyone was. And while had an idea to find out, it involved asking questions he would have rather avoided. Still, lives might be on the line.

"Trish, can I ask a favor?"

"Sure."

"I need to know where everyone is inside your house. Where the bad people are, and any of your family. It will be really hard for you to see all this again."

In Abe's mind, he heard Trish sob a tiny bit.

"I know. I'll be right back."

Abe got out of the truck, and Sgt. Burke walked up, holding out an extra police jacket. Abe looked down at it.

"Sorry, I don't think it's going to fit."

Burke chuckled darkly, lifted a sleeve to reveal a 12-gauge police shotgun and ammo belt.

"I like to think that this is exactly the right present for you."

"No, I'm more comfortable with my pistol. It has silver rounds in it, which will mess up vampires."

Burke gave him a concerned look.

"Real silver rounds? Yeah, not standard police issue, I'm afraid. I have a deer rifle in the trunk, some 12-gauge slugs. Will those do the trick?"

Abe shook his head. Only a few days, and now he was the resident expert on vampires.

"Uh, don't worry about the rifle. As I understand it, vampires have a really hard time moving in daylight. They can, but not too much." He studied the house from a distance.

"They give their blood to their human servants, though, and that blood makes their workers really tough and fast. They call them ghouls, and they don't have as much of a problem being up in the daytime. Use the shotgun, and if it bleeds normal, hit it hard. If it doesn't, hit it twice as hard, and do not stop. Head shots."

"That explains a few things. By the way, I was out there at the church, when your tall Santa went up against the LorenCo folks. Your buddy gave 'em hell. Okay, give me a minute, I'll be right back." The sergeant went back to his squad car.

While he was gone, Abe heard the voice of Trish again.

"They have Mommy and my brother and sister in my room. My mommy is acting weird. I think she gave a lot of cough medicine to my brother and sister. There are four people in the house. One is sleeping in Mommy and Daddy's room, two are in the kitchen, and one is taking a shower in my mom's bathroom."

Trish's voice trailed off.

"I looked in the garage." Her voice sounded very thin, and Abe heard Trish start to cry.

"Trish, you never have to go in there again." Abe mentally said a small prayer to St. Nicholas.

Abe had the distinct feeling something was watching them intently, but his panic receded marginally when he looked up to see a large raven sitting on the nearby telephone pole.

"Trish, why don't you go over to that pole over there, stay out of the house, and keep an eye on things for us."

"Okay."

Sgt. Burke returned, now wearing a few extra pieces of tactical gear.

"What's the plan?"

Abe drew a rough layout in the dirty snow, pointing out to him where he thought everyone was.

"And you know this how?" asked Sgt. Burke. "Wait, don't tell me. It's that 'Naughty or Nice' thing?"

Abe chuckled and then it occurred to him. Yes, he actually did have a general sense about that.

"Okay. I take the front door," said Sgt. Burke, "and you go in through the back. I'll deal with the ones in the kitchen, and you head straight down the back hallway. I'm guessing the one in the bed is the vampire, and you have the magic bullets. If you hear my whistle, give it a one, two, breach on three."

"Mind if I say a short prayer first?" Abe asked.

Burke fished a medallion out from under his tactical vest.

"I don't mind at all, but no offense, Nick, I'm asking for help from St. Michael."

Together, they prayed in silence. As he finished mouthing the words, Burke stuffed his medallion back under his vest. Sgt. Burke laughed poignantly as he prepped his shotgun.

"On my list of things to do today, I did not have 'Kill Vampires with Santa.'"

Abe smiled and pulled on the two metal gauntlets he had been given. Burke's eyebrows went up, but he said nothing.

"Yeah. Until recently, my Christmas plans were really different, too," Abe admitted.

The two of them looked at each other and headed towards the house.

The crunch of the snow underfoot threatened to give the men away more than once, but by some divine providence, the two soon found themselves at their respective doors. Abe heard the *wheet* of a whistle and counted to three. The back door opened easily in Abe's hand, not so, the front door. Abe heard Sgt. Burke yell, "Freeze! Police!" followed by gunfire. Abe immediately stepped through the laundry room and saw a trail of blood on the stained carpet that led to the living room. There was more gunfire, and Abe caught a brief glimpse of Burke as he flew past him towards the dining room. Abe headed down the hallway, going the opposite direction.

Abe was halfway down the hall when a door suddenly flew open, and a surprised looking man wearing nothing but a towel stepped out, gun in hand.

Abe continued charging forward, firing as he did so. The man looked down at the three smoking holes in his chest with even more surprise and fell.

With barely a moment to react, the woman on the bed sprung up in a whirl of fangs and claws. There was a sudden flash, and her head flew across the room, finally rolling to a stop on top of a dresser.

Having heard a scuff behind him, Abe spun, nearly impaling Sgt. Burke on the great sword. The room was filled with a soft light coming from Abe. It took a second to register, but Abe had drawn the sword and decapitated the vampire in one fluid motion. Sgt. Burke backed away.

"Woah! Serious pigsticker you have there, Santa!"

"The other two?"

"Down. Wouldn't you know it, they both went for their guns."

"Were either of them... different?"

"I don't know, I was kind of busy. I shot them both in the head." His eyes flicked over to the woman's head on the dresser. "Yikes. Those are some teeth."

Abe found a hand towel, wiped the sword down, and carefully stowed Illuminator back in its stocking. Sgt. Burke took a moment to check the garage, returning soon after. His face was grim.

"Yeah, clear. Some victims."

Abe walked over by the door that was labeled Trish! in bright colors. A woman inside was curled up with her two children, dazed and confused. Abe looked over at Sgt. Burke. He had no idea what to do at this point.

"Sergeant?"

Burke did a quick calculation.

"I only have one or two people on the force I still trust. I don't think calling this in is a good idea at this point. Anybody on the force could have a hand in this."

"And the vampires and friends will be coming back here soon, I think. We should get Mom and the kids out of here, probably grab them some clothes, and maybe some of the presents under the tree." He paused for a moment. "Do you know any elders on the reservation you trust? I think this family is part Native American."

"I do, in fact. Good idea." Burke's jaw was set and his eyes haunted. "I'll take care of this and get them out of here to somewhere safe. Good luck, Santa."

Abe handed him his .45, with two extra clips of silver bullets.

"Here's an early present, share the love if you need to. Good luck to you, too, Sgt. Burke. Once you're done here, I suggest you get you and your loved ones as far out of town as possible."

Sgt. Burke took the 45. "Thank you. But I already did that. My family is headed to Minneapolis, as we speak. I had to come back."

Abe looked at him, nodded, and then left. As Abe got into the truck, he called out.

"Trish?" A moment later he heard her voice.

"Yes?"

"Trish, thank you for all your help. Can you go with your Mom and your brother and sister? That is, if you want. If you have any more problems, come find me."

"Okay, Santa. Are the bad men gone?"

"Yeah, but there are other bad people out there, so Santa is going to go deal with them."

"Okay. Love you, Santa."

"Love you, too, Trish. God bless you."

Abe was unsure quite how he knew, but she was gone. As Abe drove back to the others, a stream of salty tears ran down his cheeks.

Walking back to the RV from the borrowed plumbing truck, Abe could hear the air ringing with Christmas music. But now, the beat of the drums and whistling of flutes sounded like a clear call to battle. Abe dashed away the last of his tears, said a prayer of thanks to St. Nicholas, the protector of children, and asked him to keep an eye on Trish and her family.

Climbing back into the RV, Jon stepped up, ready to give Abe an earful. When he saw the look on Abe's face, however, he stopped pre-rant, turned around, and brought back a cup of tea.

"When you're ready, Abe."

* * *

32. All About the Presentation

The LorenCo Vice President of Operations stood at the door alongside a security officer and looked at the man who had been bound and gagged, stripped to his underwear, then summarily tossed inside a vacant, windowless room. With a plain wooden desk and two faux leather chairs, it could have been mistaken for a bureaucrat's office, save for the partially nude man lying still on the floor.

"Can you rouse him? I would like to have him interrogated before all the kindred wake up."

"We tried," answered the dark clad security officer, "but from the bruises on his face, he's already been slapped around pretty good. He'll be lucky if he doesn't have serious brain damage. We're looking for a doctor to check on him, but everyone we call tells us to take him to the ER."

Vice President Fenley gave the security man a look of irritation and eyed the two gray uniformed guards standing outside the door as well.

"We can't very well interrogate people if you beat them senseless, now can we?"

The senior security officer re-slung his assault weapon meaningfully.

"First of all, it wasn't *my* men who roughed him up. It was de Rais, and that was when he personally caught this man. You want to bitch, feel free to take it up with the Baron, by all means. Secondly, I believe you were at home sleeping when all this hell broke loose. It was the House of Swords that dealt with this mess, and you can take that up with my boss any time you like."

Fenley stood his ground, slowly and visibly sizing up the bigger man.

"Rest assured, Mr. Florentine will be made aware of *all* the details when I speak with him this evening."

The two held their face off a moment longer, but Fenley broke eye contact first to look at the man on the floor again.

"The *minute* he wakes up, contact me." Fenley stalked off with his security. One of the two door guards reached in and closed the door firmly.

After a moment, the man lying on the floor cracked an eye open. Having determined he was alone, he placed his back against the wall and let out a ragged sigh. Top took a deep breath, and with a sickening pop, he dislocated his shoulder, bringing his hands around to his face. With a practiced crunch, he pushed his arm back into its socket, grimacing as the waves of pain rolled over him. Once sensation returned to his fingers, he ran them through his hair, seeking a small plastic lock-pick that they had failed to remove. A short time later, the handcuffs clanked to the floor.

He examined himself carefully, wincing as he soothed his badly battered cheek and jaw, which were possibly broken. Moving quietly, Top searched the room. Finally, a little luck. The room had been just another office, in a row of offices. Climbing up on the desk, Top found a place where he could jostle a group of ceiling tiles, and he did just that. Sure to collect the gag, tape, and handcuffs before making his exit, he pushed the chair away from the side of the wall, making it look as though he had just disappeared. Once he was secure resting overhead, he returned the ceiling tiles to their original positions.

Moving carefully across the wall partition above the false room, Top quietly shimmied to an adjacent room. It contained a latched window and several cubicles for what appeared to be the offices for the North Dakota Boomers, the new LaMoure franchise B-list hockey team. Making every effort at stealth, Top soon found himself with some marketing merchandise, including a pair of baggy sweats and a "Boomer" ball cap. Sadly, he could find no shoes. While the hat would allow him to create some illusions, he could not summon helpful items out of it like Rick could. With the help of a picture on one of the desks of someone he assumed was in management, he used the cap to cast the illusion on himself.

Top took a chance and peered out of the window. He could barely see two guards, neither of whom looked exceptionally aware. Probably locals, since an experienced mercenary would never leave a hostage unwatched. Top turned to look at the phones in the room, then consulted the list of extensions taped to the wall, along with a map. He knew exactly where he was now; practically everyone in this neck of the Midwest had followed the construction of the LorenCo sports arena.

Top lifted up the receiver on the phone, and the line lit up on the other phones too. Cursed quietly, he set it back down quickly. Looking at the display, it read 3:45 PM. Hell. Sunset was around 6 o'clock, and this was Christmas Eve. The vamps were going to be up and moving already. Top had to move. Hurriedly, he pilfered all the nearby desks, thankfully finding a few other useful items like tape and a boxcutter. Even better, after burgling a locked desk, he had a ring full of keys, handily labeled.

"Ho-ho!" He allowed himself a small smile, which hurt like hell.

Following a few moments of silent struggling, Top again found himself above the false ceiling. Still barefoot, he quietly made his way down around the curve, and lowered himself down into a room stacked with foam fingers and foam cowboy hats. When he landed, a cardboard cutout of the team's center almost gave him a heart attack. Peeking around the corner, he was far enough away from where he had started and so he made way down the wide corridor.

Top found a room labeled "Guest Relations." He rifled through his keys, and it looked like he was blessed with a little Santa luck. Here was a security desk, along with "Lost and Found." A few minutes in the wired cage, and now he had shoes, a jacket, and quite happily, an assortment of cell phones and confiscated weapons.

Top took a moment to bust up a wooden chair, to quickly fashion himself some stakes. Right before he made for the hallway, he stuffed a few more hats in his pockets, just in case. As Top walked back to the door, he heard the crackle of radios and the sound of running boots. He was pretty sure he knew why. He barely had time to flatten himself against a wall and hide as the door swung open. Top pulled his hat over his face, blending seamlessly with the room.

Two security guards marched in with guns drawn, searching. Over their earpieces, Top could hear a voice blasting instructions.

"...don't know, don't care. Supposedly he was with the Santas. For all we know, he could be one. I want this place searched top to bottom, and I want that little bastard found before the kindred wake up, which only gives us ten minutes. Not that I should have to repeat this, but for Chrissake, stay the hell out of Liberty Hall. Do not go in there! Understood? Team two, where are you?"

The two men finished their cursory search and darted back out. Top quickly changed his illusion to the likeness of one of the security guards he had seen earlier, following them out a few moments later. They headed one way, he went the other, and there he saw the service doors, surrounded by dozens of carts that lead to the production entrances of Liberty Hall.

Top stepped behind a column and surveyed the area. There were many guards, suited in both black and gray styles, and other various employees weaving through the area. He quickly pulled out one of his newly confiscated cell phones, created a text for the Caestus, and sent it out via their secure server.

> Top alive. In the new sports Arena. Tons of LorenCo Security. Something big going on in Liberty Hall. Vamps are going to wake up any minute. I am going to see if I can sneak a peek, then get out. This phone toast.

With that, he calmly removed the battery, pulled out a replacement phone, readied it, and then cast another illusion over himself to assume the guise of one Baron de Rais.

Top strutted with full confidence to the most heavily guarded doors, and people blanched, shuffling to get out of his way. As he stepped into Liberty Hall, a wave of energy almost made his knees buckle, and for a fraction of a second, his illusion wavered. What he saw took him a few seconds to comprehend. Against one wall, stacks of shipping containers were stacked high, with another batch piled opposite them, and all had all been painted with a Christmas theme. He quickly snapped some photos with one of his new-to-him phones.

The cavernous hall had itself been turned into a very intricate ritual staging ground, a stage floor carefully carved. On one side was a small structure, consisting of an overlapping circle and an X shape, restraints fixed at the furthest points. Nested in the larger circle was a smaller circle, complete with a Santa chair along with a beautifully decorated Christmas tree, but not a present to be seen. It looked rather lost and alone in the big room. At various points around the scene, robed figures chanted in a low, droning chorus. Top took a moment to snap more several photos and then hit send.

The false Baron looked up and in one corner, he spotted a few robed people in a glassed off VIP booth, clearly in the middle of some introductions to some obvious civilians. In ghastly silence, he saw the civilians start to scream as the vampires began to attack and devour them. Top tore his eyes away from the carnage. He had not been keeping track of the time.

Top started for the door, and again, he was waved through. Rounding the corner towards a downward loading dock, he was almost at the exterior door when he instinctively froze. A split second passed before he realized he had just passed the real Baron de Rais going the other way. The two of them did double takes.

"Hello, handsome," purred Baron de Rais from behind him. Top tried to walk away but felt himself being pinned by an arm over his shoulder. "My friend, I absolutely love your choice of characters. I scare myself, I am *so* good looking."

The real Baron de Rais reached over to reveal the stake that Top was trying to ready under his coat.

"Did you get me a stake for Christmas? You are sooo kind; but since you mortals are so fond of them, I simply must insist, you try one first." Gripping Top's hand, the Baron shoved the stake slowly up under Top's rib cage.

Top tried not to pass out from the pain.

"I... I... I'm... glad you approve. I'm glad to... sh... are...."

Baron de Rais smiled charmingly, showing just a hint of fang.

"Heh. You know, that always makes me laugh. Do you know how many times I have seen would-be vampire hunters use these to murder absolutely innocent people? Hundreds of times. It's hilarious, no?"

Baron de Rais twisted the stake and kept pushing. Top could only flail with his free hand, desperately clutching at his pockets.

"It's true, my little illusionist," said de Rais with a ghoulishly malevolent smile. "Stakes work just as well on humans as they do on vampires. Better, perhaps." This he said as the last traces of life fled from Top's eyes.

Once the man had gone limp, Baron de Rais casually tossed the body onto an electric flatbed cart, leaving a trail of blood splattering along its trajectory. He walked over to the security officers by the door as he licked the blood off his hand. The Baron recoiled, making a sour face.

"Ugh!" He turned to the officers. "You. Your problem has been resolved. Clean up the blood back there, have the body put someplace cool, but not freezing. Search it. Also, do not allow the ghoul crew eat it just yet. I may have a use for it later."

The security forces scrambled to do his bidding.

* * *

33. This Just In

Everybody jumped when there was a knock at the door of the RV. Jon peered out, spying a tall man with a hooded parka pulled up over his ball cap, Morozko standing close behind him. Jon waved his hand, and the group hurriedly stowed all their scarier items. Jon opened the door, and the stranger smiled and offered a hand, his voice a deep baritone.

"Hey there! Mike Spur, just call me Spur. A mutual friend contacted me, and she said you had some questions about some pipelines and such."

"Yes, indeed," Jon said as he returned the smile and shook his hand. "Welcome, Spur. You work with one of the companies in town?"

Spur flipped back the hood, revealing kind, brown eyes and a bone-deep tan.

"Yes and no. I'm a consultant for refineries and such." Spur nodded at Morozko, clearly they knew each other already. Spur continued.

"I was in Kyrgyzstan only a few weeks ago. I get around. Our mutual friend Commander Lira and I met when I was consulting on some safety issues a while ago. What can I help you with?"

Jon unfurled the map that Compass Rose had helped create.

"This map is going to be a little odd, but we saw a pattern here, and wondered if it corresponded with some of the local pipelines and such."

Pastor Carl offered Spur a cup of coffee, which he sipped and set away carefully, before leaning over the map.

"Alright, let's see what you've got here."

After a few moments, tilting his head one way and another, his eyebrows shot up. He lifted the paper and looked at it sideways, on the oblique.

"Okay, I have to say, whoever made this map has a very odd way of looking at the world." He pulled a large tablet from his satchel. "May I take a picture of this? I have an idea." Jon nodded at him to give permission.

Spur snapped some photos, then did some tweaking on the tablet screen. A few minutes later, he placed the tablet down on the table and called up an image.

"Here's your original map." He touched a few more buttons, frowned a moment, then adjusted it again. "Now, here's a map or three that I've just combined to save my own sanity." With two fingers he pulled the two images together.

"And here's where we overlay the two. Your mapmaker did an amazing job of figuring out where the underground piping is, as well as where most of the junctions the city and industrial piping meet."

He stood up straight again and nursed his coffee, taking in all the white beards in the room.

"I'd been brought in to consult on some problems with the plant, and I did. But, as I was getting to know the area, I realized that this city was pretty much built around, like literally around, a storage facility at the refinery. The whole area has an abundance of oil tanks, gas, LNG, and so on. The crazy part is, normally, industrial engineers work really hard to keep all these systems away from each other, as well as population centers. Look at your map."

Abe saw what looked to be a spoked pattern—part wheel, part snowflake.

"So, the city has a lot of pipes running through it? Under it?"

"Yup," Spur said and looked up soberly. "Until I saw this, I wasn't quite sure, but this is something else. Someone must have been paid off. I mean granted, this sort of stuff happens when you overlay an old system with a new system, and no one wants to pony up the money to retrofit the old one. Not the issue here."

Rick leaned over and moved the maps back and forth.

"Spur, what are these circles?"

Spur expanded the images.

"My guess is that they're pumping stations—junctions and switch valves—that sorta thing. My maps weren't real explicit."

"Can we get a copy of this?" Jon pointed to the overlay.

Spur took another sip of coffee.

"Make sure it never comes back to haunt me, sure. I had to fight to get what you see here."

Over the next few minutes, the two worked to transfer the contents to Jon's thumb drive.

"Here's the part I really don't get: This is North Dakota. Nothing but space. This town was pretty much just agricultural before the second wave of oil boomers arrived." Spur pointed at the maps. "Why the hell build a city on top of all this pipe if you have all the space in the world?"

"It probably wouldn't be a bad idea to find out where all this was being controlled from," Jon remarked. Spur grinned.

"That's the easy part. All their control systems are state of the art, fiber optic. And they have dual stations—one in a corporate office and a backup out by the LorenCo private retreat." He put the coffee down. "I get the feeling that something is rotten in Denmark, here?"

"Yeah," Jon said, looking him in the eye. "In fact, it'd probably be a good idea to get out of town before the storm hits."

Spur grabbed his hat and stood up.

"Well, that was my intention anyway. The managers I told about the problems I saw seemed otherwise occupied. They handed me a big ass check, and now I have a prop job waiting for me at the airport. With a little luck, day after tomorrow, I'll be drinking a margarita and watching the sunset from Redondo Beach." He shook hands all around and headed for the door. He stopped and turned back to the men.

"Depending on how you did it, you could probably flood most of the municipal systems here with natural gas. If that happened, I think this whole town would go up like a giant fuel-air bomb. Think… like a nuke. A good sized one. After that, a lot of nasty leftovers might be let out, like H2S, hydrogen disulfide, and other toxic substances." Spur stopped to make eye contact with them all.

"Be very, very careful, gentlemen. Merry Christmas."

With that, Spur stepped out onto the snow, walking away with purpose in his gait.

Jon's phone buzzed.

"It's a text from Top!" Jon said with a relieved smile.

Everyone cheered to hear he was still alive. By the time Jon had finished reading the text, all had begun to pack up for their rescue attempt.

The photos Top had taken poured in. Jon showed them around.

Carl looked at the one of Liberty Hall.

"That. That's what this is all about. They're planning a major league ritual of some sort."

They started to examine the other pictures, when they all felt an icy-cold, negative touch in their hearts. They all felt a member of their Caestus die. All of them staggered.

Jon slammed his fist down on the table.

"Dammit! Why the hell didn't he stay hidden?!"

Pastor Carl shook his head, resting a hand on the young man's shoulder.

"Jon, it wasn't in Top's nature. He was always curious. This info just gave us a big edge, and I think he took that risk for all our sakes. Let's take a moment and pray for him. I can light a candle as well."

Pastor Carl dropped his head, quietly delivered a prayer for their departed brother, every member concluding with an Amen.

For a long moment, no words were spoken. Jon broke the silence.

"Afterwards? After all this is done? We're going to have one mother of a blowout for Top."

The other members said nothing but stared into whatever was in their hands.

The four remaining members of the Caestus turned to look at Rick as his computer chimed again. Top's photos had finally been downloaded in full size.

"Guys, come check this out."

Jon and the rest gathered around Rick's screen. Pastor Carl pointed at the Christmas themed chair and to the X.

"I think I know what's going on now. They're going to summon Santa and capture him."

"Wait, what?" Abe asked with surprise written all over his face. "How is that even possible? The way Ron explained it, Santa doesn't even have a real body, right?"

Pastor Carl looked angry.

"Not certain, but," Carl said as he pointed at the screen, "I think they put a Santa in the chair, then summon the Spirit of Christmas. Once it joins the person there, they'll bind it."

"Probably Santa Steve, from the mall," Jon added.

"And so it is St. Nicholas, Father Frost, Santa Claus, all in one spirit they are going to capture?" asked Morozko.

"The Spirit of Christmas. I think it all overlaps on Christmas Eve," Pastor Carl said with a shrug, uncertain.

"This doesn't make sense," Abe exclaimed. "I mean, first of all, why? Why would a bunch of vampires want to kill Santa? Are they even powerful enough to do that? There are like, what, 570 million people believing in Santa right now?"

Pastor Carl studied the pictures further.

"That's true. That's a lot of power. Especially tonight, and for the next twenty-four hours or so. Some potent magical energy there. Maybe they aim to tap into that somehow?" Pastor Carl started scribbling some notes and symbols in a notebook.

Rick flicked back and forth within the series of photos when his face turned white.

"Uh, guys. What do you notice about the shipping containers?"

"The doors. The door openings," Morozko said as he leaned in.

"Right, they open from the inside," Rick finished. "Nobody there to open them from the outside."

"Motherf... hamster biscuits," Jon uttered. "Anybody got an idea how many coffins you can fit in one of those?"

"My guess is twenty-four in a twenty-foot container, if you are trying to keep them nice."

Everybody turned to look at him.

"What? I'm a pastor, I work with funeral homes all the time. Besides, that's only if they aren't stacking them, or just shoving them in dirt-lined boxes. You could fit a lot more vampires in there, then."

Morozko quickly counted shipping containers.

"So, what, a hundred and forty-four Vampires? *Baise-moi!*"

"We don't know that all of those are full of vampires," Jon argued. "It could be gear, could be ghouls. One hundred and forty vampires would be very hard to feed."

Abe felt a cold weight grow in the pit of his stomach.

"You mean like a whole sales convention of people?"

"Or whole city," Morozko added, "if you don't really care. We are out in the middle of nowhere to begin with."

Rick tapped a few keys and leaned back.

"I just sent this info to the Knight Commander. We'll see what she has to say, but at this point, I think our only option is to nuke the arena from orbit. It's the only way to be sure."

"That's not even funny," said Jon. Absently, he added, "Besides, even if we were to get a Mark 12A warhead from a Minuteman III out of Minot, it would weigh about 800 pounds, and lifting it from a hundred-foot-deep concrete bunker, then...."

All the other Santas were looking at him now, worry growing on their faces. Jon grimaced.

"Oh, sorry. Once a Jarhead, always a Jarhead."

The men exchanged glances. It was obvious each man was processing the gravity of the situation in their own way.

Abe had been sitting quietly when an idea struck him.

"I think I know why they have that makeshift X thing."

Pastor Carl looked up from his calculations.

"Yes?"

"Krampus. They're going to put Ron's street performer in the Krampus suit on it. They'll put Santa in the chair, and then Krampus on that cross thing. They're going to summon both of them."

"Okay, why?" Rick asked. "Summoning Krampus seems patently stupid. I mean, on top of summoning one of the holiest beings on the planet, an actual Saint, when you're a group of the undead."

"Power of some sort," Jon concluded. "With the vamps, it's always about power. I can't see them feeding on Santa. Any true-of-heart Santa is going to taste like peppermint and gasoline to them. That's why they don't bite us, or at least, not more than once."

Abe looked at the wooden X once more, then gestured to the St. Nicholas and Krampus illustration that Rick had framed in the RV.

"Krampus ain't a white light kinda guy, right?"

"Not that I know of," Pastor Carl replied. Then realization swept over his face. "This isn't about Nicholas. It's not! It's about Krampus. He's originally pre-Christian. He's had a belief base for thousands of years. They want *him*. He's got blood, magic, and he's powerful. He's still physically in our realm. If they can compel Santa, or rather the Spirit of Christmas, to call on Krampus? That's a call he cannot deny."

"Why tonight?" asked Morozko, "when Father Christmas is most powerful?"

"Maybe, it's not tonight?" Rick pondered. "Some ceremonies take a while to execute properly. Maybe afterwards? I mean, kids might think that Santa will be extremely tired after delivering all the toys. So, still lots of power, but that belief of him being exhausted could make that exhaustion very real."

"But why Krampus?" Abe asked and looked at all of them. They all looked back at him unsure.

Jon looked at the Liberty Hall on the screen again.

"Top died to get these photos to us. Because of his courage, we know they'll pull the pin on this thing sometime in the next twenty-four to forty-eight hours. If we can't stop what they've got planned, we might not just be saying goodbye to the holiday. This could end in a paradigm shift for the whole human race."

Morozko looked around and laughed.

"Easy-peasy. We have four Caestus left, two dogs, mebbe a fairy or two." He patted Rick on the shoulder. "You maybe have small tactical nuke in Santa bag of yours, da?"

"No," Rick answered with no small amount of disapproval in his voice, "and I'm not going to ask."

"No problem," the Russian chuckled, "I know what to do if we need a big boom."

The computer chimed again, and Rick responded with a tap on a few buttons.

"It's from the Knight Commander. Looks like we've got out orders." He read out the list.

"Priorities are as follows. One: Do what you can to slow down or terminate the Vampiric ritual. Two: Do everything you can to protect innocent lives. Three: Anticipate reinforcements. Estimated time of arrival is not certain. Four: When reinforcements arrive, do what you can to assist, but keep your team alive and intact. We will need them for a specific mission."

"What the hey does that mean?" Rick wondered out loud. He continued the list again. "'Five: Remember that the Order of Nicholas Thaumaturgus operates anonymously. Attached is our estimate of approximate apex and nadir for when the vampiric ritual will be active.'"

"Well, that's about what I expected to hear," Pastor Carl remarked. He did his best to smile while eyeing the crucifix hung over the door of the RV. "Until they make it here, what's our first move?"

Jon waved a hand at the darkening sky outside.

"Santa Steve should be finishing up at the mall in about two hours. Let's say we head over there, ASAP, and try to stop the vamps from taking him."

Nods of agreement were shared, the four men arming themselves and bundling up for a cold winter's night. When the door swung open, it was obvious in the crispness of the air that a heavy snowstorm was arriving. Abe grumbled to no one in particular.

"Wonderful. Just when we don't need a White Christmas."

* * *

34. About Those Reinforcements

At the Abbey of the Order of Nicholas Thaumaturgus in Eastern Europe, Christmas Eve had already come and passed. People and assorted beings were coming into the great hall to worship, or were heading towards various nooks and altars located on the second ring of the monastery.

The Knight Commander waited in the wings, away from the incense. Too much gave her a headache. After a moment, the Abbot of the monastery walked by, several brothers trying to match pace with him. Commander Lira fell in beside him, having no trouble keeping up.

"It does not go well. I fear Cosimo has been planning this for ages. Intelligence has it that there may be around 140 vampires there, maybe more."

The white bearded Abbot shook his head and kept moving.

"Then we need to call in some favors."

Lira gave him a slightly exasperated look.

"Father, I am. I am mobilizing everything we have in the area, but they have chosen their location well. LaMoure, North Dakota is well out into the great northern plains of the United States, in an area enduring a formidable snowstorm on top of that."

The older black man turned to look at the Knight Commander, his creased eyes sharp, yet gentle. His snowy beard shined against the darkness of his complexion.

"I have spoken with our magus and those of our number who have the gifts. They say some form of haze is also at work in the storm. Rather odd timing, wouldn't you agree?"

"Weather magic?" asked Lira. "Have the vampire houses gotten that powerful?"

"Yes and no. I know there are still some witches up in the Orkneys, and a few places elsewhere, who will perform weather workings for a price. It usually involves a knotted rope, as I recall. A few of those could do the trick. Much more prevalent in the days of sails, I would imagine."

The two brothers who had been accompanying the Abbot shot annoyed looks at the Knight Commander and one pointed to a timepiece. The Abbot had to be ready for mass on Christmas morning, which would be arriving shortly. Lira pointedly took the Abbot by the arm and pulled him away from his assistants.

"Abbot, we are about to have an epic problem, and I know you are aware of the gravity of the situation. There is a spell being cast, and its target is the

Christmas Spirit, possibly Krampus himself. Can we let the higher powers know, so they can do something about this?"

The Abbot held Lira's hand.

"We are trying. Our Lord and Savior is remaining very... ineffable at this time. While I would say that this seems unusual, it has been my personal experience that when world altering events are about to take place, it is God's will that we should sort it out for ourselves, especially when it could go either way. It's just kind of how the Almighty handles things," he finished with a sigh.

"Minor miracles are my department," the Knight Commander responded and pointed a finger at the Abbot's chest. "At this point, the best I can manage is a delaying plan, and maybe not even that. I do have some resources headed their way, but it will be too little, too late. In this organization, the big miracles are supposed to be your department, Abbot. They need our help, and if Cosimo and his mages manage to summon the Christmas Spirit and bind it, I have no idea how that will affect the Caestus, provided they are even still alive at that point. Nor how it could affect the rest of the world, for that matter. Are we going to ask these four men to defeat over one hundred vampires?"

The Abbot considered all this, his forehead wrinkled in thought. He had fiddled with his religious stole as the Knight Commander of the Order had been speaking. When she finished, he stopped rubbing one of the worn tassels, a questioning look on his face.

"I wonder...?" The Abbot paused and looked straight up to the heavens, then back down at her. "Actually Commander, you've reminded me of something." He turned to the two monks.

"I am sorry, but I will be delayed. Have Declan start the festivities and tell him I will be there as soon as I can." The Abbot turned to the Knight Commander, "Shall we?" The elderly man bunched his robes up and started moving at a trot. Lira jogged alongside him. Behind them, more monks started following, looking perturbed.

"When you said a hundred vampires, you reminded me of something," said the Abbot.

"What?"

"When the accords were signed, there were many vampires there, too."

"Wasn't that a bad thing?" asked the Knight Commander.

"It was," he answered. They turned down a hallway into one of the oldest sections of the Abbey. "But I believe there are some conditions that were written into the accords. Let's see if we can dig up the document as quickly as possible."

"Father, while I love digging through our dusty records," the Knight Commander said as she pulled him to a stop, "I must attend to our issues in North Dakota. If you would, let me know when you have something concrete."

"Lira, you have always been good at deciding what needs to be done, and by whom. Go ahead, and may God go with you. I will get help, hopefully... to find some help."

The Knight Commander turned and started jogging back to the Order command center.

* * *

35. Focus Hocus Pocus

The somewhat skeletal figure of Avice stopped what he was doing, and paused for a second. He turned to his assistant and held up a finger.

"Who is killing people out in the hall?" he asked offhandedly.

The assistant looked around the ritual floor and saw some security people heading towards the exit.

"I don't know, but I will check, Lord Avice."

"Do."

Avice continued placing the group of vampires who had gathered outside the containers, one by one, in specific numbered spots, and handed them a numbered piece of paper, as he placed them.

The assistant came back.

"Apparently the Santa that was captured got loose, and Baron de Rais found him and killed him."

There was a hiss from under Avice's ragged hood.

"Stupidi crassi porci gallici! Scitisne nihil de tenebris? Metus? Asini!"

The assistant tried to translate the rapid Latin, but Avice had already snarled and pushed him aside, just as one of the vampires in the arrangement tapped him on the shoulder. Avice whirled and loomed over the man.

"WHAT?!"

A rather seedy looking vampire in a pleather jacket held up the paper he had been handed.

"Sorry, I'm not certain I know how to pronounce all this stuff. I'm not a book sorta guy."

Avice stopped looming, turned to place the next vampire, and handed her a sheet of paper as well. He answered the man as he directed one more vampire after another.

"Are you hungry?"

"Starved. Seriously, most of us who took the slow boat are damned hungry. We've been down for a while."

"Damned hungry," Avice dryly chuckled at the pun.

"Excuse me?" said Mr. Pleather Jacket, clearly confused.

With a few long strides, Avice was back in front of him. He waved his arm slowly, taking in all the preparations.

"Do you know anything about early Greek magical rituals?

"Uh, no boss. I'm a cabbie from Boston."

"Ah, well then. I would not suggest I know anything about how you drive your nags, your ramshackle carriage, nor how you negotiate the glorious pox-filled brothels of Long Wharf for your clients. But I assure you, that if you and your colleagues assist us now with alacrity and diligence, you shall see a powerful working that will impress us all."

"Uh, sure boss, whatever you say. I'm just saying, we got a bunch of different houses here, and some of the folks I'm looking at look are about an inch away from goin' full frenzy. Meaning no disrespect, course, but controlling your inner beast is hard when you ain't ate."

The hooded form of Avice looked around and took a second to actually assess the clay he was sculpting with. After a moment, he nodded.

"I see. Yes, that could be problematic," Avice answered. He stepped back and clapped his hands.

All the vampires being positioned around him stopped talking and turned to look at him.

"Right. I understand your hunger, and that shall be alleviated shortly, I promise. My assistants will be entering the room. They will help you with the words and with garb."

Avice held up a bony finger, as if instructing a class.

"In fairly short order, you will be given a kine, whom you will smite with the laurel branch you are going to be given, at the right moment. They are completely unaware of what is going to happen next. Do *not* reveal your true nature. When you hear the flute music, you will slice their throats and make certain that their blood completely covers the symbol in front of you."

All the vampires in the room looked down at the symbols at their feet, and Avice continued.

"Once that has been done, you all may feed. Once that step is concluded, you will drop the bodies to the left, and we will all chant together. We will be starting," Avice consulted the hourglasses arrayed by the altar, "in a few minutes."

One of the vampires standing next to Pleather Coat was handed both a branch and a hooded cloak. She spoke as she added it to her wardrobe.

"I feel like I'm in a bad Hammer movie, or in my high school production of Godspell."

Pleather Jacket waved the laurel branch around experimentally.

"Hey, if the ancient leaders of our houses tell us to do the Hokey Pokey, I'm going to do it. I just need to eat, and soon!"

The sound of tinny, long overplayed Christmas music came from overhead. The vampire known as Angela led the remaining humans from the sales training program, who all looked exhausted, drunk, and elated. She took a spot on the floor, pointing for them to go stand next to the hooded figures.

There were various comments from the crowd of bemusement, and more than a bit of nervous joking. As they walked to their assigned positions, Angela counted, keeping her loud conversation going.

"That's right! We have one more big surprise for you tonight: A bit of a special graduation ceremony. In just a few moments, you will be given your certificates, your bonus checks, and we will be heading towards your flights. You've all been given numbers, please go stand next to the staff with the corresponding number."

One of the women looked at her number and stepped up to Mr. Pleather Coat.

"I believe I'm with you?" she said perkily. "Hi, I'm Margaret." She gave him a little wave and turned around to face the center of the room. "Wow, this company is big into ceremony! This is getting a bit weird-cultish. I hope they hurry. I'm famished!"

"I know exactly what you mean," Pleather Coat replied and laughed.

Avice strode out to the center of the pattern on the floor and Angela gave him a thumbs up. He surveyed the pattern with a critical eye, then picked up a carved staff, holding it like a conductor's wand. Ancient music started, as well as the beating of drums.

"Does everyone have their laurel branch?" Avice intoned in a sepulchral voice.

One hundred cloaked vampires raised them up in response.

"Excellent! Now, on the count of three, we shall all tap the person in front of you with the branch. One, two, three."

At that point, there was the sound of one hundred branches swishing through the air, and some giggling, along with a muffled "ow!" and "again!"

Avice motioned to the ceremonially robed flute player.

"Then let us begin."

A tune started, played on an ancient flute built by Pythagoras himself.

As the odd music began to fill the LorenCo Liberty Hall, so did the spraying of blood and the screams.

* * *

36. One Santa, "To Go"

Jon looked over at Abe and the rest of the Caestus. There was one advantage to the cold weather, and to the snowstorm coming in. The Avalon Mall was already clearing early, and nobody paid much attention to the group of men with long coats and scarves around their faces, coming in for a last-minute round of "guy shopping."

As they had agreed, Morozko would take the top floor, Rick would take the east door, and Pastor Carl would take the west. It was obvious from the foot traffic that most of the other doors were already locked to funnel people out of the mall on Christmas Eve.

Abe and Jon headed towards the elevators at the center of the mall, only a stone's throw from the food court. As they came in, they could see the line to see Santa was down to the last ten families or so. Some of the kids were in pajamas, and everyone in the queue looked tired. The photography staff were all business, as were the two elves assisting.

"The vampires are going to be here any moment to collect him," Abe remarked and looked around nervously.

"Over there, by the coffee place," Jon said as he surveyed the area with care. "If stuff goes down, I want you to flip that stone bench and get down behind it."

Abe sighed and headed over to the bench, but did not sit, as that would have revealed the stubby assault weapon under his coat. Instead, he pulled out his phone, and pretended to look at it.

Minute after minute ticked by, and slowly the line shrank. Families with cranky children had their photos taken and were being waved out of the mall by security with repeated cries of "Merry Christmas."

As the last family left, Jon started walking toward the Santa chair. Santa Steve stood up and applauded his team. He looked tired but elated.

"Well done, folks. Thank you all for a wonderful season! It's been great, and I hope you will all come down to California and see me sometime. I have a few small presents for you!"

Steve turned and spotted Jon, who was no longer wearing a scarf around his face. Echoing down the hall towards them, an irritated voice yelled out.

"Excuse me! The mall is now closed. Folks, we are closed. Santa has to go deliver presents."

A different voice answered.

"We know, and technically? Santa has already been delivering presents all over Europe and Asia for hours. Why the folks here haven't figured that one out, I can't say. Calm down, mall-cop, we're here to pick up Mr. Claus." The conversation echoed down the empty halls.

Santa Steve's eyebrows went up as he stepped down from the stage and he ducked around the full-sized plastic reindeer. He looked at the white bearded man in front of him.

"You are Jon, right?"

Jon nodded yes and held up his hand so Steve could see the Caestus symbol on his palm. For good measure, he showed it to the rest of the people there as well, making certain that the security personnel could see it. They all responded with a look of curiosity but seemed to accept his authority.

Jon called out to the two mall security folks.

"Take all these people and get them to your security office. Lock it up, and don't open it for anything, not anyone, for the next twenty-four hours. You need to move now!"

The senior security officer dropped the present he was opening and was all business.

"Those people coming in, what are we talking about here?"

"Terrorists," Jon replied, and he took Santa Steve by the arm. "They want to make a statement by killing Santa on Christmas Eve."

With that, one of the elves had begun to cry, but the two security officers wasted no time and started herding the photo team and Santa's staff towards the office.

Santa Steve shook off Jon's hand.

"Look, I appreciate what you guys are trying to do, but I'm just an old guy in a suit. If it can save lives, let me just go with them."

Jon unlimbered the assault weapon under his suit and mumbled something under his breath. Santa Steve caught a glimpse of the gun and went very still.

"Steve, this ain't about you, it's about Christmas," said Jon. "The bad guys are going to try to use you to stop Christmas. They've already been killing people all over town. Santa Ron died this morning." He looked at Santa Steve's face, which had paled to match his beard.

"Besides, the Order never leaves behind a Brother or Sister in Red behind if we can help it."

"Well, damn," said Steve, his face completely serious now. He peeled off his glove on his right hand. "I'm a vet. Got an extra piece?"

Jon produced a wicked looking pistol from somewhere underneath the coat.

"You've got seven shots, one already in the chamber, and the safety is on. Only shoot if they are right on top of you and do your best to tag them in the head. Go over there with Abe."

From around the corner, there was the sound of something heavy being thrown, and a group of six people strolled around the corner. One of the intruders held up his hand, stopping the others. He surveyed the scene calmly, then sighed.

"Damn, it's the Santas. Go get help."

With that, the mercenary in the rear started to retreat. In a fraction of a second, he flipped backwards, as he was shot in the head by a high-powered rifle. There was a blur, and the remaining vampires split up, going in various directions, moving faster than was humanly possible.

The sounds of screaming and gunfire filled the mall.

One of the vampires took three rounds to the chest, but barely slowed down as he closed the distance between himself and Jon. As he approached the men, he seemed somewhat perplexed when he slowed down to human speed. Jon brought out his axe from under the jacket, letting the gun clatter to the floor, the runes on his axe and on his coat glowing faintly green.

"Forgot to mention that, did they?"

"What the hell?" the vampire growled as his mouth and jaw extended out.

"When you fight this Santa, we move at the same speed."

The vampire gurgled a laugh, brandishing hands full of claws.

"Fine by me. Let's dance, Fat Boy."

Jon brought his axe around in an overhand flip and smiled with a feral grin.

"Ho, ho, ho!"

A flurry of blows ensued, and a short moment later, Jon was bleeding from several cuts. The vampire, however, was missing a forearm and had wrenched Jon's axe away, due largely to it being embedded in its collar bone. It ran. Jon cursed.

"Again? Dammit, come back here!"

Jon sprinted to pick up his gun and pursue the thief.

Across the mall, there was the roar of a running battle. One of the vampires came somersaulting over the balcony, covered in thick frost, barely able to move. As it tried to stand up, Abe and Santa Steve both unloaded on it. Abe emptied his clip, and Santa Steve darted towards the security office where everyone else was heading. Abe ran past the frozen vampire, grabbed Steve, and turned him the other way. The two of them ran down the hall, aiming for one of the exits.

Abe reloaded as he ran, both of them skidding around the corner as they neared the exit. They heard the crack of distant explosions and saw Rick having a full on wrestling match with two of the vampires. The big man saw them out of the corner of his eye.

"Run! I got this."

The vampire attempting to bite him laughed.

"Like hell!"

Rick picked up the vampire bodily and sent it through a plate glass window, then turned to face the other one. On his hands were a pair of smoking silver brass knuckles. The vampire looked at the hulking Santa and shrugged.

"So, an autograph is out of the question?"

The sound of barking accompanied Morozko and Pastor Carl running up to join them, along with the two dogs. They all arrived just in time to watch the vampire flee. Morozko had a fanged head tied to his belt, and Pastor Carl's coat was still smoking.

"You have the Santa. Good. Where's Jon?

"I don't know," Abe said, holding up his hands. "He ran off after a Vampire who had his axe in his neck."

Pastor Carl pulled out his phone and tried dialing Jon, but to no avail.

"Goddamn it."

All three men looked at the Pastor with wide eyes.

"Really?" Pastor Carl shook his head at them.

Around the corner, there was an audible crunch as Rick impaled the vampire he had thrown through the window with a piece of Christmas tree. He turned and waved, prompting Morozko to join them, trailing smoke from the long sniper rifle he was carrying over his back.

"You go, I will go after Jon," Morozko said. "Get this Santa out of here. We will meet you at rendezvous." He turned and spoke to the dogs in Russian. The pair barked in unison and started tracking.

"He's right, we have got to move," said Rick.

Pastor Carl, Rick, Abe, and Santa Steve headed outside. A blast of icy cold air met them, laden with snow. The air was filled with the sound of distant sirens and "Frosty the Snowman" over the mall sound system. The ground already had a decent covering of powder on it.

As the men headed towards the truck, Abe spotted multiple figures moving fast across the parking lot. There were at least a dozen vampires, maybe more.

"Uh, guys. Heads up."

The Caestus members slowed. Pastor Carl looked out at the approaching figures.

"Just how many vamps are there in this damn town?"

Rick looked at the older minister.

"Language, Father."

Carl laughed in spite of it all.

"Right. Okay, you guys head the other way, I'm going to slow this group down."

"Father, are you sure?" Abe balked.

Two bright but gentle blue eyes shone back at Abe.

"Son, I am sure that I am not going to be able to run very fast with two artificial knees, and running is just what you need to do."

With that, he pulled out his ecumenical stole and started praying loudly. As he did, a phosphorescent light surrounded him, glowing like a mini aurora borealis. The glow of it reflected in the eyes of the approaching vampires. Rick whirled.

"Okay, you heard the man, let's boogie."

The three of them spun and made a break for it.

Abe couldn't resist glancing over his shoulder as he ran. Pastor Carl was surrounded in a neat circle of vampires. All of them were standing around mesmerized, as if unable to move. Abe had the feeling that if the prayer stopped, it would not be a good thing for the older gent.

They rounded the corner, and Rick tapped Abe's shoulder. Abe looked where Rick was pointing and saw off in the distance more cars pulling up, more dark figures pouring out. Santa Steve wheezed.

"Guys. Leave me. Or kill me. They can't do much if I ain't alive, right?"

"Screw that," Rick snarled, also gasping for breath. "How about I start pulling a bunch of presents for them out of my bag, instead."

"What?" Santa Steve looked at Rick, dumbfounded.

"His power," Abe answered, "...he can pull almost anything out of his bag." Abe laughed darkly.

"Oh," Santa Steve replied, still breathing hard. Then he asked Abe, "What's your power?"

"Uh, I don't really know," Abe replied and blinked with surprise. He hadn't thought about it consciously. "Luck, I guess? I can hear ghosts and stuff."

Rick had pulled his Santa bag out and was grabbing gifts that looked an awful lot like ribbon-bedecked hand grenades, stuffing them in his pockets.

"Who the hell gives hand grenades for Christmas?" Abe sputtered.

"Rednecks and drug lords. Abe, if luck *is* your power, why don't you give it a push?"

"Right, luck," Abe muttered and shook himself.

Abe closed his eyes, reached out, and felt for the Christmas Spirit. Gradually, a warmth grew inside his chest. His mind grabbed the power and focused... and then pushed.

Off in the distance, there was a screeching sound, followed by a *Vrrrrrrrroooom.*

Abe heard a roar, his eyes shooting open in time to catch a white government van as it pulled up in front of them. It sported a vinyl magnetic banner on the either side, emblazoned with the words "TOYS for TOTS, sponsored by the United States Marine Corps." A voice came from the passenger's side.

"Excuse me, Santas. It looks like you guys can use a ride."

In the front passenger seat, in full dress blues, sat a highly decorated Marine Gunnery Sergeant.

The three Santas turned and grinned at each other like idiots. Abe held up his hand so they could see the Caestus sigil. The side door slid open and the Marines waved them in.

Santa Steve was at the side door in a flash. He looked up at Rick.

"I don't know about your power, but I have to say, the kid's is a doozy!"

"Yeah, that was pretty good," Rick answered with a smile as he climbed in, "but just you wait."

The three Santas clambered into the spacious interior, and the van roared off across the mall parking lot. After quick introductions and a bizarre, albeit brief explanation, the Gunny just shook his head.

"I don't know why, but we've been trying to get home all day, and we kept getting lost. I guess it's just your luck that we were still in the neighborhood." He looked back at the three Santas. "And as crazy as it sounds, we totally believe what you just told us. The Santas have always been there for us as his little helpers, so it's only fitting that we be there for you. How can we help?"

"We have to go back and save our friends," asserted Abe.

The Sergeant behind the wheel laughed.

"Yeah, uh, we have a van full of toys, not a lot of combat gear."

Rick laughed, deep and rich, and shot Santa Steve a smirk.

"I can handle that. Let's roll. It's about to get very crowded in here."

A short time later, Pastor Carl was still managing to continue his ceremony, and the circle of vampires surrounding him had not moved an inch. His voice was hoarse. Behind one of the attackers, he saw a flurry of movement, and his eyebrows shot up with concern. There was a brief commotion, and the next thing he felt was himself being physically tackled, suddenly being thrown into a snowdrift, his religious stole fluttering.

Over the shoulder of the figure tackling him, he saw a belt full of objects land where he had been standing, followed by a bright explosion and a clap like thunder.

The air then filled with the sound of gunfire, and he found himself being pulled to his feet a second later.

Pastor Carl righted himself, and quickly brushed off the powdery snow. In stunned silence, he watched as six Marines in full winter tactical gear did battle with the disoriented and burning vampires. Carl shot a look at Rick.

"Where...?"

Rick handed him a fresh pistol and a cross.

"Abe. And Toys for Tots."

"Oh, okay."

In no time, the whole group was speeding around to the back of the mall. They spotted the other two members of the Caestus. Morozko was holding a wounded dog, and Jon was slumped by his side. The Marines charged out and dragged the two men into the vehicle, the anxious dog following close behind. Abe moved to the back and crammed himself against the back door with the mounds of "Toys for Tots" presents. Pastor Carl swiveled to help Jon. Jon's voice was gravelly and uneven.

"Move. Move now, for the love of God."

Abe saw a reflection in the glass, where something dark loomed, flickering. The Sergeant driving stomped on the accelerator, but just as the van started to roll forward, there was a massive crash as something unseen T-boned the van with a massive *CRUNCH*, sending it spinning sideways, sliding across the icy parking lot. Glass, people, presents, and uniforms flew through the air as the back doors flew open.

Abe saw the world in slow motion, as yet another car slammed into the van from behind. He felt himself sailing through the air, then bouncing off a black hood at high velocity, and the loud and snowy world went dark.

* * *

37. The Enemy of My Enemy

When Abe awoke, he immediately regretted it. His vision blurred and spun, and it was all he could do to roll on his side and before he retched.

Somehow, he knew in the back of his mind he must have a concussion. Concentrate on breathing, he thought. That should help the waves of nausea go away. After the world took its sweet time coming to a standstill, the pain subsided a bit, allowing him to open one eye. He was half laying, half hanging off bundles of cardboard, next to a pile of uncrushed ones that were heading for recycling. Two industrial dumpsters bookended his nest, and there was a wicked snowstorm in progress. His whole body felt numb.

"Says nothing, makes no noise," said a high voice not far from his head.

Another deeper, more familiar voice spoke as well.

"I would do as she says, Abe. You need to get up and get going. If the Caestus magic wears off, you might freeze to death."

Abe slowly, quietly, made his way to a better position, his stomach and head protesting all the way. As his vision cleared, he saw his friend Ron standing next to the dumpster. Next to Ron, almost invisible, was the small fairy, Compass Rose, looking at him impatiently. At her feet, lying near the dumpster, was a vampire, seemingly paralyzed. Hundreds of small cuts had cut it to the bone, and many of the wounds had nasty black thorns embedded in them. He looked back up at the fairy, then back to Ron.

It took a bit for Abe to register the fact that Ron had snow passing through him.

"Uh, Ron?" Abe whispered.

"Yeah, I'm dead," said Ron. "I told you, Christmas magic is all about ghosts." The spirit of Ron stepped over to look at Abe with concern.

"And you just came damn close to becoming one yourself. Remember Dickens? A Christmas Carol? Christmas Past, Present? Well, right now, I'm the Ghost of Christmas Get Your Ass Up and Get Moving. The coast is clear for now."

Abe did what he was bid, staggering, keeping an eye on the small but deadly fairy. She watched him with strange eyes, hard as flint.

Ron started walking, motioning for Abe to follow.

"I think your power saved you. You bounced way further than you should have. After the bad guys hit your van, I think Morozko used his weather power for real. There was a massive fight inside a pocket snowstorm with almost no visibility. Believe it or not, the Jarheads managed to get the rest of the Caestus out of here, but almost everyone got hurt." Ron flickered for a moment and then came back.

"It looks like the vampires managed to get Santa Steve, after all. The team tried to find you, but there were even more vamps in the area, and so the Caestus team had to bail. I think Pastor Carl said a prayer for you, and then *POOF*, I found you." The Ghost of Ron looked a little bit defeated.

"And just in the nick of time. I tried to intervene, but no dice. I can't seem to affect the material world." Ron nodded to the little fairy zipping back and forth impatiently.

"Fortunately, I spotted Compass Rose here, and she took out the vampire that found you before it could kill you and drag you off."

Abe started to turn to thank the fairy, but Ron held up a warning hand.

"We do not *T. H. A. N. K.* the fairies, okay? You can complement her though."

Abe thought about it.

"Your work was exquisite," he said, nodding back towards the collapsed vampire.

The small fairy darted past a power box near them.

"Faugh. Murfeo."

She spat. A glob of something black hit the corner of the metal box, and hissed as it ate at the metal. For a moment, however, it seemed slightly less likely to kill Abe as well.

Abe pulled the phone from his pocket. The screen was seriously fractured, entirely failing to light up. He sighed. Ron kept motioning him forward.

"You've been out for a while. It seems one of the few advantages to being a ghost is I can get around pretty quick. The big ritual the vampires have been working on has been moving forward, and there's been a lot of death and anguish building up in that hall. The Caestus team is headed to the sports arena to stop it, but the vamps have brought in at least a busload of children into the arena. Some hunting parties of other vamps have already headed out into the town and are hunting people. They have some ghouls with them, so they can get into houses without being invited in."

"Well, crap," Abe replied. He felt a bitter ache in his chest. Now, every moment the Caestus worked to save Christmas, they were leaving more kids like Trish at the mercy of those monsters. He felt nauseous again.

Abe quickened his pace, slogging through the snow as fast as his battered body would take him.

"Where are we going?"

Compass Rose pointed to a park that was across the way.

"Dair, Nin, Huathe!"

She sped off into the storm.

Abe turned to look at his ghostly companion.

"Say what?"

"That sounds like Gaelic," said Ron. "Not my strong suit."

Abe finally cracked a smile. After all, it really was good to see his friend again.

"Wow. The Great Knower of All Christmas Trivia lets me down?"

"Really? I'm dead, and now you're giving me grief because I can't understand an ancient fairy?" Ron gave Abe a slight smirk. "You know, laughing boy, I've just had a rough couple of days..." Ron's ghostly face looked particularly hang-dog.

Abe's head slumped and tears started to form in his eyes.

"Ron, I am... so sorry."

Ron straightened up, chuckling.

"Relax, Abe. Seriously, I'm just messing with you. Just so you know, I went out in style and took a tough vampire son-a-bitch with me. I'm cool with that. Beats the hell out of rotting away in an old folk's home, jammed full of tubes and having someone else wipe your ass." Ron waved a ghostly hand through the snowflakes, which ignored him.

"Now, if you can just manage to live and share my epic story with the others, I would appreciate it."

As they slogged through the snow, across the treacherous roads, Ron filled Abe in on what happened to him. Abe laughed at the appropriate places, but part of his heart could not help but notice that behind his friend, there were no footprints.

They arrived at the park, and near a large grouping of stones, there was plaque that indicated this place may have once been a place of inter-tribal trading between local Indian tribes. Among the large boulders, there was an even larger stone, surrounded by several trees, some that looked like they had been there a while, surrounded by newer, smaller ones, fighting to stay upright in the storm.

Compass Rose zipped up and pointed to three trees nearest the big stone.

"There: Oak. Ash. Thorn." The fairy then pointed to a drawing that looked like she had scratched it on the face of the rock. "Your blood. Draw symbol. Place hand here. Say, 'I invoke the compact and summon Ilbereth.'"

Abe shot a glance over at Ron, who seemed to be hanging a healthy distance from the area.

"She's telling you to open a magical gate to the In-Between. Sorta like a limbo that touches a lot of magical realms," said Ron as he tried to get closer, but could not.

"Sorry sport, I can't seem to close the gap here. But I do know that Ilbereth is one of Santa's big-time elves, if that's any help." Ron's voice sounded distant and echoey.

Abe lifted up his hand to look at the sigil. His other hand blossomed with pain.

"OW!"

Compass Rose flew in front of him, holding a wicked looking thorn.

"Your blood! Now! On stone! Draw!"

Abe shot her a hurt glance. Hand dripping red, he drew the design as she showed him before. Abe had no idea if this was going to damn him to hell, or maybe summon Cthulhu if he got particularly unlucky. The wind started to pick up around them. When Abe finished, the fairy flew back and forth across it, inspecting it. After a moment, she nodded.

"Say words! Place hands!" demanded Compass Rose.

"I summon Ilbereth and invoke the Compact!" quoted Abe with as much intent as he could muster.

Abe placed his hand in the center, and the stone felt raw and empty. A pulse of energy flowed through Abe's body from earth below him, roiling up through him, then exiting through his hand. The symbol glowed a bright unearthly green.

Compass Rose giggled, which was an altogether unpleasant sound.

Ron called out distantly.

"Hey Abe, you might just want to take a step back." Ron added something else, but it got lost in the rush of energy flowing around Abe.

There was a cracking sound, followed by a burst of glowing verdant energy. It swirled, creating a circle of darkness blacker than black, that opened up on the face of the boulder. Out of the darkness, hundreds of forms, strange, hideous, bizarre, and beautiful, came lurching, looming, padding, skipping, whispering and cackling, moaning, and clicking. Abe watched as a gigantic hellfire-belching black horse with eyes of flame turned itself into a large white rabbit, which gave him a wink and then jumped back into the rushing mass. They swirled around the area, circling the stone, and after them came a tall, slender individual. It spotted Abe upon surveying the area, walking over to him. It resolved itself into a spindly humanoid, in wearing what might be some form of Edwardian formal dress, its colors darkly iridescent, reminiscent of a beetle's wings.

"Ah, that was faster than we expected," it crooned in a low, liquid voice.

"I may be called Ilbereth, and your Knight Commander Lira has invoked a part of the pact, requested a boon: That this group of Fay, and their allies, are to help protect this city from the vampiric forces, and to assist your Order. I am here... to supervise."

Abe felt every hair on the back of his neck stand straight up as hundreds of terrifying creatures spun and stomped around him, whispering, tittering, and sniffing him. Hungrily.

"That's very nice," he said. He was just about to say, "thank you," but caught himself. Not knowing why, he instead bowed deeply. At that, all the creatures around him slowed to a stop and looked at him curiously. Ilbereth raised a perfect eyebrow, entirely nonplussed.

"Ahem, how gracious. We are honored," it responded, offering the slightest tilt of its head.

Ilbereth drew some glowing symbols in the air and studied them for a moment.

"The Fairie Host cannot enter the stadium, in addition to several other places. Those sites have magical protections. It would seem the vampires and their mages have been at this a while. But we can amuse ourselves with some of their hunting expeditions and protect some of the human domiciles."

Ron chimed in, although his voice seemed barely audible to Abe.

"Protecting the innocents! Leaving the civilians alone, correct?"

Abe repeated what Ron said, and Ilbareth nodded with a thin smile.

"Just so," Ilbareth agreed.

Abe looked at the circle of strange creatures surrounding him.

Ilbareth spoke, or maybe sang, in a beautiful language for a moment. When he concluded, an uproar of strange moans and garbled laughter rose from the sea of fairy creatures.

"The Hunt is yours to release."

Abe hesitated, and a fear that felt primal, sharp, and deep ran through his body, only to be cut short by the memories of the vampires and what they had planned for the townsfolk. Abe swept his hand outward.

"Go."

Unearthly screams of delight filled the dark winter storm, and the Fairy Host rode.

* * *

38. Game Time

Outside the LorenCo Sports Arena, the Caestus moved under the cover of the storm. Morozko took the lead, and as he moved forward, the wind and the snow shielded them from prying eyes. Behind him was a group of twenty-three people. Jon followed a few strides behind the group, his face battered, and an arm in a sling. Pastor Carl quietly prayed and blessed members while they moved. As he touched them, the cold seemed to affect them less.

The Marines had split forces and were now each leading a group, their divisions consisting of what few reinforcements the Knight Commander of the Order had been able to marshal up out of the surrounding territories. Jon looked at them, simultaneously sad and amazed. There were nowhere near enough, and yet, during a blizzard on Christmas Eve, these brave souls had answered the call for something that would seem insane to most people.

Jon surveyed their number. They were a varied collection of men and women, mostly older folks, all sharing a look of grim determination. They all were well equipped, and some of them were decked in modern armor stuffed under hunting clothes, and few had select pieces of medieval plate. All were packing firearms just the same. Among them was a tall woman with several quivers and a bow, a sword strapped across her back, and a few older men that looked decidedly "Claus-ish."

Jon spotted Sergeant Burke following the group, trotting to catch up. Morozko brought them all closer as they neared the complex and waved to them to take cover. Jon gathered them quietly.

"Pastor, check all these folks to make certain they have their Sigils working."

"Everyone lean in here, and put one of your hands in," Pastor Carl instructed. "I know I've said this before, but bless you and protect you, and thank you for coming to the call of the Order."

There was a shuffle of gear, and everyone did as requested. Pastor Carl wrapped his stole around his hand and set it on top of the all-hands-in, intoning a prayer. The tall woman seemed annoyed but kept her hand in regardless.

After he finished, everyone withdrew their hand, and for a second, the Caestus symbol glowed on each. Jon addressed the group.

"As we mentioned back at the RV, this is how we will tell the bad guys from the good guys. If they have this symbol, you can trust them. If they're a vampire or a ghoul, put your palm against them, and you'll know if they've been naughty or nice. Remember, there were some innocent civilians in there, and we don't want to kill any lucky stragglers." He took a deep breath. "Since it's Christmas

Eve, you might be able to tell just by looking at them. At this point, I don't think there are many innocent adults left in there."

Jon drew a crude map in the snow with the butt of his axe.

"Okay, one more time. Gunny, your group is going over by the side door at the back. Go in guns blazing and get their attention. Once it gets too hot, drop smoke, flash, concussion. Do a fighting retreat out the front, then run out to the ditch out front here and get ready to cover us when we come out. After that, back to the RV park for the rendezvous."

The Gunny nodded, and called his team over, which included all the Marines.

"Right. Squad leaders, on me."

The Gunny gave a thumbs up to Jon and started prepping the units one last time before they got ready to move.

"Y'all have your ear protection, right? Holy water?"

Jon stepped away and turned to the muscular, rangy woman. She looked as tough as barbed wire.

"You're magic sensitive, correct?"

"I have magical heritage," she admitted.

"Will you have any problems if they have wards up?" asked Jon.

"Maybe. It really depends, I have some Craft skills of my own."

Jon nodded. The woman seemed untroubled by the cold, and little emotion showed on her face, craggy in the artificial light.

"Much appreciated, you coming out for this, Skyia. How the heck did you make it here?"

"Motorcycle."

Jon looked at the surrounding snowstorm and considered saying something, but just let out a soft chuckle. Her reputation preceded her.

"Okay, Skyia, your team is with the Pastor and me. Our goal is to disrupt the ceremony, and rescue Santa Steve if at all possible.

"For our team, it's all about shooting the folks in charge while we stop their fun. The Pastor will do his best to help us counter any spells they have active, hopefully breaking any ritual drawings. The ritual has been up and going for a while, however, so chances are we're going to be dealing with a lot of really dangerous creatures. When the dam does break, there'll be a lot of magical backlash, including some truly well-prepared Elder vampires."

Jon approached three of their infantry in particular.

"I want you three to keep our pastor alive, got it? Help him do what he has to do, and know that if he dies before you do, you're getting coal for Christmas."

The third of the trio moved over to stand next to Pastor Carl, who looked a bit embarrassed. Jon looked over at a man in his forties, dressed in dark clothes, fencing armor underneath.

"Rabbi, you have a sword?"

"I do, and I know how to use it," the Rabbi said as he pulled his saber. He smiled and pointed to the tip. "That end goes in the bad guy, if necessary."

"Can I bless the blade?" Pastor Carl said with a wink.

"We're good," Rabbi Ramirez replied, with a warm smile for the Pastor.

Jon waved over the Police Sergeant.

"I think you two already know each other?"

Sgt. Burke smiled at Rabbi Ramirez.

"We do."

"Good. The children are probably somewhere in one of the executive suites. Sgt. Burke, I want you and the Rabbi here to go and find them. Your team's goal is not to get into firefights or get stuck. Get in and get out with the children, and any innocents you can. After getting as many as you can, get the heck out of this city. Morozko set up a bus for you. It's in the back, and it's idling with the heater running. That will be your ride. You guys will be going in over here, by the VIP entrance."

"Got it," Sgt. Burke answered, and he took a deep breath.

Rabbi Ramirez bundled himself up, stepping away to check on the others.

"Comms check," Jon said as he tapped his ear. "Can everyone hear me?" Various clicks and responses came back to him. "Rick, did you copy that?"

Within the warm confines of the RV, stealthily nestled between snowbanks in a nearby parking lot, Rick pulled himself up to the microphone. A cumbersome splint ran along the length of his hip and leg. The car crash had not been kind to him.

"Yeah, I copy." Rick checked the revised radio set up again. "Everyone who can hear me, look at your radio and press the blue button once. That gives me a numbered pulse."

The RV filled with tiny trills from the radios. Rick looked at the read out with satisfaction. When he felt his phone go off in his pocket, he paused to take the phone call. He laughed after a brief exchange and grabbed the microphone.

"Heads up, Jon, you've got two more recruits. The fuzzier of the two is gonna join you in a minute."

Out of the darkness behind the group came two figures. One a very large wolfish looking creature, the other hiding his bulk under a parka emblazoned with a dozen patches. It was the chemical engineer, Mike Spur. The humor of the situation made both men laugh as he shook Jon's hand.

"I know you'll find this amazingly hard to believe, but my plane was grounded due to the storm. So I figured, 'Hey, if I can't fly, I better damned well help.'"

Spur pointed to the huge wolf who was politely sniffing Morozko's two dogs.

"According to your friend Rick, that's, uh... that is Jason, who is a local."

Jon smiled and took the big man's calloused hand and shook it.

"Thanks. We can really use your help, Spur. After your chat, we did some scouting, and it really does look like the vampires have this whole town wired to blow. We need to stop them."

"Yeah, I figured as much," Spur answered. He adjusted the pack on his back. "Fair warning, I know some pyro, but I am not a bomb-tech or EOD guy."

"I know, but right now, Spur, you're what we have. Plus, Morozko knows quite a bit." Jon waved to the pastor and pointed to Spur. "Carl, can you sigil him up?"

Sgt. Burke looked over at the massive wolf, then at Rabbi Ramirez, who was standing nearby.

"When he said 'local,' what did he mean by that? I've been patrolling this town for a while now, and I've never seen Cujo here."

"The Brewhouse?" the Rabbi answered, leaning forward and grinning.

Sgt. Burke looked at the wolf who gave him a disquieting, knowing grin in return. Its tongue lolled out for a moment.

"Huh? That's Jason's wolf?"

"No, that *is* Jason," the Rabbi said and laughed.

Sgt. Burke did a double take, but the wolf only smiled, cocked an ear, and said nothing.

The sergeant gave the beast a long look.

"So, it I mean, he, Jason, is a werewolf? How did you know that?"

"I'm a Rabbi. It's my job to listen."

"My town is full of vampires, the Santas are monster fighters, the only decent craft brewer around is a werewolf," Burke ticked off the list with exasperation. "I am the last to know anything in this town, apparently. Great detective work, me."

"Sometimes not knowing is a hell of a lot less stressful." Jon patted the sergeant on the shoulder. He turned to Spur and the wolf. "You guys go with Morozko, do what you need to do.

"May the spirit of the season guide us, bless us, and protect us. Move out!"

As Sgt. Burke and his team pressed forward, Jon heard him grumble to the rabbi.

"Werewolf. Hell, I didn't even know he was Jewish."

"He's not," the Rabbi said with another chuckle.

"Then how...?"

The team disappeared into the swirling wind.

Jon turned to his team.

"Skyia, you lead us in."

The warrior woman put the bow in her hand, along with several arrows, and started loping easily across the snowy ground, moving from cover to cover. Heading in a different direction, the wolf pack sped into the night, with the big engineer and Morozko following at a fast pace.

The siege had begun.

* * *

39. Baby, It's Cold Outside

Teams of vampires, ghouls, and human minions were busy out on the streets of LaMoure, North Dakota. Soon the grand ritual would be over and, while some of the petted few were going to be direct benefits of the great working, others would not be so lucky.

As a consolation prize, the leaders of the Vampire Houses had given several groups permission to go out and feed as they so desired with no concern about revealing themselves to mortal eyes. That made sense, as word was that their project concluded with the entire city being destroyed. Along with the joy of an uncontrolled frenzy, they had been given instruction to bring back a fair number of humans as refreshments, and to kill anyone who resembled Santa Claus immediately.

For the vampire community, many of whom had spent hundreds of years looking over their shoulders, this event was a rare treat indeed.

Several of the vampires were dressed up festively in Christmas clothes, gleefully dragging unconscious victims, all of whom were bound and gagged, and tossing them into the backs of vans unceremoniously. Other poor souls were being culled and drunk, openly tossed aside like so many beer bottles. Methodically, the LorenCo security teams, a blend of human servants and ghouls, followed behind them with automatic livestock injectors, zip ties, and trucks.

Allison was from the House of Dance, and it showed. She laughed as she bounded across the lawn of a picturesque house. Her team was awfully close to its quota, once it had been met, she would be allowed to run and play as she chose, free as a bird. Allison has found herself waiting impatiently all through the evening, as her human companions struggled to keep up with their vampire superiors. Tyler was a human she had known before she was turned, and being a younger vampire, having friends, even human ones, was a good thing. Tyler and his two ghouls slogged their way up, breath painting the air behind them. She had an earbud in one ear with music blasting, allowing the rhythm to catapult her into a little pirouette of joy.

"Best. Christmas. Ever!"

"Not so much for them," Tyler muttered, and he rolled his eyes.

"Hey, at least they can give a blood donation before being burnt to a crisp. That should count for something," responded Allison. She knelt down to squish the cheeks of a teenage boy, puppeteering a nod to accompany hers. "Do we appreciate your contribution? That's right! Yes, we do!"

"That is so morbid," Tyler grimaced.

She stood, but before she could offer a retort, she reflexively turned, whipping a nasty looking pistol out, silencer attached. She cocked her head, waited a second, and then fired two shots through the door. *Ta-Ack! Ta-Ack!*

She pressed the barrel against her temple and listened.

"Dogs. Big ones. No longer a problem. After you, boys, and hurry, please?"

Tyler stepped to the side, having pressed his air-powered battering ram flush against the door.

Pa-crunch!

The door lock disintegrated. Tyler gave the door a shove, and as it swung open, he quickly stepped inside.

"I invite Allison and all of her friends in," Tyler stated with a small measure of boredom.

From the staircase above, they could hear the faint clicks of an older man fumbling around with a long-barreled revolver, bringing it to bear on the people entering his house. The human, Tyler, looked up at him, dropped the ramming device, and shouted up at the old man.

"Freeze! Police! We have a search warrant! Drop your weapon!"

The older man looked stunned.

"What? Why are the police search..."

His sentence went unfinished, as he was already sinking to his knees, his throat ripped open. Blood ran thinly down the vintage wallpaper in all directions. Allison stepped past him and plucked the gun out of his hand. She blurred away, searching, and returned to the bottom of the staircase.

"Four upstairs: One in there, two there, one in the room at the end of the hall. Leave that teenager alone."

"Why?" one of the ghouls said as it paused partway up the stairs, brow furrowed in confusion.

"Because I said so," Allison spat out as her eyes narrowed, completely black and hard as obsidian.

"Yes, ma'am. Of course!" The ghoul immediately ducked his head.

Allison's eyes returned to normal.

"He's an Irish dancer, lots of trophies and everything. Maybe he'll live through the explosion? Anyway, too few guys do Irish dance anymore. They're an endangered species. It's like killing a unicorn."

"House of Dance," Tyler said with a smirk.

"Yeah, yeah," Allison responded, smiling back at him. "By the way, I found this at the last house: Catch."

Tyler snatched his gift out of the air, a thick stack of hundreds, the tips spattered with blood.

"Thanks!"

"Beats the fuck out of being a paramedic, doesn't it?" She bowed gracefully.

Tyler sighed. He started to say something, but then thought better of it, changing course.

"Well, this'll finally pay off my college loans, I think."

"We still have a few hours of dark," she laughed. "Let me see what else I can come up with."

Tyler nodded and got out of the way of the ghouls. Allison blurred past him to scout out the next house, and so he took a load off while he waited. The ghouls were a hell of a lot stronger than he was, anyway; let them carry the bodies. Five more people after this should do it, he thought. Tiptoeing over the two large dead dogs by the door, he saw both of them had been headshot with great accuracy. Tyler shivered. Other vamps had told him that his friend Allison was "to the Blood, Born," as in someone who was just meant to be a vampire. He could see what they meant.

* * *

Only a few blocks away, two vampires drove past a high school and a recreation center. To their surprise, they saw a burly man with a face full of shaggy whiskers roll past them in a truck. The bearded man pulled into the local recreation center and headed toward the building marked "LaMoure Aquatic Facility." As the man walked through the snow, the two vampires looked at each other.

"What is he doing up so early?" said the heavyset black vampire. The smaller vampire, with wan blue eyes and a slight English accent, shrugged.

"As long as he's not a Santa, who cares?"

At that moment, as the man fished for his keys, a Santa cap fell out of his pocket. He put it on, once he had brushed the snow off it.

The two vampires looked at each other.

"Well, fuck," said the bigger one. The smaller one sighed.

"Right. Let me go first, see if I can get him to let us in. You park around the side and pop the trunk."

"Got it."

The smaller of the two stepped nimbly across the snow, giving the door a few short raps. He got out his phone and waited.

A minute or so later, the man with a Santa cap opened one of the double doors.

"Hey! Can I help you? Uhm, Merry Christmas!" said the man looking up at his cap with a grin. The limey git grinned back.

"Happy Christmas to you, sir! My friend and I have been driving for hours, and we are lost as all hell. This bloody storm is a menace! The GPS on our phones is messed up, and we're almost out of gas. Could you let me make a phone call? My sister's here in town, and she's expecting us."

The man in the Santa cap smiled.

"Absolutely. It can be my first Santa good deed for the day. My name is Bob. I run the facility here. You were lucky you caught me, I'm only here because this is the only place I can hide my family's presents without them finding them. I'm going to load up, then make a break for home. You'll need to make this quick. If you have an address, I can get you some directions, and then point you to a gas station that's still open."

The slender man shook Bob's proffered hand.

"Thanks, Bobby. My name is Alan. That would be amazing. My sister's family will be so surprised to see my friend and me."

Bob pushed the door farther open.

"Come on in. I must warn you though, we have three pools here, and it's about a hundred percent humidity, warm too. When you head back out, head for your car quick, otherwise you're going to freeze up and look a lot like Jack Frost."

"I'll let my friend know. Our sincerest thanks," Alan said, standing inside the door.

Bob turned and headed to his office. As he did, out of reflex, he looked up at the big glass ceilings over the pool, and the corner mirrors that he and the other lifeguards used. Bob looked again. And again.

Bob felt his whole body go cold. Something in him told him to keep moving and chatting, which is what he did. As he headed into his office and supply room, he took a slight lead, and grabbed the memorial baseball bat off the shelf, stuffing it under his jacket.

Alan stepped in behind, quietly, as did his large companion.

"Santa Bob, this is Max. Max, Bob."

Bob kept moving around the desk and pushed the phone towards them.

"Hey Max, Alan, here's the phone."

He pushed a pen and paper over to Max.

"Max, if you have the address, write it down and I will see what I can do."

Max just looked at the paper.

"You make a good-looking Santa, Bob. Ever thought of doing it professionally?" said Alan.

"Thanks, that's nice of you. I mostly do it for charities, family, friends, and all that. I wouldn't call myself a pro by any means."

Alan nodded and snapped the phone cord out of the wall.

"You sound like a real Father Christmas to me, Bob. Santa's in the heart, y'know? Max, what do you think?"

"Too right, Alan," Max said to Alan, smiling, his fangs becoming more pronounced.

Bob pretended not to see the change, cheating his body away slightly.

"You fellows sound like Brits. You should know this will be a local call..."

In the briefest of seconds, Bob pulled the baseball bat out from under his coat and hit the smiling vampire with a powerful backhand swing, right in the center of its mouth.

Max reeled back, cursing and swearing. He was spraying black blood everywhere, and his mouth was smoking slightly. Alan leapt backward, catlike, fangs out, onto a cabinet.

"Whoa! What is that you have there, Bob?"

Bob looked from one to the other and shook his head.

"Go. Leave this town. It is Christmas Day." Bob's voice seemed to ring with unusual authority.

In answer, Max snarled, grabbing the desk and flipping it out of the way with one hand.

Bob brought the bat up, swung it easily, and both the vampires smirked, stalking a few inches forward. Bob edged backwards, feeling his way with one hand.

Alan held up a hand.

"Bobby, easy! Easy, lemon-squeezy. We just want you to meet our bosses. Won't hurt you, not as long as you cooperate." He blurred a bit closer. "You really don't have much choice."

Bob looked at Max, the big man with the mangled mouth.

"Yeah, I don't think your friend is going to go along with that."

Max stepped forward, his teeth slowly knitting back into shape as he did.

"Ee's not as stupid as he looks."

Bob pretended to trip over something, and as he did, he popped the shelf full of pool chemicals with a clean strike, and with the expertise of a recreation coach who had hit thousands of pop-flies to baseball teams, struck the tub of powdered chlorine dead on.

"Go long!" cried Bob as he dove backwards.

It exploded in a white cloud, filling the air and hitting the faces of the vampires. Bob ran for his life.

A short few seconds later, two very pissed, chemically burnt vampires came after him, all semblance of humanity now gone.

"Where did he go?" Alan tried to dig the chalky substance out of his ear.

"Fuck, if I know. All I can smell is that goddamn pool cleaner. Dammit man. This is my favorite jacket. Completely fucked," said Max.

Alan looked down, spotting tracks in the powder and a sign on the door it led to.

"Hmm. Stupid wanker's not as clever as he thinks."

The two vampires advanced into the pump room. Massive, insulated pipes joined to move water through filters, heaters, and other strange devices. Max moved down one side of the long narrow room, and on the other side of a massive set of pipes, Alan moved down the other. Towards the end of the pipes at an intersection was Bob. They watched as the slightly pudgy Santa clambered up on top of the biggest pipe, the others surrounding him humming with pressure, his back nearly against the wall. He was ungainly, but he managed to do it while still holding the baseball bat, his Santa hat barely on his head.

"Sorry about that, guys. I really don't like fighting, especially on Christmas Day. Celebrating Jesus's birthday and all."

"You really are dense, aren't you?" Alan snarled and kept walking forward.

"How so?" Bob said and looked at Alan quizzically, continuing to scoot backwards.

"Shepherds in the field with their flocks? Not during the bloody winter, they ain't. The Bible says your J-man was born during the spring, and it gives no fucking date. So, it's a bit un-fucking-likely that your baby Jaysus was born in the middle of fucking December, innit?"

Bob leaned back and flipped the latches on some nearby panels. Max and Alan watched him suspiciously. Max kept advancing as well. His mouth had repaired enough to speak.

"Catholic Church. They decided when Christmas is. I have a question for you, Saint Nick. How is it that you're Saint Nicholas, and his bones are in a tomb in Italy? Been to Bari, Italy I have. Is it Zombie Claus that's riding around delivering toys? Huh?"

With that, the two vampires easily jumped over two thick pipes that hung horizontally in front of them, leaving Bob at the back of a bisected square, standing on the big pipes.

"Yeah, I have to admit," Bob answered, "that I was always glad that none of the kids ever asked me about all that. They just want to know about reindeer and stuff."

Bob reached up and pulled a wall-mounted lever, causing several droning noises to fill the room, pinging and whooshing coming from the pipes all around them.

At that, Max leapt across the room, attempting to snatch Bob down with one clawed hand. At the height of the jump, it was like he hit an invisible wall, and slid back down in cartoonish fashion.

He stood up, looking amazed. He barked orders at Alan.

"Don't just stand there, get the motherfucker!"

Alan moved more cautiously, but as he sped up a nearby ladder, he quickly hit another invisible wall.

Bob looked at them with the corner of his mouth curling up slightly.

"You fellas are right, I'm not the sharpest tool in the shed. But I do remember some things you might have forgotten. Could be you don't know yet. I did tell you to leave town."

Alan and Max were rapidly moving around inside their respective boxes, probing quickly, fear mounting in their eyes.

"I'm going to figure this out, and I'm going to shove that bat so far up your ass you're going to look like a popsicle," Max snarled at Santa Bob.

Bob eyed the bat with a bemused look. It was signed, with a prominent Saints logo printed across its face.

"Hey now, this was a gift. The winning bat, from my winning season I coached for the Saints. Father Murphy gave it to me himself." Bob admitted with a hearty laugh.

"It figures. Catholic Private School. I bet he blessed it, and his team prayed over it every day."

Bob chuckled and looked down at the two vampires.

"Here's the thing you don't know. These swimming pools are fed by a natural spring. That stream is right below you, just under those caps, and as I recall, vampires can't cross running water. There's a maze of stream-fed water flowing all around you now."

The two vampires shot looks at each other. Alan brushed himself off, a layer of chlorine lingering in the air. He nodded affably.

"Bob, we were under orders. We've gotten off on the wrong foot. Now, if I push myself, I can probably jump high enough to reach the roof and get out. How about you let us out yourself, and we go our merry way?"

"Maybe," Bob said with a shrug, "but maybe those walls go all the way up to heaven. We shall see."

Max growled and started beating on the pipes around him.

"Maybe I make enough noise, my friends come looking for me. Or maybe I break this place."

Alan laughed, smacking his forehead.

"Duh, I am such a muppet. I forgot all about that. Hold up, Max."

Alan fished out his cellphone and turned it on. He hit speed dial and paused.

"You had your chance, Santa Bob. Our friends are going to be here soon."

Bob reached up and pulled on some gloves and what looked like a tinted safety visor.

"Well, since you're inviting company, I guess we need to turn on the Christmas lights."

Bob flipped open the two big panels, lifting back the protective mirrored flaps.

"What are you doing, Bob?" Alan's face fell when he looked up.

A bright blue glow streamed from one box, and when Bob flipped the switch for the second, the room was filled with an intense flood of violet-white light.

The vampires howled and started to smoke, running around frantically. Bob looked down at them from behind the mask.

"Fun fact: A lot of pools are using super powerful UV-A and C lights pumps to kill bacteria, viruses, and all sorts of nasty things. It kills diseases, the bad stuff, you know? But no chemicals, nonpolluting. We just got these in. I guess they work!"

Bob doubted they could hear him explain over their screaming.

About ten minutes later, Bob hosed down the room with a serious sunburn on his face, and washed their remains down a manhole into the sewer. A little while after that, a jolly man with a bag of presents, a baseball bat, and a big UV light assembly climbed into his truck. Whatever else happened that morning, Santa Bob of the LaMoure Aquatics Center was making damned sure his family was going to get their presents.

* * *

40. Invocation

At the LorenCo Sports Arena, things were going well. Henry Raymond was wearing a festive vest and coachman's hat adorned with a sprig of holly. Mrs. Schmidt had been entrained by one of the Vampire Lords, and she was being amazingly cheerful, making the job of Elaysa so much easier. Henry took a peek around one of the walls, and there was a pile of children, dressed in pajamas and housecoats, watching *Rudolph the Red-Nosed Reindeer* on the fake set that had been built for them. The children had been woken early, given a chance to freshen up, and then presented with generous cups of cocoa and cookies. A faux window, complete with shutters, sat next to the beautifully decorated Christmas tree, a scarlet Santa chair built into the wall only a few feet away. The stockings hung above the fireplace, its artificial flicker tying the whole scene together. One had to acknowledge that Avice left no detail to chance. Raymond could feel the anticipation of the children. They were waiting for Santa, and they *knew* he was going to come.

Raymond silently stepped back and closed the side panel, shifting his gaze to the other side of the large chamber. The wall of acoustic foam was working like a charm. The children had no idea that, on the other side of the very same wall, there was indeed a Santa—one who had been very carefully tied into the rune-covered chair, not less than thirty feet from them. Santa Steve did not look well, having been seriously battered when the vampires rammed his getaway van and roughed up during the ensuing firefight as the vampire team summarily dragged him away. He looked tired and old, and the fact that he was now wearing the old and worn vintage Santa Suit of the original Santa Joe did not make him look any more spry. Raymond had to admit, though, the man did look and somehow feel like Santa in some ineffable way.

Avice now stood between the Santa chair and the wooden frame suspending the Krampus reenactor. Dozens of people in robes were arranged at key points throughout the room. At their feet, the carved lines in the floor now shone with visible power, shimmering with faint energy that hurt the brain to look at. By the back wall was a semi-sized dumpster filled with bodies of the recently sacrificed.

Henry looked over to the far corner. Stevens from the House of Measures turned to meet his gaze and gave him the thumbs up. Good. That meant the foraging teams had successfully brought in more live feed. Overhead, cheerful Christmas music played, mixing with the soft chanting of the ritual. Around the great hall, vampires, ghouls, minions, and victims were all waiting. They did not have to wait for long.

Duke Cosimo and the other House Leaders strode into the room, all of them wearing robes. Each of them flowed gracefully, but with the speed and precision of ancient predators. All eyes turned to follow them.

Without interrupting his chanting, Avice gestured to their marks from his place on the stage. The leaders assumed their positions, awaiting instructions. Duke Cosimo looked over to Henry.

"Henry? Are we ready?"

Henry held up a finger as he checked his tablet again. He frowned.

"Your Grace, I must apologize, but we seem to be having some problems. Several of the foraging teams and their accompanying security have not checked in yet. It could be the storm, or the power of the ritual." Henry tapped the screen, refreshing it. "We've stopped or jammed all communications into and out of the city, except for a few key frequencies. We could be getting some crossover. I can do some checking, but it will take at least ten minutes."

Duke Cosimo cocked his head and looked at the other House Leaders. He tried to keep his irritation from rising to the surface. It had taken him decades to get their help in this grand design. The arch vampire from the House of Mirrors hated being in the company of any large groups and was visibly twitching. The leaders of the House of Wheels and the House of Swords looked ready to attack each other at any moment. Duke Cosimo looked over at Avice, whose dark eyes were much larger than normal, and he seemed to be exuding a sense of grinding determination held back by sheer will. Avice finished the piece he was chanting and bowed.

"Duke Cosimo, Master of the Houses, we are ready." He gestured with a hand at the scene.

But something itched. Duke Florentine Cosimo could sense it. Something was wrong, however, now was the time.

Avice nodded and spread his long, skeletal arms wide. Bells rang, platters of holly, mistletoe, laurel, and rosemary fell into cauldrons, and candles burst into flame.

Duke Cosimo stepped very carefully towards the Santa in the chair, careful to stay within the lines.

"Hello, Steven. My name is Cosimo, and I need you to see something."

The Duke presented a handheld screen depicting the children in the next room. Cosimo nodded to Elaysa and Baron de Rais. They acknowledged the signal with a bow to the Duke, and they exited through the side door, appearing on camera alongside the children a moment later. Baron de Rais gave a creepy little wave to the camera. The video feed showed the children turning to see their entrance. Baron de Rais was not their much anticipated Santa, so the children went back to watching Rudolph on the flat screen.

"As you can see, those children are in the next room. Whether they live or die is really up to you at this point."

The video camera was pointed towards Baron de Rais, whose face contorted from spoiled aristocrat into that of a nightmare with jagged teeth and then back again. The grin remained, however, brimming with dark intent.

Duke Cosimo spoke very matter-of-factly to Steven.

"The children are going to start calling for Santa Claus. Here, in this room, in you, the Spirit of Christmas will be manifested. If you choose to fight this process, the children will most certainly die; but if you, in your heart of hearts, truly believe in the magic of Christmas, and ask Saint Nicholas to come? There is a chance that you can save those children. If you fight this, we will start sacrificing the children and force the issue in other ways. I would rather not harm the children if we can avoid it. My suspicion is that you feel the same."

Cosimo motioned to the old Santa suit they had dressed Steven in.

"You can probably already feel the power of the suit you are wearing—an heirloom of great importance, saturated with mystical energy. It's why I'm confident you can do this. You can help bring the spirit of Santa here. Who knows? Maybe he can help you. He should. This is, how do you Americans put it? 'A decision well above your paygrade.'"

Duke Cosimo leaned in closer, still careful not to cross the line. Around the room, hundreds of eyes like amber beads gleamed as they stared at the old man in the chair.

The ruler of the Vampiric Houses held up the video again. It showed Baron de Rais, now rocking a sleepy little girl in his arms. As they watched on, he looked into the lens, his eyes went black, and bent down to smell her hair.

Santa Steve bucked in the chair, tears running from his face. He nodded emphatically, unable to speak past the tape over his mouth.

Duke Cosimo stepped back.

"Do what this person says."

Avice leaned over and looked at Steven intently.

"Excellent. Now, I am going to say some words, and you are going to repeat them in your mind. I need you to stay very focused."

As Avice started intoning the words, he pointed to the door.

In the other room, Mrs. Schmidt paused Rudolph. She addressed the room full of smiling children.

"Alright boys and girls, do you want Santa to join us?

"Yes!"

"Then we need to let him know! Say this with me, 'We want Santa! We want Santa!'"

Scampering to their feet, practically bouncing in anticipation, the children embraced the chant with a will.

"We want Santa! We want Santa! **We want SANTA!**"

In the ritual room, Santa Steve began to glow.

* * *

41. Witching Hour

Across town, Abe was doing his best to trot towards the sports arena. In the small hours of the morning, he could find nothing that looked like transportation. While he was not sweating to death, nor freezing, he realized that it could take an hour or more to get to where he needed to be. His hand still ached from where Compass Rose had cut it. Abe heard a voice near him.

"Abe! Heads up!"

He turned and saw the ghostly form of Ron, partially lit by a lone streetlamp.

"Abe, there are a bunch of vampires in the houses ahead of you."

Abe stopped and looked around.

"Can you find me a way around them?"

"Nothing that won't slow you down. You are pretty exposed out here in the snow." Ron walked over to him. "Did you close that magical gate after you opened it?"

"What? I just turned and started looking for you or Rose."

Ghost Ron smacked his face.

"Yikes. I don't know much about magic, but I think you were supposed to break the line or something. When you popped the cork on that thing, it was like there was a great wind, and it blew me a few miles away. I can still feel it."

"Well, how the hell was I supposed to know that? None of those... friends of ours told me anything!"

Ron chortled.

"Yeah, I don't think they care if there is an open pipeline to the fairy realms or wherever. In fact, they're probably enjoying the hell out of it."

"Great," Abe sighed and his head slumped. "If the vampires don't kill everyone, then the fairies might. Way to go, Abe," he mumbled irritably.

Ron leaned in close, his eyes intense. "Abe, you really don't have time to feel sorry for yourself. Your friends need you."

"Uh, in case you haven't noticed, I've been running my ass off. I'm exhausted."

"'McFly. McFlyyyy?'"

Abe's head shot up, the absurdity of getting a pop movie reference from a ghost throwing him off.

"What?"

"Use your power! It's Christmas Day, Abe. You're a member of a Caestus of the Winter Order!"

"Oh, right. Duh."

Abe took a deep breath, closed his eyes, reached inside himself, and felt for what he called his Santa Heart. Like a snow globe of happiness within him, he sensed it. He drew on the power, fanning the flames of energy within him, and as the feeling of joy grew, he lifted his head, and opened his eyes. Two driveways down, there was an object resting on a trailer, covered under a tarp and snow. Somehow, he knew that was what he needed.

"I think I have something. Hang on."

Abe trotted over to the trailer and pulled the cover off. Underneath was a vintage John Deere Liquifire snowmobile, a stag emblazoned on it. The hood had been custom painted with a *"Run-Run-Rudolph"* tagline, and the deer had a red LED nose.

Ron laughed.

"Okay, that's a pretty handy ability you have there. Heh. And it's a reindeer. Nice."

Abe searched the area, finding the set of spare keys. The modified racing sled purred to life. Abe left his business card tucked into the trailer with a note hurriedly scrawled on the back.

Sleigh in shop, will return Rudolph soon. -Santa

A few minutes later, Abe was bent over behind the windshield as the snowmobile roared through the still night air at 70 mph and picking up speed. For whatever reason, Abe somehow knew everything he needed to know about driving this custom piece of machinery. While he suspected it was because of the skis, he figured it might be because it had a reindeer painted on it.

With a *WAAAAhhrrrrrrrrrr*, he flew through the quiet streets. Briefly spotting a group of people he suspected were vampires, he cherished the surprised looks on their faces as they turned to face him. Abe laughed out loud, grinned, and punched the throttle. He flew past them, with a rooster tail of snow flying up behind him, the wind buffeting his smiling face.

Without warning, a huge rabbit suddenly zig-zagged in front of him, flashing in the light. Out of reflex, Abe jerked the snowmobile to the left. As he did, Abe did not see the lithe female Vampire who had come out of the darkness, suddenly standing in front of him in order to clothesline him across the throat, arm catching him like an iron bar. Abe flew through the air, the snowmobile sailing several hundred yards straight ahead without Abe. He was left lying on the ground, stunned and struggling to breathe. Allison walked over and looked down at Abe.

"Rough morning, Santa?"

Abe could only answer *Ghkthth!* among other choking, gasping noises.

The vampire woman saw something move a few yards away. It was the big snowshoe hare that Abe had avoided.

"Thanks for the assist, Bugs. Stick around, I'll eat you later!" crowed Allison with a toothy smile.

The rabbit looked back at her stoically and flicked an ear at her, unconcerned.

She casually reached down and lifted up the semi-conscious Santa, casting him over her shoulder. As she walked back to join the others, the frustrated Ghost of Ron stood in the darkness with his fists balled in anger. As he watched the group of people tie up Abe and throw him in the back of the truck, he noticed that the rabbit had developed a decided grin, along with feral red eyes to match. It shape-changed into a black greyhound just as it sped off into the darkness.

Ron said out loud to no one in particular, "Rabbit season."

* * *

42. Strike Up the Music

Along with their LorenCo security escorts, two more teams of vampires made their way into yet another part of the LaMoure suburbs. Lester, of the House of Wheels, stepped out of his vehicle and called everyone over.

"Alrighty, then. I need two vamps and a minion or ghoul on each team, please. Two teams can start down there," Lester said, pointing to the end of the block. Turning the opposite direction, he added, "Let's also have two teams start two blocks up that way, working your way to the middle. Feed if you have to, but let's keep it quiet. We are going to need these humans later, so save most of them for the truck that's coming."

Lester handed out bundles of zip ties and some odd devices with hand grips.

"These are called Snaps. Remember the old injector guns they used to inoculate folks? Those turned out to be pretty good at spreading infections from one person to another. So, a smart company figured out a way to make the part that touches the patient disposable." He pulled back his sleeve and pressed its tip against his skin, then pulled the trigger. There was a sharp *snap*. He flipped a lever, the cartridge ejected, and a new one was loaded in its place. He grinned.

"Now I don't need to worry about my tetanus shot. LorenCo bought the technology, and we have drug cartridges that will knock out most humans in under a minute if you inject them in an arm or leg."

"You load a clip like this." He demonstrated deftly, and then handed the red labeled clips out to the teams.

"You want to knock somebody out even quicker? Shoot them in the neck. Takes about ten, twenty seconds. They'll stay down for quite a while. If the person is really big, hit them twice, once in the neck, once on the body." He fastened the button on his sleeve again as he spoke.

"There's a marker here at the bottom. Be sure to draw a line on their forehead or their hand once they've been snapped." He smiled at the gathered crowd.

"Oh, and this is important: don't feed on anyone who has been injected. It's not a huge deal if you do, but I did once, and I was wobbling around, couldn't feel my tongue for hours. Save yourself the trouble."

He pivoted to address the few that remained unassigned.

"The teams go in, drag people out, and you guys ferry all the happy meals out to the trucks." Lester gave everyone an effusive grin. "Merry fucking Christmas, and let's roll!" The teams gave a half-hearted cheer and started off.

Not far away, in the darkness among darkness, a strange creature skulked that looked not unlike a centaur made of bits of straw, clay, and meat, covered in rags, and with an antlered skull with red dots for pupils studied the scene. Its rags swirled in an invisible wind, the shadows around seething. It spoke to the dark wind roiling around it, a staccato voice of whispers and pain.

"Flit-lings, little knives, go protect the mortal human lives, feast the black-bloods, yes indeed. With speed, with speed."

There was a rushing in the darkness, and the sound of twittering and hissing floated towards the vampires out on the street. Playing faintly on the wind were sounds like crickets whispering, "Feast, feast, feast!"

The ragged creature turned to study the shadows again.

"Korred, are you here?"

"Aye."

A massively wide-bearded figure covered in wiry hair and rags stepped out of the darkness.

"Destroy the blood-drinkers' carts, and any who would brandish iron against us. Use your glamour to confuse them."

"Hempen, Harken, Stampen. This I Will Do." The figure picked up an enormous scythe and headed towards the vehicles.

More figures came forth from the darkness, and with further swaying of skeletal arms and lilting rhymes, the creatures were dispatched to their missions. Dullahans, grogochs, leshe, lila, creatures of all sorts sped away, and then it was quiet except for the sound of wind and snow whistling across the Northern landscape. The antlered creature stopped, twisting to regard a few more creatures stepping out of the lingering darkness.

"While I have no command of you, I think this task does not displease you. Do as you like, but do not harm the innocent mortals of this realm."

Out of the darkness came a short, bearded man in fine antique armor, accompanied by a short, plump smiling woman dressed in brown, a beautiful shawl draped over her shoulders, casually creating thread on a drop spindle.

The antlered being bowed its head ever so slightly.

The bearded man turned to the woman and nodded.

"Mother Holle, will you be joining me? I feel a game of Shinty needs to be played."

Mother Holle looked at him with keen brown eyes.

"No, not today, Fin. Perhaps later." Fin bowed, accepting her answer.

The short man produced a sword, twirled it in hand, which turned into a Hurley stick. Finvarra, Rí na Daoine Sidhe, the King of the Leprechauns smiled and started to head off when Mother Holle coughed politely.

"Fin, your armor?"

"Oh, right!" He laughed.

He cracked his knuckles and his helmet turned into a flat cap, his armor now a tweed coat over a Rugby jersey emblazoned "Legion." Aside from his height and muscular broad build, he looked like a fairly normal, if short, modern human.

"Sorry, my glamour here is a touch out o' practice."

Mother Holle swung the drop spindle up and around on its axis and consulted the patterns it made on the snow. She nodded to the others.

"Good luck to you all."

Fin touched the brim of his hat and vanished.

The small woman turned and regarded the homes in the neighborhood. One of the mailboxes had been yarn-bombed with bright festive colors. Mother Holle smiled and headed toward it, humming and spinning on her drop spindle. As she walked, beautiful snowflakes like goose feathers fell around her.

The antlered creature turned to look around the area, sniffing the air. It stood motionless there for a time, a macabre statue, until it spun in place, galloping back into the shadows.

* * *

43. We May Have a Problem

Spur pushed back the access cover to the pumping station and climbed back out. On the ground outside was a field of bloody snow, strewn with various body parts he chose not to examine too closely. He looked around and spotted the immense wolf on top of one of the pipe fittings, watching the area. Spur shuddered a bit. A short time ago, he had seen what a fully grown werewolf and two trained attack dogs could do to a vampire. Spur pushed that memory back, way back, and called out.

"Morozko?"

Morozko stepped out from concealment.

"So, what do we have?"

In answer, Spur pulled his phone out and showed him pictures.

"At first, things kind of made sense. The pumps are designed to fail over, keep pressure up via alternate lines. Then I looked at some of the metal in the housings. All of this stuff will just be turned into fuel, should anything go really wrong."

"And it will go wrong, yes?"

Spur nodded emphatically.

"It starts here. There's a metal box wired into each of the pumping stations. I managed to get a look inside. Manganese dioxide and aluminum. It's essentially a thermite charge, and when it melts, it'll get up to 9000 degrees. That melts straight through the two pipes below, both of them will start burning and release a ton of pressurized LPG, and scarily enough, burst the water pipe. Then the shut-out valves slam shut, and now you have the whole mixture building up pressure."

Morozko held out his hand, and his two dogs ran to sit next to him. He absentmindedly scratched their heads, despite their bloody muzzles.

"Wait, this thermite, it will not go out in the water?"

Spur stowed the phone and opened his hands wide.

"Anything is possible, and I don't know how they made it. There's something else in the mix too. Most folks use aluminum, but with all the LPG, the oil adjuncts, the aluminum mounts... I have no friggin clue. Add in the cooling, and my best guess is that this thing will build a massive amount of pressure, burst the seals, and start a chain reaction. People forget that water does not compress, and so... boom, first seal goes, rams water and air forward, builds to a critical temp, and boom, boom, boom: Dominos. I think the whole town is over a giant, spoked, half-buried wheel, and all these bottle bombs are linked to the refinery. It's possible we could see a reaction that breaks the water down into oxygen and hydrogen. When that happens, there's going to be the mother of all shockwaves, even a secondary reaction. It'll be like a big wheel, starting at the center, and pushing out all the way to the outer limits of the city."

Morozko drew a deep breath.

"So, you think that this is hub, and each, what... spoke has detonator?"

"Yep," Spur agreed as he looked up. "Whoever designed this took their time and built in redundancies. Seems to me like they have backups on their backups. I don't think there's any way for us to get to all of them in time." Spur shook his head, looking a bit defeated. "I dunno. Remember, I'm just a refinery safety guy, not a bomb squad guy."

They sat quietly looking at each other for a moment, each trying to come up some solution. Morozko got up to inspect the inside of the pumping station. Spur followed him, looking over his shoulder. The old Russian pointed to a pipe.

"That is water pipe? If I break it right now, no boom, correct?"

Spur looked back and forth.

"I guess not. Everything in those housings looks pretty waterproof and well-sealed."

"Good. I have an idea. Be right back. Take this. Safety is on."

Spur took the rifle, automatically checking to see if a round was chambered, and that the safety was on. Morozko smiled at his cautious habit.

Less than a minute later, Morozko had returned with a staff that looked naturally ornate, with icicles and snow still covering it.

"Mr. Spur, you watch what I do, and maybe we will need to run."

Morozko's face took on a white cast and his beard and eyebrows filled with frost. Outside, the wolf and dogs whipped into a chorus of howls and barks. Grandfather Frost leaned over and rested the staff against the pipe. Patterns of frost crept up and down the casing, and snow began to flutter down from some impossible place inside the tunnel. There was a groan, creaking, and a crescendo of metallic cracking as the water pipe broke. Morozko cursed curtly, the temperature around the area plummeting. Morozko's face was filled with fierce determination and covered with hoarfrost. Spur shivered and leaned over.

"Grandfather Winter? Wait until the water gets up to the orange junction box before you start to freeze it. If you can, have it all expand upward. You need to cover all the electronics over there with ice. Really thick, and I mean really thick. The purer the water, the colder it is, the less likely that ice will conduct electricity."

"Da," Morozko grunted his answer. Twenty yards of pipe and metal started to twist and bend.

Spur watched as razor sharp shards of ice punched up from beneath the ground, and tons of metal started to screech and moan dangerously. Morozko seemed oblivious, but as a piece of debris fell dangerously close, Spur reached down and pulled the man and his staff away, his shoulders biting cold to the touch. Spur grabbed and lifted Morozko, dragging both of them forcibly back into a snowbank.

There was some cursing, and Morozko came out of the snow spitting. Spur held up his hands and pointed to where they had been standing. There was wreckage everywhere.

"Sorry, Morozko, I had to move you."

Morozko's face started to drip water and look more human.

"Yes, I understand." The older man sagged against his staff. "This is very hard thing to do. Will it stop the bomb?"

Spur surveyed the damage. It was impressive.

"Assuming that they only rigged the outside spokes and not every section, probably. My guess is they have another set of charges at the center exchange and the refinery."

"I can maybe freeze all the spokes, but you will have problems finding the bombs. But my dogs are trained for this, yes," Morozko said with a tight smile.

The refinery safety engineer unfolded the map.

"Yeah, and you have a lot of ground to cover. For the most part, the roads travel along the spokes, not between them," said Spur, pointing to the key locations.

The two of them looked down at the map. A deep voice came from behind one of the metal sheds.

"I can help, I think."

Morozko whirled, a gun raised in his hand with lightning quickness, Spur close behind. The two dogs barked happily.

"It's Jason. I'm the werewolf. Don't shoot."

A muscular man stepped out from cover, stark nude and steaming. Despite being mostly bald, he had more than his fair share of body hair. He approached them carefully.

"We need to split up. We rig up a sled with some rope, and we put Morozko on it. Spur, you take the two dogs. I've already explained to them that they need to help you find bombs. They'll do what we ask."

Both the dogs barked once.

"But they aren't happy about leaving Grandfather Winter here," Jason added. Morozko laughed.

"Of course not. They are my comrades. We work as a team." He petted one. "You know that in Russia, Grandfather Frost is pulled by Troika, with three horses pulling sleigh side by side by side?"

"Hey, if you can whip up a sleigh and three fast horses, go for it. Break out the magic. If not, I'm going to borrow Spur's Leatherman and rig you up a sled from that fiberglass housing lid over there."

"And you are going to pull the sled?" Spur asked skeptically, looking at Jason.

Jason looked back at him with a jovial but determined expression.

"As a werewolf, I'm pretty damned fast and strong, and I can get around things really quickly. Just promise me, no one ever, ever mentions this to anyone.

If it got back to my pack that Santa was being pulled around on a 'one-wolf open-sleigh,' I would never hear the end of it."

"Maybe, but you may also be the person who helped save the whole city." Spur smiled at him.

"What about Spur and all the vampires in town?" Morozko asked.

In response, Spur pulled some cylinders out of his pockets.

"These are kinda basic, but I took the liberty of borrowing some things from the rigs on my way back into town. These are improvised flash and stun grenades. If they work, they'll be overpowered as a sonuvabitch, but they should blind anything that can see; probably stun them too. If I need to, I can toss these and we run like hell."

The two dogs barked again. Jason looked at them, then at the two men.

"The dogs will do their best to keep him away from the vampires."

Morozko shook his head with a boney grin.

"As I told Rick, 'Best Dogs In The World.'" He turned to Jason. "You and I, my friend, we are going to have a drink! I want to have a conversation with my dogs!"

"If we survive, sure," Jason agreed with a smile.

The three men took no time in putting themselves to work. A short time later, Morozko was sitting on the top of a fiberglass instrument housing lid, having rigged up his staff as a rudder. Strips of hose and thick rubber padding had been macgyvered into a harness. Returned to wolf shape, Jason stalked around the corner, patiently standing on all fours as Spur rigged up the harness.

"Thanks for doing this, Jason."

The wolf just grumbled in reply. Morozko looked over at Spur.

"Silver bullets in your pistol. Maybe steal a car if you can. Good luck. Blessings of St. Nicholas the Wonderworker upon you. Purga, V'yuga, *pozabot'sya o nem, pozhaluysta.*" The dogs stood at attention, their mission to protect Spur already underway.

"You gents as well. Good luck!" Spur called out.

At that, the werewolf snarled and leaned forward into the harness. In just a few steps, they were already moving at a fair clip, and Morozko was hanging onto the handles for dear life.

"Baise moi!" was all that escaped Grandfather Winter as he hurtled over a snowdrift and into the darkness.

Spur looked down at the two dogs, who returned his attention with remarkable focus.

"I'm not much of a runner. What say we go steal a vehicle?" The two dogs barked in the affirmative, and the engineer lumbered off toward the suburbs.

* * *

44. In the Big Chair

Santa Steve could faintly hear the sound of the children on the other side of the wall. Tears coursed down his face as he screwed his eyes shut and listened to the words the tall creature to the right of him said with slow emphasis. The unfamiliar words of the chants rang through him like a tuning fork, and a warmth and calmness started to fill him.

In his mind, Santa Steve could hear a voice that sounded like a collective of many, and it slowly resolved into a gentle, human voice in his mind.

"Steven, I am here."

"Lord?"

"Errr, no. I would be what some might call The Spirit of Christmas, a part of which now might be called Santa. No amount of their chanting could force our Lord and Savior down here. I am here to help if I can. However, I am far less powerful than the Almighty."

"Santa? I mean, the real St. Nick, St. Nicholas? Santa Claus?" asked Santa Steve.

"Sort of. It's complicated. I know you have felt the magic of Christmas before, Steve. Don't worry."

Steve's mind went a little sideways at that. The voice in his head was Santa, and twenty-seven years of playing the role had never prepared him to hear it.

"Don't worry? The vampires have pulled you down here. Can you help us save the children? Please!"

The voice in Steve's head sounded sad, tinted by anger.

"I will do what I can."

"You got to do it!"

"Steven?" said the voice of Christmas Spirit.

"Yes?"

"Did you have fun portraying Santa?"

In the chair, Santa Steve sat up a bit straighter.

"Yes, it was amazing. Thank you."

"Thank you, Steven. There were times where you really made a difference. But now, you are going to go down the path that the believers of old had to tread."

"I don't understand."

The voice of Christmas took an ironic note.

"Saints usually suffered and died in interesting ways, Steve."

"Oh. Yeah, right." Santa Steve stopped crying, managing to swallow a shaky breath. He knew that, at times, he had been less than a perfect person or even Santa, but he knew he shared a Santa's heart.

"Relax for a moment and let me speak physically, if I may."

"Let's do this," Steve nodded as he replied in his mind.

The sound of sleighbells filled the room, pure and silvery. The tape on Santa's face fell off.

The figure that was Santa Steve now shone radiant, and his face looked like it had been carved from stone by a master. A placid but strong voice came from him.

"I am here."

Around the room, the chanters faltered for a moment, but Avice waved an impatient hand at them, and the chanting picked back up.

Duke Cosimo flipped open the book next to him, then peered at the seated figure.

"If you are indeed Nicholas Thaumaturgus, were you there with your Abbot at the treaty stone?

"I was in spirit."

The Vampire Arch Lord leaned forward, looking a bit skeptical.

"What did I complain about?"

"That your shoes were getting ruined by the mud." The Santa figure shrugged. "Duke Cosimo, you knew even back then that you should never wear your nicest outfits while traveling."

"Well met, Nicholas. It has been a while." Cosimo smiled.

"What do you want? Why abuse this poor man in this chair? How will summoning me help you?"

Duke Cosimo glanced over at Avice, who proceeded to drape several knotted cords over the Santa figure.

"Actually, you are but the method to the means." He glanced over to the Krampus reenactor. "I want you to summon your colleague, Krampus, right here, right now, in the flesh, or the children start dying."

The Santa figure shook its head.

"First of all, I don't know where he is. Secondly, Cosimo. You and I have both seen thousands of children dead before their times. Wars. Plagues. Famine. And I could not intervene then. And I can't intervene now. I cannot." said the Santa voice with sadness and frustration.

Cosimo nodded, as if this had been expected.

"Avice?"

The cadaverous vampire leaned forward and tightened the knots on the ropes. The old man secured; he had little issue carving a rune on the Santa's forehead.

"Let the two speak as one!" Avice intoned.

"Funny thing, Wonderworker," Cosimo said and raised his eyebrows. "Just as you can speak from the body you are currently cohabiting, you can also feel what he feels. Little known fact. So, he is lending you voice, but did you know that if we manipulate this mortal shell, we can influence you as well? As above, so below, and so on. The connection goes both ways. He accesses your strength, your power as well."

Avice sprinkled the Santa with something from a basin, and then carefully took a red-hot blade and touched it to the surface of the water in the basin.

The Santa writhed in pain.

Inside the mind of the figure, Santa Steve called out.

"Something's wrong. It hurts, it hurts!"

"I know, Steve. I can't stop this! I am trying. Hold fast."

"I'm so... sorry..." Santa Steve's voice came back thin and thready.

After a minute of watching the figure in the chair fight his spells, Avice pointed a finger at the Santa.

"Summon the Krampus now, and the pain will stop."

A cracked voice sounding like a very human Santa Steve full of anguish cried out.

"Dancer in the Woods, Krampus, Narrenfresser, Bette Noir, I summon you!"

The voice had a double tone that rang out across the hall and kept echoing.

Avice stepped over to the person on the wooden X and studied him intently. The person in the Krampus suit was starting to glow a faint purplish color.

"It should not be long now, Duke Cosimo."

Cosimo looked at the other heads of the Vampiric Houses, and all grinned at the imminent triumph.

Thunder filled the hall.

At that very moment, one of the teams of the Order tossed a mixture of flash and stun grenades into the hall where the ritual was taking place and filled the air with a hail of bullets. The entire hall roared in unison, and a great deal of screaming ensued.

As bedlam set in, Duke Cosimo pinched the bridge of his nose and huffed.

"Damn it!"

On the other side of the fake wall, Rabbi Ramirez and Sgt. Burke waited out of sight, holding their team back. As the muffled booming noise signaled the attack on the other side of the wall, they watched as three of the vampires quickly fled with their security details.

Sgt. Burke heaved a sigh of relief when he saw that familiar sadist, Baron de Rais, cock his head, then slink away swiftly and silently. Some of the children were starting to raise their heads and look around for the source of the muffled booms. Mrs. Schmidt looked at Elaysa, who thumbed up the volume of the Christmas music. The children kept their chanting up.

"We want Santa! We want Santa!"

Sgt. Burke looked at the people behind him.

"Any of you have a Santa suit with you?"

The group looked at each other blankly. One of the ladies raised her hand.

"There was a dancing Santa statue back there, and a couple of other Christmas props laying on a chair, if that helps."

Sgt. Burke addressed the Rabbi.

"I hate to say it, but it'll be a lot easier to get these kids out of here if we have a Santa."

"Yeah, we should have thought of that."

Sgt. Burke looked back to the woman.

"Please, go get the suit and a beard, and get back here as fast as you can." She nodded and ran.

Sgt. Burke addressed the team.

"You two, when we head down, you take the pretty lady and shoot her if you have to." Motioning to another pair, he said, "You two, take the big lady. Hold them if you can, try not to shoot them in front of the kids. Rabbi Ramirez, you and I are going to escort the kids to the bus out front."

A brief moment later, the woman returned with the cheapest possible polyester Santa suit and a horrible fake beard, complete with an elastic strap.

"I'm sorry, this is all I could find. The Santa suit is really small."

Everyone turned to look at the compactly built Rabbi Ramirez. Having anticipated God's little joke well in advance, he shook his head and held out his hand with a sigh.

"It wouldn't be the first time."

A minute later, the team snuck around the corner. Sgt. Burke and the world's worst-looking Santa stepped in front of the room.

"Hey kids!" Sgt. Burke bellowed out. "Look who's here! Santa!"

With all the ambient Christmas magic in the air, Rabbi Ramirez seemed just like the real deal.

The children responded by cheering and mobbing Santa. While the children were distracted, the team members snatched up Elaysa and Mrs. Schmidt. Luckily, they disarmed Elaysa without incident, and discreetly jammed pistols in the backs of the two women.

The kids were cheering, oblivious to what was going on.

Rabbi Ramirez gave them a hearty "Ho! HO! HO!" Thinking fast and scooping up the bag next to the chair, Ramirez stuffed his rapier into it.

"Guess what, kids?"

"What?" they cried.

"We're going to be in a *movie!!*"

The boys and girls looked at each other confused for a second, and then started bouncing up and down excitedly.

Rabbi Ramirez played Santa like everyone's lives depended on it. He slipped off his glove and showed the sigil on his hand to the children.

"Alright, let's have some fun! I need you to follow me, and we need to move fast, just like bad guys are chasing us! After that, you'll all get your presents! Are you ready to help Santa?"

The kids cheered and some commented on how Sgt. Burke looked just like a movie cop, while a few of the older kids started to notice how some of the people around the room looked unhappy.

Sgt. Burke noticed as well and knew they had scant few seconds before all the questions started.

"I'm Officer Burke! Everybody ready to help Santa? Okay, all you kids! Ho! Ho! Ho! Let's go!"

Two of the team members pushed open the industrial double doors that led to the entrance ramp, and as they did, the sounds of the running battle filled the room. Rabbi Ramirez scooped up the smallest child and headed up the hallway. As the crowd of people neared the exterior door, a voice called out from the closed snack bar behind them.

"What ho, Santa? Where are you taking all our little elves?"

Sgt. Burke and Rabbi Ramirez spun. Leaning casually against the wall with an easy smile was Baron de Rais.

Santa Ramirez turned and handed the child he was carrying to Sgt. Burke.

"Go."

To the children, he laughed heartily and handed over the bag, minus his sword.

"Well, bless my soul! It seems like Santa has to check to see if this big boy is on the naughty or nice list!" Rabbi Ramirez handed his bag to the biggest young person. "You older children take Santa's bag of presents. I will be right behind you."

The children started to protest, but the oldest of their ranks had already started to sense the danger of the moment and started hustling the kids forward. As they went, the children yelled.

"Am I on the nice list?" asked one.

"Oooo, he's in trouble!" said another.

"Santa, come with us!" said one of the youngest.

Rabbi Ramirez shouted to them.

"Don't worry, Santa will be right there! Go get your presents!"

Baron de Rais flashed a sardonic simper, leaning casually against the counter.

"It will be a Christmas miracle!"

Rabbi Ramirez waited until children were shoveled around the corner, then tilted his head to face the colossal predator. As he did so, he gracefully pulled the beard down and, tucking the Santa hat in his belt, he drew his sword.

"I heard you were a knight, once."

"*Oui.* Once."

"Do you have a moment to dance with me?"

The vampire lolled his head sideways, and a longsword suddenly appeared in his hand. Baron de Rais strode casually towards the tiny man.

"I don't believe I've ever crossed blades with a Santa. How wonderful."

Rabbi Ramirez settled back into an open fencing pose.

"*En garde.*"

Baron de Rais chuckled and waved Ramirez forward.

"Certainement."

The Baron's face grew more monstrous and vampiric.

Ramirez stepped to the right, bringing the saber tip up in a medium guard. Baron de Rais sucked through his teeth, made a slow feint, then followed with a blindingly fast thrust. To his surprise, Ramirez had stepped inside the line, claiming a counter cut as the vampire had withdrawn. The wound smoked.

The odious creature snarled.

"Blessed and silvered? How thoughtful."

Ramirez nodded and said nothing about his own bleeding shoulder.

"It was a gift."

"From your kindly Order, no doubt. How will it feel, Jew, to be slain wearing the suit of a Christian Saint?"

Ramirez gave the vampire a grin.

"Very ironic. But I hope you don't mind..." Moving with speed, he angled his saber in and up, carrying through with a fierce linear attack, "...if Santa attempts to amuse you in the meantime."

Baron de Rais spun to the inside but found the smaller man rolling his blade over the line of the longsword in a tight and efficient counter.

Baron de Rais brought the long sword around in a blurring figure-eight pattern, and at its conclusion, he was suddenly to the right of the little man, and his sword hit Ramirez's hidden gorget with considerable force. Ramirez flew backwards, choking and dropping his blade.

The vampire lumbered back and nodded with recognition.

"Ah, the contra-contrario. A student of the Fior di Battaglia, and Fiore's famous Flower of Battle. Nicely done. Did you know, as a young man, I studied under one of his students."

Baron de Rais used the tip of his sword to flip Ramirez's saber back to him.

"For a mortal, you are not half bad. I rarely meet a suitable match these days. I don't suppose you would consider becoming a vampire? I have so few friends who want to play with blades with me anymore. It's a shame, really."

Rabbi Ramirez pried back his gorget a bit, caught his breath, and scooped up the blade, bringing it to a defensive guard.

"Sorry, I doubt it would be kosher. I don't suppose I could talk you into discussing fencing with me over a glass of wine? I would love to talk to you about the various schools."

Baron de Rais gave him a tiny, sorrowful smile that seemed almost genuine.

"My apologies."

The vile duelist brought his sword up in a salute, and then, with a flip of his wrist, brought his sword across the flat of Ramirez's saber so fast and hard that the blade snapped in half.

"I have some matters to attend to." The Baron danced back.

Ramirez barely had time to register his broken blade.

As the second half the blade hit the floor with a *tink*, the Vampire Lord was back across the room, and his sword was cleanly plunged through the chest of the man and out the back. As Baron de Rais tried to disengage, to his surprise the blade did not slip free easily. He looked down at it, vaguely annoyed.

Ramirez looked down at the object through his chest. Blood started to trickle from his lips. He coughed, hanging limply.

"*Hrrk*! Titanium trauma... plate... Kevlar weave. Apparently... *not* sword proof," he gasped.

Baron de Rais lifted the man on his sword easily and went to push him off the blade.

"Ah, pity. It was probably not vampire tested," he chuckled.

Ramirez choked and nodded. More blood issued forth, and as Baron de Rais put a hand on his chest, Ramirez suddenly grabbed the sleeve of the sword arm and hoisted himself forward down the blade, slamming the remaining half of his broken blade into the neck of the monster.

Baron de Rais screamed and threw the man twenty feet away. Ramirez hit the wall with a bone-snapping crunch, his body twisted in unsavory ways.

The blade of Rabbi Ramirez was now solidly lodged in the corner of the neck and collarbone of the vampire, and where it met the neck, it was smoking. Baron de Rais' face was grotesque.

With great effort, the Baron spun, twisting and turning, trying desperately to yank at the sword's hilt, which burned his hands as well. Snarling, he tried and tried unsuccessfully. In great pain, the Baron de Rais spat at the swordsman and headed after the children.

A short moment later there was even more cursing, as the vampire discovered that the bus with the kids was indeed flying away down the road as fast as the driver could go.

The hall reverberated with the sound of other battles. Baron de Rais cursed through a ragged throat and turned to head towards them.

* * *

In the long hallway, the third team led by the Marines had done fairly well while the element of surprise had been on their side. Flash and stun grenades having done their part, and they were now left with a lot of very pissed undead running towards them.

"Salcedo, light em' up!"

The younger Marine put his back against the wall, then leaned around the corner with his M-27 and emptied a whole clip before pulling back. Screams and cries erupted down the hallway. The corner he pulled back around exploded into splinters as the LorenCo security people returned fire. The vampires and ghouls were already recovering from the effect of the grenades, and two of the vampires had tossed wall lockers and desks into the hallway to stop the Order's team from getting closer.

One of the older men who was covering their back let out a gurgling scream and disappeared. The Gunny looked back, and several of the people who had been behind them were suddenly missing.

The team looked in all directions, and then the Gunny looked up. Several of the vampires were now scuttling across the ceiling, batlike, and two more were busy killing the humans they had just grabbed. The team swung their guns up, and the corkboard ceiling rained down on them. These particular vampires were not used to fighting people with blessed and silvered ammunition, and as a result, all screamed, fell, or retreated. As they swapped out magazines, Gunny cried out.

"That's it! We are outta here. Fall back, two by two, let's go!"

The civilians in the team kept firing the shotguns, backing out of the room. The Marines were just about out the door, when a humongous creature burst through the wall next to them and dragged a Marine back through. The Gunny grabbed the last two Marines and stopped them from going after their friend, having caught glimpses of several pairs of predatory eyes in the dark.

"No! Out! Now!" he ordered. The Gunny tossed a grenade into the room as they pulled back.

The ghouls of the various houses ran forward to prove themselves for their lieges, and as the Order team fell back through the doors, the Marines tossed several cans of CS tear gas and smoke as they exited.

The Gunny pulled the doors closed behind them. He looked back at the team he was leading. Half were gone, and the remainder were mostly shot or otherwise wounded. Things did not look good.

"Everyone, head toward that truck. Whitsell, get ready to pull out."

As he and the remaining Marines reloaded, they started shooting at other figures that were coming around the side of the building, pouring out from other exits. The Gunny bent down to do something while the remaining Marines covered him.

"Okay, get ready to boogie."

They saw more of the doors start to move and sank several three round bursts into them.

Turning, the Gunny pulled something up, and then started running.

"Let's not wait for them! Haul ass!"

The other two Marines snapped their safeties on and started sprinting.

* * *

Behind the cargo doors on the opposite side, Mr. Fenley, one of the senior House of Measure vampires, was quickly inspecting the two people who were just captured. Neither looked important. He turned to the LorenCo security officer.

"I need the rest of those people captured."

"No," the House of Swords vampire soldier shook his head. He turned away and started directing the others.

"Nick, Rolf, the rest of my team, you're with me. We just got called to help in Liberty Hall. The rest of you security people can go after the mortals." He turned to leave.

Fenley looked at the group of other vampires and minions surrounding him and decided he was unimpressed, as the clouds of teargas and smoke roiled up around them.

"No! I am giving you an order!" Fenley shouted.

The House of Swords officer just pointed to the various weapons lying around.

"Listen, you've got guns, you've got vampires. Hell, you are a vampire. Nut up. They're just fucking humans. Take charge and go get them!"

The conversation ended there, as the House of Swords team promptly turned and started jogging away.

Fenley looked around the room, standing out in his gray business suit. He scooped up a gun, inspected it, and waved to the mix of vampires, ghouls, and minions around him.

"Fine. Follow me. Everyone, let's go!"

With that, Mr. Fenley hoisted the gun and pushed through the double doors, only to witness humans running as fast as they could towards a truck with its engine running. Several of the minions and ghouls ran past Fenley, howling in hot pursuit. Fenley, on the other hand, had always been a vampire with an eye for detail. When he ran forward, he slowed to notice the four small green rectangles in the snow around them, the words *Front Toward Enemy* embossed on their casings and a chalk cross. Before he could say anything to stop his compatriots, there was a very bright flash.

Inside the LorenCo Sports Arena, the vampire from the House of Swords looked at his companions as they trotted towards the big hall. He smiled at one of his colleagues.

"What an asshole. Yeah, they are 'just humans.' Very fucking clever humans. Tactical rule number three: Never chase a Jarhead."

A big explosion boomed up the halls, echoing from outside.

The rest of the House of Swords team grinned and nodded, maintaining their running speed.

* * *

In the big hall, all hell was breaking loose.

The main Caestus team ran into the room. The team tossed flashbangs in all directions, and Jon and Pastor Carl were glowing as they moved quickly toward the chair containing Santa Steve.

Jon's axe spun and twirled, and Pastor Carl raised something in his hand that shone with an impossibly bright luminousness, which the vampires in the room could not approach.

Duke Cosimo and the other Vampire Lords looked at each other, and as one, they took off their ceremonial robes and started to change, blur, or disappear. The Order fought to get past the outer rungs of the ritual, and as they did, the magic emanating from the lines started to crackle and shift colors, resulting in some of the cauldron fires going out.

Jon's axe flashed as he cut his way past two of the robed figures, and saw in a glimpse that the team that had come in with the Order was starting to be picked off by the elder vampires. Two of the Vampire Lords morphed into monstrous creatures, some faded from view, and some of the team simply began to crumple. Pastor Carl saw what was happening, and loudly called out a prayer. The white light in his hand flew above the humans, and a circle of white light surrounded them. The attacks stopped for a moment.

Duke Cosimo blurred to a stop in front of Jon, who was standing over a recently decapitated vampire, breathing heavily. The two stared at each other through the glowing shield.

"You come at an inopportune time, Nicholite."

"I am *so sorry* we're late," Jon said as he looked around the room. "Invite got caught in the spam filter, you know how it is."

The skeletal figure of Avice kept his hand going in ritual moves, but he stepped over to address Duke Cosimo curtly.

"We don't have time for this. No witty banter. Kill them all and get them away from my spell circle."

Pastor Carl glanced at Jon and then down. When Jon did the same, he saw that one of the glowing lines was right next to his foot.

Duke Cosimo motioned with a finger, and the various vampires in the room cocked their guns, readying the next salvo.

Jon lowered his axe slightly in preparation.

"What are you willing to bet that this axe can bite far enough down, it can cut through this magical line and mess up whatever it is you're doing?" asked the warrior Santa.

Avice whirled and snarled. Cosimo's hand came up quickly, bringing a moment of pause.

"You came in here prepared to die, if necessary. What do you want?" Duke Cosimo asked in deadly, somber tones.

Jon carefully surveyed the room.

"All innocents, the children and all hostages, leave with us, and we get safe conduct out of town. Stop this ritual."

Cosimo sighed, irritated.

"You know we are not going to stop the ritual."

At that moment, the person dressed in the Krampus suit started to twist and shake, growing in size.

Jon brought his axe slightly closer to the line.

Cosimo tilted his head slightly.

"Wait. Children, freed. Any hostages not currently in the ritual, freed. Safe conduct out of the city after daybreak, done. Any Kith and Kin controlled by myself and the others here will leave this city as well."

Jon tensed his arm, preparing to chop with the axe.

"The ritual stops now!" Jon replied.

There was a guttural, pain-filled roar, animalistic and intense.

Boom.

Attached to the frame was a huge beast, hairy, horned, with clawed hands and hooves. Steam poured off of it. It roared as it tore at the chains attaching it to the structure, and the whole room shook. Krampus had arrived, and he was pissed.

"Everyone. Stop fighting for a moment," Cosimo yelled out to the room in a commanding voice.

Jon saw the vampires and their allies back up.

"Do it," Jon said to the forces of the Order.

Sudden stillness filled the air as everyone stopped fighting and backed up, looking for advantage or cover.

Duke Cosimo looked back to Jon.

"We really are close to what we need here. How about I give you the Santa after the ritual, alive and intact, and you leave this room *now*. Last chance."

The Krampus stopped roaring and reached down, wrapping one of its huge, clawed hands around one of the chains. Giving it an experimental pull, its muscles flexed, and concrete and rebar at the base of the structure started to crack and buckle. Avice motioned, and one of the acolytes pulled an ornate looking dagger out, placing it ceremoniously against the chest of the Santa sitting in the chair.

Duke Cosimo turned to look at the creature and spoke to it calmly in an old tongue.

"Krampus. Keep pulling at that chain and our associate there will take that very special dagger and stab him in the heart. Listen carefully. That blade is known as *The Abyss* and the magic contained within predates even your verdant god."

Krampus stopped struggling to look at Cosimo, snarling. Duke Cosimo continued.

"It will destroy the soul of your friend, the forces he represents will lose their focus and dissipate, and the mortal housing him will die in a totally absolute way. Oblivion. Since you are magically bound to Nicholas, I daresay there is a very good chance it will drag you away as well."

Krampus growled. Its voice was low as unsteady earth.

"Nicholas, is this true?"

The Santa in the chair looked down at the dagger for a moment and inspected it.

"It seems possible," said the voice of Nicholas dryly.

The Santa looked over at Cosimo, his voice clear and gentle.

"Cosimo, why are you and your Houses doing this? Why have you broken the pact, again, after so many years?"

Cosimo gestured with his finger pointing up.

"Daylight. A chance to rejoin the world we left so long ago." Duke Cosimo pointed to Krampus. "Your friend here is one of the few older gods still around, kept here, ironically by your bond and the belief in you. The ancient blood and power in him is not part of your Christian magics. If we drink from him, we will again join the land of the living. We have been in the darkness for so, so very long. We refuse to be cold."

Krampus stared down at the vampires in the room.

"Will I survive?" Krampus hissed.

"We don't know, but you are very strong. Possibly," said Duke Cosimo with a shrug.

Krampus hefted the chains in his hands and looked down at Nicholas.

"A life for a life, Little Man. I would be free of you, finally."

Nicholas looked concerned, and the rest of the room shared in the surprise as well.

Nicholas lifted his head to look up at the creature and started to say something.

"My friend, I would not..."

Pastor Carl continued praying softly but caught the eye of Jon. He shook his head ever so slightly.

Jon looked over his shoulder and nodded into the shadows outside of the ring of light. Out of the shadows, a dark, long-shafted arrow flew swiftly and silently. The vampires turned to react, but not fast enough. The arrow flew into the chest of the Santa in the chair.

As people started to react, Jon brought down his axe and struck the floor hard enough to bisect the groove. Lines and sheets of magical energy started to crackle around the room, burning, flashing, and freezing as they did.

In the mind of Santa Steve, there was a voice.

"Steven, I am so sorry," said the Spirit of Christmas.

"It's weird, I have an arrow in my chest, but it doesn't hurt that much," Steve answered. "Are you doing something?

"Yes, but you are still dying."

"Ah, figures. At least we won't both be taken out by that knife. Does that mean you get to go free?" Santa Steve sounded hopeful.

"I don't know. I think we are both magically bound here for now."

"Oh. Well, hell, I figured my heart or the diabetes would get me soon anyway. An arrow through the chest is a hell of a lot more dramatic. I hope no kids saw this."

"Agreed."

Another ghost materialized near the chair, watching everything. It was the Ghost of Top.

"Hey guys. If it's any consolation, the kids did get away."

The two spirits in the chair looked up at him.

"Oh? Excellent!"

"I've been trapped in the magical boundaries of this building," Top explained. "When that boundary got cut, I could move." The Ghost of Top gestured around. "I figure this is going to end pretty soon, one way or the other."

The three of them looked at each other as chaos and battle filled the room.

* * *

45. Not Silent Night

In the outskirts of the city, a running battle between the Fay and the vampires plus their human forces turned the snow-filled night into a warzone. The vampires were fashioning themselves metal weapons out of posts and car doors, huddling next to the vehicles that had not been destroyed by the Korred, who had no problem with dealing with metal. The Fay were having a delightful time picking the creatures off one by one. Inside this house or that, people were waking up.

In one house, the noise outside woke the children of a family. The kids ran downstairs to see the Christmas presents that were sure to be beneath the tree, but instead, they saw a kindly looking woman with dark brown eyes, spinning yarn on a drop spindle. The door busted open with a crunch, and a man dragging a woman staggered in.

"I invite her in!" he yelled as he pulled her across the threshold.

The three children stood frozen for the moment. The woman with the spindle looked at the siblings and gave them a reassuring smile.

"Not to worry."

Mother Holle lifted her spindle and pointed it at the two of them.

"It doesn't really work like that, darlings. Traditionally, it has to be someone who lives in the house or is a guest of theirs. You are neither."

Two threads flicked out, rapidly intertwining the two figures, and Mother Holle did not stop spinning.

The two cocooned figures made horrible sounds, and then fell to the floor as woolen mummies. The room went back to being quiet.

Mother Holle calmly turned to the children.

"Jack, Serenity, you two head back to bed, Santa has not come yet." The youngest children knew authority when they heard it and did as they were told.

"Is that Mrs. Claus?" asked Jack.

"Does it matter?" replied Serenity.

The small woman moved her hands, and there were balls of yarn in baskets waiting to be woven.

"Cora, be a dear and have a seat next to me. I have to tell you, I am so impressed with your spinning. Are you ready to spend some time weaving with me?"

Cora sat down, wide eyed and slightly breathless.

"Can you show me how to do the tanka ch'oro technique?" the young girl asked.

The elfish woman smiled with delight.

"What a lovely surprise! Up here, I'm usually asked about European techniques, but I have been learning from my Andean colleagues. I would be delighted! Okay, so your first jákima is never perfect...."

* * *

46. Then It Went All Celtic

Further down the road, two groups had faced off over one of the trucks. On one side were a group of vampires and ghouls, and on the other side, a group of mostly humanoid fairies. In front of the biggest truck was the Korred, hefting its scythe meaningfully.

The one named Fin was sitting on the roof of the vehicle, sharing a pocket flask with a man-sized rabbit. A conversation was happening in the middle of the snowy night.

"Hurley. Shinty. Irish field hockey. It's dreadfully easy. That waste bin over there is your goal, and that wheelbarrow thing over there is ours. We each have fifteen players when we start," said Fin with an easy-going grin.

The tall vampire woman looked up at him.

"And?"

"And all you have to do is get the ball in the bin three times. Ya do that, you get all these mortals in yer wagon, and ye fly away like happy hamsters."

"Bats," interjected the rabbit.

"Oh, right. Bats." Fin nodded his head in agreement.

The vampire looked at the people behind her, all of whom looked scared and frustrated. Shooting the Fay creatures had turned out to be not all that effective, and the battles had not been going well for them thus far. On the other hand, she knew that at least three of the vampires who were with them were of the House of Dance, and two more were House of Swords. Fast and strong, and they had all recently fed.

"Fine. Let's do this," said the vampire woman.

Fin handed over the flask to the rabbit, clapped his hands cheerfully, and hopped down. Taking off his hat, he brushed the snow off, and as he did, a stack of sturdy and worn hurley sticks clattered onto the ground.

Suspiciously, the vampires came over to pick them up.

Their leader looked around.

"What are we going to use for a ball?"

Fin looked inside his hat. While he did, the tall woman motioned to one of her teammates, who hopped over a car to one of the mangled bodies lying by the side of the road, and there was a snapping, gristly sound. A few seconds later, the head of the ghoul who had been lying there rolled between the two teams. Its eyes blinked.

Fin laughed.

"Ah, a traditionalist! Excellent. This will be a *grand* game."

He set his hat on a fencepost and winked at the people inside the truck, including a very groggy Abe. Abe–who was hogtied, partially drugged, and gagged–blinked at Fin woozily. Fin pulled Abe partially out of the truck so he could see the game and turned to walk back to the others.

The small stocky man picked up a hurley stick, tapped the snow off of it, and smiled.

"We back up three paces and cry, 'Lay On!'"

The vampire woman held up her hand.

"Wait, what about the rest of the rules?"

"Och, yer right. Too right. Ah, don't touch the ball with yer hands. First one to three goals wins. If one of your players gets knocked out, they can be replaced, but ta other side gets a replacement, too. If it's a civil game, then no weapons of the true death on the field."

"That's it?"

"That's it."

She turned to look back at the vampires and ghouls, her cohorts now showing a whole lot less humanity. They looked positively vicious. She turned back to give him a toothy grin.

"Fine."

"LAY ON!"

Abe's head started to clear in the cold air, as he watched fifteen elves, fairies, and "not-terribly-certains" run towards fifteen ghouls and vampires, grinning and screaming.

As the game commenced, two things became fairly obvious.

One, the fairies had been playing this game for thousands of years. They were very good at it. Two, the vampires had speed, strength, and ferocity on their side, and most of them were bigger. As the "ball" sailed back and forth, the fairies were the first ones to score with a loud *CLANG* from the goal on the side of the vampires.

The tall woman called for two of her team members as they lined up for the next round.

"Seth, Talbert, swap sides and shift forms."

The two vampires from House of Swords started to twist and shape into unruly fanged horrors. The fairies back up a bit. Fin stepped up in front of his players and pointed his hurley at them.

"Ye call that a warp spasm? Faugh. I played against The Hound, Cuchullain 'imself, ye great furry idjits."

He nodded over his shoulder and gave them a wink.

"On me, lads."

The cry lay on went out again and this time, game or outright battle, the fairies were faster. But they were getting knocked bodily across the field, as the vampires were moving and working together well. The wooden hurley sticks were now being used more as swords to counter the claws and fangs that were now at play.

Over by the truck, Abe looked to his left and saw the Ghost of Ron.

"Well, this is something you don't see every day."

"If you have any energy, I would try using your power," Ron answered Abe. "Things at the arena are not going well, but it's not a lost cause yet. They could really use you."

Abe tried to ignore the commotion of the game and took a deep breath. The world slowed and snowflakes drifted to crawl in the air. Abe took a deep breath and mentally pushed. Ever so slowly, the real world sped back up again.

At that moment, Ron noticed the giant rabbit finishing off the rest of the flask.

"YOU!" he roared.

The Rabbit seemed a bit confused as he focused on the very angry ghost. Ron stepped past Abe, and as he did, Ron's hand came up with a very real, very solid looking revolver in it.

The rabbit's eyes opened wider as Ron brought the gun around.

"Listen, you furry menace! You're supposed to be on our side! I saw what you did back there! You help my friend here or, by God, I will blow your crazed little brains out!"

The rabbit jumped back, startled.

"I- I- I can't! The game! You cannae interfere with the game. Your friend is part of the prize!"

"I don't care! Untie him, now!"

The rabbit's head tilted as he got into an argument with himself.

"The mortal cannae leave, but treasure can be improved. His bonds are part of his clothes. Clothes can be presentable. Yes!"

The rabbit touched Abe briefly and then turned to the ghost.

"He can untie himself, but he *cannae* leave until the game is over," the rabbit said emphatically. As he did, he transformed into a giant hellfire-breathing black horse.

"The mortal stays until the game is *over*," said the Horse in a horrible voice. The ghost and the horse stared at each other balefully.

Abe looked down, now adorned in full Santa suit of high quality, and he found that his bonds were silk ribbons that untied easily. He looked over at Ron.

"Uh, Ron, how are you holding a real revolver?"

Ron glanced at him, and then back to the Pooka.

"I'm really angry right now. This thing tripped you up, which is why the vampires caught you. Emotions have power, I guess." Ron cocked his head, thinking about it some more. "And I did happen to bless this gun in the church, and I did die with it in my hand. On holy ground. Fighting supernatural evil. Sooo?"

"You created a holy relic?" Abe asked Ron, eyes wide as saucers.

A voice chimed in from nearby.

"More likely it was some sort of Santa magic."

The slender vampire stepped out of the shadows. The Pooka caught her in his fiery gaze.

"The mortal stays until the game ends," the Pooka snorted with words of fire.

Allison the vampire held up her hands.

"Hey, hey, come on My Little Pony, no worries. My team is winning anyway."

Just then, there was a clang, and the vampires cheered as a head careened off the fairies' goal.

"Crap," said Ron and Abe simultaneously.

Down on the playing field, the fairies were definitely getting the worst of it. Several of them were seriously damaged, and the ghouls and vampires were able to sustain many wounds that would normally kill a mortal.

The tall female captain of the undead team looked at Fin.

"Tied."

"Tied," Fin agreed and nodded.

He spat out a tooth from a battered face and looked at the woman with a smile of respect.

"Pity you are no longer alive."

She gave him a pointed smile in return.

"I hear fairy blood is tasty, crazy stuff."

At which point a small beeping was heard. Everyone turned to look at the source of the sound.

One of the vampires held up a phone.

"My bad, sorry. Ninety minutes till dawn, everyone."

"Thank ye, good to know!" said Fin with a broken grin. He nodded to the other fairies who nodded back knowingly.

The vampire woman shook her head and backed up three paces.

"Lay on!"

Now, the game had changed. The Fay were playing defense, and they had gotten remarkably good at blocking shots and passing.

Time passed, and one of the twisted vampires reached over and ripped a rusty *"Pick up after your dog"* metal post out of the ground in rage and frustration. Swinging it, he hit one of the fairies who had just blocked a shot, and the collision making a solid metallic *Bwhank!* sound.

The fairy screamed in pain, its wounds smoking.

As one, the fairies made a keening sound, crying out.

"Cold iron! Cold iron on the field!"

Fin was mid-pass when he saw this, and he stopped to look at the Captain of Team-Dead.

"Ye brought this on yer'sel."

The woman looked at the smoking, writhing fairy.

"Wait, you said there were no rules other than the ones you mentioned."

"I did." Fin stepped back and rolled his shoulders. He took a blood red pointed cap from his pocket and put it on his head.

"Cute," the tall vampire woman said and giggled, despite herself.

"Ye think?" Fin laughed with her darkly.

He offhandedly took his hurley stick and smashed it against a rock.

The woman eyed the now very pointed end of the stick.

"Wait!"

She held up her both hands, but there was a glimmer, and she was already flying backwards into a telephone pole, staked through the heart.

She gurgled, trying to say something as black blood poured out of her mouth.

Fin leaned in and pushed to make certain the stake would stay.

"One of the finer points of the game, m'lass, is ye don't bring killing weapons ontae the field. Ye dent use any of yer strange magics, and neither did we. But, ye bring cold iron... tch. Tisn't done. Very bad form." He wagged a finger in her face.

"We Fay have our vulnerabilities; cold iron is one. I've heard vampires have their weaknesses, too. Wood, say." He turned to the rest of the fairy team.

"I believe we now go into what the humans call 'sudden death.'"

At that, the fairies barreled towards the vampires, and both Ron and Abe found their looks of abject terror very refreshing.

Fin flickered back to where Abe was standing, pulled a handkerchief out, and started wiping the blood off his face.

"I believe you were headed somewhere, lad?"

"Yes?"

The smaller fairy man looked over at the giant black Pooka.

"You deprived him of a ride, tis only right that you give him one and deliver him safely to where he wants to go."

The Pooka reared, whinnying and snorting flame. It did not look happy.

"I know, I know, but ye brought that bit wi Fionn MacCumhal yerself. You owe this one a deed."

Abe looked at the small man, the terrifying horse, and at Ron, who had put the gun away for the moment.

"Uh, actually...."

Before another word came out of his mouth, the Pooka grabbed Abe, tossed him high into the air, and ran after him. Abe landed on the Pooka's back, screaming and hanging on for dear life. The Pooka bellowed evilly and flew like a spirit into the night.

The vampire woman Allison turned to Fin.

"Err, I did not promise to protect that mortal."

"No, you did not." Fin sniffed indifferently.

The vampire sped off into the darkness after them.

Thumping filled the air as the remaining fairies dealt with the last of the vampires and ghouls. The telephone pole was now covered with them, with impaled vampires and ghouls strung around a ghastly Christmas tree. The display was helped by the loan of some Christmas lights from a nearby yard the fairies had borrowed.

"Very nice," Fin complimented their work.

One of the fairies smiled a bit too brightly.

"Too bad, it was a good game. They almost had us."

The other one stabbed a hurley stake into a vampire whose scream turned into a sigh as it was impaled.

"Aye, but they always cheat."

"Aye," several of the fairies sighed and shook their heads.

Off in the distance, one of the Fay yelled, "Guinness!" and the Fay team smiled and disappeared.

* * *

In a flash, the Pooka was across the plains, cantering near a side entrance to the sports arena. Abe could barely speak, his face and hair wind blasted straight back. Suddenly everything was still.

Abe slid off the Pooka while clinging limply to its side, plopping into the snow by the side of the building. The Pooka snarled, its eyes blazing orange.

"The deed is done, and you delivered."

With that, it spun and disappeared into the darkness. Abe floundered in the snow, and though he tried to stand up, he tripped over something. It was the semi-frozen corpse of Top. Abe screamed and staggered back against the wall, staring.

"Woah! Easy, big guy. Don't step on what's left of me, amigo."

The Ghost of Top faded in, looking at Abe with concern. Abe's gaze darted back and forth between the ghost and the remains.

"Yeah, sorry about that, Abe. Until you touched my body, I had no clue you were out here. The whole plan in there has gone pear shaped, so it's all hands on deck. They really could use your help. In the back of my jacket, there on my body, there are a few things that might prove useful. Grab them and follow me."

Abe felt sick to his stomach as he flipped his friend over.

Top stood by, impatient.

"Yeah, right, it's gruesome, got it. Come on, come on."

There was a gust of wind and cold, and the Ghost of Ron showed up in front of Abe.

"There you are! God, it's nuts in th... Oh, hi Top!"

"Great. Yeah, old home week. Hi. By the way, Ron, there are all sorts of magical lines in there that will mess up us mostly ghostly types. Guess I can sum up. Short version?"

"There's a bunch of old school vampires in there, and they have the Spirit of Christmas trapped in the middle of a ritual inside Santa Steve's body. They used the Spirit of Christmas to bring Krampus here because he's some sort of old god, and they want to drink him."

Abe looked at the two ghosts, bewildered, and stepped past the body of his friend squeamishly.

"And I am supposed to do what, now?"

The two ghosts looked at each other and shrugged.

"Good point. Uh, do you need to think of something specific when you use your power?" said Top.

"I think it helps, but honestly, just recently, I just took a deep breath and just sort of... prayed? Or mentally pushed something, if that makes any sense?"

Ron looked at Abe intently, the heavy snowstorm swirling through his image.

"Abe, we've asked a lot of you. This is a lot bigger than any of us imagined. We need to disrupt their ceremony, free the Christmas Spirit, and save Krampus. Your sword might be able to break their bonds, but only if we can get you close enough, and yeah, there's a lot of bad guys in there."

"What we need is a distraction," Top suggested. "That used to be my department."

Top paced, frustrated, tilting his head back and looking skyward. His eyes widened, and he snapped back down to the others.

"Guys, this place has skylights!"

"Oh yeah, solar too!" Ron started to smile.

"What?" Abe looked at Top.

"The room where the ceremony is happening has nothing but a roof above it," Ron pointed upward. "A roof with skylights. We go up and over, drop you in right on top of them!"

"Wait, I don't have any rope with me, and I don't fly," Abe reminded them.

Ron blinked out for a moment and then popped back in.

"There is some serious snow up there, but I think you can grab one of the cables attached to the solar arrays and peel it off. That might work."

"In a pinch, your big Santa buckle could work as a carabiner," added Top.

"Great, I'll be Spider Santa or the great Santa Piñata, woo." Abe did not look enthusiastic.

"Over there, Abe," Ron pointed to an access ladder a short distance away. "You guys need to go now. I'll join you in a second."

Abe ran for the ladder.

* * *

Inside the hall, the Vampire Lord for the House of Mirrors was carefully stalking Skyia the archer. The warrior woman was halfway up the pipe rigging, set up, and ready to loose another arrow. The Elder vampire appeared almost on top of her, clawed hand ready to strike. Skyia instinctively turned and released. The arrow flew through the creature unimpeded, and sailed across the hall, hitting Pastor Carl in the side with great impact. The illusion of the creature smiled at Skyia as it disappeared. She cursed and looked down to see the vampire illusionist again, and immediately notched another arrow, but the vampire smiled, bowed, and disappeared.

Pastor Carl staggered sideways, the light in his hand dimming and beginning to falter. The hall flickered, and as their circle of protection shrank, the ring of vampires, ghouls, and minions started drawing in closer on the Winter Order's team.

Avice called out to several of the acolytes, who promptly assumed different positions, their chanting taking on a different note. As the battle between humans and vampire forces raged around them, Avice pointed to Duke Cosimo, who moved quickly. Krampus turned to see the Vampire Lord standing beside him, glaring as the vampire lifted the rusty chains and manacles that had manifested when Krampus first appeared, pulling them tighter.

Krampus roared as Cosimo yanked the chains down, connecting them to thick stanchions, while the goat-man thrashed so hard that the surrounding floor started buckling, causing the impaled Santa to fall over from the chair, and leaving the ghostly Spirit of Christmas still sitting upright, spellbound in it.

Avice pointed to several of the vampires.

"Someone must be pulling the chains at all times to maintain their hold on the creature. Do *not* let go."

Avice produced a small journal from his robes and intoned a phrase in Greek. The rusty chains began to glow, and Krampus stopped moving, silent, eyes wild in anger and rage.

Avice motioned and a chalice and a dagger were brought forth. As Avice approached, readying to slice the throat of Krampus, acolytes with other cups drew near.

The sudden silence from Krampus caught Jon's attention, despite the firefight that surrounded him. Jon clicked his earpiece and called out tersely.

"Rick, anybody who can hear this, we are losing in here. Carl is down, and…"

Jon's gun jammed. Cursing, he surged forward, gripping his axe with both hands, swinging in short, economical strokes that left a tide of blood and vampiric remains. Storming towards the platform, Jon became a maelstrom of blessed metal, swinging his axe powerfully from the hip.

Duke Cosimo glanced up and, lifting a piece of broken flooring in his offhand, clubbed Jon with it expertly. The warrior slammed down into the floor with a crash, rolling a few feet away.

The Duke cast an appraising look at the fallen Julemanden, then turned back to Avice, his face stoic.

"Continue, please."

* * *

47. Home for Christmas

Out in the snowstorm, Grandfather Winter raised his hand and pipes burst and buckled with shrieks of twisting metal that reverberated down the steel pipeline. A mile away, on another section of the structure, the reverberations traveled to pique the interest of two dogs, drawing their attention away from the bomb they were focused on.

Inside the pumping station, Spur patted one of the dogs on the head and stepped forward to examine the device. It was formidable. Heaving a deep sigh, he wiped the sweat from his brow, carefully shrugging off his backpack.

"This is going to take me a bit." The two dogs sat down, patiently.

* * *

Six miles away, on the Wapitah access road, a small bus forced its way through treacherous roads, obscured by snow. In an effort not to disturb the children, the bus driver called back to Sgt. Burke in a hushed whisper.

"Heads up. We have company."

Burke saw flashing lights ahead, the outlines of several vehicles, and figures standing in the snow on both sides of the roads. None had cold weather gear on.

Sgt. Burke whispered to the driver, an older Hispanic man.

"Those are not good guys. Those are LorenCo forces, and some of our police force that they've turned. Whether or not they're vampires, they're all monsters of some sort."

The man nodded and checked the knife and gun under his coat. He looked up ahead solemnly.

"We are screwed, aren't we?"

Sgt Burke stepped next to the driver as he surreptitiously reloaded his gun.

"Yup."

Burke looked over his shoulder at the kids, most of whom were bundled and curled up with each other, most of them asleep.

"I'll do what I can to draw them to the side. This road is covered with snow and ice, we have a lot more mass. Ease up as much as you can, but don't stop. You let me out here, I run ahead and try to talk us through. If things start to look wrong, you hit the gas, throw it in low gear, and push right through those two vehicles. You forget about me, and you keep going. You don't stop for nothing until you are way the hell away and in broad daylight. Then find a church."

"Yes, got it. Go with God," the driver agreed.

"I sure hope so. You, too."

The driver pulled up a cross from around his neck and kissed it, slowing down the bus to a crawl. Burke leaned out and swung into the snow, nearly losing his footing. After righting himself, he ran out into the blustery snow, the flashing lights ahead an eerie counterpoint of color in the dark haze. One of the figures near the dark vehicles walked forward to meet him, warily.

"Sgt. Burke?"

Burke advanced slowly, his hands in his parka, hood up. Burke recognized the person as one of the LorenCo Security officers.

"Yeah, Miller, right?"

"Right."

"Yeah, I need you to let me and the bus pass," said Sgt. Burke.

"That's not going to happen," said Miller, thumbing the safety on his assault rifle.

Burke nodded, scrutinizing the LorenCo officers and the turned cops who were starting to edge towards the bus. Burke looked at the vampire officer.

"You know, you don't have any jurisdiction here. I'm a duly appointed officer of the law for this town, and you need to stop this nonsense right now."

Burke hooked a thumb back to the bus, playing for time.

"Besides, if your guys get any closer, I have a friend in the bus who is going to drive it into the ditch, and we've poured gasoline right down the center. We may not live, but you won't get those kids. I hear your folk don't like fire."

The LorenCo officer gave Burke a toothy smile.

"Really?"

Miller looked past Burke to the bus, studied it for a second, and then looked back.

"You know, funny thing about being a vampire. Super keen sense of smell. Really good hearing, too." He looked at Burke with playful malice. Burke shrugged, blew on his hands, shivering with an unconvincing smile.

"Sergeant, you don't smell like gas, and I don't hear kids screaming," Miller continued. "Four of us deadites can pull that bus out of a ditch. I should know, we've been pulling our trucks out of the snow all frikkin' night."

Burke shrugged and put his hands back in his pockets.

"Hey, it was worth a...."

Burke fired through the sides of the parka, the two pistols in his pockets smoking as he unloaded into Miller's chest.

The vampire spun left and then right as the bullets hit him, but that did not stop him from flying forward and slamming Burke effortlessly onto the hood of the bus. The rest of the LorenCo forces began their march forward, and although the bus roared and started to roll forward, several of the vampires were immediately in front of it, slowing it down.

At the sounds of the gunfire and the tires slipping, the children started waking up and looking around, frightened. The driver leaned forward and dropped the bus into a lower gear, swearing in Spanish.

The vampire named Miller pointed to one of the other LorenCo officers.

"Get in there, you idiot. Throw the driver out here, but don't damage the bus. We'll need it."

The man nodded and moved toward the side door, ignoring the body of Burke on the hood. He sprouted short, curved claws, and moved to peel open the side doors of the bus.

There was a loud bang on the top of the bus, followed by the sound of something hard-shod walking across it. A hooked blade reached down and tapped the vampire on his head from above.

The vampire looked up to see the horrific shape of something with antlers— part human, part quadruped, with smoldering eyes fixed on him. It was covered with rags, and all around the area whispering sounds grew louder, more manic. The creature looked down.

"*Under our protection,*" it growled in a crackling voice.

The vampire staggered away from the windows, and the other vampires became distracted, gawking up at the creature. The bus started to lurch forward.

"Shoot it! Fucking shoot it!" Miller yelled out, pointing to the top of the bus.

Somewhere underneath the glowing eyes, a droning, wheezing laugh filled the air and strange hymns started to mingle with gunfire.

The children on the bus watched the scene unfold through the frosted windows, witnessing slender and unearthly creatures running over the top of the snow, bad men being snatched up, spun in the air, or dragged off on their faces.

Five-year-old little Olivia tugged at seven-year-old Peter.

"The elves are here, and they're beatin' up the bad guys! I told you we were still in the movie!"

Peter heard the odd laughter and screams. He was not convinced.

"They're scary. And when I get home, I am going to ask my mom and dad to get rid of that elf on the shelf. He's creepy, too."

The driver kept rolling forward and with a crunch, pushed the bus through the blockade, much to the delight of the kids.

There was a polite knock on the door.

The driver could not see anybody at first, but when Sgt. Burke finally came into view, the way he moved alongside the bus was odd, to say the least. The driver stopped the bus and opened the door, and a flurry of snow came in, carrying the unconscious body of Sgt. Burke with it, dropping it in the nearest available seat.

A tall creature in elegant clothes stepped disdainfully onto the bus. The kids all stared at it with wonder. It looked at the children curiously, and then turned to address the driver.

"You are safe for now. Drive to the nearest city and take him to a hospital. He lives, but he is damaged."

The driver looked up equally wide-eyed but managed to nod. One of the children spoke up.

"Are you an elf?"

Ilbereth turned to look at the child.

"I am."

The children looked at one another, then unleashed a hundred questions at all once. One broke out of the pack.

"You're not an elf! Elves are shorter, and they have curly shoes and stripey socks." This observation brought a fresh round of discussion among the other children.

Ilbereth looked at the child in question.

"What I am, or am not, is not for you to say. However, I am helping someone you know: Nikolas."

The children puzzled over that for the briefest of seconds.

"Santa Claus!" They all started cheering.

"When are we going to get our presents?" one of them asked immediately.

Ilbereth raised an eyebrow.

"After you wake up, of course."

"What?"

The Seelie Lord waved a slender hand, and the children sank into a deep sleep.

This amazed the bus driver, and something akin to a smile flickered across the face of Ilbereth as it watched over the bus full of now dormant children.

"A useful glamour."

"Agreed!" the driver echoed.

Ilbereth turned to leave the bus but stopped short.

"Ah, the promise delivered." The tall elf whispered into the wind, *"We have a present for the children."*

There was a rush of laughter, cackling and twittering, and suddenly, the bus was rolling down the road and the door was closed. Surrounding and festooning the children were all sorts of items that would delight a fairy. Hubcaps, lug nuts, rearview mirrors, police lights, handguns, Christmas lights of all descriptions, and assorted vampire body parts.

The driver glanced into the overhead mirror, shook his head, and returned his concentration to the road in front of him.

"Well done," Ilbereth commented as they gathered at the road stop. He raised an eyebrow. A few of the creatures looked furtive.

"Ahem."

A creature moved aside to reveal the sleeping girl it was trying to stuff into a bag.

"We are sworn to do no harm, and despite how badly they treat their children, we are not allowed to play with the ones here," Ilbereth said.

The fairy creatures groaned. One of them stroked a little boy's hair and whispered, and as it did, the boy started to fade.

> *Come away, O human child!*
> *To the waters and the wild*
> *With a faery, hand in hand*

"Put it back," Ilbereth said sternly.

The creature wrinkled its face and disappeared in a puff of mist. Ilbereth looked off towards the arena.

"We await."

* * *

48. In the Darkness

Inside the sports complex, the hall containing the ritual had gotten much quieter. The forces of what was left of the Caestus and their teams were quickly running out of ammo. With Father Carl down, the blessed light that was forcing back many of the younger vampires was no longer present, and any humans that got too close to the shadows were grabbed and dragged back into the darkness, kicking and screaming.

Several of the Vampire Lords stood quietly waiting, as an acolyte handed an ancient, ornate chalice to Avice with a bow, the vessel brimming with blood drained from the hulking form of Krampus. Avice made some gestures over it and poured it into a second container as equally venerated. As the blood of Krampus mixed with the contents of the second container, the entire repository glowed. The mage analyzed the change, then sealed the reaction with the lid, carefully placing it aside. Avice turned back to the assembled Vampire Lords.

"Its blood is indeed dangerous and potent, but you can consume it."

Another chalice of blood was drawn and handed to Duke Cosimo, ruler of the Vampiric Houses.

Duke Cosimo looked to his left and right. He presented the controlling chains of the struggling Krampus to his consigliere, Henry Raymond, who pushed back his hat and leaned in to keep the chains tight, bracing himself as Krampus tried to break free.

Duke Cosimo de Florentine, Lord of Vampires, nodded to his accursed brethren, his eyes black as a starless midnight. He raised the cup to the ghostly figure of the Christmas Spirit glowing in the chair, concluding his toast by lifting the chalice to his lips and draining it. Black liquid ran from the corner of his mouth, and he dabbed at it with a silk handkerchief. His eyes flashed green, and then faded completely white, and he swayed like a reed. The other vampires stepped back, but Avice leaned in with avid curiosity.

"Ready one of them, our Lord may need to feed," said Avice, glancing at the humans being circled.

Duke Cosimo wavered and, for a moment, his skin rippled. After a long breath, he opened his eyes, which now shone with bright green circles around the irises. Composing himself, he addressed the others, his words slightly slurred and thick.

"It is a potent draught. Do not drink it, if you do not have absolute control over your form."

The other Arch Vampires looked at each other, and Lord of the House of Measures stepped forward.

"I am ready."

Another cup of blood was handed down, and the vampire took it, drinking greedily. While all looked on, the vampire showed his shark-like bestial nature and leaned back to utter a warbling hunting cry. Black blood started to pour from its nose and eyes. It started to twist and shake, its body cycling through one predatory phase, then another. For just for a second, it looked human again, and then seemed as though it was looking to Avice for help.

Avice's gaze remained wide and indifferent, and he pulled the sleeve of his robe up in anticipation. The hapless Arch Vampire exploded messily, and there was a small cheer from the group of encircled humans.

Duke Cosimo shot them a scowl.

"Quiet, you."

Santa Jon, who was being propped up by one of the team members, chuckled.

"Some folks just can't handle their eggnog."

Another cup was handed to the Arch Vampire for the House of Dance. She drank it calmly and handed the cup back with graceful fingertips. She stretched and wriggled, as a set of black leathery wings manifested and stretched out. She giggled and brought them in to fold around her like a cloak. More blood was drawn.

In the group of humans, Santa Jon felt something being pressed into his hand. It was a high-tech grenade. He nodded. Looking down on the ground, he spotted a plastic Christmas ornament. He had that handed to him as well.

The Arch Vampires were all given their cup, and Duke Cosimo turned to Henry.

"I will take the chains. You must get your reward, old friend."

At the moment the two handed off chains to each other, Santa Jon leaned out.

"Well, since it's Christmas, and we're exchanging gifts and all..."

He whirled and threw something at Henry and Cosimo, and then spun to the right.

"Grenade!" one of the vampires shouted.

Henry sidestepped and caught the object with inhuman speed, pitching it back at the humans. He shook his head.

"Idiots."

The object bounced off Jon's head. It was the Christmas ornament.

"Well, don't I feel silly. I threw the wrong one at you!"

Jon grinned and looked down at where the actual grenade was rolling between the two bound spirits, near the altar. Jon grabbed a bunch of people near him and threw all of them towards the floor.

* * *

49. Up on the Housetop

Abe slogged through the incredibly thick snow on the roof. The large skylights had mechanical deicers, which jutted through the snow like giant translucent beetle backs in a long row, spanning this section of the arena. The Ghost of Top blinked in ahead of Abe, moving from one skylight to another. Finally settling on one skylight in particular, he pointed down.

The wind and snow were pushing against Abe like a pro defensive lineman. The Caestus symbol kept most of the cold at bay, but he had to lean into the wind heavily to make any headway at all. Stepping near one of the nearby solar arrays, Abe pulled the candy cane from his Santa belt pouch, revealing the sword *Illuminator*.

Distant Christmas lights flashed across the flat of the blade. Stepping back awkwardly, he made a few strokes and then pulled on the stiff electric cable that he had just sliced through. In a few short moments, the brittle clips holding the cable gave way, and soon he had a considerable length of cable wound up. Top appeared at his shoulder.

"That should be enough. You will need to cut through the housing… Oh crap! Incoming!"

Abe barely had time to turn as the very large and very angry Baron de Rais trudged through the roof snow as if it were nothing. His hair and eyebrows were thick with ice, but the hilt stuck in his neck still steamed whenever snowflakes hit it. The vampire was on top of Abe before he could do more than drop the cable. With a backhand, Baron de Rais knocked Abe across the roof a good distance, sending Illuminator flying out of his hand. The Baron then walked over to look down through the skylight. Below, a majority of the Caestus forces stood gathered, and Duke Cosimo could be seen raising a smoking chalice to his lips.

The Vampire Lord smiled and turned to look at the Santa who rolled backward, aikido style, and shoved himself back to his feet. Abe shook his head, trying to get the ringing out of his ears.

"I need to kill you and get down there. Someone is buying me a very rare vintage, and I would hate to miss my opportunity," said Baron de Rais.

Abe's eyebrows furrowed. Without thinking, he looked down to see a candy cane sticking out of his pouch. When he reached for it, the second it was drawn, the sword he saw across the roof in a snowdrift disappeared in a flash and was now in Abe's hands again. Abe brought it around into a mid-guard and started toward the vampire. Baron de Rais laughed.

"Really? Two sword fights in one night! This really is Christmas!"

The Vampire leaned forward, as if to rush Abe, but only moved a few paces.

Abe nodded, his thoughts torn between the present and his memories of the dark, lonely place this bastard had thrown an innocent little girl without a second thought. There was no attempt made to hide his contempt.

"Lucky you. You're fighting a member of the Caestus, remember? No vampire speed advantages here. I like your piercing, by the way."

The Marquis snarled and slogged over to meet the Santa. Blades flashed and rang. Baron de Rais danced back, chuckling. Abe followed, overextending the sword, the long blade hitting pieces of roof and solar domes with a *SNIK*, creating the odd spark here and there.

Baron de Rais did a moulinet, bringing his blade easily within Abe's guard. He pinked Santa Abe and now drops of fresh crimson started decorating the snow. Red blood marred the white fur of the suit's cuffs.

As he backed up, Abe started becoming more and more desperate, swinging more wildly, and again, the Baron lightly reached out to pink him again, wearing that sadistic grin, droplets of blood becoming steady trickles. Baron de Rais stepped back, sweeping his leg to get ready for a lunge.

Abe followed doggedly.

"I know what you're trying to do. You are trying to wind me, make me slow down so you can get closer. Not going to happen."

Baron de Rais nodded amiably, and instead corkscrewed around Abe, dodging the formidable range of the sword with serious focus.

"Really? From the way you are swinging that clumsy rake, I can only assume you are the very master of that blade. Well done."

Abe grimaced, keeping the blade going in big arcs, forcing the vampire back around the dome. The blade collided with things with apparent abandon.

"Nope. It's a Christmas present. I just got it, and so I'm sorry I can't go all Highlander on you right now."

The vampire suddenly stopped backing up, spun like a top, and darted inside the range of the blade. Abe barely got the cross guard down in time to stop the Baron's attack. The two of them held the position for a fraction of a moment.

"I may not have my speed, but I do still have my strength, it would seem."

The Baron pushed Abe sideways into the dome of the skylight. Abe's eyes grew wide as he lost the battle of strength. Skittering sideways, he glanced over the vampire's shoulder and grinned.

"Well, I have something you do not."

The vampire forced Abe's blade into a bad position, and for just a second, he shot a glance in the direction Abe was looking. With immaculate timing, Top materialized next to the big vampire and shouted "BOO!"

The Baron fell backwards onto his ass, bewildered.

Top laughed out loud.

"Remember me, you cheese-eating surrender monkey?"

Abe pressed his advantage, bringing the edge of the blade over the top, chopping at the vampire repeatedly. Abe landed a blow on the thigh, but even down on the ground, the Baron was an excellent swordsman.

"Cute. I have ways of dealing with ghosts too, you hack conman," said the Baron.

Abe continued swinging and missing, as the vampire spun himself back up into a standing position. He had a plan.

Top started to say something, but the wind roared, and a rumble and moan filled the air.

The Baron reversed his guard, skipping step forward, and slammed his foot down as he lunged at Abe. The slender blade tip skipped off the massive belt buckle, and punched through the suit, grazing Abe, but passing through the thick leather of the Santa belt.

Abe turned and brought down the hilt in a pommel strike, unable to move effectively. It connected with the vampire solidly, leaving half a burning "S" symbol on the snarling vampire's face.

Baron de Rais twisted his sword hand, pulling Abe into an embrace.

"Oh, look. I am inside your guard."

The Baron de Rais belched a low laugh, his free hand reaching up and grabbing Abe by the collar of the Santa suit and orienting his throat. He opened his mouth inhumanly wide, showing a mouth full of jagged fangs, his eyes tar black.

"Santa, shall I tell you what I want for Christmas?" The vampire went for the kill.

In response, Abe brought his sword overhand, slicing into the roof once more. Out of the corner of his eye, he could see the circle the two of them had made around the skylight.

"Sure, come and sit on my knee!" Abe taunted back.

Closing his eyes, Abe concentrated on using his power. Dropping the sword, he rolled backwards, flipping the vampire into the damaged dome, which crashed with a massive popping sound, and the Baron flew through it with a scream of frustration.

There was a sudden roar and a moaning, groaning sound of tortured steel as Abe stood up. The Ghost of Top was looking at him and giving him the thumbs up while trying to yell at him. Abe yelled into the wind.

"What were you saying? What was that noise?"

"The roof! I think the roof is going to..."

Metric tons of new snow cascaded downward, enabled by the recent slices made in the roof, and met the ritual below with a deafening slam. Abe's plan had worked all too well, his chopping having indeed weakened the over-strained roof.

Abe barely had time to look down, before he, too, fell into the arena beneath with a yelp.

The Ghost of Top looked around at no one in particular, floating in mid-air and sighed.

"Give in. The roof is going to give in," he finished saying and dematerialized.

As Abe fell, one part of him was screaming, while another part was curiously calm. His brain ran a calculation. Accounting for at least one foot of snow on several thousand square feet of roof, many tons of snow, steel, and air conditioning were about to crush those below. Not to mention all the lighting, sound equipment, and AV displays hanging underneath the roof. This was not going to be pretty. He suspected that the vampires would be able to survive the damage a lot better than the humans. In one massive BOOM, a good percentage of the roof collapsed. Abe spun mid-air and as he fell, he prayed.

"Dear Lord..."

With a blow he felt across his whole body, he hit something soft then something hard. There was a sudden flash of odd color, and all became black.

In the eerie light of the few working emergency lights, door lights, and battery powered Christmas lights, Abe's eyes opened to a sliver of frozen hell. Around the hall, snow had fallen like a giant hand, and the air pressure of the roof had blown back a massive number of bodies and gear. Pieces of lumber and speakers punched up through the snow like art-deco Christmas trees. Part of his shoulder felt completely numb, and he could see fancy gilded wood smashed to bits all around him, along with scraps of binding containing magical writing that laid in the debris. His brain was foggy, but something seemed truly odd. It felt as if he was not alone.

"Abraham, you need to get up right now," said a calm voice.

Abe groggily looked around. As he tried to stand up, the odd flashes of color floated around him again. They eventually dissipated, but he was not certain whether he was hallucinating.

Halfway in and out of a pile of snow and debris to his left was The Baron, who was partially buried in the snow, a large shard of Plexiglas piercing one of his legs. The Baron turned to look at Abe and smiled.

"I will be right with you."

Adrenaline and fear brought Abe's attention back in a flash. His sword was nowhere to be found. Abe rolled over his hip with a whimper of pain and saw Santa Steve buried in the snow, dead. Others from the Order's rescue mission were also strewn about, as if a bored child had just dropped his action figures aimlessly.

"Abraham, Abe, we need to free Krampus. We need to do it now."

Abe again looked around and saw no one, not even one of the ghosts.

He staggered to his feet. His left leg was damaged, and he could hardly put any weight on it.

"Who's talking?" he asked quietly.

"Nicholas. Nicholas Thaumaturgus, acting on behalf of the Spirit of Christmas."

Abraham felt a wave of calmness and something like love flow through him. The voice was coming to him from inside his head.

"I am currently with you, alongside you. Don't be alarmed. I will leave any time you ask. I am here to offer advice and help, if I can."

Abe faltered and grabbed the arm of a broken chair to lever himself upright. Abe looked back, seeing a multitude of vampires using their strength, claws, and accelerated healing to dig themselves out.

Abe exhaled weakly. Things could hardly get much worse.

"Okay, the St. Nicholas? *The Santa Claus*?" he asked in his head.

"Well, yes, but there are several Nicholases. We can discuss the finer points later. You need to move quickly. I can lend you some strength, but I will only be able to stop some of the pain. We need to free Krampus, right now."

Abe used the chair detritus as a crutch. He paused to wipe snow and blood off of his face. Over to his right, he could see that the great crash of snow had flung Krampus backwards in a wave of snow and debris, still attached to the massive steel structure. The chains that Krampus had been restrained with were buried, and Krampus himself was pinned sideways.

Abe heard a soft chant coming from his own mouth, that same luminous quality that had touched Santa Steve now enveloping him.

He felt his exhaustion leave him for a moment and, though the pain in his leg and shoulder flashed through him every step, he was mobile. As he shuffled forwards, he saw one of the vampires move to intercept him.

"Abe, keep moving. I will deal with him."

Again, a voice that was and was not his spoke out, in a language Abe could not identify.

Abe felt his free hand go up, and the glow grew in intensity. The vampire, one of the guards in a uniform, had little time to fear the light before his body crumbled to smoking ash.

"There are some advantages to being a Saint," said the voice with a slight chuckle.

"Holy crap! I just turned the undead," Abe thought to himself, continuing to hobble forward.

"Well, yes, but that was a minor one. The more powerful ones are a different story."

As if on cue, a piece of wreckage was tossed aside, and the Arch Lord of Vampires, Duke Cosimo, emerged from the rubble, brushing himself off. The creature looked around the room, noted Abe and started walking toward him.

Nicholas spoke quietly to Abe again.

"Abe, I believe your Caestus power was the power of synchronicity, was it not?

"Yes?"

"Now is the time. Focus on delaying that creature."

Abe slowed his limping and breathed in, like he was focusing his chi for martial arts. His brow furrowed and he felt the energy build... and then release. There was a roaring sound and light swept across the wreckage as a massive RV punched through the wall of the hall. Abe gave a startled scream, trying to leap out of the way.

Archduke Cosimo, however, turned just in time to be hit by several tons of stylish Winnebago, being driven by a crippled Santa Rick, *"Jingle Bell Rock"* playing loudly out the windows.

"Impressive," said the voice of St. Nicholas, incredulous.

Sleet, debris, vampires, and gear flew everywhere. Abe made his way to the side of Krampus. The wild creature was pinned in the debris. Even though Abe's body was crying out for him to stop, he used the piece of gold-leafed Santa chair to pry away enough of the metal that pinned the large, hairy spirit. The Krampus was groggy, trying to find itself some leverage. It stared at him with narrowed animalistic eyes, filled with rage. Abe heard himself speak with the voice of Nicholas.

"Hold still, my friend. This is going to hurt."

Abe reached down into the wreckage, found the rest of the chains including the manacles, unearthing them in their entirety and freeing Krampus. Bracing himself, Abe offered a hand to the giant creature, who snarled and took it.

It pulled itself up to its full height, blood and shrapnel matting its fur.

"Again, you save me," it growled.

"Of course not. You were coming to save me. You were merely delayed," said the voice of Nicholas cheerfully.

"I am weakened, and these Strigoi have taken some of my strength."

Abe looked up at the creature and Nicholas responded.

"Sadly, once they are away from here, it will be very hard to stop them."

Krampus nodded and started to growl. He leaned back his head and let forth a bellowing cry that were equal parts bear, great elk, and some unknown terror. The roar echoed around the shattered hall, filling it, and spilled out into the night. Krampus turned and looked down at the vampires in the room.

"You summoned me! And now you hide? Earn your blood, you parasites!"

With that, Krampus spun and shook himself, his fur bristling. Krampus reached down and picked up the iron chains and manacles and, wrapping them across his shoulders, he kept the ends free to act as a flail.

Krampus took a deep breath, smelling and scenting. His horned head rocked back and forth. A clawed hand shot out to the right, tightly squeezing the invisible throat of a vampire from the House of Mirrors. Krampus lifted it up in the air, ignoring its hissing and clawing, and with a snap, twisted its head clean off. Allowing the body to slip from his hand, he turned to look for more.

Abe was sprayed with black blood, some droplets hitting his open mouth, and he recoiled, gagging and staggering backwards. He bumped straight into the back of Henry Raymond, who spun and whipped out his wrist, a pistol appearing in Abe's face. Abe squeaked and continued spinning backwards, bringing his ersatz crutch up in defense, just in time to see it shatter with a bullet strike. He examined the end of it helplessly. Raymond, emotionless, cocked another hammer and brought it to bear. Two consecutive cracks of thunder tore through the air, Raymond's arm and part of his neck exploded as blessed silver dimes tore through them.

Rick leaned on his crutch from inside the RV door and yelled at the vampire, holding a smoking shotgun.

"It's not nice to pick on the handicapped!"

Henry Raymond staggered back, looking at Abe with malevolence, unable to speak. Abe leaned back, a bit terrified, when the voice of Nicholas spoke.

"Happy coincidence. Abe, observe. You have a stick."

Abe looked up at the part of the gold-leafed Christmas chair he had been holding, and the bullet had left him holding a jagged piece of sharp wood. Abe shook his head.

"Oh! Right!"

Abe spun the wood in his hand and impaled the vampire, who was now pulling a nasty knife. Henry looked surprised and fell backwards, paralyzed, a stake of his own design through his heart. Abe looked down at him.

"I'm sorry, I really am," Abe said and then shook himself. "Wait, uhm, never mind. Not sorry, actually. Um, Merry Christmas?"

Abe started limping away.

Not far away, an extraordinarily annoyed Vampire Lord picked himself up from the debris for a second time and turned to see Avice standing next to him. Avice bowed, unruffled by all the chaos happening around him.

"Duke Cosimo, at this point, I think we've done all that we can do. It is Christmas morning, and the sun will be rising soon. While some of you may be able to withstand the sun now, many of us will not. I suggest we depart."

Duke Cosimo sighed wistfully.

"This has not gone the way we had hoped, but at least we have our clean up planned for. Have all our ranking notables meet me out there, have the rest fight a delaying tactic."

"Indeed." Avice bowed like a gothic arch.

Duke Cosimo pushed his way past the debris and out into the winter storm. As he left, many of the figures that remained in the hall turned to follow him into the night.

Abe spotted Jon, half buried in and out of the snow. He made his way toward Jon, happy to give Krampus some space. Admittedly, Krampus seemed to be in better spirits, thundering around the hall, roaring and chasing down remaining ghouls and vampires, one after another.

Abe found a heavy plastic tube for a replacement crutch, and he hobbled over to help Jon. Out of the darkness stepped Baron de Rais, his wounds visibly healing on his face. He gave a mirthless smile as he stepped on the staked and paralyzed body of Henry.

"Tsk, tsk Santa. I am afraid you and I have unfinished business."

The Baron's blade flashed for the briefest of seconds.

Abe winced, searching for a weapon as he turned to face him, and finding none. Abe looked back at Baron de Rais resignedly.

"You really are a single-minded son-of-a-bitch, aren't you?"

Baron de Rais looked at him with dark eyes, the half handle of the previous sword battle still sticking out of his neck.

"You have no idea. In the end, only willpower matters."

In his mind, Abe heard the voice of St. Nicholas.

"While I am a bit rusty, perhaps I can help you?"

"Now is the time, if ever. I'm unarmed," Abe responded out loud.

Baron de Rais raised an eyebrow, not comprehending the exchange.

"As if I would arm you," he chuckled. "Ah, another martyr for the cause. Well, then."

The Baron's blade flew toward Abe in a blur, his full weight behind the lunge. Abe threw himself sideways, tripped, and fell underneath a Christmas tree in the wreckage of the roof.

The Baron stepped over yet another random body, preparing to strike again. Abe started crawling on his back and happened to look up. At the top of the Christmas tree was an old vintage angel, and hanging off of the angel was a candy cane.

Abe scrambled sideways, twisting and smacking the tree. The candy cane fell in slow motion. He took a deep breath, focused his power, and held out his hand. To God and anyone else who was listening, he whispered.

"Please."

There was a flash of light in the hall. Baron de Rais blinked as the heft of the blade pierced him. He staggered back, a geyser of foul-smelling black blood pouring from his smoking wound.

From beneath the Christmas tree rose Abe, dressed in his battered, bloody Santa suit, holding the blade of Cormac, the sword known as *Illuminator*.

The Christmas Spirit, also known as Nicholas, shared his lifetimes of knowledge with Abe, allowing Abe to move the unwieldy blade a lot more gracefully.

Baron Gilles de Rais hissed as the glowing blade raked across his arm, leaving a smoking wound. The vampire stepped left and feinted right, watching Abe carefully.

"It would seem we are not alone. I've seen this style of sword work before. Two against one, not very sporting."

"Life isn't fair," Abe answered, "you should know that better than anyone."

The Baron tried a couple of false attacks which Abe did not fall for, and Abe continued pushing the Baron backwards. The Baron snarled in Latin.

"And who is the spirit within this humble shell? Do I have the honor of addressing the Hidden Nicholas? I know you've been looking for me a while, oh Protector of Children."

Abe felt a well of anger overflow within him, as if a centuries-old book was being reopened. Memories flitted across his mind: Memories of death, destruction, and hideous wickedness caused by the creature in front of him. Gilles de Rais was a serial killer of hundreds of children from the 14th century to the modern day.

"If I may, Abe," said the voice of St. Nicholas.

"Hey, by all means, play through."

In Latin, a voice cried out that was not Abraham's.

"By the power of the Lord and the strength of the Lamb, I bind thee. Thou shall not leave this circle of light!" The words boomed with holy authority.

Illuminator thrummed with a light that created a perfect sphere around the two of them.

The Baron replied with a thin-lipped, fanged smile. He began to smoke, ever so slightly.

"How wonderful! Finally, after all this time, Santa has come to bring me a present," he said in a voice as soft as silk.

The two figures collided, and a whirl of blades spun around them. Abe caught several blows, but the power of the larger blade was not to be denied. In a puddle of dark blood and snow, the vampire spun left and right, looking for an opening. As he did, he spoke.

"Nicholas, is this any way for a man of peace to behave? Did you forget that, out of all those hundreds of dear, sweet children I played with and all the hundreds of people I tortured, I shared my treats and made some powerful friends?"

With that, his attacks became more furious, words of a dark and foul language issuing forth from the Baron's bloody mouth. His eyes shone like embers, his skin hardening into a mottled charcoal gray, and the dark maroon that now outlined his silhouette was unquestionably demonic.

Nicholas spoke in Abe's mind.

"No. We cannot let him finish his incantation. We must separate to defeat him. Push him straight back into the circle behind him, but don't step in and don't let him out!"

"What? No, I can't hold him. Are you crazy?"

St. Nicholas was already gone, and all the extra energy and sword skills went with him. The sphere disappeared, Abe's arms sagged, and a plethora of wounds suddenly screamed out to him.

The hellish figure facing Abe grinned. It loomed over him, flexing long, black talons that curved like sickles.

"Typical. Of course, your precious Saint abandoned you. No worries, I shall find him soon enough, and I will drink my fill of your Krampus! Oh, then, what a wonderful crimson pageant of innocents I will put on!"

Abe saw a ghostly figure behind the demonic Baron, unsuspecting lines forming in the slush below. The snow in the room began to swirl and gather. Abe summoned what was left of his power and funneled into it what little energy he had left. Abe's hand glowed faintly.

Behind the left foot of the demonic Baron, the gust of wind dislodged a toy car from the debris.

Abe blinked and then jumped at the Baron, screaming.

"AAAAAAAuggh!" Abe flailed with the sword.

The chimeric demon surprised, flinched for a second and stepped on the toy, staggering backwards, rending part of Abe's suit with a clawed hand. Abe swung Illuminator overhead and heaved it downward. The creature toppled backwards into the circle, blood streaming and smoking.

A flash accompanied the sound of bells as the spectral image of Nicholas Thaumaturgus disappeared. Abe heard the voice in his head again.

"Abe, we must move fast."

Acting as one, the two Santas bent down and touched the ring of symbols pressed in the snow.

"May this sign be bound!"

The Demon de Rais howled and sprang up to charge him, looking to eviscerate Abe with the crooked talons that were once his fingertips. Abe staggered and jumped back just as The Baron collided with an invisible wall.

The creature screamed and jets of flame erupted as it tested the circle.

"I Shall Burn You All in Hellfire!" the creature roared.

Fire filled the circle. Abe peeled his attention away long enough to catch the soft outline of Nicholas standing beside him. It smiled gently at Abe and pointed down. Inside the dome, the snow continued swirling and falling. And where it touched hellfire, water and steam poured forth. As it rolled over the creature, the maddened beast began to smoke and burn.

The voice of St. Nicholas spoke to Abe again as the image of Nicholas faded.

"For the Winter Order, holy water can, in fact, be made with snow in a pinch."

The creature inside went insane, the trapped heat creating gallons of holy water for it to stand in. A miasma of sulfur and flame roiled within the bubble, its light too intense to look at directly. Abe stepped away, shielding his eyes, the screeching within hitting an ear-splitting crescendo. Soon, there was nothing left but the smoking, glowing symbol on the ground, and the crackling, charred skeleton of Baron de Rais.

Abe started searching for any other survivors. Rick and Jon hobbled up to join him, both looking equally damaged. A ghoul flung itself out of the darkness, but it was summarily thrown back with an arrow through its heart. All three of them turned to see Skyia as she strode past, notching another arrow. Rick marveled at the spot where Baron de Rais had been destroyed, hitching his Santa bag over his shoulder.

"'I'm meltinggg, I'm meltinggggg!'" Rick said and smiled for the first time since sunset. He reached into his battered Santa bag and handed Abe some things wrapped in cloth.

"What are these?"

"Holy wafers, some salt, blessed oil, and a blessed iron spike covered in silver."

"Oh." Abe looked at Rick, tired and confused. "Why?"

Jon coughed.

"Standard stuff you need when destroying a really powerful vampire or demon."

"Oh. Oh, wait a second. Won't the holy water do the trick?"

Both men shook their heads, sighing.

"If you would grant me the honor, I will show you," the voice of St. Nicholas said quietly.

Abe had the feeling that this was something that had been coming for a very long time.

"Of course."

The Spirit of Nicholas guided Abe and, taking the package, stepped forward, sword in hand. Abe watched himself cut the line of the circle. Immediately, the demon-infused vampire corpse started to recover. The blade was already in motion however and, in one beautiful arc, it came back around, cleaving the head off Baron Gilles de Rais, separating skull from body. The head fell to the ground. And in movements swift and sure, the body was spiked, holy wafers were stuffed between its curled lips, a symbol drawn on its forehead, and words of power were spoken throughout. There was a crack as the spike was driven home, and snow fell gently from the opening of the roof, a gentle benediction. The wind fluttered through the hall, bringing a chill with it.

Abe stood back, feeling himself sob for a moment. He regained control while staring at the aftermath, allowing relief to wash over him as the weight of his promise lifted from his shoulders.

"Merry Christmas, Trish," Abe said softly, thinking of the little girl and his promise to her.

Jon and Rick bowed their heads, and as they did, the ghosts of Top, Steve, Ron, and Pastor Carl appeared. They all stepped away from the body, and Santa Jon spoke looking at Abe.

"The Winter Order, and St. Nicholas, have been looking for that bastard for a very, very, long time. Well done, Abe."

The Ghost of Carl looked around at the circle.

"Where is Morozko?"

"He's still out there, dealing with the bombs the vampires left, I think," Jon replied.

"Abe, did we see the Spirit of Nicholas Thaumaturgus next to you?" Pastor Carl asked.

"I think he's still around," Abe said as he nodded.

Top held up a ghostly hand.

"So, just to recap: The town could blow at any moment, and there is still a butt-ton of vampires around here plus Krampus."

Rick leaned and added quietly.

"And several of you are dead, and it's Christmas morning." Rick paused and added in a sarcastic voice, "And I think some of those chief vampires got a big cup of blood from Krampus."

"Thank you, Rick," Jon winced and waved everyone together before proceeding. "First order of business, we need to find the vampires who drank from Krampus, and we need to do it before they leave town."

"Hey, Abe," Top coughed. "That cell phone you found on my body. Still got it?"

"Yeah. I got that off of that sick French bastard over there." Abe fished it out.

Top smiled and jerked a ghostly thumb at the remains of The Baron.

"It has the numbers of most of the head vampires. If the power is still on in the RV, I can probably show you how to track them down, if they have their phones near them."

Everyone looked at the phone then the Ghost of Top, offering him a round of golf claps. He bowed.

Jon looked around again.

"Okay, there's still a town full of vampires, ghouls, and the humans that work for them out there. Possibly some in here too, if Krampus hasn't killed them all. We also have a lot of wounded and dead that need our help."

"And we need our bodies retrieved," Pastor Carl added quietly.

"Some good news," Rick said as he held up his hand. "We have more reinforcements coming, and with them, a full crisis team from Bismark." He addressed Abe.

"The vampires outside are tussling with some very nasty fairy folk. Someone opened a fairy trod, and the whole city is a madhouse. Kinda funny, if you think about it. The vampires really don't like it when they are the ones being hunted and played with for a change."

"My heart bleeds," Jon laughed grimly.

"That big hairy fella, Grumpus or whatever and a few others from our side, they're still chasing down the vamps in here, I think," added Steve. As if to confirm what Steve said, they all heard the familiar cycle of a roar, gunfire, and screaming, followed by silence.

"Well then," Jon concluded, "It's not done yet. Let's go find their leaders, and I'm going to ask you folks who have crossed over to go check on Morozko."

"Not that I'm bitching," Santa Steve interrupted, "but I was never part of the Caestus. Why am I still here?"

"You are now officially a Ghost of Christmas Past," Top replied. "You're probably almost done, just not yet."

"Oh joy," Steve grumbled, "figures I would die at the *end* of my season."

Top patted him on the shoulder.

"Yeah, I'd consider this a pretty shitty retirement party. Sorry, dude."

"It's the power of the Caestus and the Season," Father Carl explained. "Apparently, we all still have things to do before we catch that last sleighride." He pointed to Abe and Steve. "You two both met the Christmas Spirit in the form of St. Nicholas. That's no small thing."

"Yeah, I guess," Steve admitted, looking pensive. "After letting them get their hands on Krampus, sticking around one more day is the least I can do."

Jon reached down and lifted his axe.

"Right. Santa has a few more stops on his list. Let's get to it."

"Indeed," said a quiet, now familiar voice in Abe's head.

Together, the remaining forces of the Winter Order, alive and dead, ventured into the night.

* * *

50. Exit, Stage Left

A small convoy of black cars slogged through the snow-filled roads towards the new airport of LaMoure, North Dakota. Inside the vehicles, several of the Vampire Lords studied their hands or sat looking as if they were meditating intently.

Duke Cosimo turned to Elaysa, who offered him a bag of blood. He shook his head, gently waving it away. As his hand flexed, he studied it with rapt fascination.

"I take it that Henry is still back there?"

"I'm afraid so. We've lost about half the kin who were in the city, and many Elders joined them. Not so much from fighting with the Santas, but as a result of doing battle with the Fay."

Duke Cosimo took a deep breath and shook his head.

"I truly hope this was all worth it."

Elaysa softly touched his leg.

"How do you feel?"

Duke Cosimo regarded his hand.

"Odd. Powerful, yet vulnerable. In all my years, I've never felt both at once."

Avice was riding in the vehicle with them. In a dry, scratchy voice, he broke his silence.

"It may take quite some time before you fully assimilate the power you have imbibed. Avoid stress, maintain focus."

Duke Cosimo looked up at the thin form of Avice.

"And you. How are you?"

"It was a great working. My magic is weakened. The sooner we are away from here and I am back in my beloved catacombs in the Vatican, the happier I shall be."

Duke Cosimo nodded.

"I have had multiple teams of snowplows clearing the runway all night, and our jets should be de-iced and ready as soon as we arrive."

As he spoke, the darkness outside lifted from the occasional streetlamp to that of a mid-sized airport. The fleet of vehicles drove straight to the runway loading area where several jets waited, engines already spinning. The snowstorm still swirled around them, large trucks shoveling the length of the tarmac.

Doors were opened, and the powerful Elders moved toward the forward Gulfstream jets, while the rank and file headed for the more militaristic aircraft.

As they moved, a man in a suit and several LorenCo security walked in step with them.

"Mr. Cosimo, you have an approved flight plan out of the country, as you requested, but..." The man trailed off his comments, looking apologetic.

"But?" Duke Cosimo slowed to regard the man.

"Huge storm, sir," the man said as he gestured to the sky. "We have a lot of unstable warm air at higher altitudes. It could be very dangerous for you to fly right now. Let us move the jets back into the hangars, and have you relax there until it's safer to clear you out."

"And you are knowledgeable about these things?" Duke Cosimo said pointedly, and the others all turned to look at him.

The man blanched.

"No, sir, but we have two air traffic controllers, Bill and Andy. Both are up in the tower. They both know the skies around here, and if they say it's a bad idea, then it is a very bad idea."

Duke Cosimo sighed, looking upwards at the brightening sky.

"Dawn will be here very soon. I want to be rid of this place. I will inform our pilot. We will be leaving. Now."

The man bowed and stepped out of their way.

Duke Cosimo and the Elders, along with Elaysa, boarded the jet. As they did, in the wind and darkness, they did not seem to notice Avice stepping away and straying out into the snowy fields.

As it turned and headed down the runway, the first jet gave a deep roar. Inside, Duke Cosimo spoke quickly to the pilot and then returned to the others.

"Our pilot has informed me that the ascent will be rather dramatic, but that he is going to take us out of this area and storm system as rapidly as possible. Hang on." Duke Cosimo turned to Elaysa. "Make certain all our windows are blacked out, please."

Elaysa walked the cabin quickly, closing all the windows, and latching them securely.

The vampires and other passengers looked visibly anxious when the jet started to shake and vibrate. Elaysa quickly sat back down and buckled herself in securely.

"Done," she said with a reassuring smile.

"Thank you." Duke Cosimo gave her a small pat on the hand and a brief smile in return.

Everything in the jet swung to a sharp angle as the jet leapt into the sky.

"A small confession," Duke Cosimo said quietly to Elaysa, "while I love the conveniences of the modern age and would never go back to the olden times, flying still unnerves me."

Her eyes got big as the jet shook.

"I understand, believe me. I'm only human. If I were Kin like you, I might survive a plane crash."

Duke Cosimo shook his head.

"A crash such as that would be hard even for an Elder to survive, my child."

Fake though it was, Elaysa attempted to give him a cheery smile.

"No need to test this on my account," she said.

* * *

Down on the ground, what was left of the Caestus was hightailing it out to the airport as well. As they flew down the road in borrowed trucks, Rick spotted a line of recognizable vehicles coming the other way as he was driving.

"Guys, we have company."

Abe and Jon were in the process of taping up and bandaging their wounds. They dove for the new weapons that Rick had recently supplied.

They struggled to get ready, but the long convoy of vehicles did not seem interested in them. Instead, the group sped past in a spray of snow and slush. Jon stayed down low, peaking over the window.

"Heads up, some of those look like reinforced tactical vehicles."

"Are they vamps?" Abe asked, exhausted and bleary eyed.

A ghostly form faded in next to him. Ron nodded.

"Some. Looks like they're bugging out, and picking up their people as they go."

As the last vehicle flew past them, one of the LorenCo security vampires flashed a toothy grin and flipped Rick the bird as they went by.

"What, are we in high school? They are so on the naughty list," Rick quipped.

The Caestus team drove into the airport. The gates leading to the tarmac were still hanging open. As they pulled in, the Ghost of Top was waiting for them.

"One jet carrying all the big cheeses, already gone. The other one is taxiing down the runway as we speak."

The men hopped out of the car to see the other Gulfstream coming around the corner on the spacious runway.

"Oh no you don't," Rick said, his face filled with determination. Jon looked hopefully at Abe.

"Do you really think someone gave someone an anti-aircraft missile for Christmas?" Abe asked incredulously.

Rick shook his head as he lumbered forward with his splinted leg.

"Not going to find out."

Rick came to the stop near one of the airport security vehicles covered in snow and leaned against it. Abe and Jon walked up as Rick pulled something unwieldy out of his Santa bag.

"Sun is finally starting to come up!" Jon said excitedly, pointing to the horizon.

Although it was just barely noticeable in all the snow, to Abe, this was the most beautiful sunrise he had ever seen.

Rick stood up triumphantly, holding something odd in his hands. It immediately gave a very nasty whine and shot straight up. Something silver was attached to the bottom, glinting as Abe watched it fly like an angry wasp.

"Drone?"

Rick nodded as he pulled the controller around.

""Yup, Mavic. Popular these days." Rick's eyebrows furrowed as he guided it toward the end of the runway. "Apparently this was a gift from a Ukranian."

The second Gulfstream roared as it shot off the pavement. In the darkness and snow, it was hard to see what was going on, but after the snow stopped swirling, the jet and the blinking lights of the drone were gone.

Abe and Jon turned to look at Rick, whose attention was fixed fully on the controller.

"Well?

"My controller is telling me that the drone isn't responding," Rick said with a shrug. "So, either it got sucked into the intakes of the jet or it got knocked out."

"Maybe we'll get lucky," Jon offered as he peered after the jet.

"Or they will get very unlucky," Abe added.

"Abe, we can't let those jets get away," the voice in Abe's head spoke privately to him.

Abe stepped away from the others.

"Um, St. Nicholas, we're exhausted. The town could blow up at any moment."

"Abe, it's still Christmas morning. There is still a bit of night in the world. A lot of power has been raised, and there are children opening presents. And remember, you have a remarkable gift."

"What?" Abe sagged, almost too tired to imagine how this could still be up to him.

"Abe, close our eyes and really, truly *BELIEVE*."

Abe looked around him one more time, took a deep breath, curled his hands, closed his eyes, and...

Off in the distance, there was the sound of thunder and, ever so faintly, sleigh bells.

* * *

51. Thunder-Snow

Aboard the LorenCo Gulfstream jet "Michelangelo," the engine quieted and started to level out.

Duke Cosimo unbuckled himself and opened up one of the side window visors slightly. It was still fairly dark outside, the jet having just broken above most of the storm clouds. In that moment, everything felt serene, passing through a valley of tall columns of storm clouds lit by starlight, the aviation lights at the wing tips and, ever so faintly, the first rays of morning. He stood, adjusted his jacket, and looked at his watch. He turned to Elaysa.

"Contact Ivitar and say to him the following, *'tó dé enechthísetai.'*"

He watched as she fished out her phone and did as she was instructed. His gaze wandered back to the window. She finished and looked back at him.

"What was that? A quote from Aurelius?"

Duke Cosimo smiled.

"Well done, part of one. *'This too will be swept away.'*" He went back to looking out the window.

"I just gave the command to have the city destroyed. The explosion should be quite dramatic."

* * *

Not far away, two men were in the process of tearing out a relay box in a large tunnel. From behind them came a loud bang, and a shower of sparks jumped from one electrical node to another. Spur's face turned white as he quickly reached out to rip a cable off a mount, and there was an electrical crack as he did. Morozko looked down, his two dogs jumping nervously at his feet.

"I am thinking they just set off bomb?"

Spur leaned back, looking at the smoking, sparking end of the cable he was holding.

"That's a fair guess," said Spur.

"*Svolochi!* Bastards!"

Spur wiped his face and looked at the embodiment of Grandfather Winter standing there before him. Cold emanated from the figure, and his beard and eyebrows were encrusted with ice.

"Agreed. In any case, we need to move right now. If we missed any of the major charges, we could be hit by a secondary explosion at any second."

For a big man, Spur climbed the metal rungs with the alacrity of a person who had been a rig-rat for years.

As soon as he got up, he turned around to help bring up the dogs. Morozko waved his hand away.

Spur surveyed the area around them. Near them were massive pipes, twisted and bent by fantastic shards of ice. The two of them watched as various pipe junctions banged or sparked, then went quiet.

"Best Christmas, evah!" Spur enthusiastically declared. As he sat down exhausted, the dogs decided this meant time for petting and tackled him affectionately.

"I don't understand," Morozko said, looking at their happy puppy pile.

"You and I just saved a good-sized city from being destroyed on Christmas morning. We defused a major death trap, and I personally took out a bunch of bombs. I did this with Frosty the Russian Santa, and I got pulled by a one-werewolf open-sleigh!"

"I heard that," a voice said from around the corner. "We agreed that we were never going to mention this, right?"

Jason was back in human form, having found a pair of overalls somewhere before electing to join them.

Spur laughed; a deep bass belly laugh that would befit any Santa.

"So sorry, I'm exhausted." He flopped backwards into the snow, laughing in a deeply exhausted and slightly crazed way. After a minute, he started making snow angels.

Morozko started laughing and fell over to do likewise.

"Y'all are nuts," Jason said with a slight smile.

The dogs yipped and jumped around them, tongues lolling out.

* * *

At the intersection of Hwy 83 and Interstate 94, a battered school bus was illuminated by the first rays of dawn as it came over the Dakota plains. Sgt. Burke had carefully disposed of all the ickier presents left by the Fay, and both the driver and he now wore looks of pure determination. The children looked angelic and slept in mounds. Burke knew they would be waking soon.

When they eventually pulled the bus over at a rest stop, Burke had found a stone washroom to relieve himself when he caught the flash of squad car lights on the other side of the bus. He readied himself and unhooked the lock on his pistol and crunched around the side, then peeked around the corner. He saw a North Dakota highway patrol officer and another man talking to the driver. The patrol officer smiled and handed Burke a cup of coffee as he approached, a donut resting on top of the lid, with sprinkles.

"Merry Christmas!"

"Merry Christmas!" said Burke, taking the coffee. The civilian pulled off his glove and turned to face Burke. He was tall, with a beautiful white beard and twinkling blue eyes.

"Santa Arnold," he said, introducing himself. Burke smiled at the pleasant handshake.

"We heard about the seven layers of hell you went through back there, and we know that the kids were promised a visit from Santa, as well as a real Christmas morning. I got together with folks from my community outreach, and we're going to make that happen for the kids here. We need to take our time getting to Bismarck, though, so they have time to finish arranging things."

Burke reached up and pinched the bridge of his nose. The weight on his shoulders slowly fell off. He looked away, just in case it looked like he was crying.

From inside the bus, the voices of several children started to call out.

"Hey, where are we?"

"I gotta pee!"

"Why do I have a hubcap?"

The four men smiled at each other and headed back to their vehicles.

* * *

Back at LaMoure Airport, the three living members of the Caestus were starting to have a hard time seeing the ghosts standing next to them, as the sun was coming up.

Rick tossed the controller for the drone back in his bag.

"Damn, I thought it was going to work."

Jon tapped Rick on the shoulder and gestured at Abe.

Abe's eyes were closed, and the wind and the snow swept up around the group. The sky rumbled.

Out of a cloud bank sprang Santa Claus, complete with a beautiful sleigh and with eight large reindeer. Lightning crackled around them.

"No. Frikkin. Way!" Rick gasped, looking at the sleigh.

"Way!" responded Jon. "Abe! Open your eyes!"

Abe remained mesmerized by the booming voice now speaking in his head.

"We have a great deal of magic potential that has been raised. With your gift, you have opened a window from the now to the in-between, and right now the magical realm is overlapping with yours."

Abe opened his eyes to witness the sleigh neatly turning on its axis. The sleigh landed expertly, dodging a car and a parked plane. The reindeer look aggressive and annoyed.

Abe was still having a hard time believing. Santa, *the Santa*, was here.

"Abe," said the Christmas Spirit in his mind. "In the last few days, you've dealt with vampires, ghosts, fairies, and saints. It's okay. Let yourself believe."

Santa pulled up the reigns and addressed the assembled Caestus, including the ghosts.

"Hello, boys. I know you all want to go for a ride, but I am still on the clock. And the Spirit of Christmas tells me that we have a problem that we need to deal with. Once the sun is completely over the horizon, I won't be able to stay." Santa turned to address Abe directly.

"You manifested me, young man. The realms won't be together for long. Let's fly!"

The other Santas helped pile Abe into the front seat, grinning like school children. They were as giddy as a gaggle of groupies at a concert. In the back of the sleigh perched a chesty elf with a mohawk, nose ring, and tattoos. Alongside him sat a slender female elf with purple hair and a clipboard.

Santa motioned everyone standing outside the sleight to step out of the way.

"Merry Christmas to all, and ...well, you know the rest," he said with a wink.

The reindeer lowered their heads and, in a blur, the sleigh was in the air and flying at an incredible velocity. Abe turned white as a sheet and clutched the sides for dear life.

Abe turned to look at his copilot, who was every bit the Santa that he had ever imagined. As he looked at him, Santa's face seemed to blend from one style of Santa to another, ever so subtly. Abe looked back at the reindeer.

"Where's our red-nosed reindeer?"

"He's the guide," Santa answered with a chuckle. "I sent him to find those jets."

As in answer to the question, off in a distant cloud, there was a flash of red.

The muscular elf leaned over and handed Abe a cup of cocoa.

"Industrial strength."

"Abe, Spike and Pixie Jen," Santa said by way of introductions. "Spike, I send in to deal with problems. Pixie keeps us on schedule and coordinates with the teams and Mrs. Claus."

Pixie cleared her throat.

"You have five minutes, Santa."

The sleigh banked into a curve, and Santa talked as he steered.

"Normally, I can't really interfere with human affairs. The emphasis there is on the word *human*. The Caestus was duly invoked, and there were enough inhumans and magic involved that I was allowed to help you. Besides, they broke the contract."

Abe sipped his cocoa. He could feel it making his hair stand on end.

"Wait, help do what?"

"Stop the jets full of naughty creatures, of course."

Abe patted himself down with his free hand and came up empty handed.

"How can we...?"

Before he could finish, Santa pointed down off the left side.

"There's one. It appears they have an engine out."

Abe looked and, sure enough, a faint stream of smoke was trailing out of one of the engines.

"What do I do?" Abe asked and scratched his head.

Santa laid a finger aside of his nose and winked.

"Spike, I am having a hard time seeing that jet. How about you?"

"Oh, yeah. I can barely make it out, Mr. C!"

"Pixie?"

"Indeed, the white of the plane mixes with the clouds."

The sleigh swooped past the jet and into the clouds in front of it.

"Back in the old days, back before all the nanosats, before I had Navstar, I would occasionally get lost in a cloud bank. Fortunately, I had a trick I used to do."

"You might want to set your cocoa down," whispered Pixie to Abe.

"Did you know that the names Donner and Blitzen, that is to say, Dunder and Blixem, actually mean 'Thunder and Lightning?'"

Before Abe could say anything, Santa cracked the reins and yelled.

"Donner, Blitzen! *Fiat Lux!*"

The two strapping reindeer closest to the sleigh leaned back, shook their antlers, and leaned into the traces. The sleigh crackled with electricity, and the clouds around them filled with massive bolts of lightning. Thunder slammed their eardrums, booming and rolling, echoing back and forth.

Santa guided the sleigh up and the jet behind them headed into the turbulence. A few short seconds later, the jet was on fire, headed downward.

"This is why you listen to the flight controllers!" Santa shouted triumphantly.

"What?" Abe shouted back, almost deafened.

Spike leaned over and patted him as if he were a bit slow. Santa ignored the exchange, then spotted another red flash.

"Time?" Santa asked Pixie.

"Ninety seconds, Santa."

"Right." His face set in complete focus.

The sleigh did the equivalent of a midair bootlegger reverse and shot in another direction. Abe almost lost what little he had in his stomach.

"Abe, do you like Christmas decorations? Especially the vintage ones?"

"I do," Abe replied, absently. "I really like those old bubble lamps in particular."

"Me too! I love those." Santa chuckled.

Pixie leaned over and handed Abe a bulky, well-wrapped present.

"Merry Christmas, Abe."

As the sleigh banked into the clouds, they swooped out in front of the Gulfstream that the Elder Vampires were in.

* * *

Inside the jet, Duke Cosimo glanced out the window again, annoyed and puzzled.

"We should have seen something. Some sort of flash, or something." The Duke turned to Elaysa. "Call and see if everything is going as planned." Before she could move, her phone rang.

Duke Cosimo looked at her expectantly, and then angrily as her face betrayed that all had not gone as planned. He reached for the phone but was interrupted. The copilot tapped him on the arm.

"Your Excellency, there is something you need to see."

Duke Cosimo, Elaysa, and several others rose to look through the window of the cockpit. In the stormy sky ahead of the jet, the were occasional flashes of lightning, heavy gusts of snow... and a sleigh.

"Avice, we need you up here! Now!" barked Duke Cosimo.

He whipped around. The other Vampires shrugged, looking bewildered.

"He's not here."

Duke Cosimo shook his head, turned, and gave Elaysa a pat on the cheek.

"My apologies, little one."

* * *

Inside the sleigh, Santa smiled.

"Go ahead, open it. All the good stuff is on the bottom."

Abe shrugged and opened the box. It was full of tinsel, lots and lots of tinsel. He pulled out handful after handful, which was ripped out of his hand by the wind and carried away. Spike watched the silver tinsel whip over his head and fly backwards with a malevolent grin. Every handful was flying right into the air intakes of the jet.

At the bottom of the box was a set of vintage bubble lights, and a small, handmade hip carrier for candy canes, one candy cane included.

"Merry Christmas, Abe."

"Merry Christmas, Santa," Abe said and teared up a bit as he grinned.

Just then, there was a roaring cough, then another mighty *chuff! chuff!* with the sound of turbines spinning down. Lightning crackled around the area. Abe spun in his seat to see the two engines of the jet in flames.

"Not only vintage lights, but that was vintage aluminum tinsel," Spike announced cheerfully. "That's the good stuff! They don't make that anymore."

"No worries, I'll get you more," Santa said as he patted Abe on the shoulder. "It never hurts to decorate for the holidays, don't you think?"

With that, he pitched the sleigh in a gravity defying arc. As it sped away, Pixie's voice could be heard.

"Thirty seconds, Santa."

* * *

The jet lost speed and continued heading downwards in an uncontrolled plunge. Inside, all the passengers looked terrified, all except Duke Cosimo. He was watching the sunrise from the window, as if it was the most beautiful thing he had ever seen. He turned to Elaysa, a hint of wonder in his voice.

"Look. My hand isn't burning in the sunlight. So. Warm."

Elaysa nodded, tears running down her face as the jet began to spin out of control.

* * *

52. Ollie-Ollie

Abe felt like he was drifting in a fog when he found himself back in the park, beside the standing stones. Santa reached out and shook his hand.

"Tell the folks in the Order, thank you." Santa sat down and picked up the reins. His voice softened, sounding a great deal like that of Nicholas Thaumaturgus. "Remember Abe, a lot of lives were lost, but countless more were saved. The world is a better place because you stepped up."

With a click of the tongue, the reindeer and the sleigh floated up and were gone in a red flash. Distantly, Abe heard, "*Happy Christmas to all, and to all...*" as he left.

Abe sagged against the stone. Ron materialized near him.

"One last thing, and then you can rest, buddy."

"What?" Abe looked around blearily.

There was a blur and Compass Rose appeared.

"You need to call them back. Close the Way."

"How do I do that?"

Another voice answered. A short stocky man with a flat cap walked over and placed something on the ground next to Abe.

"My name is Fin," he said. He pointed to the stone and the horn. "Ye blood the rock, then blow the alf-horn, and blow it three times. It's very important ye blow it **three** times."

Abe picked up the horn. It was long and silver, with a strange, unnatural curve to it.

"Right." He turned to look at the rock, and then looked at his hand.

There was a flurry of movement, and Compass Rose stood on a nearby rock, holding a bloody thorn. She smiled viciously. It took Abe a second to register the pain.

"Damnit! Ouch!' yelped Abe, and then he pressed his bleeding hand next to the first mark, wincing. The air between the standing stones turned silvery.

Abe picked up the horn and took a deep breath.

"*Baaaarrrooooooooooooooooo!*"

The sound of the horn echoed across the fields, bounced off the rocks.

From around the bushes, out of the trees, and from the shadows, Fay creatures began to head toward Abe. They were beautiful, terrible, and frightening. Many of them carried souvenirs equally as disquieting.

Abe took another hurried deep breath and sounded the horn again, feeling his strength fading.

"Baaarroooo!"

Whispering and shrieking, gibbering and clawing, the fairy host retreated back through the portal. Abe could barely stand. Compass Rose watched him hungrily.

The voice of Ron came to him from a distance.

"Abe, if you thought the vampires were bad, the fairy host will make the vampires seem like a pack of Girl Scouts. You need to finish it."

Abe lifted the alf-horn one last time.

"Baaaaaarrrrrrrooooooooo!"

A macabre, ragged creature staggered through the gate. The Pooka, holding a screaming vampire hostage, flew through the gate. A small woman dressed in sensible brown and patterned clothes, winding thread as she came, calmly walked through the gate. She was followed by the short man with the flat cap, who gave him a knowing wink.

"Well done lad, well done!" He tipped his hat and stepped through.

The horn echoed and echoed. As the sound was dying out, the tall and elegant Ilbareth appeared, bowing reverently and deeply.

"We have come as bidden and this boon is filled, opener of the Way."

Abe staggered forward to hand the creature the horn. It demurred with an odd smile, and the horn shrank to a third its size in Abe's hand.

"It is lent to you for now. It must be returned. If you sound it, we will come."

With a final nod, it stepped through the gate and exited the world of men. The wind rose and fell.

Compass Rose flew about an inch in front of Abe's face. With a few quick movements, she grabbed a hold of three hairs on Abe's beard. She tittered, gave him a genuine smile, and zipped away.

Abe watched the sun rise and could hear all sorts of interesting noises from the city. Everything was covered in a beautiful coat of dazzling white frost. The morning sun glistened.

"Abe, you can't stay here. You'll freeze to death," said Ron, his voice fainter and fainter.

"Right. *Feeze to deffth*. Just let me nap for a second," Abe muttered. His head slumped to his chest.

The Ghost of Ron sighed.

"I'll go get help."

* * *

53. Prey and Prayers

In dark woods near a railroad trestle, a figure stirred, emerging from the broken old cellar of a long-abandoned house. Avice brushed himself off, slowly turning to survey the area. He was about to move when his head jerked up, wrenched to the right suddenly, just in time to feel a blade pressed against his neck. Looming out of the darkness was the form of Krampus.

The horned creature had golden eyes that gleamed in the darkness. A deep purr sounded as the hand without the blade pinned Avice.

"Did you think I could not smell you, sorcerer? That I had forgotten what you had done, how you humbled me, how you made a fattened calf of me for your lords and masters to suckle on?" uttered Krampus in a voice full of menace.

Avice took one bony finger and pushed back the hand holding the blade a bit.

"Be careful with that blade. Even the slightest scratch is deadly." Avice paused. "My sincere apologies. I have been under the thumb of Duke Cosimo for hundreds of years. He was holding me hostage. It was I who put the weaknesses in the altar-stone and made sure you stayed conscious. You will note that I did not board the aircraft with the others."

Avice bowed slightly and turned to look at Krampus.

"My senses tell me you are still seriously injured. Perhaps I can make amends?"

"I have no reason to trust you, and even more to destroy you." The horned head of Krampus cocked slightly as he regarded Avice. Avice gestured to the world around them and sighed wearily.

"There are so few of my House left. I swear on my True Name that I just want to return to my libraries and cats."

"Cats?" he growled.

"Cats," nodded Avice. "I take in a few strays every ten years or so."

Avice saw the Krampus hesitate and pushed his advantage. He pulled something from his robe, slowly. It was the container from the ritual.

"I thought I might be meeting you again. This contains a quantity of your blood, magically preserved. If you drink this, it might restore some of your strength."

"Mine," Krampus snarled and snatched it out of his hand.

"Indeed. Let me go. I will return to my books, and if you have need, I can answer questions for you in the future. You play at being the wild beast Krampus, but I know that you sat beside Chiron and have danced with Enkidu. Spare me, and I will trouble you no more."

Krampus held up the ancient dagger and pointed it at him.

"And what shall happen the next time the vampires aim to force your help?"

Avice smiled slightly.

"Courtesy of your friends, I will have time to move my important possessions to someplace else. I can generally sense the future enough to avoid most people."

With a twitch, the dagger flew from Krampus's taloned hand, twirling, spinning up. Avice shot a worried glance up and, then surprised, stepped back into the arms of Krampus.

Krampus twitched his head and a line appeared on Avice's sallow cheek. Viscous black blood dripped from the cut made by Krampus's horn. Krampus reached out with a long, snake-like tongue, and licked it up. His eyes darkened and his nostrils flared.

"I have tasted you, and I have scented you. There is no place that I, 'hunter in the clouds, dancer in the woods,' cannot track you. Do not trouble me or mine again."

"Agreed." Avice winced.

"Go." Krampus stood back.

Avice slowly walked away. Several minutes passed. After a while, Krampus loped up the stream bed, and found a tree branch to sit on. Taking his time, he unbuttoned his clothes and inspected his various wounds.

He opened the container and sniffed it, the contents smelling strange and enticing. Krampus looked out to the woods and then lifted it in a toast, before drinking deep and long. To a random rabbit that was wandering by, Krampus swayed as his vision blurred and said, *"I taste better than I'd supposed!"*

The rabbit said nothing.

It was at this point Krampus doubled over. The spasms that rocked him shortly thereafter were accompanied by many screams of pain and anger. Any creature that heard them ran for their lives.

* * *

54. Candlemas

February 2

As Abe stepped into the diner, he glanced down at his bag of medications, the drugstore bag still stapled shut. Abe always felt a bit weird after the holidays and did not want to leave the bag in the car to freeze.

People glanced at him, took in his Santa appearance, and they smiled politely. Their facial expressions betrayed their silence with a look that clearly said, "It's over, go put yourself in storage, or shave the stupid beard."

While shaving was often a tempting thought following the season, he had resigned himself to the burden. Since human facial hair typically averaged only a quarter of an inch a month, it would take several years to grow back to its current length.

Abe sat at the table where Ron and he used to meet, holding discussions long into the night, laughing until the staff made them leave. Abe sighed and looked even more forlorn.

A lot of people had died, a lot of people had lost their jobs, and there was a whole lot of confusion around a cover story of an evil corporation and a chemical spill. One upside, however, was that in light of the evil doings at LorenCo, the remaining assets of the company had been put into a public trust fund. All the remaining citizens of LaMoure were now receiving monthly stipends from the trust, which helped a great deal. Abe toyed with his spoon while he waited.

"Ahem," Abe looked up from his reverie. It was the new waitress, an older woman with interesting Celtic tattoos.

"Hey, Abe."

"Hey, Kathy."

Without asking, she put a thermos of coffee in front of him, poured him a cup, and put down three metal servers of cream. She handed him a menu.

"I wanted to show you a picture."

"Yeah?" Abe looked up at her.

Kathy tapped her phone to show him a man with blue eyes, white hair, and fluffy white beard.

"That's my sweetie, Colum. He's the air-traffic controller in town. I keep telling him he's got the look and personality."

"Yup, prime Santa material. I imagine he makes a lot more, doing what he does."

"Yeah, but how do you think he got all his white hair?" she smiled mischievously.

"Air-traffic control is a hard job, but I hear it's rewarding, in its own way."

Another voice spoke up.

"They say that about my job."

Abe turned to look. It was the new head of police for LaMoure, North Dakota, Captain Burke.

"Join me, Captain?" Abe motioned to the table.

"Sorry, I just ate, and we're still overseeing a ton of clean up." The captain looked at Abe and shook his head. "You would not believe some of the things we've found."

Abe pointed to something on the menu, and Kathy smiled and started to walk away.

"Speaking of some things I found, I gave these two a ride in. Thought you might want to see them." Captain Burke smiled and turned for the front door. He sided past two figures, one was tall and lanky with his gray beard and old hunting clothes, while the other was huge, wearing a long overcoat and big leather hat.

Abe recognized Morozko immediately, but not the other. The bigger one walked oddly and kept his head down. Morozko, as per usual, smelled of too many campfires and not enough showers. Both of the figures smelled of dog.

Kathy came back to get their orders.

Morozko patted Abe on the shoulder and turned to Kathy.

"Darling Kathy, good to see you! Tea and all the sugars. Barbecue. The special." He glanced at the figure by his side.

His companion pulled his collar back but left the hat on. The face looked feral, with strong features, a thick close-cropped beard, and piercing yellow eyes.

Abe almost fell out of his chair. It was Krampus. Sort of.

Kathy smiled at the big man.

"You're a big one. What will you have?"

"Meat. Lots of it. Rare. And a salad," it said in a deep, melodic voice.

"I'll save all the bones for the pooches," the waitress replied as she headed back to the kitchen.

"Spaceba!" said Morozko. The Russian addressed Abe, "Do you recognize our friend?"

"Um, well you look a lot different."

Krampus sniffed the air around him, and then looked back at Abe.

"I had another encounter with that damned sorcerer." Krampus looked uncomfortable at the admission.

Morozko jumped in.

"He drank his own blood, but in the jar was the blood of all the other vampire Elders for test," Morozko explained. "Plus, other magic ingredients. They wanted to be more human. So, now, he is more human."

Krampus lifted his hat to show his horns, which were diminished but still visible.

"Not entirely. At night, I am... More."

"Wow," Abe blurted and just blinked at the two of them.

"This is why we need your help," Morozko said, eyeing Abe intently.

Abe looked at the two of them, two of the deadliest Winter Order members he could possibly imagine.

"You are going back to the Monastery of the Order, no? To complete your training?" asked Morozko.

"Yes, once I clear up some stuff here and finish healing."

"Good. You need to bring 'K' here back with you. He needs to go back to Europe. His lands are not these lands. He will heal better there."

Kathy brought in plates of food, and all three of them ate with a healthy appetite. Morozko managed to eat and talk with all the skill of a professional ventriloquist.

"You need to take him. He has no papers, no ID. He is very big and very obvious. I cannot help him. Everyone in this town is scared bad from the killings, no?"

Abe finished what he was chewing.

"And how do I do that? They just sent me a stipend. I have only enough for my plane ticket there."

Morozko shook his head and wiped his beard.

"You don't know. You are now the 'Opener of the Ways.' K will guide you. You go the In-Between way."

Abe poured himself more coffee.

"I don't know anything about this stuff, and the Fay are as dangerous as hell."

"Da. That is why he will take you. You open, follow him."

At that, Krampus finished his third plate, leaned back, and yawned, showing teeth that would put a panther to shame.

"It is dangerous, but I cannot stay here."

Abe looked around the restaurant. Kathy came over and left a bill for him, along with a greasy bag of bones for Morozko, which K looked at a bit longingly. Morozko handed him a thick bone, which the wild spirit crunched down happily.

"Okay, I mean this with no offense, but why would you trust me or want anything to do with me?"

Krampus looked around the cafe once and then opened his coat. Around his shoulders sat lengths of the iron chains.

In a flash, a memory of Nicholas Thaumaturgus slipped into Abe's mind. He remembered what it meant to wear those chains.

"For now, Abe, he and I are linked to you," a voice in Abe's head said quietly.

"I heard that! Damn it, I knew it." Krampus growled and thumped the table.

Abe fished some money from his wallet and slapped down a big tip.

"Right. Well, let me get some things together, heal a bit, and then we can go."

Morozko picked up the bag of bones and smiled at him.

"You will have much fun. Is like a trip to Disneyland."

"Tinkerbell generally doesn't try to kill the customers," said Abe.

"In the Fairy Realms, sometimes death is preferable," Krampus said as he raised an eyebrow.

"Same thing at Disneyland, if you get stuck in the really long lines," Abe replied.

The three of them stepped out into the cold and snow. Morozko's two dogs were waiting for them, their tails wagging excitedly.

Abe looked at his car and then back at his "new" friends. He just knew his car was going to smell like goat and dogs for weeks.

* * *

Acknowledgments

Many of the characters in this novel are influenced and inspired by all of the crazy characters I have in my day-to-day life. Some characters are composites of multiple people, and some are straight up constructs. If I've killed you gloriously, it's always a sign of affection!

It took a lot to get this book out and to keep me mostly on the rails. I just want to say from the bottom of my nerdy little heart, thanks!

First, many thanks are lavished on my family (both bio and chosen): My lady, the brilliant Cat Ellen—editor and general wrangling of all the squirrels and fantasies. A thousand thank yous to her lovely family and all the love they've shared with me.

Heaps and heaps of love and gratefulness to my son, the mighty Boyo, RJ Ryan-Seutter. Years of storytelling between the two of us are clearly obvious in these pages, as is his devilish editing, too. What a lovely assistant editor you've become.

I cannot thank my own family enough for the years we've shared together: Mom (Rita Shaw), Joe Shaw, Christine, Brian, Will, and so many others.

No book is the effort of just the author, and those who've inspired and helped me along the way include (in no particular order and not limited to): Michael D. McCarty, Chris Spurrell, Gillian Cameron, the Legendary Kings (Rachel and Ronnie), Myk and Nola Price, Bob Bulick and Jocelyn Whitney, James and Lori Kay Kiser Dinwiddie, Michelle Durant and Michael Keesling, Ramsay Cowlishaw, and Don Fasig. The serial numbers may have only been partially filed off, but you've each influenced so many parts of my life.

All hail the mighty Meg Burns for the Latin proofreading and insight. As always, find actual Latin teachers and pay them well.

To the many organizations and groups that have left indelible marks on me: The Society for Creative Anachronism, the CPW Alumni Crew, IBRBS (International Brotherhood of Real Bearded Santas), FORBS (Fraternal Order of Real Bearded Santas), NSN (National Storytelling Network), the Celtic Arts Center, the Los Angeles Science Fantasy Society, the TPG group, the Secret M Group, the SoCal Ren-Faire Community, and the late, great, Queen Medb Encampment. Medb, much of this is in your memory.

To my specific Santa mentors over the years: Ron Breach, Stephen Hollen, Gordon Bailey, Phillip Wenz, and Tim Connaghan. You invested in my world, and I'm thankful for your worlds.

To the various Santas (who go by many names) who have inspired my own understanding of the Christmas spirit: Tracy J. Alger, Stephen Arnold, Jim Biedle, Johnathon Burton, Shawn Coley, Andy Farr, Miguel Garcia, Chuck Gill, Mark Larson, Cortney Lofton, Melissa Lynn, Jason Marks, Allan Siu, Matt Spaulding, John Stout, Stanley Taub, Patrick Turnbull, and Scott Whitesell. And to the various embodiments of Mrs. Claus (who are wonderful by any name) who keep so many Santas on track: Jacki Chamberlain, Kimmie Claus, Cat Conner, Carol Crosby Baker, Genma Holmes, Jen Kersey Ziegelman, Tosombra Kimes, Maggie Nitz, Trish L. Schuler, Natasha Spencer Coley, and Margie Wolczak. Plus a special thanks to the Elves and other assorted Fay and Magical Creatures in my life: Marlan Clarke, Julia Clayton, Alicia Glass, Virginia Hankins, Dr. Mona Hanouni, Myke Hutchings, Clau Orona (and the Orona family), Skyia (Laura Dranes), Jess Starwood, Aarene Storms, Mary Wang-Boucher. The Magical North Pole would not be the same without you.

A hearty shout-out and three cheers and huzzahs to my entire SCA community and family, but especially for these characters and treasured friends: Sean "Sheridan" Richards and Maureen McQueen, Suzy Snowden and Courtney White, Tanya and Sean Wilson, Jay and Tonda Kubena, Chris Taylor, True's Crew (Toad Corners, Snails, and all the Gnomies), Jeff Jacobsen (fencing Maestro!), Marcus Barber (always pick an excellent nemesis!), Roberta Ashley, Bridget Lucia MacKenzie, Jonathon Hopf, Rosa Ruiz and Stryker, Christine Seelye-King, Laura Hopf, Saul Dudley and Amy Wert-Dudley, and all my fellow SCA Bards (Whiskey Bards, too).

For my fellow jar-heads: Col. Amber Lehning, SSGT. Bob Young, and SSGT. Christopher Stricker. You've been in the trenches, so you know.

Kudos to the original photo crew who've been there for me: Suzanne Stuedle Gonzalez, Crystal Olguin, and Stephanie Gill. Your passion for your craft has brought out the best in me.

To my fellow nerds: Susan Fox and Gene Turnbow, Julia Clayton, and Matt Tice. You keep the nerdy fires going, and I appreciate you so much for this.

Finally, no author gets out of the library without having been influenced by the authors who came before him. In my case, a tip of each my hats to: Patricia Briggs, Catherine Briggs, Jim Butcher, Neil Gaiman, Dafydd ap Gwilym, S.P. Hendrick, Benedict Jacka, Terry Pratchett, Rumi, John Scalzi, Maggie Secara, William Shakespeare, J.R.R. Tolkein, Catherynne Valente, and Roger Zelazney.

Robert Seutter
August 2024

Biography

Robert Seutter, aka True (as in True Thomas the Storyteller) LOVES myth, legend, and folklore. He is a Traditional Spoken Word Storyteller, a Professional Christmas Performer, and Christmas Performing Instructor. His previous incarnations include working in the video broadcast industry and as a Marine Sgt. He believes in tilting at windmills plus stepping up to make a difference, especially for lost causes. Travelling to and occasionally fro with Christmas Performer Workshops and as a Storyteller, he does his best to bring some storytelling magic and share the art with others.

He lives with his brilliant and lovely lady, Cat Ellen, and hopes to spend even more time with his talented son, RJ Ryan-Seutter. He hopes someday to have a little heirloom apple grove, critters, and a firepit to tell stories by.

www.ingramcontent.com/pod-product-compliance
Lightning Source LLC
Chambersburg PA
CBHW061557170626
46811CB00001B/232